RED
ON THE
RUN

A "Syndicate-Born Trilogy" Thriller

by

K.M. Hodge

RED ON THE RUN
The Syndicate-Born Trilogy – Book 1

THIRD EDITION SOFTCOVER
ISBN: 1622532465
ISBN-13: 978-1-62253-246-9

Editor: Sue Fairchild
Senior Editor: Lane Diamond
Cover Artist: Kabir Shah
Interior Designer: Lane Diamond

EVOLVED PUBLISHING™

www.EvolvedPub.com
Evolved Publishing LLC
Butler, Wisconsin, USA

Printed in Book Antiqua font.

BOOKS BY K.M. HODGE

THE SYNDICATE-BORN TRILOGY

1 – *Red on the Run*

2 – *Black and White Truth*

3 – *True Blue Son*

4 (A Prequel) – *The Sally Ride Chronicle*

THE BOOK CELLAR MYSTERIES

1 – *Walker Texas Wife*

2 – *Texas & Tiaras*

Save the Date

DEDICATION

This book is dedicated to my family, who has always believed I could do this... even when I didn't.

Prologue

Church Hill
Richmond, Virginia
June 15, 2025
4:00 PM

I want to scream, to fill the room with my anguish, but for her sake I don't. She wouldn't want me to make a scene. Instead, I sit in the back of the room, away from the other mourners, in an ill-fitting black dress that I borrowed at the last minute. I've never been a details person, so when my best friend told me she was dying I didn't think to plan out what to wear for her funeral.

I still can't believe this is really happening. She doesn't belong here in this dark cave. I want to pick up her lifeless body and animate her into the woman she'd been, but would never be again.

For as long as I had known her, she had worn the millstone of grief around her neck like a family heirloom. Loss was all she knew. We were alike that way, except that she accepted it and kept going, rather than rage against her fate or lament it as I do.

"Life is too short, Ellie," she would say. "Choose joy all day, every day."

Fate brought her into my life when I needed a friend the most, and her love and support saved me from myself. She, and the glimmer of hope she had brought out in me, became the very foundation I stood upon.

Now, without her, I feel as though I might crumble and fall back into the abyss. Why am I still here? Why is she gone? I'm left behind, again, alone with my grief and painful memories.

Maybe I should start smoking. I think about it often these days, but no one takes up cigarettes in their late 40's. Out of habit, I check the time on my phone—the service was supposed to have started twenty minutes ago. People are sitting in groups quietly chatting, remembering, some of them familiar but the majority of them strangers.

She'd been a vivid storyteller, prodigious with her correspondences after I moved away and our regular sessions stopped. She had lived a life filled with one tragedy after another. During her weekly sessions, and then later in her phone calls and letters, she would artfully lay out each tragic landscape, stacking them one on top of the other, a veritable Lincoln Log house of horrors.

In the beginning, the evocative imagery conjured by her life stories would leave me awake at night, bringing home for me the experience of secondary trauma.

As her therapist, I had crossed some basic ethical boundaries by taking her on as a client and then becoming friends with her. Our shared experience of having lost a child bound us together in a spiraling transference that should have caused me to lose my license forever.

Just the thought of those early days brings all the pain up anew, and I instinctively touch my stomach—another empty vessel.

The sound of mournful music playing out of old speakers in the front of the room brings me back to the present. The service has finally started, and the minister is talking, but I can't hear a word he's saying. Seeing her lying stiffly in the oak casket, with a waxy, yellowed pallor makes it hard for me to breathe. My heart is racing, my breath is coming in short gasps, and the room suddenly feels as if it's closing in on me. I need to get out of this cave, this tomb, before it consumes me.

I make a beeline to the exit right behind me, and the heavy wooden doors give easily as I push them out.

The cool spring air immediately stings my burning flesh, and my wobbly legs implore me to sit down on the funeral home's stone steps. My heart rate slows and my vision returns to normal as the panic attack abates. From my seat at the top of a hill, the city lays spread out before me, a barren, lifeless landscape, a ramshackle center of yesteryear—ruin porn. Death is everywhere here, following me around like a persistent black cloud.

Steeped in grief and self-pity, I didn't hear the door open behind me or steps coming towards me, so I jump when he speaks my name in his deep baritone voice and the tips of his fingers brush my bare shoulder.

"Ellie?"

I look up at him. The skin on my chest and arms prickles and my heart skips a beat.

His deep brown eyes capture mine and his smile deepens as he speaks it again. "Ellie."

A smile, curved inside book-ended parentheses, greets me. In one swift motion, he removes his hat, unbuttons his jacket, and lowers his large frame beside me. He's aged but his smile and intense gaze, and the effect they have on me, are the same. Time slows almost to the point of stopping, expanding to envelop us in this moment.

I somehow regain control of my vocal cords and acknowledge him in a half question, half proclamation. "Christopher."

Simply saying his name awakens my senses. I feel my face flush, and look away from him. His rounded shoulder playfully taps against mine. He had once been my respite, my port of call from the storms of life. My heart is heavy with grief and I long to burrow inside his embrace—cleave to him—like I had so many times before. I no longer had that right, though. I walked away, I remind myself.

How is this possible? Why now? My brain is in hyper-drive trying to process this odd happenstance. "Are you really here?"

"In the flesh," he replies. As if to reassure me of his true presence, he takes my hand and brings it to his lips.

Sometimes seventeen years can feel like a breath away.

He nods his head towards the doors. "My mother passed away."

His news constricts my already grieving heart. "I'm sorry."

For the first time since he spoke my name, he turns away from me, trying to hide his pained expression.

"Yeah," he says with a long exhale. His grip on my hand tightens as he clears his throat. "Today was the viewing, or whatever it is they call it."

In that moment, I remember seeing the other family across the hall. I close my eyes and try to remember what she had looked like, the sound of her voice, and the smell of her kitchen.

He brings our clasped hands back up to his mouth, brushing his lips against my fingers. A lone tear falls from his cheek onto my index finger.

I stop breathing, but the heady silence is broken by his tearful laugh, and I finally breathe out again.

"What?" I ask as his sweet, soulful, brown eyes meet mine.

He smiles. "I was just thinking about how much my mother hated you, and about what she would think about my holding your hand like this."

I can't help but tearfully laugh back even if it is at my own expense. "Yes, she would be none too pleased."

We look away from each other and instead gaze at the city at our feet—our city, our home. Well, it used to be my home.

He clears his throat and nods his head behind us. "What about you?"

My voice sounds shaky—not my own. "My friend Katherine passed away. I don't know if you remember her or not." A sudden shiver ripples through me as my body remembers.

Without a word, he places his jacket over my shoulders, pulling me closer to him. His large arm encircles me while the ministrations of his fingers on my arm begin to calm my overworked nerves.

I let out a breath I didn't know I had been holding. My fingers brush the scratchy polyester jacket of his uniform just under the lieutenant insignia; he has done well, been promoted. I want to touch the cool brass bars, but years in the service have trained me to leave them unmarred by the pads of my fingers. He chuckles at me as if he can read my thoughts, making my cheeks hot and red. The visual show of my arrant embarrassment serves to fan the flames of his laughter, causing me to join in with him despite myself. As it dies down, we fall into a companionable silence. Like magnets, our heads are drawn together, deepening our embrace.

His free hand finds the hem of my dress and works it between the pads of his thumb and forefinger. "I'm sorry about your friend."

I look up from the spot I had been studying on the step in front of me and meet his intense gaze. Our foreheads lightly press together.

My response comes out in a hoarse whisper. "She was Alex's...." I take a deep breath and continue. "She was the one who lost the baby."

His eyes lower in remembrance.

I reach with a trembling hand for his. "What she went through...." A ball of unresolved emotions chokes my throat.

He sighs and his heavy-laden lids, still at half-mast, avoid my searching gaze. "Alex," he says under his breath, a name that holds such meaning to us both. Looking up at me at last, he asks, "Do you want to talk about it?" His voice implores me to open up to him.

I clear my throat, preparing to tell him the whole of it and unburden myself, and present to him my elegy to her.

Chapter 1

Nin's Bar
Danville, Virginia
February 29, 2008
7:30 PM

The clock radio on her 2003 Mazda 626 dash read 7:30. Katherine let out a deep sigh as she turned off the car. She was late for her meeting with Alex Bailey, the new FBI field agent assigned to be her partner. He had called her earlier that morning to tell her he was finishing a case in Richmond, and wondered if she might want to meet up later, before they were assigned their first case on Monday. She had agreed and suggested meeting in her hometown of Danville, Virginia in a high-end bar nestled right off of I-95.

She hated to be late, but that had been out of her control tonight. Her thumb rubbed at the spot where her ring had been all her adult life—so many years wasted with a man she had never even loved. She closed her eyes and let the tears slide down her cheeks. She swiped at her cheek, took a deep breath, and got out of the car.

The cold February winds whipped at Katherine, causing her to grip the side of the car for balance, and to wonder if even nature was conspiring against her.

She scanned the dimly lit bar and spotted him at the far end, fingering an empty shot glass. He had wavy, dark brown hair cut in a style that was outdated but looked perfect on him. His tall lanky form, five o'clock shadow and rumpled Men's Wearhouse type of suit looked almost comical next to the excessively wealthy regular patrons, in their tailored Armani suits and Donna Karan ties. There was something else, though, that made none of the other stuff matter: he was one of those guys that exuded sex. His good looks and no doubt charm had most likely left many women waiting for a call the next day.

She had heard through the Bureau grapevine that he was one of the hottest agents to ever step foot in the D.C. office.

***

He tapped his tar-stained fingers on the bar and mentally cursed whoever had initiated the smoking ban for this small town. Signs posted all over the bar warned patrons not to light up inside or within 200 feet of the entrance. He hated waiting, especially when he couldn't smoke. It had been a long day, and the cigarettes he smoked in the car on the long ride over hadn't quelled his anxiety. Since that was out, he'd decided to drink instead, and two shots of Bushmills Irish Whiskey later his anxiety had only worsened.

The clock on his phone told him she was already twenty minutes late.

A cold blast of air hit his back, and he turned on the bar stool to face the front door. The woman who had kept him waiting stood in the entrance. *Maybe some things are worth waiting for.* He took in every detail, as if he hadn't pored over her personnel file with a fine toothed comb, memorizing every detail.

She stood five-foot ten—six feet in those heels—with a small athletic frame. He'd heard she was part of the FBI running club, ran upwards of five miles a day, and it showed. Her fitted black suit probably cost more than his entire wardrobe. The red soles of her expensive-looking shoes matched her long curly hair, which reminded him of the bald cypress trees in the fall.

She was beautiful, prepossessingly so.

He swallowed hard as he took her in. *Damn.* He adjusted his thrift store tie and smoothed out his suit, suddenly concerned about his own appearance and what she might think of him.

She blushed under the weight of his heavy, inquisitive gaze, but regained her composure and walked towards him with her hand extended in greeting. "Special Agent Bailey?"

He took her hand in a firm grasp and smiled. "Please, call me Alex. You must be Katherine. Do you want to sit at the bar or get a table?"

"The bar is fine."

Alex, ever the consummate gentleman, nodded and held out his arm to let her go ahead of him. He couldn't help but notice her toned calf muscles flex as she took her seat at the bar. He shook his head to try and regain his focus.

The bartender, Nin, smiled at Katherine as she took her seat at the bar. "Usual?" Nin asked.

Katherine nodded and he turned back to pour her a glass of tonic with a twist of lime. When he returned with it, she took a sip of her tonic water and set it back down.

Without thinking, Alex ordered another drink. He had begun to find it harder and harder to keep it together, and tonight's drinks were only adding fuel to the fire that was already threatening to turn into an out of control blaze.

He rotated his stool inward towards his new partner. "So, Special Agent Ka-ther-ine Mitchel, what brought you into the FBI?" His words began to slur together a little, not drunk, but on the fast track to getting there.

She tilted her head slightly. "I was recruited right out of school. I had been in Cambridge, here in Virginia, getting my Doctorate in Psychology."

"Yes, but what made you choose law enforcement?"

"My father was a US Marshal. He died on duty when I was a teenager, and I was impressed with the FBI agents that handled the investigation."

He brushed her hand. "I'm sorry, that must have been hard losing your father that way at such a young age."

"What about you? Why did you join the FBI?"

He took a sip of whiskey. "I wanted to have a cool badge."

Katherine's cheeks pinked as she chuckled at his joke. "The word around the Bureau is that you're on the FBI fast track, having solved some pretty high profile cases, and that you were one of the top agents in the Counter Terrorism Division."

"Don't believe all the rumors you hear."

She let out a short laugh, covering her mouth with her hand. Her right brow arched up. "All of the rumors? I've heard other more *interesting* ones."

He flashed a smile and finished the rest of his shot. The sober part of his brain advised that he needed to slow down before he slipped and made a fatal error in judgment. The louder part of his brain screamed that he should focus only on the beautiful woman in front of him and the sound of her laughter. A part of him wanted to make her laugh for the rest of his life, even if it was at his expense. He must be drunk already, he thought, because he was starting to sound like one of those ridiculous men in the awful Nicholas Sparks books Sara always read out loud to him.

He needed to snap out of this. Women had always been his kryptonite.

The small band in the far corner of the bar started to play a slow romantic tune, *At Last*. His impulsive streak kicked in, and he took her by the hand towards the dimly lit dance floor.

As he led her into a slow waltz, Katherine leaned into him. He pulled her small frame up against his and persuaded her body into a conversation that left both of them a little breathless.

His voice a bit husky, he whispered in her ear, "I love this song."

"Me too." Her face and neck flushed to match her hair.

Alex smiled, encouraged by her response. Katherine was a perfect partner, so he added small turns and dips that made her smile. The lessons he had taken in college were coming in handy.

All the twists and spins began to be his undoing, though, as his knees started to wobble and the whiskey that sloshed around in his gut threatened to make a reprise. He swallowed hard and tried to focus on her, on her smell—gardenias. His train of thought followed a myopic track of wanting and, engrossed in her smell and touch, he didn't see it coming.

The first punch caught Alex square in the jaw. His hands went up to cup his wounded face as he shot an angry glare at his assailant. "What the fuck?"

A blonde, stocky man about half his height grabbed Katherine by the arm and yanked her out of the way, then served another sharp blow to Alex's jaw.

Though stunned at first, the second punch sobered Alex enough to respond. He rushed with all his weight into his assailant's center of gravity, his momentum causing them both to tumble against the back wall of the bar. His pointed shoulder bone dug into the other man's solar plexus.

The dance floor cleared, with one of the couples helping a stunned Katherine to her feet, and the band stopped playing. Everyone stopped what they were doing and watched the fight unfold, leaving the grunts and movements of the two fighting men the only sounds in the bar.

The bouncer stepped in to break up the fight. At 6'5" and 300 pounds, this took little effort.

The collar of Alex's shirt jerked back, choking him.

His assailant turned on Katherine, grabbing her arm and pulling her up close to him. "You bitch!" He reached into his pocket and pulled out a letter and an engagement ring. "What the hell is this?"

Her eyes widened in fear. "Charles!"

Nin stepped in and gently placed a hand on Charles's taut shoulder. "Everyone is watching, sir. Perhaps now is not the time for this."

Charles looked at Katherine with disgust and released her from his grip. He shrugged off some of the anger and walked over to Nin, addressing him with a controlled rage. "I don't want either one of them to ever come in here again. Is that understood?" Charles commanded as he straightened Nin's tie.

"Of course, sir," Nin replied, strangled from the tightened necktie.

"Tiny, take him out!"

Tiny? Why are only giant men called Tiny?

"You heard the man. Time for you to go sober-up, little buddy," the man said to Alex.

Alex stared up at him. "Are you fucking kidding me? *He* started it."

The giant man kept dragging him out the door.

"Why aren't you throwing him out, too?" Alex demanded.

The bouncer shook his head. "Mr. Charles owns the place, and you were dancing with his girl. You pissed off the wrong dude, my friend."

As the bouncer yanked him out the bar door, Alex heard Charles say to Katherine, "Don't think I'm finished with you, and next time there won't be a crowd around to protect you."

Tiny tossed him out of the bar—like a bag of trash—causing him to stumble and almost fall on the concrete. The rush of cold air sobered Alex up. He walked over and sat on the nearest parking stump to wait for Katherine, cursing himself as Charles peeled out of the parking lot in his over-sized truck.

Katherine stepped out of the bar and stopped outside the entrance, watching as the taillights of Charles's truck disappeared down the long dark highway.

Alex rose from his hiding spot and touched her arm, startling her. "Sorry, I didn't mean to scare you." Katherine nodded in a haze as he continued. "I hope I didn't mess things up between you two."

"No, that had nothing to do with you. I... I left him tonight." A small sob escaped her tightly clasped lips.

Alex reached into his jacket and handed her a crisp white handkerchief. "Hey, are you going to be okay?"

She nodded. "I'm fine, Alex." She examined the handkerchief, thumbing over the cross-stitched monogram on the corner, and dabbed at her eyes.

He gently reeled her into his open embrace and she let him. As she looked up at him and began to pull away, he lowered his head and placed a chaste kiss on her lips.

Katherine startled. "Alex...." She put her hand on his chest to put some space between them.

He rubbed his forehead and winced. *Time to sober up, indeed.* "I'm sorry."

Katherine frowned and her eyes narrowed as she stood in front of him clutching the handkerchief.

He sighed. "I'm sorry, I think I might have had one too many tonight." He hiccupped back a burp.

She exhaled and rolled her eyes a little at him. "Come on, I can't very well let you drive yourself home."

Twenty minutes later, they pulled into Alex's apartment parking lot.

"Want to come in... for a cup of coffee or something?" he asked, stepping out of the car.

She offered a kind smile. "No, I think I should get going. I'll see you on Monday."

Alex flashed her a thousand watt smile and headed up to his apartment.

Jason's Apartment
Danville, Virginia
February 29, 2008
10:00 PM

After a long day at the newspaper, Jason Knettle had at last settled in for the night with a glass of scotch and a good book, when his cellphone rang.

"Knettle speaking."

"Hey, Knettle, it's me," Katherine said. She sounded frazzled.

"Hey, Red, what's up?"

"Can I crash at your place for the night?"

Jason's heart raced at the thought, and he answered without question. "Of course you can."

He heard her breathe in deeply. "Great. I'll be there in a bit."

With that she hung up, leaving Jason with the phone still pressed against his ear. Feeling foolish, he tossed it on the sofa.

He and Katherine had been friends for years. The day they met had been an unseasonably hot and humid day. It seemed like eons ago. Jason worked as an intern for the Danville Press, which his family owned, and was on his first assignment to cover the class of '94's homecoming game. Katherine was a freshman in college at the time, and her sister Addie was a junior at the high school.

Katherine had volunteered to work the concessions stand. She had worn her class of '93 fighting Bobcats tee shirt and a pair of faded blue jean shorts that brought attention to her long tan legs. Her wavy red hair hung in two short pigtails that brushed against her shoulders when she moved.

It had been one of those freak fall days where the temperatures shot into the eighties.

***

Jason arrived already dripping with sweat from his walk from the parking lot. He made a beeline for the concessions stand—desperate for a Coke—and found her instead. It was love or lust at first sight—he wasn't sure. Instead of mentally cursing his father for making him sit through a high school football game, he tried to come up with something clever to say that might win the heart of the beautiful woman before him.

When he reached the front of the line, she smiled at him, making his world turn upside down and inside out.

"You look like you could use something cool to drink," she said. When she smiled, her perfectly aligned teeth glistened, mesmerizing him further, but her smile faded, perhaps after seeing how peaked he had become.

"Sir, are you alright?" she asked.

No sooner did she say this, he fainted right there at the counter.

The next thing he knew he was lying down in the shade with his head in her lap. As she cooled him down with the wet rag, he wondered if he had died and gone to Heaven.

"Here, take a sip of this water," she said, and looked him in the eye.

Jason smiled back at her and complied with her wishes by taking slow sips of the cool water. "What happened?" He tried to sit up, only to have the dizziness overcome him, and he lay back down again.

"Take it easy. You fainted," she said.

He felt his cheeks flush with embarrassment as he groaned. "I'm supposed to be covering the game for the Danville Press." He flashed his press card.

She smiled. "You really weren't dressed for the weather." She nodded towards his white oxford shirt and black dress pants, which clung to him like a second skin.

Jason smiled back at her and laughed a little to himself. "No, I suppose I wasn't. In my defense, I did leave the suit jacket in the car."

When she smiled back at him with a wide easy grin and a short chuckle, he thought he might be in danger of fainting again.

"My name is Katherine, by the way." Her eyes squinted as she looked down at him.

After an awkward pause he found his voice. "Jason. Jason Knettle."

They ended up watching the game together. Jason even bought and changed into a Bobcats tee shirt and baseball cap. They found out they knew many of the same people, but had never met because he had gone to a private school for boys in Rhode Island. They talked for hours about what their plans for the future were and what they wanted to accomplish.

Katherine told him how she planned to go to graduate school for psychology, and how she planned to pursue a career in law enforcement.

Jason told her about his dream of being a novelist like his grandfather, and how his father had his mind set that Jason would take over as Editor-in-Chief of the Danville Press. He offered to show her some of his short stories and a novel he had written.

***

Through the years, their friendship had grown and, even though she had never shown any sign of reciprocating his feelings, he loved her beyond reason. He'd remained single through the years, and dated so infrequently that people at the paper were beginning to wonder if he might not be gay.

A knock at his apartment door made him jump. Even though she had her own key, she always knocked—another way she kept him at a distance.

He took a deep breath and raked his long lanky fingers through his short dark hair, then rose from his overstuffed sofa and answered the door. The moment he opened the door, Katherine rushed through it and into his arms, almost knocking him down.

"Oomph," he noisily exhaled from the force.

He held her tightly to him as he led her over to the couch, helping her sit down. It took him several minutes to calm her down. When she at last stopped sobbing, he pulled a blanket off the back of the couch and wrapped it around her. She curled into his arms, and he held her the entire night without saying a word.

***

The next morning, Katherine awoke to the morning light shining in her eyes. As she began to wake up, she became aware that she wasn't in her apartment. Groaning, she rubbed her face with the palms of her hands.

This morning habit woke Jason, who was sleeping beside her on the sofa. "Red...?" he asked, half awake.

Katherine groaned again as yesterday's events came back to her. "I left Charles," she blurted out.

After a long agonizing pause, Jason responded, "Do you want to talk about it?"

She sighed. "No, not really." Almost to the point of tears, she continued. "I...."

Jason knitted his brow. "What?" he asked more forcefully this time.

Katherine shook her head and mumbled, "It's nothing."

Jason's eyebrows lowered and his eyes narrowed. "No, if it was nothing you wouldn't be so upset." He called out her BS, as usual.

Katherine clutched the edge of the couch.

He covered her white-knuckled grip with his hand in an effort to comfort her. "You can talk to me." His voice carried a soothing tone that made her heart hurt.

She feigned a smile. "I know. It's just...." She choked on her words.

"He didn't hit you again, did he? Because if he did—"

She held up her hand. "No, no it wasn't like that."

"Then what is it, Katherine?" He again knitted his brows in frustration.

Katherine diverted her eyes from his intense gaze and instead looked at her shoes.

"Katherine...."

She turned to face him, forcing back unshed tears. "Please just drop it, J. Can you just be happy with the fact that I left him?"

Jason's face sank. "Yes, yes... I'm glad you aren't going to be hurt by him anymore."

She could tell by the look in his eyes that he was growing weary of this never-ending conversation with her. He didn't understand why she stayed with Charles, and to be fair, she didn't quite understand her reasons for staying, either. She was resolute this time that she would not be going back to Charles, shivering at the thought of all he had done to her and to others. No, she wouldn't be running back to him this time, no matter what he said to try and get her back.

As Jason rose from the sofa, Katherine grabbed his hand. "I'm sorry, Jason. You're such a good friend to me. I know you just want what's best for me."

Jason wordlessly nodded and, after a few seconds, broke her hold on his hand and walked away.

She hated to keep secrets from him, but her fear of involving him in this mess kept her from telling him the truth. Trying to regain her sense of self, she rose from the sofa and called out to Jason, who was in the kitchen making coffee. "I'm going to go for a run. Wanna join me?"

After a long pause, he at last responded to her. "No, I think I'll sit this one out. I should probably go into the paper today and get some work done. Make yourself at home. I don't know when I'll get back. It might be late. Don't wait up for me."

Katherine's heart hurt at his response. She'd hoped that they might be able to spend the day together, as they'd often done in the past after she and Charles had fought. Wanting to give him his space, she ran down the stairs of his complex and out to her car to get her suitcase and her gym bag. A long run would help clear her mind.

After her five-mile run she returned to Jason's apartment. She would have to look for a new place to live, but couldn't bring herself to deal with that particular consequence of her actions.

Much to her dismay, Jason ended up spending most of Saturday and Sunday at the paper, leaving Katherine to sit alone in his apartment and think over the events of the last few weeks.

She was so eager for Monday to start, she awoke at 4:00 a.m. to go for another five-mile run and then work the weight machines at the gym before going into work. The routine was brutal but it helped clear the fog from her mind.

FBI Headquarters: Hoover Building
Washington, D.C.
March 3, 2008
8:00 AM

From his spot perched at the corner of her desk, he watched her walk in a daze through the busy bullpen. Her red and puffy eyes suggested she had been crying, and she carried a Kennedy Center travel mug. Maybe she liked the opera, he noted.

When she saw him, her steel blue eyes turned icy.

Uh-oh, he thought, clutching the files in his hand even tighter, bracing himself for the impact of the inevitable angry words.

"Excuse me, Agent Bailey, but would you so kindly get your ass off of MY desk!"

Alex flashed a lazy smile as he stood up. "You're not a morning person, huh? That's cool."

Katherine sank into her leather chair and took a sip of her coffee, gasping and touching her red lips with the back of her hand.

He thought of making some off-handed comment about coffee being hot, but thought better of it. Something told him that she wasn't one to take teasing well.

"What do you want?"

Alex held up the case file with a smirk. "I'm here to work, Agent Mitchel."

She sighed and slid further down into her chair with a scowl on her face. "Right," she said under her breath.

Alex handed her the case file. "A little girl's body was found in the woods behind her house. She was reported kidnapped seventy-two hours prior. There's been a string of murders of little girls all along the eastern seaboard in the past three months. ASAC Richards handpicked us for the taskforce. Of course my first case in the Violent Crimes Unit is going to be a child murder," he said, his mouth drawn in a tight, grim line.

She flipped open the case file, and glanced up at him with a look that made him think she might want him to scram.

"I'll leave you to get acquainted with the particulars. ASAC Richards scheduled the first briefing for this morning. You've got thirty minutes before we're needed in the ready room."

"Thank you, Agent Bailey," she said in her professional tone.

He could see the wall she was putting up between them, no doubt as a result of his kissing her the other night. He nodded back, adjusted his tie, smoothed out his suit, and walked back to his desk.

The briefing took three long hours and left Alex in dire need of a cigarette. He had known that the transition to the Violent Crimes Unit would be hard, but he hadn't prepared himself for working on child abduction and murder cases.

Alex jogged down the back stairs and out the side door unnoticed. The bright afternoon sunshine almost blinded him. He leaned against the cold stone of the FBI building, took long drags of his cigarette, and watched visitors mill around the outside--taking pictures of themselves behind a cardboard cutout that looked like an FBI badge.

As he exhaled a large ring of smoke, a familiar form came into view.

Charles MacAvoy walked briskly out of the FBI building and headed in Alex's general direction.

He put out his cigarette and stepped out of the shadows and into Charles's general line of sight.

Charles's jaw tightened. "Agent Bailey," he said through his clenched teeth.

Someone had been doing a little Googling, he thought. Grinning from ear to ear, he sauntered over with the intent to push some buttons. "Charles, you miserable twat of a human being."

The other man's face contorted with pure rage. "Motherfucker!"

His heart rate rose as Charles came at him, pushing him against the wall of the building and pinning him there with his forearm. Alex hadn't anticipated him being this responsive.

"I read up all about you, you miserable sack of shit," Charles said. "I know your name. I know where you live. You do not want to fuck with me."

Alex snickered, "You're right about that, but it's not you I want to fuck. Your girl is pretty hot, and not a bad kisser."

Charles jammed his arm further into his throat, constricting his breathing. Instinct kicked in and Alex brought up his knee with a quick hard jab into the other man's scrotum, and smashed his own foot down hard on Charles' foot, releasing himself from the chokehold.

Straightening his tie and jacket, Alex looked down at Charles with a look of disgust. "It was a pleasure. We should do this again some time."

Not wanting to wait around for him to recover and retaliate, Alex went back into the building and up to his desk to finish up his expenditure reports.

Chapter 2

O'Malley's Bar
Ocean City, Maryland
March 8, 2008
7:20 PM

Katherine sat in her FBI-issued sedan outside their suspect's last known address, and checked her watch for the third time in the last half hour—he was twenty minutes late for their shift, breaking FBI protocol for surveillance of a suspect. She studied the information they knew about their suspect and tried to memorize his face, but her back was stiff and she was tired from the long week. Couch surfing at Jason's apartment had begun to take its toll, but she had been too busy with work even to think about looking for an apartment.

A tapping on the passenger side window startled her out of her reverie. *Alex*. She reached across to open his door.

He smiled and slid into the seat. "I know I'm late. Sorry." His cheeks and nose were red and his teeth chattered together.

His charming smile disarmed her, something that after a week of working long hours together was becoming a habit between them. The boundaries that she clung to had become tiring, and she'd let them slip against his relentless charm.

"I'm hoping you will forgive me when you see what I brought." He held up a white, greasy takeout bag like a prize. "Mr. Sandwich, your favorite. Meatball sub for me. Veggie Delite for you." He reached into the bag and handed her the smallest of the two sandwiches. "Oh, and coffee, of course. It's cold as shit out tonight." He held up a large thermos with two nested cups on top.

Katherine raised her eyebrow in a mock-irritated way. She couldn't let on that his charm had actually managed to work on her. "Tell me something I don't know. I've been freezing my ass off." She smiled despite herself. She enjoyed his company and, in spite of her best efforts to keep him at a safe distance, had grown fond of him.

His emerald-colored eyes twinkled from the light cast off by the street lamps. When her eyes met his for a brief moment, the side of his lip curled up into a small smile.

Her heart skipped a beat. "Don't worry, you haven't missed anything. It's been rather uneventful. Unless you count watching a bunch of frat boys piss in the alley an event," she mumbled through a mouth full of food.

Alex snickered. "I'm sorry I missed that."

Katherine settled into her seat as she watched people coming in and out of the bar across the street. The subtle sounds of Alex beside her, chewing, shifting in his seat and crumpling his wrappers, comforted her.

***

A companionable silence set in. Alex had wolfed down his sub in record time, astonishing even himself. Then he remembered that he hadn't eaten anything since breakfast, and that had only been a bagel with the nasty fat free cream cheese that the office clerical staff kept picking up.

He reached between his legs and pulled up the thermos. With great care, he poured steaming hot coffee into one of the cups and handed it to Katherine. Their fingers brushed each other in the exchange, causing a blush to blossom across her freckled nose and cheeks. Alex looked away, smiling. He didn't need the coffee anymore; a warm alertness settled into his bones.

He pushed his seat into a reclining position and burrowed into the worn leather interior in preparation for a long night of sitting, waiting, and watching for their suspect to show up. They had spent the last several days working up a profile, phone canvassing and interviewing witnesses, which led them to suspect a thirty-year-old white male, who lived above O'Malley's Bar in Ocean City, Maryland. They were assigned the first twelve-hour shift.

Alex soon found himself fighting sleep even though it was only 8:00 p.m. In an effort to stay awake, he decided to probe Katherine and find out about her ex's unexpected visit on Monday.

Trying to sound casual, he cleared his throat. "Hey, I forgot to tell you I ran into your ex the other day, outside, during my smoke break. You two are getting back together?"

Katherine set down her empty thermos cup on the dash in front of her. "He brought me my service weapon. I had forgotten it at the apartment when I left on Friday." She turned and looked at him with a joking grin. "Not that it's *any* business of yours."

He lifted his hands in defense. "Just making conversation, Agent Mitchel."

Just as he said this, the suspect sauntered out of the bar across the street and headed in the direction of the abandoned field next door.

Katherine jumped out of the car first and ran towards the suspect with her gun drawn. "FBI, *stop*!" She then followed at a fast clip as the suspect bolted in the direction of the alley.

As per primary tactical procedures, Alex sprinted around the back of the bar and came out through the alley in an effort to corner the suspect.

While in pursuit, the suspect reached into the band of his pants, pulled out a small pistol, spun on his toes and pointed his weapon at Katherine. She raised her gun, trained to shoot him if necessary. The suspect shifted back and forth on the sides of his feet with his weapon pointed at Katherine, creating a standoff.

"FBI. Drop your weapon! *Now! Drop it!*"

The suspect's weapon hand shook.

Shit. Alex tried to close in on the suspect and do a quick visual sweep of the perimeter, and he caught sight of some movement in the direction of the dumpsters. His mind raced as he glanced up, still keeping his gun trained on the suspect. His heart thundered in his chest as a surge of adrenaline flooded his body.

There. A beam of reflected light from the street lamp gleamed against the metal barrel. *A gun!* A car's headlights illuminated the scene for Alex. A sharpshooter was poised on the landing of the fire escape above them, aiming at Katherine! With only a second to respond, he lifted his 9mm SIG-Sauer P226 pistol and called out to the sharpshooter.

"FBI. Drop your weapon. I will shoot."

The sharpshooter glanced down at Alex before returning his attention back to his sights—his target, Katherine.

Alex fired off his weapon and expertly took down the sharpshooter, who never got a chance to fire.

The loud echoing sound of his service weapon jolted the already skittish suspect, who wildly fired his weapon, missing Katherine by a wide margin.

Katherine pulled the trigger on her Glock 23, but the gun jammed. Alex aimed and fired his gun, taking down the suspect, who crumpled to the ground between him and Katherine in a flurry of curse words.

Katherine holstered her useless weapon and moved the suspect's gun out of reach with the handkerchief from her pocket.

His handkerchief, he realized. Alex reached down to pull up his right pant leg and handed Katherine his Kahr CM9 from out of his ankle holster. "Here, take this."

While Katherine held the suspect in place, he walked over to the fire escape, pulled down the ladder and climbed up to where the downed sharpshooter lay sprawled on the landing. He sank down on his haunches and felt for a pulse. Nothing. Pursing his lips, he looked down at Katherine, who was reading the suspect his rights.

The man kept ranting about pressing charges while she called first for an ambulance, and then to her ASAC.

Alex patted down the sharpshooter, looking for any kind of identification, and then climbed down the ladder as Katherine was hanging up her phone.

"He didn't have any identification," he said.

She wet her lips with a smooth sweep of her tongue. "My gun jammed."

He frowned and rested his hands on hips. "I noticed. Have you had trouble with it before?"

She shook her head, taking on a defensive posture. "No. I always clean it and keep it oiled."

Alex worked his bottom lip as an idea started to germinate.

Katherine nodded to the man on the landing. "Do you think he was an accomplice? None of the profiling or research indicated that he was working with anyone else."

He looked down and nodded at the suspect, who had lost consciousness. "If he's an accomplice, which I don't think he is, hopefully he'll talk."

Katherine sighed, but before she could say anything he touched the sleeve of her coat.

"The sniper was aiming at you. He has no identification. I'm not a weapons expert but I think his weapon is a military grade sniper rifle." He worried his bottom lip again, reluctant to continue his train of thought. "I... I don't think he has anything to do with this case. I...." He couldn't bring himself to say what he was really thinking. She wasn't ready to hear it—he could tell.

The sound of the ambulance pulling up got him off the hook. He turned away from Katherine and strode with purpose towards the EMTs, leaving her alone to consider the possibilities.

Twenty minutes later, the Evidence Collection Team was busy at work roping off the scene, collecting, cataloging, and referencing the evidence, including Katherine's service pistol. A tactical officer on scene was able to confirm Alex's suspicions that the sharpshooter's weapon was a Blaser R93 LRS2, a military grade weapon. Forensics took the sharpshooter's prints to enter into the FBI's Integrated Automated Fingerprint Identification System, or IAFIS.

The lead forensic investigator caught up with Alex on his way out of the roped-off crime scene. "We'll let you know if we get any hits."

"Thanks, man," Alex said with a sigh. He wasn't expecting any hits. Some people didn't exist, and he had a feeling that shooter was one of those faceless, nameless people.

The agent nodded as if he too wasn't holding his breath. "You were both damn lucky that neither of you got hurt."

Alex huffed. "Yeah, lucky."

FBI Headquarters: Hoover Building
Washington, D.C.
March 9, 2008
12:30 AM

Several hours and lots of paperwork later, Katherine packed up her stuff to go home.

Alex grabbed his things and walked out with her. He even held open the door for her as they stepped out into the brisk March air.

She started for the curb, but Alex reached for her arm and stopped her. "Hey, it's been a rough day, and I don't know about you, but I'm way too wired. Want to go out and grab a bite to eat? The RFD on 7th is open for another hour."

Katherine sighed. "No thanks, Alex. Maybe next time. Goodnight." She lifted her arm and waved down a passing cab, and got in.

"Where to?" the cabby asked.

It was late and not a lot of places were going to be open. She thought for a second before replying. "Fado, 7th and H." She pulled out her cell phone and dialed Jason's number.

"Knettle speaking."

"You have no idea how good it is to hear your voice."

The cab driver looked through the rearview mirror and caught her eye.

After everything that had gone down that night she couldn't help but be suspicious of everyone—even the nosey cabby.

"That bad of a day, huh?"

Katherine lowered her voice. "Yeah, you could say that. I.... There's something I need to talk to you about, but not over the phone. Can you meet me somewhere?"

"I thought you were on surveillance all night?"

"That's part of what I need to talk to you about. Can you meet me?" She could hear the desperation in her voice, but it couldn't be helped.

"Of course, where?"

"Fado?" She knew the moment the words left her mouth that Jason would be concerned about meeting her in a bar, but she needed to meet with him in a public place and, at the late hour, bars were her only choice.

"Okay. Should I be worried?"

She looked to the rear of the cab again to see if any cars had followed. She didn't think so, but she hadn't paid close enough attention. "We'll talk about it when I see you."

"Give me twenty minutes."

"Okay." She ended the call and placed her trembling hands in her lap.

Grand Hyatt
Washington, D.C.
March 9, 2008
1:00 AM

Alex sat in the lobby of the Grand Hyatt, a place he frequented when he didn't want to go home. He had just relayed to his superiors the events of the evening and they were none too pleased, but the mission was still a go. To help alleviate his mounting stress, he took short puffs off his cigar and knocked back heaping gulps of Jack Daniels straight from the bottle.

His cell phone vibrated, making him jump, and he jumbled through his pockets and answered it right before it went to voicemail. "Bailey."

The voice on the other end, distorted by a voice modifier, made the hair on his arms stand up on end. "You won't always be there to save her. Drop it or she won't be the only one who ends up with a toe tag in the morgue." The click and silence that followed was deafening.

Alex put his phone down on the arm of his chair and, with a trembling hand, downed the rest of his minibar whiskey in one long swallow.

He quickly thumbed through his contacts until he found the one he needed. "Hey, yeah, sorry to wake you, Danny, but I need you to trace the last call that came in through my cell. Yes, thanks. If you could get me a number by tomorrow that would be great."

When his phone buzzed again two seconds later, he jumped, but after seeing the familiar name and number pop up on the screen, he tried to calm himself. "Hey."

The sultry female voice on the other end did nothing to calm his racing heart. "Hey, baby, where have you been? When ya gonna come back to my bed?"

Alex rubbed his temples. "How 'bout tonight? Meet me at the Grand Hyatt. I'm in room 344."

The woman chuckled. "Don't worry, baby, I'll make you forget all about your troubles."

He ended the call and turned off his phone so that he wouldn't be disturbed. A night with Sara was just what he needed, he thought, as he placed his phone in his pocket and stumbled towards the elevator.

Fado
Washington, D.C.
March 9, 2008
1:00 AM

Jason sat side-by-side with Katherine in a booth at the far end of the bar, to avoid having to shout. He looked at her out of the corner of his eye while he rotated his coffee cup—a nervous habit. The worry lines etched across her forehead, and her wide blue eyes, made him anxious. He took a deep breath and reached for her hand, which she gave freely.

A heady silence had settled in between them. He tried to be patient with her, but was becoming restless.

She fidgeted with her cup until at last she cleared her throat and spoke up. "I've resisted telling you any of this for your protection, but I can't do this alone anymore, and you're the only one I trust."

He tightened his grip on her hand.

She opened her mouth and closed it again, as she seemed to struggle with finding the right words. "You asked me earlier why I left Charles. It isn't for any reasons that you might think." She took a deep breath and looked down at their linked hands. "I left Charles because of the things I found out about him, things that I found on his computer—something that trumped my fear over what he would do to me if I left him."

Jason's eyebrows knitted together. "What did you find?"

He listened as she told him about the information she had found and saved on two thumb drives.

She drank the remaining coffee in her cup, pushed it away from her, and let go of his hand as she sat forward at the table. "Half of it is encrypted, but he's a part of an organization called The Syndicate. I don't know exactly what his role is, but I learned enough to know that this group is dangerous. There were a lot of high profile names on some of the documents. I think he knows that I'm on to him, and tonight I was almost shot by a lone gunman. It could be nothing, but I think they might be trying to take me out."

Jason was left speechless. This was too much information for him to process all at once. Without realizing it, he had turned away from Katherine and faced forward. He twisted and knotted the paper wrapper of his straw.

"I'm thinking of turning in the drives to Alex."

Her new partner... whom she's known for all of five minutes! Is she crazy? Jason shook his head and huffed. "You just met him and you trust him that much? I would think that, if anything, this whole thing would have taught you not to be so trusting." He ran his long fingers through his hair. He didn't mean to be harsh, but sometimes he didn't know how else to get through to her.

She nodded in agreement. "Maybe you're right." She looked around the bar before slipping two thumb drives into the palm of his hand.

He felt as though she were handing him a live grenade.

She caught his eye, a serious expression etched across her face. "If anything happens to me, I need you to get these to ASAC Richards with the FBI and tell him everything. I don't know for sure, but I think he can be trusted. Like I said, there are so many high profile names attached to this, including people at the FBI and CIA. It even looks like high-level government officials are involved." She took a deep breath and sighed. "But you're right... I can't just give this to anyone. I trust you to hold onto them until I figure out a plan."

Jason put the drives in his dress pants pocket. "We can't go back to my apartment tonight. If Charles or someone else is trying to kill you, he will definitely try again, and it's no secret that you're staying with me. We'll have to stay somewhere else, like with that cop friend of yours, Lisa's girlfriend. What's her name? Marianna?"

Katherine pulled out her phone and texted Marianna.

Of all of Katherine's friends, Jason liked Marianna the best.

They worked their way through the crowded bar. He kept one hand inside his pants pocket, fingering the thumb drives. As they stepped out into the cold, the loud crack of gunfire erupted from a black sedan parked nearby.

Katherine looked at him with a startled expression before crumpling to the ground, where a dark pool of blood formed around her still body.

Jason's heart hammered in his chest as he squatted beside her. He took off his jacket, wadded it up and pressed it down hard on the wound that bubbled blood at an alarming rate.

"Don't just stand there!" He looked up at the growing crowd of people that had formed around them. "Someone call 911!"

He turned his attention back to Katherine. "Come on Red, stay with me." Soon he could hear the sound of the ambulance coming. "Just hold on."

The cacophonous sounds of ambulances, police cars and a fire truck drew closer to them. "They're on their way. Do you hear that?"

Her pale face added to his alarm.

"Just stay with me, Red."

FBI Headquarters: Hoover Building
Washington, D.C.
March 9, 2008
9:00 AM

Alex trudged into the Hoover building to finish up the paperwork from the bust and to find out where things stood with the suspect. He clutched his second triple-shot of espresso in his right hand, hoping it would give him the energy he needed to get his work done; he hadn't exactly gotten much sleep last night.

When he rounded the corner on his floor, he was confronted almost immediately by his ASAC. "Where have you been and why aren't you answering your phone?"

Alex mentally ran through all of the possible excuses he could give to his superior, but unable to come up with a good excuse on the spot, he chose to evade the question. "Is something wrong, sir?"

ASAC Richards sighed in a mixture of frustration and concern. "Special Agent Mitchel has been shot. She's at Pendrell General Hospital."

Alex's stomach bottomed out. "What? Is... is she okay?"

Richards nodded, his mouth drawn in a grim line. "It was touch and go for a while, but I just got off the phone with a friend who was there when she was shot, and he said she made it out of surgery okay and her doctors expect her to make a full recovery."

Alex let out the breath he'd been holding. The *what ifs* flew through his mind as he tried to think of how he could have prevented it from happening. It was his fault.

Without acknowledging his superior, he turned on his heel and stalked out of the building. Richards called out to him, but he kept walking.

Pendrell General Hospital
Georgetown, Maryland
March 9, 2008
10:00 AM

Alex stood at the door watching a man, dressed in scrubs, caressing her cheek. The tall, lanky man had close-cropped brown hair and large features. On his nose perched a pair of glasses.

Jealousy bubbled up inside of Alex and his fist clenched involuntarily. *This is silly.*

He cleared his throat, startling the man, who turned to face him. "Hi, I'm Agent Alex Bailey. I'm Katherine's new partner at the FBI. And you are?" He walked towards the man with his hand extended in greeting.

"A friend," the man said, ignoring Alex's extended hand.

Alex lowered his hand. *Wow, what's this guy's deal?*

A nurse came in and gave the man a look of deep concern. "You're still here? You should go home and get some rest or at least get something to eat. I promise we will call you if anything changes."

"You're right. I think I am a little hungry." The man stood and stretched his long limbs. "Excuse me." He breezed past Alex, almost knocking him over.

Alex watched as the man left the room.

The nurse caught his gaze. "He hasn't left her side all night. It was touch and go there for a while."

"Is she going to be okay?"

The nurse narrowed her eyes. "Are you family?"

He shook his head and flashed his badge. "She's my partner at the FBI."

She nodded, but still seemed unsure. "We're only supposed to release information to family."

"What about the man that just left?"

She looked in the direction of the door. "He's her friend and medical proxy. Poor dear was with her when it happened."

He smiled at the nurse, doing his best to lay on the charm. "Can't you just break the rules this one time?" He threw in a little suggestive wink for good measure.

The nurse blushed, her resolve softening. "You aren't supposed to be in here at all. I don't even want to know how you managed to make it into the room."

Alex pressed his hands to his chest as if in prayer and pleaded with her. "Please?"

A small smile crept up the side of the nurse's mouth. "Okay, but you didn't hear this from me."

He mimed zipping his lips, which got him another shy, rosy-cheeked smile. He hadn't lost his touch.

"It was touch and go for a while since she lost so much blood. She was lucky that there was only minimal internal bleeding that they were able to take care of in surgery. They did have to remove her spleen, but otherwise she is doing very well, considering."

The nurse performed a quick vitals check while she talked. "If it wasn't for her friend's quick response, though, she would be dead." She placed her stethoscope around her neck and started for the door. "Five minutes!"

Alex smiled and held his hands together in supplication. "Thank you."

Once she had left, he brushed his fingers against Katherine's.

Her eyelids fluttered. "Hmm... J," she mumbled in her half-drugged sleep.

Alex squeezed her hand. "No, Katherine, it's me, Alex."

Katherine mumbled in response—too doped-up to communicate.

He reached behind him and pulled the chair closer to the bed, and sat down beside her. All he could think about was the phone call he'd received last night. If only he'd been with her, maybe this wouldn't have happened. He felt like Alice, with every fiber of his being urging him to plunge down the rabbit hole.

It was getting harder and harder to stay the course and not let her in. It wasn't just a case anymore—all he could think about was her.

***

Jason took a bite of his hospital cafeteria tuna salad sandwich, and called one of his sources. "Hey, Pete, I need a favor. I need all the information you can give me on Special Agent Alex Bailey of the FBI. Yes, it may be an alias. Yeah, thanks... I think she's going to be okay. All right, thanks again. Talk to you later." He hung up and took another bite of his sandwich, but his nerves caused him to choke and gag on the sandwich. He was done.

He walked into the room only to see Alex stroking Katherine's hair. He felt his cheeks flush with anger. "You're still here?"

Alex put down her hand with care and rose from the chair. "Yeah, I was just going to leave."

When Jason didn't say anything, Alex continued. "I hear you're the one I have to thank for saving her life. She's lucky that you were there."

Jason's stiff posture and scowl made him start to feel foolish. He uncrossed his arms and let out a small sigh. "Yeah, I guess so."

Alex nodded, worrying his bottom lip.

The shame of Jason's childish behavior prompted him to lower his defenses and extend his hand. "I'm sorry I didn't introduce myself earlier. I'm not myself today."

Alex nodded, accepting his extended hand in greeting.

"I'm Jason Knettle, an old friend of Katherine's. She's been staying with me the last couple of days."

Alex nodded. "It's nice meeting you, Jason. I really should be heading back to work. I promised the nurse I would only be here for five minutes. When Katherine wakes up, can you tell her I stopped by?"

He shrugged. "Yeah, sure."

Alex looked at him as though he didn't quite believe Jason would follow through with his request. "Thanks."

With one last sideways glance at her, Alex walked out.

Jason waited until he could no longer hear the other man's footfalls, and then went back to her side. The thought of almost losing her was almost more than he could bear. He ran his fingers through her hair and combed it behind her ear. In a half sleep, Katherine snuggled against his hand and his heart leaped. He was powerless to stop himself from tracing his index finger along the fullness of her lips.

At his touch, she shifted, still half asleep. "Alex...."

Her words broke him. He was tired, not himself. He needed to go home.

FBI Headquarters: Hoover Building
Washington, D.C.
March 9, 2008
3:00 PM

ASAC Richards fingered the now curled-up corners of his stack of papers; the forensic evidence from the arrest the previous night had come through. He had also put in a request to the local PD about the shooting incident with Agent Mitchel. They had to be connected, but he was missing the puzzle piece that would prove his theory correct. His phone's shrill ring shook him from his train of thought.

"Richards," he answered.

"Agent Richards, A.D. Fullmore would like a word with you."

"I'll be right up," he said with a deep sigh.

He gathered up all the files and paperwork he had on the two incidents, put on his suit jacket and headed up to the executive floor. Before going inside he adjusted his tie.

"Agent, he'll see you right away," the assistant said.

He walked into the office and was greeted by his superior. "Take a seat."

"Yes sir." He sat down across from the Assistant Director.

Fullmore shuffled the files in front of him, making himself look too busy to actually look Richards in the face.

Richards hated this man and his arrogant nature.

"I understand you have the suspect in custody and that he has confessed to the murders."

"Yes sir." He rested his files on his crossed legs.

His eyes rose to acknowledge Richards. "And one of the agents under you was shot last night in an unrelated incident."

Richards cleared his throat. "Actually, sir, I believe the two incidents might be related."

He opened the file and pulled out the sheets he wanted his superior to see, but was disheartened when Fullmore held up his hand and waved the papers away. "Agent, I don't see how these incidents are connected, and would like you to drop any lines of inquiry you might have on the case."

This is ridiculous! He could feel his blood pressure begin to rise, and he felt the vein on his forehead pop out like it always did when his frustration skyrocketed.

"With all due respect, sir, you're wrong. One of our own was shot down in cold blood in a well-lit area where someone should have seen something, but no witnesses have come forward. The weapon used to shoot her was left at the scene, but ballistics is saying we've got nothing. You can't tell me the sniper incident earlier that night isn't related. Someone wants her dead and no one seems to be doing anything about it," Richards said, trying to temper his growing irritation.

Fullmore cleared his throat and looked Richards directly in the eyes. "Agent, you investigate what I tell you to. Senior Agent Toddson is availing himself to the D.C. police in regards to Agent Mitchel's shooting. You're not to investigate this incident any further. Is that clear?"

Richards rubbed the stubble on the end of his chin. "Yes sir. Crystal."

Fullmore nodded. "Good. In the meantime, I have a case I would like you to put your attention to—another child abduction case. Depending on how well this one turns out, I don't see why you can't be promoted to Section Chief when Fox retires. But that will only happen if we can work together on getting *this* case solved."

He handed a case file across the desk and began to give him the details and specifics of the new case, but Richards barely heard a word. All he could think about was how he had been told to drop the investigation of Katherine's shooting.

Why? Everyone knows Senior Special Agent Toddson is a stooge.

There would be no investigation, and that made him more determined than ever to find the connection between the two. Who wanted Katherine dead? And why did his boss not want him to look into her attempted murder?

FBI Headquarters: Hoover Building
Washington, D.C.
March 9, 2008
4:45 PM

Alex put away his notes on the shooting in his desk drawer and locked it up. The investigation into Katherine's shooting and the caller who threatened him had gotten nowhere. Danny hadn't been able to trace the call, saying something about dropped packets or some encryption software. All Danny could tell him was that it originated in D.C. and that it hadn't been on a land line. In other words... nothing.

On his way out of the Hoover Building to the parking garage, he pulled out his cell and finger-swiped his way through his contacts until he found the number he was looking for.

After three rings a woman picked up. "Hey, Alex."

He smiled. "Hey, Doc, do you have time to grab some dinner? I've got something I need to talk to you about."

"Alex, you need to get yourself a real therapist."

Her halfhearted chastisement made him smile. There would never be another therapist, only Doc. "You know it isn't as simple as all that."

The sound of her familiar sigh filled his ear. "Okay, how about you come by for dinner? We can have a couple beers and throw some burgers on the grill."

He chuckled. "It's freezing outside and you want to grill?"

Doc laughed. "Who said anything about *me* grilling? You want to talk you have to earn your session."

"Yes, ma'am! I'll see you in a few." He ended the call and sighed as he slipped into his car. He'd made a lot of progress in the last few years in dealing with his problems, but he knew he still had a long way to go. Having Doc provide him therapy and medication on the side allowed him to function on the job without fear of losing his security clearance or his rank of Chief Special Agent at the CIA.

As a CIA agent undercover, he needed to assess Katherine and Charles as threats and uncover who within the FBI was allowing an organized crime group to go unchecked. As part of the agreement between the two agencies and the Attorney General, he was also to avail the FBI of his expertise in criminal profiling. He had helped to capture over ten criminals during his short stint as a law enforcement officer.

In all his planning, though, he hadn't figured out how to keep a boundary between himself and Katherine. The lack of protection left him vulnerable to his natural wants and needs as man, especially in light of his oftentimes crippling addiction. Despite Doc's best efforts to help him control it, he spiraled out of control too often.

Over the last year he had grown envious of Doc and her husband. He yearned for things most men his age wanted, but nothing ever come easy for him.

He came into the world the son of a crack-addled mother and a meth-head dad. From an early age, he knew he had two options, succumb to his lot in life or rise above his heritage and be something better. It really wasn't a hard choice for him.

As a naturally gifted learner and someone who worked harder than most, he was able to pull himself out of the situation in which he'd been born. When he was sixteen, he was accepted o-n a full ride to Howard. To make up for what the scholarship didn't pay for, he had to work two jobs, but he still managed to get near-perfect grades every semester. In record time he received his bachelors in Criminal Justice and his Masters in International Affairs. While at Howard he became fluent in Arabic, Mandarin and Kurdish.

At age twenty the CIA recruited him and he took on the identity of Alex Bailey—his mother's maiden name. After he went through training, he traveled the world doing undercover operations during the second Gulf War. Two years ago, his superior, Supervisor Magellan, assigned him to a long-term undercover position within the FBI at the age of thirty-one. At the request of the Attorney General's Office he was placed within the FBI for training and then assigned to the Counterterrorism Division, and more recently the Criminal Investigative Division.

At a tipping point in his career, and his life, for that matter, he knew it could go either way.

As he pulled out of the Hoover Building's parking garage, he reminded himself of all he had overcome, and how he had it within him to be successful. Doc had been working with him on resetting the internal dialogue tape in his mind, which whispered to him that he was a failure, a degenerate....

...Like his old man.

Chapter 3

Church Hill Neighborhood
Richmond, Virginia
March 9, 2008
7:00 PM

Alex pulled up to the curb in front of a two-story, Federal-style brick home just west of Chimborazo Park. He loved this house and the people inside. He had met Doc and her husband, Chris, over ten years ago while on assignment in the Middle East.

Even though it was a direct violation of protocol, he continued to socialize with them even after he'd taken his current assignment under light cover at the FBI. He had his suspicions that his supervisor at the CIA knew of his association with the Forester family, but chose to look the other way. His reputation for uncovering impossible-to-get intelligence afforded him a little leniency, which he tried to not take advantage of.

Doc was one of the few and necessary luxuries he allowed himself. For years he'd been going to her for "under the table" therapy and medication to manage his addiction and the underlying anxiety that went along with it—a perk of having a psychiatrist as a best friend.

This current mission required him to be on point at all times, which meant he needed to keep his sexual predilections in check. If everything went well, a promised promotion to the rank of Junior Supervisor awaited him, something unheard of for a man his age. He just had to keep his shit together.

He shoved his keys and phone into the deep pockets of his wrinkled dress pants and reached into the back seat for the grocery bag full of goodies.

The security light on top of the garage lit up the stone path to the front porch, where Doc stood waiting for him. He couldn't help but smile his first genuine smile in days.

"Well, well, well, Alex, it took you long enough. I'm starving!" She smirked and stepped aside to let him in.

"Sorry I'm late, but I did remember to pick up some Dogfish Head beer and those ridiculously expensive chocolate truffles you love." He shot her a full-toothed charming smile—his go-to response.

"You're forgiven!" She offered a weary smile in return.

Alex rolled up his eyes in mock relief. "Phew!"

She rewarded him with a little laugh.

"All right, Doc, let's get the meat on the grill before we both starve to death."

"Have at it. You know where everything is." Her tiny stockinged feet shuffled along the oak wood floor through the living room and into the spacious kitchen.

He hummed to himself as he put the beer and chocolates away and took out the hamburger patties. The simple domesticity of it comforted him; he could be himself with her, and that in itself was a relief.

"So, dear Alex," she said, "do you want to talk about it now or wait until after dinner?"

He bit his lower lip, as her direct question caught him off guard. *Two can play at that game.* "So, uh, when does Chris get back?"

Doc's brow furrowed as she opened up two beers and poured them into her favorite frosted beer mugs.

Alex snatched one from her grasp on his way out the screen door to the patio. A shiver ran through him. With the sun gone, the air bit in a way that went right through him despite his wool jacket. The welcomed heat of the grill warmed his hands as he placed the patties on the bottom rack.

She wrapped her heavy wool sweater jacket around her and stood in the open door frame. "If you must know, Chris is in Germany right now. He should be home by Tuesday." Doc pursed her lips and shuffled her foot in front of and behind the other. "Make them rare."

"Yes, ma'am, your every wish is my command."

She responded with a swift kick to the back of his knee, making it bend.

"Dammit woman! You want me to burn myself?" His yelp made her giggle. "Never mind. Forget I asked."

He shuffled back and forth to stay warm. "It's been a long and difficult day, so be nice to me." He took a generous sip of his beer—the hoppy taste lingered in his mouth.

After a long pause, Doc finally spoke up, "So why were you working so late on a Sunday? I thought you pulled the first shift for surveillance?"

He paused and took another sip of his beer. As much as he wanted to talk to someone about what was going on, he still felt himself resisting her. Yet if he didn't just say it now, he never would, so he let the sad truth come out.

"So I guess the employee assistance program didn't get the memo." He paused and took a deep breath. He couldn't look at her so he looked instead at the burgers. "Katherine was shot last night."

Doc gasped. "What?"

Alex nodded and cleared his throat, hoping to dislodge the lump of unexpressed emotions that had begun to form there. The playfulness of moments before was gone. Their session had now begun and she became his Doc, a role he knew she secretly loved.

"Oh, Alex! What happened?"

"It's a long story, but it might be connected to my mission."

"Is she going to be okay?" Concern emanated from her body.

"I—I think so," he said, unsure if he really believed that. "At least for now."

A silence fell between them, making him anxious. She always did that with him, and he hated it. He couldn't help but fill the silence. "When I asked for this mission, I knew it was going to be hard, but I didn't think it would be *this* hard."

She leaned against the doorframe and gave him her full attention. Her long, straight black hair curtained around her oval-shaped face.

He inhaled and exhaled to hold back the tears that threatened to fall before he continued. "I'm having a hard time being objective in this case when it comes to Katherine." He half-mumbled into his beer glass, "I might have feelings for her."

She tried to catch his eye, but he looked away. "Might?"

The glass *clunked* as he slammed it down on the table beside the grill. "Okay, I do. I do have feelings for her!" He held up his hand to keep her from talking. "I know what you're gonna say, that it's normal for me to develop feelings for her after spying on her for the last two years, that I've had to develop this false intimacy to do my job."

"But it's more than that?"

"Yes." He turned off the grill and put the finished burgers on the platter.

"I'm... I'm sure this isn't going to come as any surprise to you, but I think I should start the process of getting out of the spy business." He looked up to meet Doc's gaze directly for the first time since he got there.

When she didn't respond right away, he tried to continue. His mouth opened and closed several times before he could tell her what was really on his mind. "Doc, I... what if I fail? What if she dies?"

"Yes, what if?" She reached out and took the burgers from him, and turned to go inside.

Alex closed and locked the door behind them, and sat down at the large oak table at the end of the kitchen, where he and Chris had played countless games of poker.

"Alex, have you talked to your mission handler about any of this?"

He snorted out a short laugh. "Nooo!"

She put their plates together and handed him his while he gulped down his remaining beer. "This case is too important for you to pull out right now, isn't it?"

He got up to get another beer—this wasn't a conversation to have while sober. "That's an understatement. Years of work have been put into this damn thing. I don't think I could walk away from it, from her, even if I wanted to. All I can think about is keeping her safe." He took a long swig straight from the bottle and added under his breath, "And making her happy."

He sat back down and took long gulping mouthfuls of the beer, wishing it was something stronger. "Mission: to save the girl." He couldn't help but think of the girl from Mosul, the one he hadn't been able to save.

"Alex," she said with a sympathetic tilt of her head.

He held up his hand to stop her because he just couldn't bear to talk about it now—maybe ever. "Can we not get into *that* tonight?"

Doc remained silent.

The incident with the woman from Iraq had changed him, and nothing he could ever do or say would erase that experience. No matter what, he'd be chasing that regret until the day he died.

Doc twisted and tore at the ends of her napkin. "Are you taking your meds?"

He hated the pills, but being off of them was so much worse. "Yeah, I'm taking them."

She exhaled and tossed the shredded napkin out of reach. "Good... and you're keeping things under control?"

Alex shrugged. "That's certainly subjective, Doc. How do you define control?"

She cocked an eyebrow at him.

He knew what she meant, but he didn't feel like getting into this with her for the hundredth time. "Well, I'm not picking up prostitutes or masturbating during my lunch hour to get through my day, if that's what you mean." He couldn't help the sarcastic tone to his response. Talking about his addiction and the disgusting things it led him to do was hardly his favorite way to pass the time.

She crossed her arms over her chest and gave him that chastising look that she seemed to reserve just for him. "What about Sara? Are you two still *seeing each other*?"

He laughed at her choice of words. "*Seeing each other.*"

"Alex!" Her tone made clear that he was pushing the limits of her patience.

"If you mean are we still fucking all the time, every chance we can get, then yes." The shame caused by his actions bubbled up inside of him. Saying it out loud brought them into the light, and he preferred to keep his private actions in the dark.

"Do you need me to adjust your meds?" Her almond-shaped eyes narrowed as she regarded him with a look of concern.

He shrugged and looked away.

She reached across the table and put her hand on top of his. "I'm worried, Alex. I'm worried that you might have a relapse, especially with all the pressure you're under in this case."

"I am too. Why do you think I'm here? Well... besides the joy of your company, of course."

Doc smirked. "Of course."

He heaved a deep sigh as he contemplated her suggestion. "I'll think about it. The last time we increased the dose, I couldn't sleep or eat."

She nodded slowly. "We could try another medication, or you could try to work the steps again."

He laughed despite the angry look she gave him.

"I know you think it's crap, but—"

"I said I'd think about it, Doc."

Danville Press
Danville, Virginia
March 9, 2008
8:00 PM

Jason sat at his desk re-reading the email he'd received from his source--a background check on Special Agent Alexander Bailey. It had come back squeaky clean, but some odd inconsistencies made his informant think that maybe Agent Bailey was really a Spook—a spy for the CIA. Jason couldn't even begin to imagine what that might mean.

A knock at his door startled him back into reality. "It's open, come in."

His door opened and his perky blonde copy editor poked her head in. "Hey, boss, I've got a copy of the police report and information you asked for on the shooting."

Jason sat up and reached out for the file folder. "Thanks, Sara."

He couldn't help but watch the hypnotic sway of her hips as she left his office, closing the door behind her.

Damn, she's hot.

He scanned the report and noted something unusual: police had found the weapon used to shoot Katherine near the scene, but with the serial numbers scratched off, and free of fingerprints.

Was this supposed to be a warning? If they wanted her dead, wouldn't they have been more precise?

From what Katherine had told him, and the research he'd been able to dig up, these men didn't seem to be the kind to make mistakes.

His cell phone—on vibrate—began to dance across his desk. He grabbed it and answered, "Knettle speaking."

"Hello, Mr. Knettle, this is Dr. Martin from Pendrell General. I'm calling to inform you that we're starting treatment for a post-surgical infection. Ms. Mitchel has what we believe to be Methicillin-resistant Staphylococcus aureus—MRSA."

"Is she okay?"

"Yes, we've got her on a round of high dose antibiotic."

Jason ran his fingers through his hair. "Thanks for letting me know."

He hung up the phone and tossed it back on his desk. It had been years since he'd been to church, let alone prayed, but today he found himself pleading with the Lord to save his friend.

FBI Headquarters: Hoover Building
Washington, D.C.
March 10, 2008
5:00 AM

ASAC Richards sat alone at his desk, reading over the D.C. Police report on Agent Mitchel's shooting. His concern for his subordinate led him to ignore the direct orders of his supervisor, something he wasn't prone to do.

He'd spent his weekend secretly investigating the failed assassination attempt on Mitchel's life. As a trained profiler with over twenty years in law enforcement under his belt, he knew all the right questions to ask and how to get the information without drawing any attention from the higher-ups in the Bureau, and he was determined to find out the who and the why.

The shrill ring of his phone bounced around the empty bullpen. "Richards."

"Hey, man, I looked into this case for you and I might've stumbled onto something. I don't want to discuss it over an unsecured line, though." His oldest and most trusted source had come through for him again.

Richards looked at his watch. "How's about I meet you at Swings in two hours when they open. I think I'll need a bucket of caffeine to hear what you have to say."

The voice on the other end chuckled. "You're going to need something stronger than that."

Pendrell General Hospital
Georgetown, Maryland
March 10, 2008
7:00 AM

Jason jogged up the hospital stairs with a bouquet of flowers in his arm, and made his way straight to Katherine's private room.

He found her sound asleep, and decided to leave her that way as he carefully placed the bouquet of roses on the table beside her bed. He noticed Charles's familiar script on one of the cards nestled inside a bouquet of daisies. It made the hairs on the back of his neck stand on end.

Are the flowers a warning? A way to throw off local law enforcement? Don't they always assume it's the significant other first?

He took out a piece of scrap paper from his coat pocket and wrote her a quick note to let her know that he'd been there.

As he was walking out of the hospital, his phone rang. The caller ID showed a D.C. area code.

"Knettle speaking."

"Hello, Mr. Knettle, this is Agent Richards with the FBI. I'm Agent Mitchel's direct supervisor."

His skin prickled with fear. What did he want?

"I was wondering if I couldn't take a moment of your time."

Jason looked at his watch. "Sure, I have a few minutes."

"Can you meet me at Swing's in D.C.?"

Jason thought for a moment. "Yeah, that's not a problem. It will take me a bit, though, as I'm in Georgetown right now." He mentally calculated the length of time and the best route to take.

"That's fine," Richards said. "Just get here as soon as you can."

Jason hung up his phone and tapped his jacket inside pocket, where he'd been keeping the jump drive Katherine had given him. She'd said to pass it on to her supervisor if anything happened to her.

Was she right to trust him?

FBI Headquarters: Hoover Building
Washington, D.C.
March 10, 2008
1:00 PM

After a short visit with Katherine that morning at the hospital, Alex had spent the rest of the day buried under piles of paperwork. His phone buzzed in his pants, startling him. *Sara.*

What are your dinner plans tonight?

Alex leaned back into the chair and texted her back.

I'm hoping you are. Your place or mine?

Her response came back almost instantaneously.

My apartment at 7pm. Eat before you come.

He chuckled to himself and slipped his cell phone back into his pants pocket. In the back of his mind he thought about his conversation the night before, with Doc—maybe he did need to up his meds and cut things off with Sara. Just as he knew the cigarettes he smoked were bad for him, he knew that Sara was too, but he was barely holding it together these days. He couldn't just let go of all his coping mechanisms at once, no matter how detrimental they were to him in the long run.

He sighed as he eyed the stacks of files and information for the new case the department was working on. He hadn't even cracked them open yet. He was so lost in thought that he jumped when Richards touched him on the shoulder.

"Hey, man, I've been calling you." A look of concern flashed across his supervisor's face.

Alex sat forward in his chair. "Sorry, sir, I guess I didn't hear you." After a moment's pause, he continued. "Is there something I can help you with?"

Richards nodded. "Have you eaten lunch yet?"

"No, I haven't." Alex pushed back on his desk and stood up.

Richards handed Alex his coat, which had been hung up by his desk. "Come on then, lunch is on me. We can walk over to Marcy Mays."

"O-kay."

Once outside, Richards leaned close to him and whispered, "I came across some information about your partner and the shooting. I was hoping that maybe you could help me shed some light on what happened to her."

He liked Richards, and from what he could tell the man was trustworthy. The fact that he was looking into the shooting was a good sign.

"You mean besides the police report about it being in retaliation for the collar of our suspect that night?"

Richards exhaled loudly. "So I'm not the only one who has questions. Well, I might have some answers for you, information about how she's in the middle of a top secret investigation by the CIA."

Alex's heart skipped a beat. *How did he find out about that?* "What?"

Richards nodded. "Yeah, I was just as surprised as you. I don't know all the particulars just yet, but I do know that it involves a large scale criminal operation. They're suspected of everything from drug and human trafficking to extortion and money laundering. There are even whisperings of it being in cahoots with some terrorist cells in Iraq, which is probably why the CIA is involved. My source didn't know for sure how Katherine's involved, so I did a little digging. Amazingly, I didn't have to look too far to get that information."

Alex tried to push down the growing panic sloshing around in his gut. He had to make sure the operation remained a dark one, but he also needed to know how much mission information had been leaked. He would have to deal with the *how* later.

He stopped in his tracks. "Sir, tell me everything you know."

Richards ran a hand through his thinning hair. "Well, like I said, I did a little digging and spoke to a few people this morning. After talking to her friend Jason, the one who was there when she was shot, I have a much clearer idea of what's going on."

"What did he say, sir?" Alex tried to keep the growing panic out of his voice.

Richards looked around them as they walked, and leaned in closer, speaking in a hushed tone that made it hard for Alex to hear. "I found out that she has information from one of the operatives from the group—bank statements, businesses and other information. It's a veritable gold mine. This group is wide-scale enough to include people here at the FBI, Congress, you name it! I have it all in a safe deposit box at the bank. We've gotta do something to protect Katherine. Her life is in danger."

Alex bit his lower lip almost to the point of drawing blood. A rapid-fire debate had begun in his mind on whether or not to let

Richards in on the mission. He enjoyed some leeway to make tactical decisions in the field, but he was pretty sure this was a bit above his pay grade.

Fuck it! "Sir, there's something you need to know."

Mack's Auto Center
Ocean City, Maryland
March 10, 2008
2:00 PM

The man smoothed out the wrinkles on his tailored suit pants. He hated coming to this place, but he didn't have a choice.

Sometimes you have to go into the sewers to find the rats.

He checked his Omega watch and looked around, not really expecting to see someone he knew.

A man can never be too safe.

He was, after all, a prominent, well-known man, even in Ocean City, Maryland.

"Sorry I'm late." Billy sauntered into the shop and wiped his hands clean of the car grease that had permanently stained his hands and nails.

The man swallowed hard and grimaced in disgust when Billy extended his hand to him. He would sooner shake hands with an actual rat than touch Billy's meaty paws. Thankfully, the dirty rat didn't seem too shaken by his rebuff.

"You wanted to talk?" He noted the hint of irritation in the mechanic's voice.

"Yeah, I want to know who sent down the order to take out Katherine."

Billy crossed his arms over his chest. "You know I can't tell you that."

"Bill, I've helped you a lot in the past. I've turned a blind eye more than once."

Billy harrumphed and looked down at a spot on the floor where oil had pooled one too many times. "My advice is you'd better get to her before his men do."

The miscreant was right. He would need to get to her quickly. "I'll need men."

"I can give you some cousins of mine, but you'll have to keep a close eye on them. They're... well, let's just say they make me look like Mother Theresa." Billy scratched at his scalp, making his hair stand on end.

"I'll take 'em." The desperate urge to keep Katherine safe propelled him forward.

He'd never wanted her to get caught up in all of this. They had all tried to keep her away from the ugliness of the business, but her curiosity had gotten the best of her and she put herself smack dab in the middle of a lion's den. As much as he loved her, sometimes he wanted to just shake her, knock some sense into her for good.

FBI Headquarters: Hoover Building
Washington, D.C.
March 31, 2008
5:00 AM

Alex secretly ordered the task force to provide Katherine—without her knowledge—around-the-clock security during the weeks she was in the hospital or at home recovering. It was just a temporary solution to a long-term problem of keeping her safe, something he and Richards had devoted two weeks of work trying to figure out. They needed to get her out of Washington and into protective custody, but they also needed to be careful not to undercut the joint task force's efforts to find out who in the government was associated with the group called The Syndicate. CIA intelligence analysts were now more certain than ever that someone high up on the FBI chain of command was on their payroll.

Until they knew definitively whom they could trust, they had to be careful about how they handled a case over which the FBI had no jurisdiction, and which they had no permission to be on. Another challenge was the fact that Director Barnes and Special

Agent Richards were the only ones at the FBI who knew that Alex was part of a CIA investigation. They were all forced to keep up the ruse, which meant long, brutal hours of work for Alex.

With the help of the task force, Agent Richards had managed to fabricate a convincing out-of-town assignment as the cover to get Katherine into the Federal Witness Protection Program. From there she would submit a leave of absence request, which Richards would file with HR once she was in custody.

Langley was in the middle of decoding and analyzing the data she'd collected. They had managed to get over a hundred names and businesses of those involved, including direct ties to terrorist cells in and out of the US, but the process was much more painstaking than anyone had anticipated. The group's tight security features could cause all the information to disappear if accessed incorrectly.

Even though the joint task force was closer to solving the case than they ever had been, they still needed more in order to get the Attorney General's Office to prosecute. Without Katherine's testimony, they would have no case at all.

So, for now, everything hinged on Katherine.

That morning her doctor, as scheduled, gave her clearance to go back to work, which set in motion the plans that Alex and Richards had so meticulously set in place—plane tickets purchased, hotel reservations made, and new temporary identities fabricated. All of it had to funnel through the FBI, which took a lot of careful paperwork on Richards' and Alex's parts, but they had everything in place when Alex left the Hoover Building that morning at the break of dawn.

As the Hoover Building filled his rearview mirror, he thought over the last two weeks and all the hard work he and his team had accomplished. Most memorable was the time he had spent with Katherine. He'd made it a point to visit her every day at the hospital, and when she got out, he found excuses to drop in and visit her at home. He would bring her dinner or lunch, or come by with a movie and popcorn. In just two short weeks they had grown close—so close, in fact, that she had asked him, and not

Jason or another friend, to pick her up from her last physical therapy appointment.

He needed to be at the hospital at nine, which left him just enough time to grab a bite and maybe pick up some flowers or something. He smiled to himself in anticipation of seeing her again.

Pendrell General Hospital
Georgetown, Maryland
March 31, 2008
9:00 AM

Alex parked outside Pendrell General Hospital and took one last puff of his cigarette before tossing it out the window of his car. He then grabbed the flowers lying on the passenger's seat and headed into the hospital.

The sound of his rubber soles clapping against the linoleum and echoing down the winding halls towards the clinic did nothing to calm his nerves. He clutched the small bouquet of flowers with his clammy fingers, and couldn't remember the last time he had been this nervous. As a seasoned agent, this type of tactical mission shouldn't have him this rattled, but it did.

He was surprised to find Katherine sitting in the waiting room. His heart skipped a nervous beat at the sight of her. *God, she's beautiful.*

She wore all black except for the cornflower-blue scarf wound around her pale white neck. The fabric perfectly matched the color of her eyes.

He bit his lip hard when she looked up from her phone and caught his intent gaze. "For you." He handed her the flowers and smiled despite his nerves. "I'm not late, am I?

"No, I finished early." She smiled back and smelled the bouquet. "They're beautiful! Thank you!"

He shrugged his shoulders and looked away, so as not to get lost in those blue eyes of hers. "It's nothing. Just, you know, a little something to celebrate your last PT appointment."

When he looked back down at her he noticed that her face and neck were now flushed red. He seemed to be having that effect on her a lot lately, which pleased him to no end. "How are you feeling?"

"Okay, I guess." She shrugged her shoulders and let out a small grimace. "I never knew how much I used my abs 'til now."

Alex offered his arm to help her up out of the chair, and winced with sympathy, the memory of his own gunshot wound from ten years ago sending a twinge of pain through his chest.

As they walked out of the hospital and through the parking lot, his hand bumped against hers and an electric shock went up his arm all the way down to his groin. *She's a live wire.*

"What a beautiful day!" She took a deep breath through her nose and tilted up her face to the sky. "Fresh air and sunshine!" She exhaled slowly as her bow-shaped lips settled into an easy smile.

Her just-be-glad, Pollyanna-esque way was beginning to grow on him. He looked around them and took in the winter landscape spread out before him. Though almost April, it had snowed over four inches the night before. Across from the hospital, in a small community park, children played a game of Wallyball and made snow angels. Despite the beautiful scenery, he couldn't help looking at Katherine instead. Her porcelain white skin, bright blue eyes, and red hair set against the world of white, took his breath away.

"Yes, beautiful," he said.

Her dazzling gaze once again met his, and her cheeks stained red once again.

She's going to be the death of me.

***

Katherine sat in the freezing car with her nose buried in the flowers. Over the last few weeks she'd grown used to Alex's company. He always seemed to find some reason to stop by every day, and at the time it seemed completely logical. It also didn't hurt that he was easy on the eyes. If the situation were different, she wouldn't think twice about actively working towards a relationship with him, but considering her situation, she thought it prudent to maintain a professional distance... even if it did leave her hollow and aching with need.

For now, though, she smelled the flowers and enjoyed the hint of spring during the dead of winter.

He scooted into the driver's seat beside her, and nodded towards the flowers while he buckled himself in. "Read the card."

Her breath caught for a moment. "Okay." She carefully lifted the envelope flap and pulled out the card stock, which was covered in tiny, neat writing.

Dear Agent Mitchel,

The information you have obtained on the jump drives is vital to an ongoing investigation. Your life is in danger. Agent Bailey will be taking you today to a safe house. From there you will be transferred to the custody of the Federal Witness Protection Program while the investigation continues. We can't be sure about surveillance bugs, so keep silent in regard to what you have just read. The CIA safe house will dispose of the note properly.

ASAC Richards

"You ready?" Alex asked.

She put the card back into the flowers and forced herself to smile as the full weight of the news began to sink in. "Yeah, let's get going."

She knew she should be thinking about her safety and how to stop the men who had tried to take her life, but all she could think about were the flowers. They had been a Trojan horse bearing bad news, not a romantic gesture after all. Her girlish flight of fancy--while in the middle of what was a real life or death situation--embarrassed her.

Everything is a giant mess. She shivered.

Alex turned the heater on full blast. "Are you cold? The car warms up really quickly."

"I'm okay," she mumbled.

A look of concern blossomed across his chiseled features.

She avoided his glance and scorned his pity.

After a long pause, he looked away from her and pulled out onto a deserted strip of Highway 95.

Katherine curled up against the heated leather seat, and watched through the side mirror as her hometown and everyone she loved in it disappeared into a singular vanishing point.

***

Alex watched her out of the corner of his eye. He couldn't understand why she had such a hold on him. He had always prided himself on being a consummate professional, capable of separating his emotions from his work. He had, he thought, perfected this ability.

He was beholden to no one. He'd never had a girlfriend, no family to speak of, and only a couple friends. Doc and her husband Chris were the only people outside of the CIA who even knew his real name.

These distracting thoughts regarding the trajectory of their relationship flew through his mind as he traversed the familiar, long stretch of road—only partly paying attention.

From seemingly out of nowhere, an eight-point buck darted out in front of his car, tearing him from his train of thought. His reflexes brought his foot down hard on the brake—a bad choice considering the slick road. They both lurched forward against their locked seat belts.

Katherine cried out.

Shit!

The brakes locked and the back end fishtailed, putting them into a spin. Adrenaline shot through his veins as he quickly drove into the spin and regained control of the vehicle.

The unscathed buck paused in the middle of the deserted road and regarded them, then dashed off into the woods lining the highway.

Alex's heart thundered in his chest as he took a deep shaky breath. He drove the remaining yards into the hotel parking lot, threw the car into park, and turned to Katherine. "I'm so sorry! Are you okay?"

"I'll be fine." Tears filled her wide eyes, letting him know that she was anything but fine.

All it took was him placing his hand on her shoulder to set off a wellspring of tears.

He deftly unbuckled their seatbelts and pulled her hard up against his chest.

After a few moments, she lifted her face off of his shoulder with a look of embarrassment. "I'm sorry."

Why is she sorry? He weaved his long fingers through her hair and tucked it behind her ear, and used the pads of his thumbs to wipe away the remains of tears on her cheek. *Just one kiss. What would it hurt?*

Time slowed to an agonizing pace as they sat frozen in the moment. His heart raced and his breath quickened as....

Life is too short. He tipped her face up to his and laid a chaste kiss upon her readied lips.

As they parted, she breathed out his name like a plea: "Alex." Her eyes, filled with desire, looked up at his in expectation and want.

He didn't waste any time. There was nothing innocent about the second kiss as he captured her mouth with his own, swallowing up any other words she might have said next.

She returned his kiss with earnest, taking his breath away in surprise. With great reluctance, he pulled away to catch his breath, and leaned his forehead against hers as their shallow breaths filled the small space between their parted lips.

Her fingertips brushed his cheek, inviting him back for more.

He answered her silent invitation with a greedy kiss that yielded nothing. Her fingers slid down his cheek to rest on his beating heart, and he smiled at her touch, unintentionally breaking their kiss.

"We... uh... should probably get inside. Maggie is waiting for us." He tried to see through the fog of lust that blinded him. He needed to be sensible about this.

A shy smile flittered across her lips as she released her hold on him.

"Wait right there." He jogged around to the passenger's side to help her out. She gasped in surprise as he lifted her out of the seat. He hadn't anticipated her to be so light, and almost lost his balance.

She clung to him with a wide-eyed expression that made him laugh a little. "Alex, put me down! I can walk."

He smirked. "I've got you."

He held her more tightly, and she relaxed against him as he carried her to the door marked 4B.

Alex's colleague, Maggie, came to the door dressed in a smart gray suit. "Alex, Katherine, right on time. Come in."

Alex walked into the room and set Katherine down on the twin-sized bed in the corner. The room was set up as an office with a metal desk, laptop, printer, phones, and surveillance equipment. He noticed that one of the screens showed active surveillance of Jason's apartment, and quickly pushed the off button for the screen before Katherine noticed.

What was Mags thinking?

"Mags, do you have our paperwork?" He tried to keep his irritation out of his voice, but wasn't too sure he had been successful.

"It's all in here: new identification, bios, plane tickets, and clothes." Maggie handed them each a small carry-on suitcase. "Katherine, you will need to change your hair color—red kind of stands out."

Katherine's face fell.

Alex was a little sad himself, sorry to see the red go. He smiled at her in the hopes of cheering her up, and pointed at the paperwork. "Did you see where we're going?"

Katherine shuffled through the papers and her face lit up. "Florida! A little time in the sun sounds lovely."

He smiled as she once again found a silver lining to cling to, his world-weary heart again skipping a beat in the presence of her undying hope.

Maggie twisted her hands. "You will be posing as a young married couple while you transition into hiding. A representative of the US Marshal's office will rendezvous with you to complete the transfer of custody from FBI to Federal Witness Protection. Katherine, you're to have no contact with *anyone* at all. It could seriously put your life in jeopardy, and others' too. Do you understand?"

Katherine's smile melted into grim determination. "Yes, I know what's at stake. My father was a US Marshal."

Because they were on the clock, they changed into their new clothes, and Katherine dyed her hair strawberry blonde. Maggie presented them with matching wedding bands to finish off the ruse. They looked every bit the married couple.

Maggie smiled at the finished product. "Good luck."

Katherine looked up at Alex. "We'd better get going or we're gonna miss our flight."

After working their way through rush hour traffic, they finally arrived at Reagan International Airport with their new identities—Mr. and Mrs. Matthew Scully, newlyweds.

Two hours later, they were on the plane heading to Key West, Florida. Alex played it up for the flight attendants by doting on Katherine. He couldn't help but imagine what it would be like to be a real married couple going on their honeymoon. Maybe her hope was seeping through his tough skin.

After they landed and secured their luggage, they piled into a CIA fleet sedan and drove all the way from Key West to Orlando in an effort to ensure their location remained unknown.

Alex's heart raced as they neared the hotel, where they had booked the honeymoon suite.

Chapter 4

Wyndham Hotel
Orlando, Florida
March 31, 2008
8:00 PM

Katherine dropped her purse at the door of the spacious, ornate room. "Wow!"

Alex brought in their bags, dropped them in the open foyer, and kicked the door closed behind him. He caught Katherine by surprise when he picked her up by the waist and drew her into a long passionate kiss.

She quickly pulled away from the kiss, even though it had already begun to unravel her.

God, he's a good kisser. "We shouldn't be doing this. The FBI is paying you to protect and serve, not to proposition and seduce." She tried to catch her breath and calm her racing heart.

She could tell by his smile that he wouldn't be so easily dissuaded.

He carried her over to the sofa in the middle of the room and laid her down on it. "Nothing wrong with practicing for being under cover. We're newlyweds, ya know?"

The saucy grin he gave her, coupled with the suggestive rise and fall of his eyebrows, made her want to lower her defenses and let him in.

His fingers ran through her now blonde hair as he kissed her—a soft, sweet kiss—and the shame and guilt that hovered just above the surface of her subconscious reared its ugly head. She needed to put on the brakes before things progressed past the point of no return.

"Alex, stop. We can't do this." Even though it pained her to do so, she pushed him away.

"You're right. I'm sorry," he said in a rushed apology.

He sprang up from the sofa and walked over to the coat in which he kept his pack of cigarettes and lighter.

The click of the lighter coming to life made her jump.

He turned on his heel, the cigarette dangling precariously from his lips, and walked out onto the balcony.

Katherine followed him, pausing in the doorframe. She felt torn between her desire and common sense, which told her this was neither the time nor the place to indulge in the bodice ripper fantasy she had playing over and over in her head.

Before she could say anything, Alex said, "This isn't going to be easy...." He took a long drag, and continued, "...playing by the rules." A plume of smoke left his parted lips. He put out the cigarette and then stormed past, leaving her standing in the doorway. "I'm going to go take a walk."

She noted more than just a small amount of irritation in his voice, and the loud slamming of the heavy door behind him.

Once she was back inside their room, she plopped down onto the pullout sofa and rested her head in her hands. Thoughts of Charles and everything left unsaid between them, including the commitments they had made, flashed through her mind. As much as Charles had hurt her, she still felt torn between past commitments and her growing desire for her partner. Alex was everything she wanted in a man—smart, funny, sexy, and a damn good kisser.

She twisted the government-issued ring on her finger. It represented a hollow union but, for a moment, felt real to her.

***

Once outside the room, Alex slammed his fist against the hallway wall, causing a picture to fall to the floor. He pulled out another cigarette and lit it as he made a beeline for the hotel bar.

The thought crossed his mind that he should call his sponsor or Doc, but he just couldn't bring himself to take that necessary step. It had been years since he worked the steps of the program, and he could feel himself spiraling even with the medication Doc had prescribed him. The rapidly building need had him balancing on the knife's edge. Just a little taste--that was all he needed—to get him through.

An hour later, he walked back into the now pitch-black hotel room. Curse words flew out of him as he fumbled for the light switch and tripped over the bags he had carelessly tossed on the floor earlier. At last he found the switch and flicked it on, causing a soft light to spill into the room, bathing it in a warm glow.

Katherine lay curled in a ball on the sofa, a prescription bottle of Vicodin on the stand next to her.

As he stood over her, he let the shame of what had happened wash over him. His obsession with sleeping with her was taking a toll on him. He couldn't help but wonder, if he gave in to that urge, if it would lessen the need gnawing at him or just consume him whole.

After Katherine had put the kibosh on their make-out session, he'd ended up in the bar bathroom with a willing and able replacement. He shivered in shame and disgust with himself, as his addiction once again threatened to wrestle the reins away from him.

The sofa groaned as he lifted her up. He carried her into the bedroom and tucked her in, and she slept soundly—a heavily drugged sleep that he knew she needed.

He washed away the smell of his failings in the hot hotel shower. As he stepped out of the shower, the harsh artificial light left his reflection in the mirror looking haggard and worn. His addiction was taking a toll on him in more ways than one.

On the way out of the bathroom, he grabbed a pillow and blanket and went back out into the living room. He set up his bed for the night, and pulled out his cell to call Doc.

She picked up on the third ring. "Hey, Alex."

"Do you have a minute?" He swiped away the tears that were sliding down his cheeks. The humiliation over his addiction and what it had already cost him was sometimes more than he could bear. "I'm having a bad night."

"Oh, Alex, did you have a relapse?"

"Yeah, something like that. I've been thinking maybe those side effects wouldn't be so bad after all."

The Mall
Washington, D.C.
April 1, 2008
6:00 AM

Even though he had access to the congressional gym, Scott still preferred to run outside. He had been an all-star track and cross-country athlete in high school, like his twin sister Katherine. They had both kept up with the running even into their thirties, something he was proud of.

His government-issued parking sticker let him park almost anywhere, making it easy for him to fit a quick run in at any time of the day. The biting cold weather awoke his senses and helped him to think more clearly. He was going to have a busy week, with several key bills hitting the Senate floor, and he needed to be sharp and on his toes.

He had surreptitiously managed to sneak in some pork belly spending for his district, and needed to ensure that the bills passed in order to make good with his campaign contributors. He spent half of his days scheming and making deals behind closed doors. Congress was an ugly place, where power and money exchanged hands at imperceptible rates, and he couldn't afford to be waylaid by trivial personal matters.

Unfortunately, the mess his sister had caused had created an unavoidable distraction.

Scott was rounding his way back to his car when his phone chimed with an incoming text message. He slowed down to check it—no text received before 7:00 a.m. was ever good. *Jean.*

Emergency meeting today at 9 in the tunnel by the kids' art.

The game of holding onto power required one to walk a slippery slope.

Wyndham Hotel
Orlando, Florida
April 1, 2008
7:00 AM

The light streaming through the cracks in the blinds awoke Katherine from a sound sleep. She squinted at the clock: 7:00 AM. *When's the last time I slept twelve hours?*

She hopped out of bed, did her regular yoga routine, and took a quick shower. With her morning rituals complete, she tiptoed out into the front room. She was relieved to see soft dark curls poking up over the pillow on the sofa. After their little fight, she had wondered if he would still be there when she awoke.

As she walked farther into the room, his body revealed itself to her in sections. When she saw him in his entirety, her breath caught in her throat and her eyes feasted on the sight before her. His firm, muscular chest, sprinkled with dark curly hair, rose and fell with each breath. A small puckered scar marring his near-perfect right pectoral caught her eye, and before she could stop herself, she reached out to touch it.

Alex clasped onto her wrist and pulled her down upon him, making her gasp. His anxious mouth searched hers out and she found herself giving in to his ardent kiss. With one arm on her back and the other cupping her head, he shifted them until he had carefully pinned her beneath him—a place she didn't mind being.

Her long legs wrapped around him, making him growl in her ear. With her lips, teeth and tongue, she encouraged his advances. She needed this.

He grasped a fistful of her hair, yanked hard to expose her neck, and his teeth connected with the bundle of nerves along her neck and collarbone.

She cried out. The intoxicating smell of his natural musk and the salty taste of his skin left her wanting more. The night before she had vowed not to allow this to happen, but once again she found herself at the mercy of her desires.

Her fingernails dug deeply into his back as he bit, licked and sucked the tender skin at the hollow of her neck. His quick and nimble fingers made short work of the tiny buttons on her fitted blue oxford shirt, and the skin on her neck and chest became hot and inflamed from the scratchy stubble on his face, as he kissed his way down the new path of exposed skin. She pulled him back up to her lips. She had lost any and all control of her body, which responded in kind to every move and thrust of his. Each touch, each kiss, left her wanting—*needing*—more.

It would be so good. What could be the harm in just one time?

A noise rose over the sounds of their moans and heavy breathing. Katherine stilled for a moment. "Your phone's ringing," she rasped in his ear.

Alex grumbled in frustration as he rolled off her and grabbed the blanket to cover himself. He moved to answer the phone.

A wave of embarrassment and shame washed over her. She had let things go too far. While he looked the other way, she stood to clasp her bra and button up her shirt.

"Hello, yes, thank you. Just leave them at the concierge desk, please. Thanks again." He hung up.

Feeling self-conscious, she crossed her arms over her chest. "Who was that?"

"A special treat I have cooked up for us."

The blanket around him fell to the floor, making her heart race once again.

"I'm going to go shower, but first things first."

He pulled her up against him for a tantalizingly short kiss that ended almost before it even started, leaving her longing for more as he walked off in the direction of the bathroom.

It would be so easy to just give in to him, to succumb to his persistent advances. Her fingertips brushed her kiss-swollen lips.

I'm doomed, she thought to herself with a small smile.

***

Once in the bathroom, Alex took his medication, hoping it would kick in quickly. Doc had advised him to take one and a half pills while he was in Florida. She would fill a different prescription for him when he got back home.

His heart was racing so fast that he thought he might pass out. His hands clutched at the bathroom sink as he breathed in and out, trying to ground himself, as Doc had taught him. As much as he wanted to sleep with Katherine, he also yearned for a relationship with her outside of the bedroom—something he had never had before with anyone. To get there, he would have to put the brakes on the physical part of their relationship and focus on building trust with her.

He thought over all the things Doc had told him last night. It was the first time in his life that he'd ever asked for love advice, or... hell... even *needed* it, for that matter. Bedding someone was the easy part. The other stuff remained a mystery to him, an "As Seen on TV Only" kind of thing.

Once his heart rate returned to normal, he started the shower and took out his toiletries bag. He hoped tonight's surprise would help turn things in the right direction for them. It would be good to get out of the hotel—so much easier to behave in public.

After he had showered and dressed, he and Katherine spent the morning catching up on all their paperwork. Alex tried with every fiber of his being to keep a respectable distance between them. He knew from recent experience that even the slightest touch would be their undoing.

At four o'clock on the dot, he brought a garment bag out of the bedroom and held it out in front of her. "Put this on."

She looked up from the book she was reading. "Excuse me, what?"

"You need to get dressed. Remember that surprise I told you about? Well, it has a dress code requirement."

She half-smiled back at him, cocking one eyebrow. "All right, I'll play along this time, but for the record I am not a big fan of surprises."

"Noted, but I think you might like this one." He dangled the garment bag in front of her, hoping to pique her curiosity.

"We'll see about that."

He chuckled and waved his hands anxiously towards the bedroom and bathroom, then playfully shoved the bag into her hands. "Get dressed!"

She laughed. "Okay, okay."

An hour later, she came out dressed in a crimson-red, floor-length gown, her blonde hair swept up in a French twist. A single row of pearls graced her pale, freckled chest, and two pearl studs anointed each earlobe.

"Wow," he said, swallowing to suppress his growing desire.

She twirled the skirt of the gown, showing off. "You like it?" She looked up at him from beneath her hooded lids.

"Yes, very much so." He dug his fingernails into his palms to keep himself in check.

Her face flushed as she flashed him a shy smile. "Me too. Thank you. It really is beautiful. How did you guess my size?"

He smiled as he tried to adjust the bow tie of his tuxedo. "I'm a trained investigator." His fingers shook a little under her watchful eye.

She tugged the lapels of his jacket and moved his hands aside so that she could fix the troublesome tie. "You clean up nice, Special Agent Bailey."

He winked. "I know."

She chuckled at his confidence.

Now that they were ready, he took her hand into the crook of his elbow and led her to the door. "Are you ready for our adventure?"

The expectant smile that looked up at him made his body hum with delight. When she squeezed his bicep, a rush of adrenaline shot through him.

"I can't wait."

Florida Opera House
Orlando, Florida
April 1, 2008
7:00 PM

Katherine reached for his hand when the orchestra began the first notes of the prelude, bringing Madam Butterfly to life. It had always been one of her favorite operas.

How did he know? Does he like the opera too, or is this just an elaborate part of his seduction of me?

She didn't want to question this moment, and instead decided to push away her nagging thoughts and let herself be taken in.

By the final scene of the third act, her carefully put together face was in danger of being put to ruins by the hot, wet tears that stung her cheeks. Alex wordlessly handed her the handkerchief from his pocket, and she dabbed the corners of her eyes, not wanting to miss the scene before her.

During "Con Onor Muore," he reached across and held her hand. The music took her far away from her own problems. It was too easy to slip into the magic of her connection with him. Her mind wanted to escape so badly that it let her heart take control—that, and it was too hard not to be charmed by this handsome, intelligent, and thoughtful man.

Seito Sushi
Orlando, Florida
April 1, 2008
11:00 PM

After the opera, Alex had a CIA town car take them to Seito Sushi. Being himself and sharing something he loved—like the opera—with someone was new for him. He felt a riptide-like pull wrenching at his heart, leaving him raw and exposed.

Is this love? It hurt, but it was a bittersweet pain that left him wanting more.

As they sat in the car outside the restaurant, she looked at him with sparkling blue eyes that made him melt.

"You really are a good investigator," she said. "Opera. Sushi. I couldn't have planned a better evening."

Alex exited the car and walked around to help her out of the car. He couldn't have wiped the grin from his face even if he tried. "Maybe you need someone who cares enough to do the investigative legwork to give you what you want."

She looked down at their joined hands, but did not reply.

The silence made him nervous, but he pushed it away and took her by the arm into the restaurant. They ordered a variety of things on the menu, and both agreed in the end that the unagi rolls with the eel were the best they had ever eaten.

After dinner, they returned to their hotel room on foot, wanting to enjoy the beautiful night air. Two CIA agents followed at a respectful distance.

"Alex, tonight was amazing. Thank you."

He paused mid-step to look her in the eyes. "But...?"

"But... I'm in no position to start anything with anyone."

He nodded, taking her hand back into the crook of his elbow. He felt her body relax as they walked back the rest of the way in a companionable silence.

It was after 1:00 AM when they finally arrived back to their room.

Katherine took off her shoes with a sigh. She looked as tired as he felt.

He took her request—to slow things down and give her time—to heart, but he needed one more kiss. Before she could make it to the bedroom, he pulled her against him, kissed her, and whispered into her ear, "I'll wait."

She shivered in response.

It physically hurt him to refrain from kissing her again. "Goodnight, Katherine."

"Goodnight, Alex."

As she walked away to the bedroom, she looked over her shoulder at him one more time. When her eyes met his, he let out a small laugh, and she rewarded him with a shy smile and blush in return.

God, she's beautiful.

The next morning, Alex awoke to the sound of his cell phone ringing. "Hello," he answered, still half asleep.

Katherine came shuffling out of her bedroom with her hair askew from sleep. "Who is it?" she mouthed.

He sighed and his lips grew tight as he handed the phone to Katherine. "It's for you." He tossed her the phone in irritation. "It's Jason."

Katherine's face lit up, which inflamed him with jealousy. In a sullen huff, he stalked off to the bathroom to clean up and cool off.

***

Katherine watched Alex leave the room in an endearing huff before bringing the phone up to her ear. "Jason? What's wrong?"

"Kat, thank God. Are you okay?" His tone quickly changed from relief to accusation before she had a chance to answer. "Why did Agent Bailey answer the phone? Where are you? Your boss won't tell me anything."

"Slow down. What do you mean, my boss?" She felt her face grow hot at his accusatory tone.

"When the police and I couldn't find you, I tracked down your boss—the one I gave the drives to. He's right here next to me. I had to twist his arm to let me speak to you," he said in a rush.

"Jason, I'm fine. This is just a precaution. Can you put Agent Richards on the phone?"

His whining voice rattled her nerves. She needed to know what was going on and she needed to know now. *What was he thinking tracking down my boss!*

"Agent Mitchel?"

"Yes, sir, I'm here."

"Are you well?"

"Yes sir. Forgive me for being abrupt, but can you please tell me what's going on?"

"Agent, I have some bad news. I'm very sorry to have to tell you this, but your sister Addie was murdered."

"Oh God," Katherine cried out, and her legs started to give.

"There was a note at the crime scene saying that you would be next if you chose to continue on your current path. We have reason to believe that they know the case was a ruse."

She stumbled back and fell into one of the hard-back chairs in the room, and began to cry.

"I'm sorry for your loss," Richards continued. "We want to do anything and everything we can to keep you safe, which means we need to move up our timeline."

She wiped her eyes with the pad of her thumb, too choked-up to speak.

"Are you ready to hear the new plan?"

"Yes, please," she stammered as she tried to calm herself.

"Things are going to have to move rather quickly. First off, we are going to need for Agent Bailey to come back to Washington on the earliest flight out."

As her superior rattled off the rest of the instructions, Katherine tried to pay attention but all she could think about was how she'd never see her little sister again. When he finished giving her the new orders, she heard a soft sigh on the other end of the line.

"I'm sorry again for your loss. We're going to do everything we can to catch these guys. In the meantime, we need to keep you safe."

"Thank you."

"All right, I'll shoot you a message when the marshal and his men get there. Be safe, Agent."

"Yes sir. Thank you again." She ended the call and tossed the phone on the sofa, then headed towards the bedroom to get cleaned up. On the way there she wordlessly pushed past Alex. She could sense his concern, but was too numbed by the news to acknowledge him.

***

While she cleaned up, Alex went downstairs and got them coffee. He wanted to give her a little space since she seemed upset.

When he returned to their room, she was standing out on the balcony. Her green cashmere sweater, tight black leggings, flowing blonde hair and piercing blue eyes made her a formidable sight.

A glass of golden liquid sat on the ledge. She held one of his cigarettes in hand, as well. He stopped at the doorway of the balcony, sensing that she had constructed a wall while he'd been gone.

She took a puff of the cigarette and turned to face him.

He walked the few feet that separated them and took the glass, which smelled like scotch, away from her and put it on the other side of the balcony, out of her reach. He placed a steaming cup of coffee in the spot where the scotch had been, and nodded toward it.

She shook her head no and avoided his gaze.

He snatched the cigarette from her hand and took a drag, finishing it off before putting it out in the ashtray on the ledge. He could tell she was getting pissed off with him, but he didn't care.

"Want to tell me what that call was all about?" He pulled her lithe body against his.

She gracefully broke from his hold and walked past him, disappearing into the bedroom.

He took a deep breath before following her back inside. "What are you doing?"

She paused, giving him an irritated look. "What does it look like I'm doing? I'm packing to leave!"

He crossed the room and reached out for her, but she inched away from his touch. "After everything that's happened, you're just going to storm out of here without giving me an explanation?"

She glared at him with such venom that he immediately withdrew from her.

"Get out. Just get out of here!"

The raw display of emotion convinced him to turn around and leave the room, but the moment he did he heard her burst into tears and collapse on the squeaky bed. He slumped down into one of the living room chairs. The sound of her sobs made his heart ache. He couldn't just sit there and listen to her cry.

This is ridiculous! He jumped out of the chair and went to her.

She looked frail, with her body curled inward and her face buried in her hands.

He tentatively sat down beside her and tugged on one of her arms, pulling her into his welcoming embrace. To his great relief, she let him hold her until the crying subsided.

A hard knock came to the door, startling them both. A soft voice announced, "Room Service."

We didn't order any room service. He reached for his gun on the bed stand and rose to answer the door, glancing at Katherine's worried face on his way out. Before he opened the door, he peered through the peep hole at the convex, distorted face of a bellhop.

"We didn't order any room service," he said through the closed door.

"I have a delivery for a Katherine Mitchel," the bellhop responded.

He threw open the door and stepped out of the way with his gun drawn. "Who sent you?"

The young man's eyes grew wide and his hands flew up in the air, causing him to drop the flowers. "Please don't shoot!"

Alex looked down at the flowers now lying in a heap on the floor. "Don't move!" He crouched down, his gun still trained on the bellhop, and picked up the flowers.

Katherine walked up behind him and took the elaborate bouquet from him.

Alex motioned the frightened young man into the room and over to the sofa.

Katherine plucked out the card and read it out loud. *"Kuriosity killed the Kat. Enjoy your little affair, Red. It won't last."* She dropped the flowers and the card and slumped into one of the overstuffed chairs. Scattered petals lay discarded around the bouquet, giving off the faint aroma of lavender and baby's breath.

"They know where you are. How do they know?" Alex asked under his breath.

Her eyes closed. "It's even worse than they thought."

He bent to pick up the card and tossed it at the bellhop. "Who sent you?"

The man shook and stuttered, "I—it was left at the desk. I—I don't know anything!"

She looked up at the bellhop. "How did you know my name?"

His fearful gaze met hers. "The man who dropped them off said to send them up to this room and ask for Katherine Mitchel. Please don't kill me. I promise that's all I know."

Alex kept his gun trained on the distraught young man while he grabbed Katherine's deactivated cell phone from her bag. He scrolled through her photos, pulled up the first one he found of Charles, and showed it to the young man.

"Is this the man who dropped them off?"

The bellhop shook his head no.

Alex sighed, lowered his gun to his side, and fished out his FBI badge from his jacket to show to the young man. "I'm going to need the surveillance tape with the man who dropped off this package. Is that understood?"

The man nodded.

"Good. Talk to your manager and make that happen. Go!"

The bellhop jumped up and ran back out the door, which slammed shut behind him.

Alex gave himself a moment to calm down, then put down his weapon and went to Katherine, who had gone back into the bedroom

When he walked into the room, she looked up at him. "My little sister.... They killed my sister because of what I know."

She clutched at her abdomen. "Jason's been trying to get a hold of me. He was worried because he couldn't find me. A note left at her crime scene said that if the investigation continued, I would be next. They know where I am, Alex. I have to leave right away."

His chest tightened as he sank down onto the edge of the bed.

She took a deep breath as she zipped her bag closed. "Jason finally tracked down Richards, who got to Barnes. Director Barnes himself is trying to get me instated into the witness protection program a day earlier than originally planned. In a few minutes, I'm supposed to meet with the Federal Marshal who's to be assigned to me. It's someone the Director knows personally, someone he trusts implicitly."

His phone buzzed with a text message from ASAC Richards.

The marshal is waiting downstairs.

It was most likely his friend Brian Williams, which made him feel a little more reassured. He relayed the message to Katherine.

She responded over her shoulder. "Barnes wants you to return to Washington on the earliest flight out."

A numb feeling settled in as he stared at the floor. "I'm sorry about your sister."

She wordlessly grabbed her bag and started for the door. The light from the living room cast against her blonde hair as she paused and turned to face Alex with tears in her eyes. "Goodbye."

He sprung up from the bed in a panic, and followed after her, catching her before she could walk out the door. Desperate for her to stay, he spun her back to face him, causing her to wilt in his arms. Her lower lip began to quiver—his undoing.

He wrapped her in an embrace, and a lump formed in his throat when she tilted her head and her glassy eyes looked up at him with unabashed warmth and desire. Without taking his eyes off her, he lowered his head and captured her lips with his own—imbuing her with his desperation.

As the kiss deepened, Katherine wrapped her arms tightly around his neck, pulling him closer to her. Her soft velvety tongue welcomed his into her warm mouth. Whatever control he might have had started to unravel as he forcefully pressed her against the door, closing it shut behind them. He heard her gasp, but from pleasure or pain he wasn't sure.

His desperate kiss crushed her mouth, but it wasn't enough to meet the deep-seated need that gnawed at him with each passing second. It hadn't occurred to him to prepare for this moment when she would leave without him. He tried to push out of his mind the nagging voice in his head that said he should stop and let her go.

As his impatient mouth explored the crook of her neck, his overeager hands worked their way underneath her shirt, making Katherine shiver and whimper in what he hoped was delight. His splayed fingers captured her breast, and she moaned deeply into his ear.

Madness. This is sheer madness.

Without thinking, he tugged her shirt up, only to be stopped by her shaking hand. "Alex... we can't."

Her words sounded hallow in his ear. Unable to stop himself, he pressed himself against her.

Instead of pushing him away again, she wrapped her arms around him and slipped her hands into the back pockets of his jeans.

His hands once again found their way underneath her shirt, making her gasp and rub against him harder. "Don't go! Just a little longer," he said, pleading with her.

Katherine cried out as his mouth once again nipped and sucked the sensitive spot on her neck, which he'd discovered the day before. When his hands abandoned her breast and started to tug at her leggings, she twisted her body away from him. "I have to go. They're waiting for me," she said.

"Can't we can just take off somewhere? Just you and me? No one will find us." His hands grasped hold of hers and brought them up to his chest, where his heart beat for her alone.

The anguished look in her eyes sliced through him, making the parting that much harder. He pulled her once more into his embrace, her hand still pressed against his beating heart, and kissed her with an aching tenderness. The salted taste of her tears filled his mouth. "Just you and me," he whispered against her lips.

She sucked in her bottom lip and looked away from him with her forehead still pressed against his. "I can't. I have to go."

His antics were just delaying the inevitable. "You're right. You should go."

He stepped back, picked up her bags, and handed them to her. Her face wilted before his eyes, and he shoved his hands into his pockets to keep himself from touching her again. "Katherine...."

She turned partway, her eyes filled to the brim with tears. "Yes?"

"I'll wait." His voice cracked but he didn't look away.

She rose on tiptoes and tenderly kissed him one last time, a short, sad kiss that did more to break his heart than appease it.

In the space of one breath, she opened the door and left.

As the door closed, he butted his head against it and angrily wiped away the tears that had begun to fall.

Chapter 5

Green Hill Cemetery
Danville, Virginia
April 4, 2008
6:00 PM

"In sure and certain hope of the resurrection to eternal life through our Lord Jesus Christ, we commend to Almighty God our sister Adeline Mitchel, and we commit her body to the ground—earth to earth, ashes to ashes, dust to dust."

Alex stood at Katherine's sister's gravesite, shivering in the cold spring wind, an unseasonable cold April day at just thirty-two degrees. He shoved his gloved hands deep into his pockets in a vain attempt to keep them warm.

As the ceremony concluded, he walked over to Katherine's twin brother, Scott, and extended his hand in greeting. "Hi, Senator, I'd like to introduce myself. I'm Alex Bailey, Katherine's partner at the FBI. I just wanted to extend my condolences to you and the family over the loss of your sister."

Scott gave him a firm handshake. "Thank you. It's too bad Katherine couldn't be here. It's as though I lost two sisters and not just the one. Have you heard from her? I don't suppose you know where they sent her?"

"No, Senator, I'm sorry I can't answer either of those questions."

Scott frowned at Alex's response. "Can't or won't?"

Alex shrugged. "Either way, it doesn't matter. All I can tell you is that, for the time being, she's safe."

The senator's line of questioning and brusque attitude chaffed him. A feeling of relief washed over him when he saw Jason walking up to them.

Scott smiled politely at Jason and shook his hand. "I'm glad you were able to make it, Knettle. It's good to see you again. I just wish it was under different circumstances."

Jason smiled politely back at the Senator. "It's good to see you too. I'm sorry for your loss. Addie was a great girl. She'll be missed."

Scott put his arm around Jason. "Have you heard from Kat?"

Jason paused with a confused look on his face. "No, I haven't talked to her since they put her in federal custody. I think that is the whole point of the witness protection program. I don't know any more than you do."

Before they could finish their conversation, Alex interrupted them. "I'm sorry, Senator, but I really need to speak with Mr. Knettle alone. Official FBI business. I'm sure you understand."

Scott eyed him suspiciously, but moved along to be greeted by other mourners offering their respects.

"Jason," Alex said once they were out of earshot of the senator. "There are some questions I'm hoping you might be able to help me with. Katherine trusted you, and therefore, so do I."

Jason's eyebrows lifted but he nodded slowly. "What can I do for you, Agent?"

"I've got kind of a hunch that I would like to run by you. I'm hoping if we all work together, we can get Katherine home sooner rather than later."

Jason nodded. "I'll help in any way I can."

"Good. I was hoping you would say that."

While walking to their cars, they arranged to meet up later in the week. He hoped Jason could shed some light on questions about the people in Katherine's life and their possible connection with The Syndicate. A hunch had been playing over and over in his mind, and they were usually spot on.

Brian, the marshal in charge of her, told him earlier that she had been safely installed in the witness protection program and seemed to be doing okay. Despite the good report, he wouldn't be assured until he saw to her safety himself.

He needed to solve this case so that he could go to her and return to what they had started in Florida. The memory of those two short days haunted him.

Sam Hill Nursery and Organic Community Garden
Aransas Pass, Texas
May 31, 2008
7:00 PM

Nothing good ever lasts.

She ripped another prickled weed out by the roots, and dug her hands deep into the soil, her body covered in coastal grit, sand and salt. It was just a way to pass the time and wait for the other shoe to drop. Her once perfectly manicured nails were cracked and muddied from the long hours she put in at the nursery. Much to her boss's dismay, she never wore gloves, as her need to feel something real—despite the damage it did to her skin—was too strong. Even the fire ant bites she left unchecked. It should all bother her, but it didn't, or at least not enough for her to do anything about it. The physically demanding work left her dirty and aching at the end of each day, but she enjoyed it.

This new life left her with lots of time to think, which scared her at first. She'd spent so much of her life trying to avoid thinking. Now her mind played and replayed the reel of all the horrific things that had happened to her over the years. There was no longer anywhere for her to run to get away from the thoughts that plagued her.

When it became too much for her, her thoughts would inevitably turn to him. She would languidly recall his distinct smell, the way he had tasted, and how his stubble had felt on the sensitive skin of her cheek and neck. She was under no delusions that she'd been in love, but she'd felt something. For a brief time she felt safe with him, and that meant everything to her. She was afraid to hope that they might ever be free to resume what they had started.

The voice of her elderly boss calling from across the rows of red leaf and bib lettuce—by her new name—broke her from her reverie. "Holly?"

"Yes, Susan?"

Susan, whose frail back was heavily hunched over, tried to stretch and straighten up as best she could.

"I'm done for the day sweetheart. Can you finish weeding these last few rows and close up for me? I need to get home to Frank and a nice hot Epsom salt bath." The poor old woman winced in pain.

Katherine—er... Holly, she had to remind herself—nodded wordlessly as her boss shuffled out to her pickup truck and drove away. She stretched her own stiff back and arms, leaned back onto her heels, and put her hands on her lower back to deepen the stretch.

The coastal wind had been picking up all day, leaving her with the distinct taste of sandy sea salt in her mouth. She hated the grit that coated her freckled and burnt flesh. After enduring it for over two months, she wondered sadly if she would ever get used to it, and her palpable loneliness made it harder and harder for her not to drink.

Every day, when she rode her bike past the Sparky liquor store, she felt the very real temptation to fall off the wagon. It would be immeasurably easier to hide from everything in a bottle, but she had worked too hard to get and stay sober. Even after a decade of sobriety, she still fought daily against that inner instinctual calling that all addicts hear. When she first arrived on the island, the need for alcohol had overwhelmed her. Having almost thrown away her nearly ten years of sobriety in Florida, she knew she needed help. In a panic, she went to the local library and used their computer to find an AA group.

Katherine had been a drunk once. She was determined that Holly would not be.

The great thing about AA was that she could plug into a group no matter where she was, even in hiding. The closest AA meeting, that wasn't in town, met on the mainland in Corpus Christi—a bit of a trek, especially given her mode of transport: a beat-up Huffy bike she'd bought second-hand.

She didn't let that inconvenience get in the way of her staying sober. The forced exercise was good for her, too.

The meetings were the only thing that seemed to help her to stay strong and work the steps of the program—something she had been lax in doing. A month into hiding, she hit her sobriety anniversary and received her ten-year chip—as Holly, of course. She carried it with her wherever she went, and whenever she felt the urge to drink, she would clutch the chip in her hand like a worry stone and pray.

The stillness of this time in hiding unnerved her. She had known chaos for so long that she felt lost in the quiet. Yet this moment of respite was just the eye of the storm passing over, and the impending eye wall was all around her—it would hit sooner or later. All she could do was wait for the storm to return and bend her to the point of breaking. The thought made her shiver, and goose flesh took residence next to the freckles spotting her bare arms and legs.

She pushed the thoughts out of her head and put her all into her work. She pulled, dug, and yanked out the weeds from the remaining rows. When she had finished, she picked up all the garden bags full of yard waste, and contemplated what to eat for dinner. It was already 8:00 PM, and she couldn't skip another meal. She had to eat.

As she locked up the nursery and got on her bike, she thought about Alex again, warm hopeful thoughts that helped her cope.

Alex's Townhouse
Alexandria, Virginia
June 1, 2008
8:30 AM

Alex shifted in bed as the sound of his phone ringing pulled him awake. A small hand with long painted nails caressed his bristled cheek.

"Your phone keeps ringing," she said.

He opened his eyes one at a time while reaching for his phone that was charging on the stand by his bed. By the time he unplugged it and pulled it towards him, it had already beeped to announce a new voice message. His free hand rubbed his face and eyes, which were too blurry with sleep to see who had called.

He rubbed his eyes again to bring them into focus. 8:30 AM. Three missed calls.

Shit. That can't be good. His sleep-addled mind played with the idea of just ignoring it, but the small voice of reason in the back of his mind won out. A tired groan escaped his lips as he sat up and stretched his long legs over the side of the bed.

Sara had already rolled over.

He yawned and stretched again, and put his feet and legs to purpose on the scratchy carpet beside the bed, still nude and in no hurry to dress. He had always been comfortable with his body. It was what lay under his skin that he kept covered up.

He hobbled into the kitchen, started the coffee pot, and sat at the beat-up kitchen table he'd rescued from the dump several years before. With a swipe of his thumb he pulled up his voicemail notification, and the sound of his boss's voice suggested it was going to be a bad day.

It's Sunday, for God's sake! So much for a day of rest.

He deleted the message and rose to pour himself a cup of coffee. Sara's soft, tanned hands and arms wrapped around his waist, and her greedy hands and skillful mouth quickly brought him to a state of arousal. He could easily take her on the counter, the table, the floor....

As he turned towards her, still trapped within her insistent embrace, she gracefully brought her arms up around his neck and wrapped her long legs around his midsection. She used her strong arms and legs to lock herself around him by her ankles.

His mind clouded with lust—his drug of choice. Even after two long, languid days and nights together, he was still wanting. They shared a strong insatiable addiction for sex, and an abhorrence of relationships, making them perfect for each other. Though they both worked for the CIA, they'd met at a meeting for sex addicts.

They had been sleeping together on and off for over ten years, depending on where Langley assigned them. He knew nothing of her day-to-day life, and she knew nothing of his. He wouldn't have it any other way.

As much as he wanted to fuck her again, there wasn't enough time. Thankfully, with the chemical help Doc had prescribed, he was able to deftly change gears. He gently reached around and unhooked her ankles and arms from around him, and placed her back on her feet.

"No time to play this morning, little bunny," he said.

Sara pouted in response—the kind of duck face pout that pretty girls made, which made him cringe in disgust. Without a word, he walked away from her to the bathroom to get ready, leaving her standing there, unsatisfied and wanting.

He derived more than just a small amount of pleasure in denying her what she wanted. He was fucked up... and he knew it.

Le Droit Park
Washington, D.C.
June 1, 2008
10:00 AM

Alex stood stiff against the cold hard pole of the Metro's green line. His boss at the CIA, Supervisor David Magellan, had requested a meeting in Le Droit Park, near Howard University. He hadn't been back to the 'Shaw' in years. It served as a halfway point between where he and his superior lived.

The familiar static sound of his stop being announced brought his attention back to the task at hand. He pushed and prodded his way out of the subway and into the morning light at the top of the stairs.

All along the sidewalk, streetwalkers and drug dealers offered him all the sex and coke he could ever want. Hookers and drugs aside, there were several new businesses that had popped up, and two brand new high-end looking condos advertised vacancy.

Yuppie revival. He rolled his eyes.

Half a mile into the walk, he saw his destination: Church's Chicken. A little bell rang announcing his entrance as he opened the door. A few patrons glanced up at him before returning to their meals. He scanned the sea of unfamiliar faces until his eyes caught the one he'd come for.

"You wanted to meet me, sir?" He slid down into the ripped booth seat across from his boss.

Magellan passed an envelope across the booth's table to him.

With a little trepidation, he reached for the envelope and laid its contents onto the table. Inside were three pictures. One was of Katherine working outside a nursery, with the name of the place visible. All it would take was a quick Google search for anyone seeing these to find out where she was hiding. The remaining two photographs made Alex's blood run cold—real game changers.

He dropped the pictures and looked up at Magellan. "Who else has seen these?"

His boss scratched his well-trimmed white beard and sighed with irritation. "That's classified."

His heart hammered in his chest and he bit his lip to control the rage bubbling up inside, as pieces started to fit together in his mind. "Are you trying to smoke them out with her as bait?"

His boss rose from his seat and placed a hand on Alex's taut shoulder. "Wait a few minutes and call Brian. Just warn him. Don't tell him what you've seen. I know you can be convincing enough." With that, Magellan walked away as if nothing had just happened.

Alex waited until he left before calling Brian to warn him that Katherine was in danger.

"Williams speaking."

"Hey, Brian, it's Alex."

"Hey, Alex--"

"Brian, she's in danger. Her location has been blown. You need to get your man out there *now*." Alex wet his lips with a quick sweep of his tongue.

"What? You're kidding, right?"

"No, I'm not kidding. Call me as soon as you hear anything." He ended the call and tried to breathe, feeling as though he had the wind kicked out of him.

A feeling of cold dread settled into his gut. He tried to keep his emotions in check as best he could, but as he got up to leave, he shoved and kicked chairs out of his way in a huff. If even one person dropped the ball, it would be over for Katherine.

The CIA was calling a Hail Mary pass play... with Katherine's life in the balance.

Chinatown
Washington, D.C.
June 1, 2008
10:30 AM

Sara thumb-tapped the wheel in an impatient staccato beat. The light was taking forever, and her head was pounding from the compounding stress of her current situation. She had gotten several disturbing emails and text messages, all before 10 AM. The photographs her boss had emailed out that morning weighed heavily on her.

Beside her on the passenger's seat, her phone rang. "Hello?"

The voice on the other end made her skin break out in goose flesh.

"There has been a change of plans. We need you to step things up," the voice demanded.

Sara sucked in a quick breath. "I know. Did you get the pictures I emailed you?"

The voice on the other end rose sharply. "Yes, but we need to talk about that later. I need the information from the jump drives. Did you get inside his apartment yet? Did you find them?"

She tried to calm her nerves. "No, I haven't. I'm going to try again tonight."

The voice sighed with irritation. "You need to get your head in the game. Don't think for a second that he won't throw us both under the bus for this. We can't afford for you to fuck up here. Drop the affair with that spook and do your job!"

"I know. I understand what's at stake here." Maybe she should be surprised that he knew about her thing with Alex, but she wasn't; he was the kind of person who just knew things.

"Good. Now listen closely. I don't want to have to repeat myself. I have to rent a car and don't have time for your bullshit, okay?"

Sara swallowed hard as her mouth became dry. "I'm listening, Charles."

Katherine's Beach Condo
Aransas Pass, Texas
June 1, 2008
12:30 PM

Katherine walked out of the library letting the rain seep through her worn skin. Other people squealed as they ran with a purpose under their makeshift umbrellas. They had places to go and people to see and didn't have time to get wet. She had nowhere to go... no one to see.

Half a mile away from her condo the sun came out, and her stomach staged a protest over the lack of food she'd been providing it. Innumerable cups of coffee and half a croissant were not enough to subsist on, but what she put in her mouth was one of the few things she had control over.

Her legs wobbled as she walked up the steep hill leading to her condo. Out of breath, she steeled herself to make it up the steep flight of stairs to her front door. The steps, treacherous when dry, were a death trap when wet.

The sound of her screen door blowing open and closed made a chill run down her spine. When she looked up from the steps, she noticed the heavy wooden door on the other side of the flapping screen—it was ajar.

Someone's inside. Instinct kicked in and she reached behind for her gun, to no avail. Her gun was back in D.C.

Cell phone. She patted her pockets, but it wasn't there. It was inside the condo. Her eyes darted about. *I need a weapon.* She spotted a loose board and crouched down for it.

The sound of gun cocking froze her in place.

"Stand up, Red."

The familiar voice was anything but a comfort to hear. She straightened, certain he could see her heart hammering against her shirt, and eyed the Glock 42 pointed at her chest. "Charles." His name tasted foul on her tongue.

"Red, if you had wanted to go to the beach, you could have just said so." Charles lowered his gun, grabbed her arm, and pulled her through the door and inside.

She didn't resist. The fight had drained out of her from the moment he spoke her name. She was deflated—done.

As the door closed behind them, he pushed her hard up against it, covering her body with his. "I missed you."

His hot breath tickled her ear.

"You're not an easy woman to find. Thankfully, I know a lot of resourceful people."

The hard point of his hips ground her thin frame against the wood door, painfully pinning her in place, making it difficult for her to breathe.

A rustling from her bedroom got her attention. She glanced over his shoulder at two armed men walking out of the bedroom.

They shared an amused look, and left the living area to do a check of the small galley kitchen.

She could hear the men rifling through drawers and cabinets, but they weren't going to find anything.

Charles' lips grazed her neck. "God, you smell good."

Despite her efforts to remain calm, she trembled.

This only encouraged him.

His teeth and lips assaulted her neck while his heavy hand molded itself to her attenuated flesh. Fingers pinched and tugged at her breast, making her gorge rise and forcing her to swallow back the coffee and croissant she had eaten earlier. When his eager mouth sought hers in earnest, she clamped shut her lips and turned away from him.

"You are still my wife," he said through gritted teeth. He made sure to punctuate his words with a hard thrust of his body against hers. "It's been far too long."

Her eyes met his with whatever defiance she had left. "If you are here to kill me, then just do it."

Charles pulled back from her, letting air return to her grateful lungs, and she slumped in relief.

"You think I want to kill you?"

"Don't you?" She looked down at the gun he still held in his hand.

He sighed and placed the gun on the table beside him, then took her into his arms. "Red, honey, I'm here to protect you. If I can find you, so can they."

She cocked an eyebrow. "They, who?"

He took her hand in his and tugged her reluctant body over to the rattan sofa. "Men like Alex and The Syndicate."

She sat still and listened as he began to weave an elaborate work of fiction.

Like most of his stories, he always came out looking like the hero. He claimed to be on a mission to save her from some men high up in The Syndicate, who wanted to stop her from taking the data to the FBI or CIA.

He doesn't know they already have it.

She knew too much about his own involvement in the group to believe most of what he said, until he started to talk about Alex. He showed her paperwork, from a private dick, to back up his story.

A lie is most convincingly placed between two truths. In the back of her mind, though, a kernel of doubt had begun to grow. What did she really know of Alex? Not much, but her instincts told her to trust Alex, and her instincts were almost never wrong.

Charles reached out and held her limp hand in his, making her skin crawl in disgust. She leaned as far away from him as she could. *I need to play along, placate him.*

One of his goons brought her a teacup and, after taking a sip, she sat it onto the coffee table in front of her. She opened her mouth to tell Charles she believed him, but nothing came out. All of a sudden her eyelids were too heavy to remain open, and darkness assaulted her against her will.

Washington, D.C.
June 1, 2008
2:00 PM

Alex sat in his car trying to talk himself out of breaking his cover. With everything at stake, he couldn't afford to make a false step. He wanted to jump on a plane and fly to Texas, but he had to stay put and do his job. He couldn't afford to end up being taken in by the CIA and held for God-only-knows how long.

On the seat beside him, his phone rang its familiar ring tone. He snatched it up and answered it immediately. "Bailey speaking."

"Agent Bailey, we have some reports in from our team members on the ground," Magellan said.

"Is Katherine okay? Did the US Marshal get her to the Corpus Christi safe house?"

The silence on the other line was deafening.

"Is Katherine safe?" he asked again.

"Bailey, someone paid off the marshal. He made up some bullshit excuse about going to a funeral but we can't seem to corroborate his story."

Alex's voice came out as a plea. "Sir, what happened?"

"They got to her before we could." His boss's voice was laced with contrition. "Someone from command will call you as soon as we get some more information. It seems like a neighbor or someone might have seen something. We are looking into it now. Okay?"

A sudden tightening in his chest made it hard for Alex to breath. "Yes, sir, thank you." He pinched the bridge of his nose and sucked in a deep breath, then ended the call and tossed the phone on the passenger's seat.

He fished out his cigarettes from the inside pocket of his suit jacket and tapped the bottom of the pack in an effort to jar loose a cigarette. It was empty—Sara must have smoked the last one.

In frustration, he threw his empty pack at the windshield. "Fuck!"

He took out his pent-up anger and frustration on his steering wheel, punching it with his fist.

Chapter 6

Brian Williams' Home Residence
Hinsdale, Illinois
June 2, 2008
1:00 PM

Brian sat in his home office thinking about the call from Special Agent Bailey. Two hours later, he'd gotten ahold of the officer assigned to Katherine's detail. The man had broken protocol, traveling three hours away to attend the funeral of his deceased mother.

Brian had promised to leave and go to Katherine. In the meantime, he alerted the island's law enforcement, but all they could do was patrol her street and try her door. There was no answer.

She wasn't answering her emergency cell phone either. He couldn't help but think of her father and all the years they had worked together. *She's not going to die on my watch. She can't.*

His ringing phone startled him. The screen displayed a Texas number. "Williams speaking."

"Marshal Williams, this is Sergeant Peters with the Port Aransas Pass Police Department. I'm sorry to tell you that Ms. Mitchel appears to have been taken from her home residence. We were able to talk to one of her neighbors, who witnessed Ms. Mitchel being held at gunpoint when she arrived at her residence this morning. The neighbor also stated that she saw three men taking her unconscious body from the home and driving off with her in a black unmarked SUV. The neighbor, Ms. Miller, is working with our sketch artist, and we'll put out an APB and some composite sketches tonight. We'll have the report faxed to your office this afternoon. I still haven't seen your marshal yet," the Sergeant concluded.

Brian rubbed his forehead. "All right, thank you for the update, Sergeant. Please call me if you find out anything else." He hung up and buried his face in his hands.

Unknown Location
June 2, 2008
Unknown Time

The sudden jarring of the SUV running over the rumble strip on the side of the highway brought her back to consciousness. She had been slipping in and out of awareness for hours. The binding on her wrists and ankles dug into her skin, and a thick strip of cloth kept her blind to what was going on around her.

During one of her moments of awareness, she'd felt a thick calloused hand slide up her thigh and underneath her shorts. As if from far away, she heard shouting, then felt a smattering of liquid hit the side of her body. It smelled like blood.

The car door opened, causing a rush of air to blast her tender skin. Now she only heard two men instead of three.

What did they give me? Where are they taking me? She felt a prick, a pinch, and then darkness came again.

As she slipped back into unconsciousness, her mind wandered back to Alex. She welcomed it, imagining that he had been with her at the beach house, that instead of suffering alone, they were together—them against the rest of the world.

In her mind's eye, they spent their days working side-by-side and their nights wrapped up in each other's arms. She imagined all these things and more... in the darkness.

Danville Press
Danville, Virginia
June 2, 2008
3:00 PM

Jason sat in his darkened office and fingered the unread stack of articles sitting on his desk. Even with the deadline looming, he just couldn't bring himself to care enough to start on his work.

A knock on his door startled him. "What?"

Why can't they just leave me alone?

The door creaked open just enough for Sara to peak her head into the office. "Sorry to interrupt. Just noticed that nothing has gone out yet, and wondered if you need some help."

Jason sighed. "Sure, sit down."

Sara smiled back at him as she scooted into his office, closing the door behind her. She picked up the untouched articles in front of him and began to scan them, pen in hand.

He admitted to himself that he was growing more and more fond of her, but for all the wrong reasons. The loneliness of his life had begun to wear thin and she was an attentive and beautiful woman. She had been insinuating herself into his field of space more and more often, and he was finding it harder and harder to push her away, to keep up the wall.

The wall—his defense against the rest of the world—was beginning to crumble. *What would be the harm...?*

Chinatown
Washington, D.C.
June 3, 2008
11:30 PM

Sara flipped through her contacts on her phone while stopped at the light by her apartment. Thumb-swiping her way through to the C's, she finally pulled up Charles' number and clicked *call.*

He answered on the third ring. "Why are you calling me, Sara?" The loud rumbling noise in the background made it hard for her to hear him.

Is he in a car? "I went through his apartment a little bit when he was asleep, and I think he might have the information we're looking for on his computer. I'm going to try and extract it next time. I think I have his trust, but I'm going to need a little medical help to ensure he stays asleep this time. He's a light sleeper." She hated the anxious tone in her voice. He always had that effect on her.

He sighed. "All right, call me when you have something." A click signaled he had hung up.

While she was afraid of crossing him, she was even more afraid of the other one. The other one saw through her attempts to charm him. He didn't want sex, he wanted power.

She didn't even want to *think* about what Alex would do when he realized she was the one responsible for giving up his girl's location.

Her position in this game was tenuous—a pawn who could be sacrificed at any time.

Joe Coffee
Grosse Pointe Woods, MI
June 3, 2008
7:00 AM

It was a brisk June morning even by Michigan standards. Locals grumbled as they entered the shop in search of hot coffee to help them through another long summer day. After a brutal winter, cold temps in the summer provided a hard slap in the face.

Tim had already set up shop in the corner, where he could see everyone who came in or left. At sixty-nine, he felt the cold down deep in his bones, especially in his knees. He'd blown them both out playing football when he was in high school, and forty years of law enforcement had only served to damage them further, making old age a bitch on his body.

He ran a hand over his thinning white hair that spiked up on top. His working man's gray dress pants and short-sleeve button up shirt made him look like an undercover cop, but he'd worn these same clothes for years as a detective and US Marshal, and he didn't feel comfortable dressed any other way. He even still wore loafers and dress socks. He had tried to wear tennis shoes, but they just didn't feel right. Halfway through his crossword puzzle, he was interrupted.

"Tim!" the man said.

He looked up from his paper at one of the men he had worked a few jobs with. "Jimmy."

Jimmy held out a bag to Tim. "Want a bagel?"

He shook his head and motioned to the chair in front of him. "Is your old man still keeping you busy?"

Jimmy nodded. "You know it."

***

While the two men exchanged small talk, a man in jeans and t-shirt stood several yards away, putting the lid on his coffee. Neither noticed when the man took out his phone and snapped several pictures of them.

The Washington Memorial
Washington, D.C.
June 3, 2008
10:00 AM

It was only 10:00 AM and already Alex had deep sweat stains on his blue oxford dress shirt. It promised to be a record-breaking hot and humid day, so he rolled the sleeves up to the elbows in an effort to cool off. It was too hot even to smoke, so he sat there grumbling to himself.

As each minute passed, he grew more and more impatient—checking his watch impulsively. The informant was late. Only the iced coffee made the waiting bearable. He stretched his arms out on the park bench and fantasized about taking an ice cold shower and sleeping naked under his ceiling fan.

Fuck the world. Fuck everything.

Just as he was going to give up and leave, a man in running shorts and a soaking wet sleeveless shirt jogged his way. He slowed to a stop and began to stretch his quads.

In mid-stretch, the man straightened, walked over to Alex, and handed him a piece of paper. "I think you dropped this."

Alex pocketed the note and smiled. "Thanks, man, it's my shopping list. I can't lose it. You never know what I'll forget."

The man chuckled and resumed his jog.

Alex slung his suit coat over his shoulder and walked with purpose back his air-conditioned car.

Unknown Location
Unknown Date
Unknown Time

Katherine had lost track of time. She thought maybe they had been on the road two days, but she couldn't be sure. They had been drugging her steadily since they first started. The recovering addict in her noticed that she was beginning to show signs of dependency on whatever drug they'd used to keep her sedated.

To add insult to injury, her unwashed skin had begun to itch, but the drugs and the restraints prevented her from doing anything about the persistent itching. It was maddening.

Each time they shot her full of drugs, she welcomed the hard pull of darkness, where she dreamed of *him.* The darkness was her safe place.

Chapter 7

Unknown Place
Unknown Time

So cold. Katherine's teeth chattered and her body shook. The tank top and urine-soaked shorts she'd been wearing for days clung to her clammy body like a second skin, but that wasn't the worst of it. The itch that had started off as a nuisance had long since transitioned into torturous insanity. They had started to space out the sedative, causing her to experience the familiar symptoms of withdrawal—twitch and ache. The tear-stained cloth that covered her eyes—a blessing—allowed her to further dissociate herself from her situation.

In a rare moment of lucidity, she overheard a conversation Charles had with the driver of the SUV. "When we get to the cabin, I'm going to need to go into town and meet with George to get the methadone," Charles said.

"All right, boss. I can handle her. She's so strung out, she won't be any trouble," the goon replied.

Charles exhaled. "No, she won't be any trouble."

Charles doesn't trust him. Katherine's skin prickled with fear at the realization, and her heart thundered in her chest as she slipped back into unconsciousness.

Unknown Location
Underground
June 5, 2008
9:00 AM

He leaned against the tunnel wall and pulled up his newest text message.

I should have the information soon. I have the falsified files ready to hand off to him.

After deleting the message, he let out a slow agonizing breath. He wanted to trust her, but was beginning to think she might be playing both sides. He couldn't help but wonder if Blondie was the reason The Syndicate couldn't find her. No one seemed to know where Charles was, either, which was concerning to say the least.

"Any news?" a voice called out in a hushed whisper.

He put away his phone and looked up at the familiar older man. "No, we still don't know her whereabouts, and we still don't have the documents."

"Once we get the data, she will need to be taken care of," the man said.

"She might not be the only one we have to deal with."

Jason's Apartment
Danville, Virginia
June 5, 2008
9:00 AM

Jason groaned in bed, rubbing the heels of his hands into his eye sockets. He must have drunk too much the night before. He and Sara had gone out to one of the hip new bars by the paper, and then had come back to his place, though he didn't remember much about what happened after that. Actually, he couldn't remember how he got back to his apartment.

Everything was fuzzy. He remembered snatches of moments, but the whole of it remained a mystery to him.

Geez, everything hurts. He had the mother of all hangovers—pounding head and nausea. *I'm gonna be sick!*

He scrambled to his feet and stumbled into the bathroom just in time to throw up the entire contents of his stomach into the toilet.

Jason laid his sweaty body down on the cool tile.

I'm too old for this shit. What was I thinking? He wasn't in his twenties anymore.

In the back of his mind, he thought he heard something in the kitchen. *Did Sara stay the night? Why can't I remember anything?*

He felt himself slip into unconsciousness.

FBI Headquarters: Hoover Building
Washington, D.C.
June 5, 2008
10:00 AM

Alex leaned against the cool concrete of the FBI headquarters, smoking his second cigarette, when Richards walked up to him.

"Bailey, bum a smoke?"

He straightened and looked at his boss in surprise. "Didn't know you smoked, sir."

Richards chuckled as he accepted the cigarette and lighter Alex proffered. "I used to be a two-pack-a-day smoker back during the war. I quit about ten years ago. This business with Katherine has me off the wagon." He lit the cigarette, took a long drag, and slowly let the smoke out his parted lips. "That source of yours... how trustworthy is he?"

Alex ran his fingers through his sweaty hair. "He's solid. We now have two confirmed sources saying he is alive."

Richards sighed. "I thought you were going to say that."

Alex stretched his long body out against the cool concrete building.

"You're going to have to go to Michigan and confirm it yourself." Richards squinted, and an array of fine lines circled his eyes like the setting sun. He looked as though he hadn't slept a wink since this whole thing started.

Alex huffed in response. His boss's suggestion was easier said than done. "And how would we make that work, exactly? We still don't know who in the FBI is helping out The Syndicate. If it's really him, we can't let anyone know we found him."

Richards put out the cigarette against the wall. His thin lips formed a grim, determined line. "You leave that to me."

Alex smirked and started to head back inside.

Richards stopped him. "If you ever want to leave the CIA, the FBI would love to have you on our team."

"After all that has happened, I think I might take you up on the offer." He was touched by his boss's offer, but he wasn't so sure he really wanted anything to do with law enforcement anymore.

Richards shoved his hands into the pockets of his dress pants. "I understand how taxing something like this is, even on a seasoned one like you, but you're good at what you do. I'd love to have you on my team permanently."

Alex smiled. "I've enjoyed working with you too, sir. I'll keep your offer in mind."

Unknown Location
Unknown Time

The sound and vibrations of the SUV turning onto a gravel drive jolted Katherine awake. The bile of panic rose in the back of her throat. In her mind, she had convinced herself that as long as they had been moving she would be safe. As the car slowed and came to a stop, she started to shake.

The cloth blindfold obstructed her view, so she had no idea where they might be. While she had been out, they had tightened the bindings on her hands and feet, leaving her skin chafed and raw. A rush of panic-induced adrenaline shot through her, giving her the strength to fight against the tight cords.

"I guess it's time for a little shot, lady," the goon said. "Can't have you trying to get away now, can we?"

She began to cry as she felt him wrap her arm with a rubber strap and shoot her full of drugs.

"Help me carry her out of here," the goon shouted.

"Let's put her there on the sofa." Charles's voice held a hint of hesitation, which did nothing to allay her growing fears. "All right, I'm heading out. Are you good?"

A ripple of fear ran through her and she shivered. *Why is Charles leaving me with a man he doesn't trust?*

"Yeah, boss, don't sweat it. I can handle her just fine."

"Good, I'm leaving the SUV here and taking the truck," Charles said.

"Sure, man."

Katherine felt the pull of the drugs as the sounds around her began to blur and fade. She fought the fog of sleep, wanting to stay alert, but soon found herself back in the darkness.

Alex!

Jason's Apartment
Danville, Virginia
June 5, 2008
11:00 AM

Jason awoke with a start on the floor of his bathroom. *What time is it? How long have I been out?*

His head buzzed and he had a sharp ringing in his ears. He needed coffee. Maybe that would make him feel a little more human.

He arose from the floor, trying to regain his bearings. "Fuck!" He pinched his eyes shut and clutched his still aching head.

It took a great amount of effort to make his way out to the living area of his tiny apartment. Much to his surprise, Sara was working on his laptop. "What are you doing?"

She startled and closed the laptop shut with a bang. "Hey, sleepy head, you're awake. Want some coffee?"

She was obviously trying to redirect his attention, but he was too messed up to care. "Yes, please."

She rose from her seat at his makeshift desk and said over her shoulder, "I just made another pot."

"I think I'll need the whole pot." He was only half joking as he followed her into the kitchen.

The effort of making it this far had been more that his body had been prepared for, so he plopped down on one of his breakfast nook chairs. He couldn't remember ever feeling this bad before.

She pursed her lips into a *duck face*. "Ooh, you poor thing!" She filled a tall coffee cup to the top, brought it over to Jason, and sat down on the seat across from him.

"What did I drink last night?" He rubbed his head. "I don't remember ever feeling this hung-over before. I don't even remember coming back here last night."

"Yeah, you were pretty far gone. Don't worry, I was the perfect lady and didn't take advantage of you...." She winked seductively. "...much."

He smiled briefly and sipped the hot coffee—a little caffeine to clear the cobwebs, his father used to say.

Sara stretched her arms up over ahead, causing her t-shirt to rise, exposing her taught abdomen and the underside of her full breast. "I think I'll jump in the shower, if you don't mind."

Jason swallowed hard—mesmerized by her exposed body. "Yeah... sure... make yourself at home."

She hopped up from the chair in a way that only a young woman could, kissed him on the cheek, and pranced off to the shower.

He watched with interest as she disappeared into his bedroom. *Damn!*

He took another sip of his coffee, and got up to check his email. His legs wobbled as he tried to walk, making him lose his balance. He caught himself at the last second, but in the process sloshed his coffee and knocked over Sara's bag, upending all the contents onto the floor.

"Shit!"

He sat his mug down and squatted—his knees popping in protest—to mop up the coffee with a tissue and to put everything back into her bag. One by one, he replaced the contents, mentally cataloging each item—comb, lipstick, tissue packet, condoms, wallet, cell phone, jump drive, and a small zip-lock snack-sized bag of little pills.

Pills? He held the little baggie up to examine the contents. They were white, small and round. He gasped in realization of what they might be: Rohypnol.

He had done an article for a magazine, years back when the drug first hit the scene, and had done extensive research on it. Had Sara drugged him last night?

His head began to spin and the coffee started to bubble up in his throat. He bolted from his chair and grasped the sides of the sink basin as he vomited up the coffee he had just drunk. The acidic aftertaste of the bile made him grimace. When his stomach spasms finally stopped, he turned on the tap and swished out his mouth.

Oh, God, what is happening to me? He held on tightly to the counter to keep from falling.

His laptop.... *What was she doing on my laptop? Did she save something onto her thumb drive?*

There was one way to find out. He stumbled over to the desk and sat down. His hands trembled as he turned on the laptop and put her thumb drive into the USB port. His knee bobbed up and down. He wanted to believe that he would find nothing, but....

FBI Headquarters: Hoover Building
Washington, D.C.
June 5, 2008
11:30 AM

Alex looked up from his computer screen to see ASAC Richards marching towards him. Richards worked his way through the busy bullpen to Alex's desk, clutching several folders in his hand.

"Sir?"

Richards extended the papers to him. "You're going to Detroit to assist the local office in creating a profile on a serial killer case they're working."

"Of course. Thank you, sir," he said.

"It shouldn't take long, so if you want to catch a Tigers' baseball game while you're there, you will definitely have plenty of time. I have a guy who can hook you up with some tickets, gratis," Richards added for good measure.

"I might take you up on that. Thanks." Alex stood up, closed and locked his desk drawer, and shut down his computer. Even though it was ridiculously hot out, he shrugged on his suit jacket to cover up the unsightly sweat stains on his rumpled Oxford shirt. "When's my flight?"

His boss—looking pleased as punch—nodded at the paperwork. "It's all in there. I included the 302 form that Director Barnes approved. You leave out of Dulles at 3:00 PM."

"I'll call you if I need anything." Alex clutched the folders to his chest.

"Yes, please keep me updated."

As Alex made his way through the building to the elevator, his phone buzzed in his pocket with a text message. He swiped the screen to pull up the text message from Brian.

Katherine's location still unknown. The black SUV had Texas plates and was most likely a rental. The sketches show that one of the men was Charles MacAvoy. Sorry, Son.

Alex's chest tightened. He still hadn't heard anything from his CIA mission handler or from Supervisor Magellan.

Fucking CIA!

Chapter 8

Jason's Apartment
Danville, Virginia
June 5, 2008
11:15 AM

Jason's hands shook as his computer shut itself down for updates. He swore his computer did this just to irritate him, and let out a resounding sigh as it rebooted, the blue screen ticking off the updated percent of completion.

"Come on... come on." He groaned in impatience, his knee bobbing up and down.

Just as the welcome screen announced itself, he heard a rustling behind him and Sara's soft, sultry voice filled the air. He whirled out of the chair, using the desk as support as he stood up.

"I was thinking we should...." She paused, wearing just a towel wrapped around her still wet body as her gaze fell on Jason at the computer, and at her open bag and the pills on the desk. The towel she had been using to dry her hair fell to the floor with a resounding plop.

"What did you do?" The anger inside of him rose, giving him the strength he needed to confront her despite his discomfort.

He snatched up the bag of drugs and shoved them in her face. "Did you drug me?"

She trembled and took a small breath. "Y-yes."

Pure rage coursed through him as he threw the bag of pills, sending them scattering across his living room floor.

She raised her hands in a defensive posture and backed up a few steps, putting some distance between them. "Jason, it's not what you think!"

He suppressed the urge to strangle her, but could find no words.

She flinched and backed up another step. "I thought it would help you loosen up. I just wanted to help us have a little fun. It was just a little X."

He had taken X in college—this was not ecstasy. The lies... he was tired of the lies. He grabbed her by the wrist and flung her down on the sofa. "You're lying! And I can prove it!" He opened up the jump drive folder and gesticulated angrily at the screen. "And this? What's this? You're stealing files from my computer?"

Sara sat mute on the sofa, looking at the wood floor where the rest of the pills lay scattered.

He quickly deleted the files with one click and checked the history to make sure she hadn't emailed it or saved it on a cloud somewhere. After he had sufficiently checked his computer he reached for his home phone. "I'm calling the police."

She shrugged in a nonchalance that drove him insane. "Don't bother. It will just be a waste of time." She nodded to the phone. "I don't exist, at least as far as law enforcement and the government is concerned."

He clenched his fist and tried to decide whether or not she was lying. He should just call her bluff.

She continued in an even tone. "They will hold me long enough for my associates to come and collect me."

Jason's hand began to tremble as he clenched his fist hard enough to draw blood. The fog in his mind began to lift and he was starting to see the truth. "You're a part of this, aren't you?"

She stood and wrapped the towel tight around her chest. "You know I can't tell you anything." She modestly bent over and scooped up the rest of the pills and put them back into her bag. Gone was the seductress act that he had fallen for—hook, line, and sinker.

As she walked past him she whispered in his ear. "The place is bugged."

He sank back down into his chair, absorbing all she had said. He didn't know what to think, what to believe anymore.

Five minutes later, she came out of the room dressed in the clothes she had worn the night before and, without saying another word, took her bag and her now empty jump drive and walked out the door.

"Goodbye, Jason," she said with a sigh. "You're a good man. Take my advice and get as far away from this as you can."

Jason felt depleted. The rage that moments before had caused his blood to boil was now only simmering. The encounter with Sara left him with a deep-seated desire to get out of town, get away from this giant mess. He threw on some clothes and grabbed his laptop, phone, and a bottle of water. He knew just the place to go.

***

Sara let out a panicked breath as the door closed behind her.

I'm a dead woman.

She hadn't gotten the information that her associates at The Syndicate needed, and she had been caught by the eyes and ears of the CIA, who were no doubt dispensing field operatives to collect her that very minute.

Regret hung on her like ill-fitting clothes as her actions began to sink in. Jason hadn't asked to be involved in any of this. He was a good man and she liked him. At least now he knew they were watching him. She'd had nothing to lose telling him. After all, now the CIA and The Syndicate were going to be after her.

She was doomed.

Ever the smart and resourceful woman, she had already begun to strategize her next best move: turn herself into the CIA, or take her chances with The Syndicate? Death, or life in prison?

Not much of a choice.

For the time being, she would hide. Like a rat, she knew how to disappear into the woodwork.

Dulles Airport Departures Entrance
Dulles, Virginia
June 5, 2008
12:45 PM

Alex stepped out of the cab onto the curb outside the entrance to the Southwest Airlines Departures curbside check in. While waiting his turn in line Supervisor Magellan called him on his cell.

"Bailey speaking."

"Hey, Alex, sorry it's taken me so long to get back to you with an update. We had an incident this afternoon that you should know about." He spoke in a hurried way that belied his normally calm demeanor.

"Sir?" He sucked in a nervous breath, not sure he wanted to know.

"Bailey, as you surmised at our last meeting, we had suspected there was a mole here at Langley, as well. Today we confirmed the mole as Senior Special Agent Horton."

Alex gasped. "What?"

"We are just as shocked as you are, I assure you. We now know for certain that she's the one who leaked the information of Katherine's safe house location to MacAvoy. We are dispatching agents now to apprehend her."

"Um... okay, thanks for letting me know. Please keep me updated." He ended the call feeling as though someone had knocked the wind out of him.

Sara! No, not Sara. He felt sick.

"Sir, are you all right?" the woman in front of him asked.

He shook his head no and leaned against a support post.

"Sir?" the woman asked again.

Alex held his hand out to keep her at bay. "I'm okay." His voice shook. "Just give me a minute, please." He reached into his pants pocket, pulled out a Xanax he'd pocketed for the flight, and chewed it in an effort to expedite its effect.

He took a long, slow, deep breath.

God, I need a cigarette.

Several no smoking signs made clear that would not happen.

He pushed off the post with his foot and walked up to the check-in, since it was his turn in line. He didn't have time to fall apart. For his and Katherine's sake, he had to keep going.

Katherine.... She has to be okay. She has to be.

If anything happened to her, he swore that he would take Sara's life with his own bare hands.

Yellow Hat Cabin
Millburo, Virginia
June 5, 2008
12:45 PM

Despite the opiate haze, Katherine felt a hard tug at her shorts and underwear. They slid down her sweaty legs with little resistance. Her shirt and bra soon followed suit, leaving her bare. Warm soapy water and a scratchy old rag began to wash away the sticky sweat and grime that had accumulated over the last couple of days. Her feet, calves, legs, breasts, and face were made clean again.

Thick, meaty hands massaged soapy water into her scalp, and cups of warm water washed away all the soap, leaving her blissfully clean. She was lulled by the motions of the hands... until she felt a soft cloth tying her hands together above her head.

A sudden hot flush of panic rose up inside her.

The hands were back, but with a more sinister intent. They kneaded her breast, making her long to escape, to return to the opiate-induced darkness. The soapy hands traversed her helpless naked flesh, parting and painfully violating her.

She tried to fight the fog that entrapped her. She desperately wanted to stop these hands from breaking her—splitting her in two. She used every bit of remaining strength to raise her free leg at just the right moment, and brought her hard bony knee up hard. It connected as she hoped it would, filling the room with a painful howl.

The hands were angry now. They wanted to hurt her back and they did. The bitter metallic taste of blood filled her mouth and made her gag. The hands grabbed fistfuls of her freshly cleaned hair, causing her head to rise.

The sound of her head hitting the floor was the last thing she heard before the darkness pulled her back under.

Highway 81, Just outside Washington National Forest
June 5, 2008
12:40 PM

Jason was lost in thought as he drove his beat-up truck to his grandfather's cabin. He knew he would pass Katherine's family's cabin on the way and found himself anticipating it. It startled him, though, to see a dusty, road-worn, black SUV parked in the circular drive outside her cabin.

He threw the truck into reverse and backed up onto the circular drive in front of the property. Out of the corner of his eye he caught movement from inside the cabin.

What the hell?

He pulled out his rifle from the back of his truck, and charged into the cabin just as someone ran out the back door.

Red. All he saw was red. Blood was everywhere.

His gaze followed the trails of blood on the wood floor to its source, a naked body.

Katherine!

His stomach lurched and he dropped to his haunches and dry heaved. When he had finished, he rose to go after the man who had done this to her, but it was already too late; he was gone.

He heard a four-wheeler in the far distance in the timber behind the house. Katherine's family had always kept one in the back. He would never catch him.

Katherine!

He returned through the blood and knelt down next to her, and discovered she had a faint pulse and her chest rose and fell with small shallow breaths.

She's still alive!

He reached into his pants pocket, pulled out his cell phone and dialed.

"911, what is your emergency?"

Chapter 9

Yellow Hat Cabin
Just outside Richmond, Virginia
June 5, 2008
1:00 PM

As Jason waited for the ambulance, he took the Navajo blanket off the back of the sofa and covered Katherine's naked body. They had used it countless times over the years to cover themselves when they sat out on the porch swing late at night drinking beers.

That seemed like a lifetime ago.

As much as he loved her, he couldn't stay in that room with her, so he waited outside. The sound of the ambulance arrived long before he saw it, a sound that would forevermore be imprinted with his memory of Katherine.

The rig pulled up onto the drive beside his truck and the SUV. The EMTs jumped out and ran to him with great urgency. "Sir, where are you hurt?"

He looked at them, confused, until he realized he was covered in her blood. "Please help her. She's inside," he finally said, still in shock.

The police pulled up minutes later. They had questions he didn't have answers to. All he could do was tell them what he saw, which didn't amount to much. He knew that he was under suspicion, but he didn't care.

"If I'd gotten here a few minutes earlier, maybe I could've stopped this from happening," he told the detective in charge.

They wouldn't find the man, he thought. No one existed, apparently. Men like him were free to roam the earth, harming anyone in their way without fear of impunity. Even if they did find the attacker, it would be his word against Katherine's. Jason had after all never seen his face, and Katherine was blindfolded, so odds were she hadn't seen him either. He considered all the rape cases he'd reported on where the man got off scot-free, and sighed.

The police began to collect evidence while the EMTs worked on Katherine. He heard snatches of their conversation.

"She's lost a lot of blood."

"Her pulse is threading."

The neighbor, Amice, a friend of Jason's grandfather, had heard all of the pandemonium from his house a half mile away and had walked over to see what was happening. Jason explained as best he could to Amice what had happened while the EMTs loaded Katherine onto their rig.

The police told him to stay behind until they could corroborate his telling of the events. After an hour of collecting evidence, they released him on the condition that he would make himself available for questioning.

Amice insisted on driving him to the hospital in Jason's truck. They sat in the surgical waiting room, while Katherine had surgery for internal bleeding.

Amice rested his open palm on his knee. "I've known you your whole life, son, and I can tell you know a lot more than you're letting on."

Jason sighed with exhaustion. He didn't want to think about what was going on, much less talk about it, even to Amice, who had always been kind to him.

"I'm worried about you and Katherine," the old man said. "I can see that you're mixed up in something dangerous. I don't want you to repeat your father's mistake."

Despite his growing exhaustion, he opened his eyes and met Amice's concerned face. "I'm worried too, Amice. I'm not sure how to get out of this, how to stop it. I feel like I'm on a runaway train."

Amice's eyes watered and his Adam's apple bobbed up and down as he swallowed hard.

Jason didn't want to die like his father, fighting a formidable foe with a flashlight and a pen. It had been all about getting the story for his father.

Amice grimaced, looking unconvinced. "I worry that your feelings for her are going to get you killed. Whatever mess she's in, it isn't your battle."

Jason shook his head. "You saw what happened to her. I can't just leave her to fend for herself."

He leaned over with his elbows on his knees and cupped his hands together over his nose and mouth. All he could think about was the red all over the cabin, and the smell of blood that still lingered in his nostrils.

Katherine's blood!

Jason dropped his limp hands to his kneecaps. His body and mind were feeling the day: being drugged, finding out Sara was a spy, his apartment being bugged, and finding Katherine nearly dead. He sucked in a breath and looked away from Amice. He couldn't let anyone see him like this.

"Can I have the keys to the truck? I can't sit here."

Amice handed over the keys. "You sure you're okay to drive, son?"

Jason nodded as he tried to still his trembling hands.

"All right then. You go on and do what you have to do. I'll have one of my VFW buddies take me back."

"Thank you." A brief feeling of guilt washed over him at abandoning the poor old man at the hospital, but he just had to get away.

As Jason stepped out into the muggy air, he looked up at the sky. The pain of the last couple of days overwhelmed him to the point that his legs gave out, causing him to drop to his knees in agony. At that moment a loud wailing sound permeated the heady afternoon air, a painful, almost inhuman sound.

It took him awhile to realize that the sound had come from him.

Renaissance Hotel
Detroit, Michigan
June 5, 2008
9:30 PM

Alex lay on top of the hotel bedspread, flipping channels, fighting sleep. A box of stale pizza lay next to him half eaten. The stress of the day had finally caught up with him. He had spent the greater part of his time putting together a serviceable profile for the Detroit Field Office and had just emailed it to the ASAC for the case.

Determined to turn in early tonight, he slipped out of bed, emptied his pockets, and swiped at his phone to turn it on only to get a blank black screen—dead. He plugged it in to charge overnight, and the smell of sweat and garlic wafted from his body. He wouldn't have time in the morning, so he stripped out of his suit and jumped in the shower.

After he had finished, he turned down the bed and fell between the crisp white sheets, but just as his head hit the pillow, he remembered that he hadn't set the alarm for the morning. Cursing under his breath, he reached for his partially-charged phone and turned it on, and was surprised to see several notification icons demanding his attention: four missed calls, three voice mails and two text messages.

He pulled up the latest text from Richards first.

Why aren't you answering your phone?!?! I've been trying to call you all evening and it keeps going straight to voicemail. CALL ME!

Alex swiped to the second message.

Pick up your damn phone!

A chill ran down his spine as he dialed into his voicemail.

"First message sent at 4:00 PM," said the automated message.

"Alex, I need you to call me. Katherine was found and has been admitted to Holy Cross in Virginia. She's in critical condition. I spoke with her doctors and they said she was raped and beaten."

Alex dropped his phone and, gasped for air.

Oh God. His right hand rose to his mouth. *Oh God.*

His eyes stung and his hands shook as he snatched the half-empty pizza box and hurled it across the room, knocking down a lamp. He then slid down the side of the bed and buried his face in the palm of his hands.

Red Dawn Casino
Detroit, Michigan
June 6, 2008
1:00 AM

Charles had been standing outside the casino for hours waiting for him to come out. With unlimited funds and a lot of determination, one could find anyone. It hadn't taken a whole lot to get Billy to give up the location of his rat cousin. The fucker wasn't stupid and had gone underground right away.

It was all his fault. If he hadn't involved these degenerates in the first place, it never would have happened. He wasn't a perfect man, but he had never wanted this. By trying to save her from one psycho, he ended up leaving her at the mercy of another kind of monster.

He was done, but not before he made everyone involved pay for what happened to Katherine.

Indie Coffee
Outside Richmond, Virginia
June 6, 2008
3:00 AM

After driving around for hours, Jason had pulled into an all-hours cafe and ordered breakfast and coffee. Lost in thought, his forgotten pancakes now lay at room temperature in front of him.

The waitress came by to touch up his coffee. "Sweetie, I know the food ain't the greatest, but you should at least try it before you pass judgment."

He paid no attention to her sarcasm.

She sat down at the booth across from him.

Jason turned away from the window first to see her nametag read Nessie, and then to meet her curious eyes.

"Do ya wanna talk about what's bothering you?"

"Don't you have to work or something?" he asked, irritated by her meddling.

The woman smirked as she looked around the cafe. "You see people I don't?"

He looked around the deserted cafe and chuckled. "I guess you don't get too much business at this hour, huh?"

"Depends. Either way, I've got time, and you look like you could use company," she said with a twinkle in her eye.

He sighed and wrapped his hands around the comforting mug of coffee. "I do, do I?"

"During this shift it's not unusual to get customers with interesting stories to tell, especially the ones that brood in the corner and don't touch their food." She nodded down at his full plate.

He hadn't touched the pancakes that had sounded so good when he had ordered them, but under her watchful eye, he took a bite.

The cute waitress smiled and pulled on one of the tight curls that splayed across her face. "Now that's a start." She winked, making his stomach flip-flop.

He couldn't help but smile back at her. "Okay...." He looked down at her name tag again and read out loud, "Nessie, how's about you guess?"

Her eyes rolled up and she gazed at the ceiling while contemplating the challenge. "It has to do with a woman." She tugged at her curls again.

This distracted him. "Yea...."

Nessie smirked. "It's always about a woman."

While she talked, Jason took large bites of the cold pancakes and toast he had ordered an hour before.

"Since I haven't seen you before, I would have to assume you aren't from around here. Which means you're running away from something."

He looked up from his now half-empty plate. "Why's that?" *Am I that transparent?*

She shifted on the bench and her long leg brushed his under the table. "I know everyone in this town, and I don't know you. When life brings you to the middle of nowhere, it ain't ever good."

He couldn't help but be distracted by her. She was devastatingly beautiful, with skin the color of his coffee and shoulder-length hair that haloed her face in a million tight curls. "What about you? Are you running from something, too?"

She shook her head, making her curls bounce, and bit the end of her finger—her mouth slightly parted. After a long pause, she released her index finger from between her dazzling white teeth and pointed at him. "You're a reporter too, aren't you?"

His eyebrows dropped in surprise, and grinned. "Okay, now I'm impressed. Am I that transparent?"

She smiled and rose from the booth. "Don't feel bad, Sugar. Everyone is transparent as cellophane to me."

Jason chuckled again.

The bell rang over the cafe door, and he was sad to see a young couple stumble in. He watched Nessie's curvy form as she walked away, and let out a breath of laughter when she turned her head over her shoulder and winked at him. Dropping a handful of bills on the table to cover his tab, he took one last swig from his coffee cup and got up to leave.

Though he left more at peace than he'd been when he arrived, nothing anyone could say, not even a sweet waitress, could mitigate the impending doom making itself at home in his gut.

Joe Coffee
Grosse Pointe Woods, Michigan
June 6, 2008
5:00 AM

Alex sat in his rental car and watched a man in his late sixties seated inside the restaurant. Alex was able to make a positive ID on the man; it was without a doubt Katherine's dad. Local records confirmed what they already knew—finger prints didn't lie. Now they would have to figure out how to bring him in and get him to testify against a group that forced him to fake his own death.

Katherine.

Try as he might, he couldn't get her out of his head. He had finally gotten an update from Supervisor Magellan that they had trusted men guarding her, and that she was out of critical condition, but some of the damage done to her might be permanent. Magellan had also said that she was on suicide watch.

It took everything in him to keep his cover, to not rush to her bedside, to not run away with her far away from all of this.

He couldn't see how this would end well for either of them. Was it all worth it to stop a group of men who were addicted to greed and power? He wasn't so sure anymore.

FBI Headquarters: The Hoover Building
Washington, D.C.
June 6, 2008
10:00 AM

Alex caught the first flight out of Detroit and went straight into the office to meet up with Special Agent Richards. They decided to meet outside so that they could smoke and talk in private. He took a long drag of his cigarette while his boss filled him in on everything he knew, along with details from the paperwork the hospital and police had faxed over.

Alex's chest tightened and he felt short of breath. It was worse than he had imagined. Everything was there in black and white.

Katherine.

Richards looked at him with deep concern. "Bailey, because of everything that has happened, I need you to talk to Dr. Forester in the EAP offices. It's standard procedure. It shouldn't take long, and it shouldn't affect your field status unless she recommends it."

Alex sighed in frustration and exhaustion. "Fine, when?"

"You have a scheduled appointment with her in two hours."

Alex huffed in surprise. "I guess I don't have a choice in the matter?"

His boss gave him a sad smile and shook his head. "Sorry, no you don't. I have to talk to her too, since you two are my subordinates." Richards smoked the last of his cigarette and put it out against the building.

Alex patted him on the arm. "I guess I'll talk to you later then." He kicked off the wall and walked back inside and up the stairs.

Before heading to the EAP office, he dropped the police report off at his desk and pocketed the detailed report from Katherine's doctors. For two hours, he read the report over and over again until he could recite it verbatim. The notes said the doctors thought she might not be able to have children. This stuck in his mind. What else would those bastards take away from her? And for what?

FBI Headquarters: Hoover Building, EAP Services Department
Washington, D.C.
June 6, 2008
12:00 PM

As the time for his appointment drew closer, Alex began to pace back and forth in the waiting room, playing over and over again in his mind the information from the doctor's report.

At 12:00 on the dot, Doc opened her door and ushered him into her office. "Come in, Agent Bailey."

Alex chaffed with irritation. "Okay, Dr. Forester."

He needed a punching bag, a safe place to be angry. In the back of his mind he knew Doc was all he had to help him get through this turn of events, but he would still fight her every step of the way.

She closed the door behind him and pointed over to the chairs in the center of the room. "Would you like to take a seat?"

He stalked towards her, but she didn't flinch. "This is bullshit, Doc, I don't have time for this."

She walked past him and sat down, but her eyes never left him. The concern she felt for him emanated from her like a strong perfume, choking him.

"You seem very agitated and anxious. Would you like to talk about that?"

Alex barked at her. "Don't pull that therapist bullshit with me, Doc. You know exactly what's going on." A part of him felt bad for unleashing all of his pent-up feelings onto her, but it had to come out.

His outburst didn't seem to bother her in the least. She sat there nonplussed with her characteristic serene therapist expression on her face. "Actually, I don't know Alex. Please tell me."

He growled. "Fucking CIA pricks! They...."

His thoughts were so scattered that he couldn't even put a coherent sentence together. If he said it out loud then it would be true.

She just sat across from him, not saying a word just like she always did—using silence to draw him out.

His awareness of this technique didn't change the fact that it always worked. He hated silence.

He stalked back and forth in front of her. "If I had been there with her, none of this would have happened."

His hand flew to his mouth as though the words of what happened might slip out between his lips. The feelings inside of him reached a boiling point, and he picked up the small pencil holder sitting on her desk and threw it across the room. Pencils and pens scattered all over the floor.

His carefully constructed, stoic facade began to crumble as hot, angry tears stung his cheeks. He wiped away at his cheeks with the back of his hand and tried in vain to hold it all in, but the sheer effort was more than his body could bare, and his legs started to give.

Doc didn't miss a beat. In seconds she was up and leading him to the overstuffed sofa, where he sat pitched forward with his head cradled in his open palms. She put her arm around him and let him lean against her—his safe place. Even after the last of his tears had fallen, they sat in silence with his head buried into her neck.

The urge to tell her, to share his grief with her, prompted him to sit up and hand her the worn piece of paper from his jacket pocket. He couldn't look at her while she read it.

"I can't talk about this, Ellie." He called her by her name, something he never did.

"Oh, Alex," she said, placing it on her desk and taking his hands into hers. "This is not your fault. There's nothing you could have done. The man who did this to her... it's his fault and his alone."

He thought of the other girl, the other one he hadn't been able to save. The memories of her and his time in Mosul had haunted him for years. Katherine was just another notch in his belt, representing all the women he had let down—another girl he hadn't been able to save.

He looked up at her with his jaw clenched tight and his shoulders curled over his chest. She placed her hand against his still damp cheek and he closed his eyes, causing a single tear to fall. His bottom lip quivered. "Sara... Sara gave up the safe house location. She...." He swallowed down his grief, trying to continue. "Langley used Katherine as bait and everything went to shit."

He needed to move, so he stood and walked across the room to the wall shelf where Doc kept her textbooks and several framed photographs. His fingers brushed over a photo of himself and her husband Chris from when they were overseas. They both looked so young then, and he didn't think many people from that time would recognize him now. It surprised him that she kept it on her shelf where anyone could see it. Not that they couldn't be friends, but still, the less people knew about their past, the better. The last thing he needed was someone asking questions about how they knew each other, though he realized that was the least of his problems at this point.

"What kind of investigator am I if I can't even tell that the woman I've been working with and fucking for the past decade was working both sides?" He could hear the whining and self-pity in his voice, but he didn't care.

"I know what you are going to say, that you never trusted her and that you tried to get me to end things with her years ago. You were right. I should've listened to you." Under his breath he added, "You're always right."

After a few moments of silence, Doc said, "Are you getting any sleep?"

He laughed and rubbed the dark circles under his eyes. "No, and even when I do I have horrible nightmares." He pinched the bridge of his nose. "If I tell you something, you have to promise that you won't get mad."

She sighed and pressed her lips together in a slight grimace. "What?"

"I quit taking the medication," he said in a whisper.

Doc sighed and dropped her gaze to her hands. "Alex, you know you can't just quit taking it cold turkey."

He nodded. "I know, I know. I just can't think when the dose is that high. I wasn't sleeping or eating."

"What do you want to do?"

Alex sighed, grateful that she wasn't going to lecture him. "Can you give me another prescription? Maybe something new? I want to get better, I really do. I've never had a need to make this work before, but I do now."

"Yes, there is a new anti-anxiety medication that might work better for you."

"Great."

"But you have to take them every day. No skipping pills, okay?" She wrote him out a script and handed it to him.

Alex nodded as he took it from her and pocketed it. "I promise. Scout's honor." He offered a sly smile and extended three fingers up in the air. It had been an inside joke they'd shared for years.

She just rolled her eyes at him. "I'm not kidding, Alex."

He gave her his most genuine smile to let her know he took her suggestions seriously. "I know, Ellie."

The gratitude he had for her made it hard for him to say the next part. He looked down at his shoes while trying to work up the courage to ask his friend for the biggest favor he had ever asked of her. "There is one more thing."

She cocked her eyebrow at him in irritation. "What?"

He bit his lip and paused before he continued. "I need you to recommend a six-month leave of absence for me."

"I really wish you wouldn't ask me to do that." Her eyes softened with concern. "A psychiatrist recommendation for even temporary leave could destroy your career. You know this."

He rested his hands on his hips. It took everything in him to try and keep his calm, but he couldn't keep the unmistakable tone of desperation from his voice. "I have to be with her, Ellie, and the CIA isn't going to let that happen. If you make the recommendation, then I don't have to break my cover. It is a win-win for all involved, if you ask me."

"Alex, maybe they have good reason for preventing you from going to her right now."

He frowned. He had thought it through and this was the only way he could be with Katherine, and at the moment, that was all he could think about. "Ellie, don't do this to me. I love her and I need to be with her."

Doc sighed and looked down at her crossed hands. "Love—"

"Ellie, you can't tell me, if this was you, that Chris wouldn't be turning the world upside down to get to you. I *know* he would."

Her eyes narrowed in warning, but he didn't heed it. "You forget I was there when he went AWOL to get to you after you...." It was then that he saw her pained expression, and knew he had gone too far.

She quickly looked away from him to hide her eyes that were brimming with tears.

He had struck a raw nerve. It was an off-limits topic, and he had known that.

Shit! The last thing he wanted to do was hurt her—she was his best friend.

"I'm sorry—"

She held up her hand to stop him, got up from her seat, turned on her computer and started typing. He sat in silence wishing he could take the words back as she pressed a key and handed him a printed off form with her neat and careful signature on the bottom. It was a request for leave. He touched her hand but she drew back her hand as if scalded.

"Get out," she said.

"Doc, I'm sorry...." His voice was laced with deep regret, but she didn't seem to care.

She shoved the paper at him. "I said go!"

He took the paper and felt shame bloom from his core. The silence between them was palpable as she shuffled papers around pretending to be busy. He paused a minute... and walked out. Once the door closed behind him, the sound of her sobbing on the other side cut him to the quick. He didn't see how he could repair the damage, but he couldn't afford to lose any momentum. He would have to mend this fence later, after she had cooled her heels.

He went straight to ASAC Richards' office to turn in the leave recommendation for him to approve and sign. With wet palms, Alex knocked on the open door.

Richards looked up from his piles of paperwork. "Just the man I wanted see. Come in and take a seat."

Alex walked in and took the seat across the desk from Richards.

"I think I might be on to something. I know the answer is buried somewhere in these files, but I think I found the leak here at the FBI. I had my suspicions from the beginning, but now...." Richards paused, beaming down at the papers in front of him as if they were the eighth wonder of the world. "I have a lot of research still to do, but I am almost certain that Assistant Director Fullmore is a co-conspirator," he whispered.

Alex nodded. "That's wonderful, sir."

His boss frowned. "Why aren't you excited? This could launch both of our careers into the stratosphere!"

He handed over the paperwork from Doc.

"What's this?" Richards asked as he skimmed the paperwork. "I don't understand. This is bullshit! You're fit for duty. I'm fighting this, Bailey." Richards reached for his office phone in frustration.

Alex stopped him. "Sir, I requested her to write me this recommendation. Just like I am going to ask that you approve it and submit it to the director so that he can get it off to the CIA."

Richards pushed back from his desk. "Am I missing something here? Why the hell would you request this? You might as well be signing your own pink slip. You'll never work in the field again after this."

"That's kind of the idea, sir."

Richards shook his head. "I'm not signing this, Alex." His boss tossed the paper across the desk towards Alex. "You're a damn good field investigator. If shit's getting to be too much with the CIA, then come over here to the FBI. You can write your own ticket. You're a young man with a promising career. Don't throw it away."

"Thank you, sir, but I'm done. This last fuck-up with the tactical mission just put me over the edge," Alex explained as he thumbed a rip in the chair. "This is just between us, sir, but I knew the mole from the CIA. We had been close.... I should have seen it coming but I haven't had my head in the game. I can't risk someone else getting hurt because I'm not in 100%."

Richards rubbed his chin and pulled on his bottom lip as he started to piece it all together. "Alex, forgive me for prying into your personal affairs, but did you and Katherine have something going on?"

Alex looked away from his boss's interrogating gaze, answering his question with his silence.

Richards sighed. "F—uck, Bailey." The agitation showed in his boss's mannerisms as he stood up and walked over to the window of his new office. He looked over his shoulder at Alex. "Is she worth it?"

Alex's eyes filled with tears. "Yeah... she is."

His boss's shoulders slumped in defeat. "Are you sure about this? I can't sign off on this unless you're absolutely sure."

"Yes, sir, I'm sure."

Richards wrote a note on the form and crossed out a whole section of the paperwork before signing it and handing it to him. "All right, but I've amended it so that you can still work for the FBI contractually throughout the course of this investigation, and on any other future case as needed. I need your help to find a way to nail that son of a bitch Fullmore to the wall."

Alex nodded. "Yes sir."

"Dammit, Bailey, I hope you know what you're doing."

Alex looked down at the form and then back at the kindhearted man in front of him. "Thank you, sir. It's been a pleasure to work with you."

Richards nodded. "I'll courier all this to you once you get settled. We'll communicate through whatever protected channels you want. Good luck, Alex." He extended his hand.

Alex gave him a firm handshake.

His boss sighed. "I can't say that I'm happy to see you go, but I get it. A man has to do what a man has to do."

Holy Cross Hospital
Just outside Richmond, Virginia
June 6, 2008
4:00 PM

Katherine lay in her hospital bed staring at a small stain on the wall. It helped her... focusing on something as inane as a spot. The room's blinds were closed and all the lights in the room had been shut off. After being blindfolded for several days, she had developed a temporary photosensitivity.

Her mind played over the myriad of causes for the mark on the wall, when a large man came bustling through her room with an irritating energy. "Good afternoon, Ms. Mitchel, my name is Edward Underwood, but you can call me Ed. I'm your assigned social worker."

The large, red-faced, elderly man ambled over to the windows and pulled the vertical blinds off to the side, letting the late afternoon sunlight spill into the cheerless room.

She grumbled at the harsh light, trying to shield herself from it with her arm.

Mr. Underwood plopped down into the chair beside her bed with a loud thump.

Katherine peaked out from behind her arm to see him working on a crossword puzzle. She shifted and turned away, burying her face in the pillows.

After a minute or two Edward cleared his throat. "Twelve across... this may be a growing science.... Hmm," he said to himself.

Is he serious?

She rolled over and looked him in the eye while she talked. "Excuse me, Mr. Underwood, but I would really like to be alone right now."

His half-moon smile and look of pity enraged her. "Katherine, I know you know that you're being held here under the 50/51 code. This means that the hospital isn't going to discharge you until they're sure you are no longer a danger to yourself."

Katherine's eyes squeezed shut as she curled into a tight ball. She wanted to shut out his words. She heard him stand and push the nurses call button.

"Can you bring in a wheelchair for Ms. Mitchel? She needs some fresh air. Tell Marcy to bring those burgers outside. We'll be in my usual spot."

The nurse at the station responded, "No problem, Mr. Underwood. An orderly will be by with one shortly."

Katherine flipped over towards him, pulling on her IV port. "Ah! Mr. Underwood—"

He cleared his throat and held up one finger in interruption. "Ed, please call me Ed."

She pressed her lips into a fine line before continuing. "*Ed*, will you please go! I don't want a wheelchair. I don't want to help you with your crossword, and I don't want to talk to you."

He pinched the bridge of his nose as the nurse brought in a wheelchair followed by an orderly, who walked over to Katherine's bed to help her out.

Though she didn't want to go, she also didn't have any fight left in her, so she complied.

The nurse adjusted her IV to a portable pole and arranged all the tubes and wires to allow for her to be mobile.

Once situated in the chair, Ed pushed her out of the room. "Let's get some fresh air, shall we?"

She slumped down in the chair and chuckled. "You say that as though I have a choice."

He looked down at her with a frown. "You always have a choice, Katherine."

She sat silent as he pushed the chair over to an outside private pavilion. Just as he locked her chair in place next to a bench, a nurse strolled up the path with two take-out bags.

Mr. Underwood pointed at the nurse. "Ms. Mitchel, our dinner is walking up the path as I speak. You will eat. You'll just have to trust me that it will be the best hamburger you have ever eaten, and then we can talk."

Katherine cracked a small smile at his persistence, and soon proceeded to eat the entire burger and the large fries.

He chuckled. "Do you want more?"

She looked down at the empty packaging. "I guess I was hungry. You were right. It was the best burger I've ever eaten."

He smiled. "Want more?"

She nodded and accepted another burger from the bag beside him.

"You need it more than I do," he said with a wink.

Rayburn Building
Washington, D.C.
June 6, 2008
6:00 PM

Charles stood outside the Senator's office door, took a deep breath, and rapped on the door. He had convinced the Senator's staffers to let him speak with him despite not being on the schedule.

"I said to hold all calls. I don't want to be disturbed, Diane," Scott called out from the other side of the heavy, oak door.

Charles opened the door and strode into the office, shutting it behind him. "I think this is a call you might want to take." He strode across the room to Scott's desk with an empty bravado.

Scott's hands, resting on his cheeks, began to draw his face downward in a look of dread. "What the hell are you doing here?"

Charles flashed a look of false indignation. "What, no glad tidings for an old friend?"

Scott sat up in his chair, his face reddening. "You know I can't be seen here with you, especially after what I heard happened! I don't know what kind of shit you thought you were pulling with that kidnapping stunt."

"I could say the same for you—trying to kill off the whole family." Charles tossed two photographs down on the desk between them. The one of Katherine in Texas had been destroyed. He didn't want anything to remind him of what happened at the cabin. He crossed his arms over his chest. "None of that matters, though, right now."

The Senator looked down at the pictures. "Oh God." His meaty hands trembled as he snatched the offensive photos from his desk. "Where did you get these?"

Charles took a deep breath and reminded himself: *I'm doing this for Katherine.* "Jane Bond, our little blonde bitch. We're going down on the same ship, Senator, so unless we work together we're fucked."

Scott's fingers pressed into the deep creases on his forehead.

Before he could respond, one of the staffers knocked and opened the door. "Senator, you're needed on the floor."

He swore under his breath. "Yeah, give me five minutes, Diane."

When the door closed again, Scott turned back to Charles. "I have to go. I'll call *them* and see what *they* suggest, and let you know later... tonight."

Charles stood and put the pictures back into his pocket while Scott put on his rumpled jacket.

At the office door, Scott turned with one hand on the knob and said, "Meet me at Old Ebbitt Grill on 15th Street around nine. I'll text if this runs over."

Charles nodded and lifted his hand to salute him, his voice filled with disdain. "Sure thing, Senator."

Scott glowered at him, then turned on his heels and headed out the door.

Charles fingered the guest pass clipped to his jacket. He walked through the halls, worrying over the meeting tonight. One of the photos was a temporary insurance policy against Scott and his goons, but he had nothing to protect himself from Sara, who posed the greatest threat to both men. Yet Scott wouldn't want her around for long now that he knew she had physical evidence that connected him to The Syndicate.

Church Hill Neighborhood
Richmond, Virginia
June 6, 2008
8:45 PM

Alex coordinated arrangements with Brian and some colleagues to fly out to Chicago, and secured temporary housing for him and Katherine. After he had finished getting his ducks in a row, he tried Doc on her cell one more time.

It went straight to voicemail.

His flight wasn't until the next morning, so he jumped in his car and drove over to Doc's house. If she wouldn't pick up, then he would force the issue face-to-face. He didn't want to leave town for an indefinite amount of time without making things right between them.

As he pulled up in front of the house, the front door opened and her husband, Chris, walked out. Alex got out of the car and met him halfway up the walk.

"I don't know what you did, but she's really upset. She said she doesn't want to talk to you."

Alex shrugged. "I fucked up, Chris."

Chris snorted. "No shit, B. What did you do? She's not talking. If you tell me, maybe I can help you out."

He followed Chris over to the stoop and sat down beside him. He needed a cigarette for this, so he fished one out and lit up. After taking a long drag, he explained the long and the short of what had happened in Doc's office.

Chris shook his head. "Jesus, Bailey!"

He groaned in embarrassment. "I know! I know! I didn't mean to hurt her. I was upset and didn't think about what I was saying."

Chris took the cigarette from Alex and took a hit.

Alex let him have it and pulled out another for himself.

"B-man, there is something you should know.... Ellie's pregnant."

Alex hung his head in shame. "Oh shit."

Chris nodded as he took another hit from the cigarette. "The doctors didn't want her getting pregnant again, but you know Ellie." He puffed his cigarette and blew it out the corner of his mouth. "She wants a baby so bad that it's all she thinks about. Now that she's pregnant, she's terrified of losing this one too. She's lost her damn mind."

Alex took long, slow inhalations of his cigarette, drawing the smoke deep into his lungs. He thought of the first baby she had lost in Iraq, when she had almost died and had been so depressed that she hadn't gotten out of bed for weeks afterwards.

"You need to make this right, B. We're boys and all, but I don't have your back in this fight."

He whined in frustration. "I'm trying, man, believe me, but I'm leaving town tomorrow morning to meet up with Katherine, and I don't know how long I'll be gone. That's why I stopped by tonight."

Chris regarded him with a coy smile. "So tell me about this girl that has you all wound up tight like a hairpin trigger."

Alex blew a plume of smoke up into the night sky as he let himself think of Katherine. "She's beautiful, smart, funny, and makes me want to be a better man." He smiled, a little shy admitting his feelings out loud. "I think I might love her."

"God, women make us crazy."

Alex chuckled in agreement.

Chris took another long drag of the cigarette and blew the smoke off to the side. "I remember when I first met Ellie. I thought I would have a heart attack every time she walked in the room. All through basic, I followed her around like a lovesick puppy. It's a good thing she took pity on this poor man," he said with a small smile.

Alex laughed and stretched out his long lanky legs onto the steps.

Chris grew serious. "I'm sorry about your girl, man. If that had been Ellie, I... fuck, I don't know, man. I don't even want to think about that." He put out the cigarette in one of Ellie's potted plants.

Alex nodded, sucking in his lower lip to stop the tears that threatened to fall. "Yeah," he said, his voice quivering.

His dear friend stood up and put his hand on Alex's shoulder. "Wait here, man. I'll see if I can get her to come out. No promises, though. She may just want your sorry ass to sit out here in this Godforsaken heat like a dog. She's crazy like that, but you already know."

"I hear ya, man. Thanks." He watched his friend go back inside to try and fight for his cause.

He sat on the steps, smoking and looking up at the blinking lights of a plane flying overhead. The sun had set and dusk had begun to set in, and he couldn't help but reminisce about the earlier years of his friendship with the Foresters. He loved them so much that it hurt, and the thought of losing his friendship with Doc was more than he could bear.

An hour after Chris went back inside, he was startled by the sound of the front door opening and closing. He put out his cigarette and waved the smoke away.

Doc walked down the steps to the bottom one and sat down beside him. Her sharp shoulder knocked hard into his.

When the second blow never came, he turned to her and spoke from his heart. "Ellie, I'm sorry. I'm a total fucked-up asshole and you have every right to be mad at me."

Doc stared at her feet and clasped her hands over her knees.

He reached out and covered her hands with his. "You know I love you, Doc. I'm going to miss you. I hate that I'm leaving with things like this." His tear-filled eyes sought hers out, but she turned her head away from him. He squeezed her hands again. "I want you to be happy. Chris told me about the baby." He paused for a moment. "I hope you get that happiness this time around."

She turned towards him, her face streaked with tears. "I want you to be happy too, Alex, and if she makes you happy then you should go to her. Life is too short and full of too much sadness to not snatch up every little bit of happiness you can get."

Alex put his arms around her shoulders and hugged her to him tighter than usual. They sat for a long time in silence, looking up at the stars and contemplating everything that lay in front of them. Alex wondered if either of them would get the happy ending they sought.

Chapter 10

Knettle Creek Cabin
Millburo, Virginia
June 7, 2008
6:00 AM

Jason parked his truck along the interstate and walked several miles up the familiar path to a rustic cabin beside a large pond. The long walk helped him clear his mind and calm his tense body, which had been on red alert for days. His heavy-footed stride crunched the brush underfoot, alerting his grandfather's golden retriever to his arrival.

The dog came traipsing across the yard to greet him. The old boy was getting on in years.

"Hey Bobo." The dog walked by his side up to the door of the ramshackle cabin, where an old, stout Irish man stood in the doorframe.

"*Howyiz,*" the man called out in the traditional Irish greeting.

Jason waved. "Hello, *Daideo*! "

His grandfather motioned for him to come inside. "Come in, lad, I've got a pot on."

Jason shuffled his feet at the doormat, scraping away the dirt and other outdoor detritus he had accumulated on his long walk. Once inside, he felt right at home.

Bobo circled the braided rug by the fireplace three times before plopping down.

The cabin and his grandfather, his only living relative, had always had a way of centering him. He slumped down onto a beat-up old wooden chair he had sat in since he was a little boy, and kicked off his shoes. The memories of days spent in the cabin as a child warmed him and brought him the comfort he needed.

His hands brushed the scarred wooden kitchen table where he had watched his grandfather and Amice play many games of chess and reminisce about their service in Korea. A well-worn chessboard sat off to the side on top of a pile of books. Perhaps Amice told his grandfather what had happened.

His quiet grandfather shuffled about in silence between the stove, counter and refrigerator preparing mashers—a traditional Irish breakfast.

The sound of Jason's stomach grumbling broke the comfortable silence between the two men. He couldn't remember the last time he had something homemade, let alone a large, rich, traditional homemade meal like the one being prepared.

While the food was cooking, his grandfather placed a chipped teacup in front of Jason. The aroma of Irish tea—Lyons, his favorite—steeping in a small teapot at the center of the table was a balm to his battered soul. He carefully poured the rich, heavy tea into the cup, and inhaled deeply the comforting aroma.

"This is amazing," he said with a smile.

His grandfather grunted in response, and Jason sighed. It had been a long time since he had genuinely smiled, felt relaxed.... *Fuck!* He raked his fingers across his face and through his hair before taking a sip of his tea. When he set it back down on the table, he rested his head in his open palm. *So tired.*

He sat there half asleep until the sound of his plate being placed in front of him startled him awake. As tired as he was, he was even hungrier. He couldn't help himself, and dug into the food as if it would be his last meal.

His grandfather chuckled. "You need a good Irish girl to feed you, lad. You're disappearing."

Jason laughed, his mouth full of mashers and eggs. "I won't argue with you there, *Daideo*."

After he had cleared his plate and had seconds, his grandfather set him up in the guest room where he had slept as a child during summer visits. His grandfather covered him with a wool blanket, which his great grandmother had made when his grandfather still lived in Ireland. His head barely hit the pillow before he was asleep.

Holy Cross Hospital
Just outside Richmond, Virginia
June 7, 2008
Noon

Katherine lay motionless in her hospital bed thinking about the session she had just had with her social worker, Ed. She had told him all the things she thought he wanted to hear, but like most depressed people, her efforts to conceal her true feelings were transparent. She felt like an open, festering wound that would never heal.

Someone stood guard outside her room the entire time.

Suicide watch. This is what it has come to.

A nurse came in with a paper cup and a glass of water. "Ms. Mitchel, I have a little something to help you sleep."

Katherine's hackles rose, and a scream of protest escaped through her cracked and bruised mouth. She thrashed away from the nurse, tangling herself in her IV line.

The nurse stepped back and called for help.

"*Noooooo*," she cried.

She didn't stop until her Ed appeared. "Ms. Mitchel, you don't have to take anything you don't want to take. You're in control. Do you hear me? You're in control right now." He repeated the phrase over and over until it started to sink in.

When his words reached the language centers of her brain, she began to calm down.

"Katherine, you are safe here," he assured her.

She shook her head. "I will never be safe." She sniffed back a sob. "Not here, not anywhere."

Knettle Creek Cabin
Millburo, Virginia
June 7, 2008
Noon

Jason ran a finger along the dusty jackets of his grandfather's books. *Daideo* was a renowned author, having published more than thirty books, both fiction and nonfiction, about the war. The whole of his grandfather's life's work, spread out before him, humbled and inspired him in equal measure. He dreamed about quitting his job and writing what he wanted to write.

Fucking paper! Fucking father leaving it to me!

He leaned his forehead against the bookcase and closed his eyes, hoping to gain some wisdom through osmosis.

His grandfather came up behind him and put a hand on his shoulder, leading him to the chairs. "What's the *craic*?" he asked in his native Gaelic.

Jason smiled. "*Daideo,* I don't know if you heard this or not, but my life is a giant mess."

They sat down across from one another. His grandfather rested his arms on his knees as he leaned in towards Jason. The fingers of his hands came together to form a triangle.

"What's wrong?"

"What's wrong?" Jason parroted back with his elbows resting easily on his knees. "Everything." Tears stung his eyes, but he was too proud to cry in front of his grandfather.

"A stor."

Jason smiled a little at the familiar term of endearment, 'my treasure.'

His grandfather rose from his seat and sat down beside Jason on the love seat. "Your Mam, God rest her soul." The old man paused to reflexively do the sign of the cross in deference to Jason's mother, who had passed away when Jason was a young boy. "*Go mbeadh do mháthair mhaith leat a bheith sásta.*" He often slipped into Gaelic when he became emotional.

Jason sighed. "I know she'd want me to be happy, but I don't know how to be happy anymore."

His grandfather cleared his throat and wet his lips. He was a quiet man by nature, and would wait for Jason to tell the whole of it before responding.

"I've gotten myself caught up in this mess with Katherine and some criminal organization. I hate my job. I'm lonely. And I am more than a little afraid I'm going to end up getting myself killed like my old man." Jason felt a little bit lighter now that he had spoken the truth out loud.

He chuckled as a single tear slid down his cheek. "I don't know what to do."

His grandfather squeezed his hand. "There is nothing so bad, that couldn't be worse, my Mam use to say."

Jason nodded and squeezed his grandfather's hand back. "*Daideo*, I think this is as bad as it gets." He didn't want to think about how it *could* get any worse.

His cell phone buzzed in his pants pocket—an unwelcome intrusion—making him jump. He pulled up the text message from a Brian Williams of the Federal Marshal's Office in Chicago, and cursed under his breath. His heart dropped.

"I'm sorry, I have to go."

He bent and kissed his grandfather on the cheek, and rushed out the door. In record time he jogged the long walk back his parked truck.

On the way to the hospital, he used his Bluetooth and called the Federal Marshal's office to get more information on the severity of the situation at hand.

Holy Cross Hospital
Just outside Richmond, Virginia
June 7, 2008
2:00 PM

Katherine sat in the wheelchair and waited for the nurse to bring her the discharge paperwork. The faxes and court orders sticking out of her medical file made it possible for her to leave against doctors' orders. She couldn't wait to leave. Her legs shook with anticipation, her body flooded with a constant stream of adrenaline.

During her stay at the hospital, madness moved in and made itself at home in her mind. It filled her with dark and dangerous thoughts. She was overwhelmed by the pervasive urge to slice open her arm just to see if she would still bleed. The small bit of logic that remained in her cautioned her against such a drastic science experiment.

She knew that just one misstep would ensure a longer stay at the hospital, court order or not, so she kept her madness in check and constructed a formidable wall that kept everyone at bay—especially Jason and his pity.

The concern from the nurses, doctors, and Jason were too much for her to bear. It managed to lacerate what was left of her dignity.

A sympathetic nurse handed her the discharge paperwork, and she suffered further. When she had finished signing the paperwork, Jason popped into the room. He was going to drive her to some place in Illinois, where they were going to meet with Brian, the Federal Marshal in charge of her case.

They had explained this to her that morning over a phone conference, but she had been only half listening. She was beginning to feel more like a rag doll, carelessly dragged from one place to the next by those directing her life, causing her stitches to pull at the seams.

Jason took control of the wheelchair and helped her into the car.

She wanted to slap him, to make him feel as worthless as she felt. Instead, she acted as limp as the rag doll she had become.

He assisted her into the car without comment or complaint.

Metro Station-Chinatown
Washington, D.C.
June 7, 2008
7:00 PM

The intersection bustled with people getting on and off the metro. No one gave him a moment's notice, even though he had on a sweatshirt—in the middle of a heat wave—with the hood obscuring his face. The orders had come in earlier that morning, and the plan was set in motion.

The higher-ups had intercepted a message she had sent her handler. She had been reluctant to come forward, but by the end of the call had agreed to a meeting at Langley—a tentative deal had been struck.

Even though she would be taking the eight o'clock train, he arrived early, not wanting to take any chances. His heart raced in his chest and his breath came in short gasps. He reminded himself that he needed to do this in order to save his own skin. She was a cornered animal that would strike out at the closest person to her, and that was him.

He tried to not think about how he was going to commit murder—again.

Interstate 70
Just outside Indianapolis
June 7, 2008
7:00 PM

They had been driving for hours.

The white lines of the highway entranced Jason, and he wished life were like a highway—with signs to guide him along the way. He no longer held stock in his own ability to discern the right path. He gripped the wheel with such ferocity that his hands began to throb in protest. He looked down at his white-knuckled grip—the hands that had played a role in un-ghosting the woman beside him—but refused to unclench them from the wheel.

She sat so still beside him that he began to wonder if she were there, or if her vessel was all that remained of her.

Eight hours into their drive, they pulled into the small town of Travis, just outside of Chicago. Brian's home wasn't too much farther. He fished for the restaurant napkin on which he had written down the directions, and had to squint in the half-light of the street lamps to read his chicken scratch handwriting, all while weaving down small, quiet neighborhood streets. He was lucky he hadn't been pulled over yet.

As he turned the corner onto a cul-de-sac, he spotted a house with the right address number on both the house and the curb in front.

Thank God.

Too exhausted even to get out of the car, he used all of his leftover energy to put the car in park, turn off the ignition, and collapse back against his seat.

Katherine sat unmoving beside him... until she saw what he saw.

A shadowy figure outside the front door stepped out of the dark and into the path of the security lights.

Alex.

Chapter 11

Brian Williams' Estate
Hinsdale, Illinois
June 7, 2008
9:00 PM

Alex's anxiety rose with each passing hour, and as those hours of waiting turned into minutes, he smoked his last remaining cigarettes. A trusted courier had hand-delivered the first batch of FBI documents earlier that day. Somewhere inside the files might lay the key information necessary to indict A.D. Fullmore. He had been pouring over them all afternoon and evening, a painstaking process made more challenging by his distracted mind.

Instead of paying attention to the work, he kept thinking of her.

The sound of the rental car pulling into the drive made him jump. He and Brian walked outside to meet them in the driveway, and his whole body hummed with electricity, shooting all along his spine as synapses fired at imperceptible rates.

Fuck, I need to calm down!

His feet, oblivious to his inner turmoil, propelled him forward out the front door and down the long driveway.

When he saw her, he froze—a statue in mid-step under the security lights on the front lawn. His stomach flip-flopped at the sight of her face and neck, which were covered in garish bruises and cuts. The sickening yellow of the interior domed light in the car made her features look twisted and pinched.

"Oh God."

Beside him, Brian also stopped in his tracks. "What?" Then he, too, saw for himself what was at stake. "Oh shit."

Alex licked his lips in determination and continued walking to her. His vision became myopic with her in his sights, their gaze locked together.

She stepped out of the car and broke into a run towards him, and they collided in an almost painful embrace. She wrapped her overly thin arms around him and clung to him with a desperation that either threatened to snap them in two or forge them into one new whole being.

It was a small comfort knowing that, at last, he could now keep her safe—even if for just the moment.

Her tears erupted in choking gasps, and he held her up as her legs gave out. Her heart made time with his, and her tears dampened his neck. They had known each other a short time, but something had happened in those scant few weeks that inexplicably bound them together—a force of nature.

So lost in her, he barely noticed Jason and Brian walk into the house.

Alone. At long last.

Out of need, he sought out her mouth and kissed her the way he had been wanting to since the moment they said goodbye.

She met his kiss with an ardent one of her own.

All of his senses took her in: taste, sound, touch and smell. *I need to see her – really look at her.*

He pulled back slightly and took in the sight of the woman before him. She was not the same person he had left behind in Florida; the light in her eyes had gone out.

He could feel her growing self-conscious under his inquisitive eye, and a violent shiver rippled through her as she pulled herself out of his insistent grasp.

Every fiber in his being buzzed with longing, but he had to give her space to heal. The new meds—coupled with his determination to rise above his addition—suppressed his instinctual urges. The night before, he'd asked Doc how he should proceed with Katherine so that he wouldn't inadvertently hurt her with his ignorance and ineptitude. She had said to take it slow and let her take the lead. So....

He took the small duffel she clutched in her hand, and led her inside.

"Brian's wife put together a room upstairs for you. Do you want me to show you? Are you tired?" He set the bag down in the foyer before closing the door behind them.

She shook her head and avoided his gaze.

He led her with a slight touch on the small of her back into the living room just as Brian came around the corner.

"Well," Brian said, "I got Jason all settled into one of my boy's old rooms. I have Frank's room all fixed up for you, Katherine. Do you want to turn in or maybe like some tea?"

"Tea would be nice." She sat down on one of the plush sofas in the living room. Her flat affect worried him.

The room was sparse but expensively furnished. Brian disappeared into the kitchen to make the tea, leaving them alone again.

Alex leaned against the mantle on the other side of the room. Now that he had seen with his own eyes the evidence of what had happened to her, he felt rudderless. He patted his jacket pocket and was dismayed to remember that he had smoked the last cigarette just minutes before. Without a cigarette, he didn't know what to do with his nervous hands, so he crossed his arms in front of him and stared down at his shoes.

For once in his life he found himself speechless. What do you say to the woman you think you're in love with after she's been brutally beaten and raped? He shivered.

She watched him with a stillness that unsettled him even further. The look she gave him made him think that she too was at a loss for words. They stayed there in silence with their naked thoughts dancing around in their heads.

Brian broke the awkward silence when he walked back into the living room with a tray of hot tea mugs in hand.

Alex shot him a helpless look, silently begging him to stay and help explain the situation.

Brian cleared his throat. "Katherine, as you know I'm a blunt man, so I'm going to cut to the chase. Alex and I have been talking about how to keep you safe and end this whole thing as quickly as possible."

Her grim expression greeted both men. "I don't see how that's possible."

Alex shuddered. *She might be right.*

Metro Station-Chinatown
Washington, D.C.
June 7, 2008
9:00 PM

"Barry, can you get the press to back up?" The lead D.C. homicide investigator, Sergeant Frank McFadden, tapped his uniformed police officer on the arm.

"They're vultures. Fucking can't give the poor girl a little respect." Barry hitched up his uniform pants over his bulbous gut.

"Tom, did you get a statement from the witnesses?" McFadden surveyed the scene before him with a look of frustration. It was a total cluster fuck, as usual.

"Yeah," the junior detective said. "They said some guy in a gray hoodie pushed her in front of the train and took off for the street. It all happened so fast, by the time people realized what had happened the perp was already long gone. The descriptions of the subject are all over the place. All we know is it was a male in a gray hoodie and black jeans."

"Great! This case isn't going to leave the board anytime soon." McFadden heaved a great sigh and rested his hands on hips. "As shitty a description as it is, let's get an APB out anyways. Maybe we'll get lucky."

"Yeah, I have a better chance of winning the lotto, sir," Tom replied under his breath.

"You have any better ideas?" McFadden barked.

"Fuck, no!"

"Do we have a name?" Sergeant McFadden nodded with his head over to the body.

Tom shrugged. "The credit card in her pocket said Sara Horton. We'll have to confirm that, though."

Brian Williams' Estate
Hinsdale, Illinois
June 7, 2008
9:00 PM

Alex knelt down in front of Katherine. "You have to believe that I won't let anything happen to you."

She leaned away from him and gave him a pointed look. "I *want* to believe that you can help me, but I don't. I don't even know you."

At her words, he stiffened and glanced over at his friend.

Brian stood up and cleared his throat. "I think I'm going to head up to bed and let the two of you talk this out." He walked out without another word.

A thick awkwardness laced the air. Alex stood and rubbed the stubble on his chin and cheeks. "Katherine—"

"Don't bullshit me. I know you aren't who you say you are... that you're keeping things from me. Charles showed me stuff his private investigator dug up. Who are you? Who are you, *really*?" Before he could answer her, she continued. "I can't keep doing this anymore. For all I know you're going to try and kill me," she said all in one breath.

She slumped and slid back against the sofa, seemingly drained by her rant. "I don't know who to trust. I just know that to get through this, I need to be able to trust *someone* again."

He swallowed hard as her words sliced through him. If she only knew what was in his heart. If he could just touch her, let his hands and body speak the words he was failing to express. But that would only make things worse.

"It's complicated, but I can assure you that I'm not going to kill you. I want to do everything in my power to keep you safe. I know you're really confused right now and don't know who you can trust, but I need you to know that you can trust me." He bit his bottom lip to keep himself in check.

Her eyebrow cocked in disbelief.

It was going to take time and a lot of convincing to get her trust. He slowly moved closer to her with his hands in the air. "I'm an open book. Ask me anything. I might not have the answers, but I will be honest."

A pregnant pause hung over them, making him even more anxious. He hated silence. In desperation, he began pacing back and forth as he again filled the air with his hurried words. "Okay, so you asked who I am. Well, as you might have already figured out, my name isn't Alex Bailey. My real name is Alexander Martin Estrella."

He paused for a second to let that sink in, and to muster up the courage to continue. It had been years since he had spoken his birth name, and he was dismayed that it now sounded so foreign on his tongue, but she needed to know what was on the line. "Katherine, you have to understand that it's against the law to tell you any of this, but I trust you, and I want you to feel like you can trust me."

What he was going to say next was a felony and could put the mission in danger, but he needed to put all the cards on the table. He continued despite her angry scowl.

He dropped his voice so only she would hear. "I don't technically work for the FBI."

Katherine's mouth fell open. "What?"

He raked his fingers through his hair as he tread on dangerous ground. "I've been working undercover inside the FBI to investigate any ties the government and the FBI might have with The Syndicate."

Her mouth opened and closed as if she wanted to say something, but nothing came out.

He held his breath as she shut her eyes for a moment. It was a lot to process—he knew that. When she looked back up at him, he let out the breath he'd been holding and continued to dig himself into an even deeper legal hole.

"I've worked in the field for the CIA for the last thirteen years, most of which I spent overseas. I'm good at my job, and before all this was up for a promotion as a Junior Supervisor, which at my age is a pretty big deal." He was proud of his service to the country—one of the few things in his life he could stand by.

"I grew up near Howard University and lived in government housing for most of my life. My mom took off when I was three and I lived with my meth-head dad until he overdosed when I was seven. I became a ward of the state, in and out of foster homes until I aged out. I got a full ride to Howard, where I got my bachelor's and master's, and I'm fluent in three different languages. I'm a recovering sex addict. I drink a lot and smoke even more. I've never been in any kind of serious relationship, and.... I know this is going to sound crazy—I know that—but I think I might be falling in love with you." As the words tumbled unbidden from his lips, the realization of what he had just said settled in.

Katherine gasped and her face reddened. "You don't even know me. How can you say that you love me?"

He sighed and shoved his hands into his pants pockets, dropping his gaze back down to his shoes. He'd told her the truth, and part of him was glad to have laid it all out on the table—even if it was embarrassing. He knew she felt the same way; he just had to be patient and wait.

Until then, he needed her to know the whole of it. "Because of the intrusive nature of my work, I do know you. I know you better than anyone."

He tried to choose his next words with care. "In a widespread effort to move the investigation along, the government put you and several others around you under surveillance. It was my part of my job these last two years to profile you. When you were cleared as a possible co-conspirator, it was deemed necessary to get to those around you by getting close to you."

"Jesus," she said under her breath, like a prayer.

Confessing exhausted him. He sat down across from her, fighting the urge to take her hand or to offer her any kind of physical comfort. "Katherine, the investigation of your father's death never stopped. It's what started this whole thing. He stumbled onto this group and was *allegedly* killed because of what he knew."

Her gaze dropped down to her hands and a single tear splashed on her thumb. "Charles... how high up in the organization is he?"

He suspected she knew the answer to her own question, but still needed to hear it. "He's one of the group's mid-level operatives. They've been mostly using him to launder their money through his various businesses and holdings. He isn't the one we're most concerned with now, though. Your twin brother, Scott, is also a part of it. The most recent intel on him is that he appears to be a high-ranking member in the group, which has been financing his campaigns through a Super Pac called The Old Dominion Fighters."

Her mouth opened in shock and disbelief, and her breathing became shallow.

Before either of them could continue further, Alex's phone rang in his pocket.

She stared at him. "Aren't you going to answer that?"

He sighed in irritation. "I wasn't going to."

Katherine folded her arms across her chest. "Answer it."

He fished out his phone and caught it right before the call went to voicemail. "Bailey."

"Turn on the TV," Supervisor Magellan said.

Great! This can't be good.

He looked around, spotted a remote, grabbed it and turned on the news. The ticker at the bottom read that a woman had been pushed in front of an oncoming subway train.

"It's Agent Horton. They took her out." His boss sounded weary.

"Oh Jesus." His hand went to his abdomen, where it felt as if he'd been stabbed. "Do we know who?"

"We don't know for sure, but my guess is MacAvoy. We think she was going to turn him in to us in exchange for immunity. She was on her way to Langley when it happened."

"Mmm hmm.... Thank you, sir." He ran his hands through his hair and shifted back and forth on the heels of his feet. "Let me know if you hear anything else."

He ended the call and sank back into the soft folds of the sofa. He could feel the hot sting of tears threatening to fall. His world was falling apart at his feet, and he was powerless to stop it.

***

In the bedroom directly over Alex and Katherine, Jason tossed and turned, unable to sleep. Every time he closed his eyes, he pictured them together. He could hear the mumbled sounds of their chatter downstairs, which his brain tried to piece together into understandable words and phrases.

Frustration and anxiety finally got the better of him, and he jumped out of bed and picked up his laptop. He turned on the computer and pulled up some of the notes he'd taken on The Syndicate case, even though he'd read them a dozen times already. When he finished skimming through them, he pulled up a blank document and began to write.

For the first time in too long, he was writing what he *wanted* to be writing, and it felt good. As a writer, the only way he could process this giant mess was to put it to paper. He tumbled down into the words and let them guide his fingers as they danced over the keyboard—telling the story they were *meant* to tell.

It was just the beginning.

Chapter 12

Nin's Bar
Danville, Illinois
June 7, 2008
10:00 PM

Charles sipped his scotch in hopes it would calm his nerves. A slight tremor had developed in his hands, making it difficult for him to hold his glass. He needed to forget what he'd done. Four drinks in and he still saw her face every time he closed his eyes, and the sound of her screaming still rang in his ears. Deep down he knew that no one would ever classify him as being a good man, but he never in his wildest imagination would have thought he could become a murderer.

The events of the last few weeks now blurred together, and the tethers of sanity were loosening, leaving him dangling over the cliff of an impending breakdown.

Scott had been texting and calling him for over a half hour, but he had yet to respond. Sara's death had made the news, and the asshole would want assurances that there had been no mistakes, and that nothing could be tied back to the great and powerful Virginia Senator.

Fucking degenerate scumbag.

He downed his glass of scotch and ordered another. Without warning, the contents of his stomach come back up, constricting his throat. To avoid spewing all over the bar, he swallowed it all back down with a grimace. He was a businessman first and foremost, and getting sick all over his own bar would be bad for business.

Business! That's what had started this whole thing in the first place. He needed out of this mess—he no longer had the stomach for it—but there were only two ways out, and neither of them was appealing. He had to do it just right, so that he didn't get branded as the scapegoat for the group's transgressions.

In his drunken state, he sent out an intercession, a futile wish to go back in time and stop himself from joining up in the first place, back when The Syndicate had first approached him. He'd been young, stupid, and ambitious. His inherited wealth and deceitful business dealings had caught their attention, and they made him an offer he couldn't turn down. At first, it seemed like a good investment, but then their demands grew more and more unscrupulous—even more so than his own—and they had ways of making a man do as he was told.

He shivered as the memories of his failings washed back over him.

Over the course of the last ten years he had done things he wasn't proud of. No matter what it was, though, he had always been able to rationalize it away—but not this business with Katherine... no matter how hard he tried. Yes, he had mistreated her—he was man enough to admit that now. He really had tried his best to keep his anger in check, but sometimes the rage inside of him would erupt. He never stopped loving her, though. She was his life.

He needed to step forward and turn himself in, turn everyone in, especially the great and powerful Senator from Virginia. It was the least he could do to make up for all the pain he had caused her.

Yet the *how* part eluded him.

I'm going to need help... someone I can trust.

Brian Williams' Estate
Hinsdale, Illinois
June 7, 2008
10:30 PM

Katherine struggled to stay awake as Alex told her about his colleague that had been murdered, pushed in front of a moving train. Her heart ached for him, despite her best efforts to put up walls between them. A part of her wondered if the dead woman had been something more than just a work buddy.

Alex sighed when his phone rang again. "Hey, Doc, yes I heard. No, I'm not alone. No, it's not like that. I'm with Katherine. Yes, I promise. I will call you tomorrow. Okay, bye."

His eyes slid closed as he placed his phone back on the sofa's armrest and rubbed his face with the heels of his palms. He looked exhausted.

She felt ashamed, but her curiosity got the best of her. "Who was on the phone?"

He paused mid-rubbing and met her scrutinizing gaze. "The ever formidable Doc." A small smile crept across his tired features, the first real smile she had seen on him all night. "She's an old friend of mine that I met when I was in Iraq. She heard about my colleague—my boss called her to let her know—and she was worried about me."

"Oh." She quickly dropped her gaze to her clasped hands. *Another "friend."*

His charming smile deepened. "Let me clarify. Doc and I really are *just* friends. I'm friends with her husband, too. They're the only ones I have actually." He cupped his mouth to catch a yawn.

She couldn't help but think about what he'd said about being a recovering sex addict. His past aggressive sexual overtures towards her made more sense, but it was far too late to be analyzing everything they had discussed that night. She needed sleep.

Alex stretched and stood up from the sofa in the awkward way tall people do. "Come on, let's get some sleep. It's been a long day and it's getting late."

Katherine's eyebrow shot up and her skin prickled with fear. *What does he expect of me? That we'll start back where we left off?*

A sad smile hung on his drawn features. He held up three fingers like a pledge. "I know my past behavior might make this seem disingenuous but, scout's honor, just sleeping. Scout's honor. I just... I don't know, after everything that happened today, I don't want to sleep alone tonight."

Her heart hammered in her chest at his request. "I don't know."

"Katherine, I just want to be near you and know you are safe. I promise."

She nodded, still anxious. The thought of being in a strange room all alone seemed a much more frightening prospect, though. "Okay."

He reached out and helped pull her up from the sofa, picked up her bag, and led her into the spare bedroom off the kitchen, where Brian had set him up for the night.

She followed with a reluctant willingness.

***

The digital readout on the alarm said 1 AM. The exhaustion, which hours earlier had threatened to pull her under like a riptide, had been replaced by an anxious wakefulness. Though desperate for sleep, she couldn't bring herself to take the sleeping pills the doctors at the hospital had prescribed.

For now, being sedated—hell, even going to sleep—was a frightening thing. She remembered what the social worker at the hospital had said to her about having patience with her healing body and mind. While she hated to admit it, she did at least feel a little safer having Alex nearby.

The depth of her feelings for him frightened her. She didn't exactly have the best track record with men. Charles had also claimed to love her, and not only did he mistreat her for years, he also kidnapped and drugged her and then left her with that madman.

She shivered at the thought, awakening Alex.

A groggy grunt escaped his lips as he rolled over to face her. "Can't sleep?"

She shook her head as a rush of shyness washed over her. "No."

He nuzzled his tired face into his pillow but kept his sleepy green eyes trained on her. "Wanna talk?"

She stared blankly back at him, not sure *what* she wanted anymore.

He wet his lips and slid his hand underneath his pillow. "Since we are both awake, can I ask you something?"

What could he possibly need to ask? Doesn't he know everything about me already? "Yeah, sure."

"First of all, can I hold your hand?"

The tenderness with which he asked touched her, and she nodded. Alex reached across the wide expanse of the bed for her hand, and after a long pause, she clasped his hand to hers.

"You don't have to answer this if you don't want to, but there's something I've been trying to figure out," he said.

"What's that?"

He wet his lips again—an endearing nervous habit—before continuing. "Why did you marry Charles? And why did you keep it a secret?"

The question surprised her. She thought back to all those years ago, and her heart became even heavier with grief. The need to unburden herself of the past was great, and for some unknown reason she trusted Alex.

"Well, I guess since you've profiled me, you already know how I was before and after my dad died. I was wild, drunk and high most of my teen years. Charles and I started dating about two years before my dad died. We partied a lot, especially after my dad was gone. He wasn't always violent, at least not at first." Making excuses for Charles and his behavior had become a reflex.

"My brother Scott didn't think we were all that serious. I guess he figured once I grew up and stopped partying all the time that I would come to my senses and leave Charles."

Scott... my brother who had been so concerned for my wellbeing. How could he be a part of all this? Both he and Charles had been deceiving her all along.

Alex squeezed her hand, bringing her back to the present. Maybe this was like ripping off a Band-Aid: she just needed to say it quickly and be done with it.

"Anyways... in our first two years of dating, he hit me a few times, but he always blamed it on having too much to drink and... I don't know... I guess I believed him. Half the time I was too drunk or high even to notice or care, but my dad noticed." She bit her lip, her eyes pooling at the memory.

"I didn't know it at the time, but my dad had made an amendment to his will right before he died, stating that if I married Charles I would be cut off from my inheritance. I guess he hoped I would choose money over Charles."

For years she'd been carrying around a deep-seated guilt that her dad died disappointed in her, but she wasn't ready to admit that out loud yet.

She took a long, deep breath before continuing. "A little over ten years ago, before I married Charles, Scott and Jason staged an intervention. They were worried that I hadn't dealt with my dad's death, and about all the drinking and drugs. They got me to see some of the ugliness that had come out of my addiction."

Alex's lips lightly touched her knuckles.

The simple act took her breath away and she had to take a short pause to collect herself. "So, I got sober and started to see a counselor. Charles got on board, quit drinking around me, and was, for the most part, supportive. That was when things got bad. He couldn't blame anything on the alcohol or drugs anymore, and I didn't have anything to numb myself against his rage." She brought the blanket up to stave off the chill that rippled through her.

"The smallest thing could set him off. I felt like I was walking on eggshells whenever I was around him. He was pretty controlling of my time and didn't like me hanging out with any of my friends, or even Scott. He was always very concerned about what I did and who I talked to when he wasn't around. It was the norm for him to grill me for hours on end. Once he woke me up at 3 AM to rant and rave at me for going to a friend's birthday party without telling him."

A small tear slid down her cheek and stained the pillow beneath her.

"One day Scott took me aside and told me about the will and how it was my dad's dying wish that I break things off with Charles. It was a well-timed conversation, because by then I was tired of living under Charles's thumb and wanted out. He had threatened me so many times about what would happen if I left, that I believed he would kill me or himself. I agreed with Scott that I would break it off in a public place, and then spend some time out of town until things cooled off."

"I can't even imagine how frightened you must have been," Alex said.

Katherine nodded. "I was terrified. He took me out to dinner that night, so I told him then, figuring he wouldn't attack me in a restaurant full of people. I was wrong. He dragged me out by my hair and slammed me up against the brick wall of the building. He almost knocked me out. Thankfully, the restaurant owner and some people on the street called the police and they arrested him. I was pretty banged up, but otherwise I was very lucky. Looking back, I can't believe I didn't press charges, but at the time I just wanted it to be over with. So I packed up my stuff and went up to our cabin—"

The recent memory of what happened in that same cabin washed over her, leaving her paralyzed.

"I'm here. You're safe," Alex said, squeezing her hand.

She closed her eyes and nodded as the anxiety washed over her. The aftershocks of it all were almost worse than the attack itself.

He squeezed her hand again and brought it up against his beating chest. His soft, emerald green eyes regarded her with such love and respect that she almost choked on the concern that emanated from them. "Just breathe."

She took his advice to heart and took a deep breath. In order to work through it all, she needed to finish the story that had been hanging around her neck. "I'm okay." She let out a trembling breath and continued.

"Jason and I were up there fixing the place up," she said, pushing past the panic attack like it hadn't just happened.

"We were alone. I always knew he had a crush on me, so I guess I should have seen it coming, but I was young and naïve. That weekend he decided to try and kiss me. Of course, at that exact moment Charles burst into the cabin. He and Jason got into it and he ended up kicking J out. I was terrified. Charles pleaded with me to reconcile. He said he would die without me, that he loved me, and that no one would ever love me like he did."

Alex squeezed her hand, giving her the reassurance she needed to keep going.

"It sounds crazy when I say it now, but at the time I was so depressed and lonely that I believed every word. I didn't think I deserved anyone better. He suggested that we marry in secret so I wouldn't be written out of my inheritance. I was stupid and agreed."

She sighed before she told the last of the story. "I moved in with him after the civil ceremony. Scott stopped speaking to me. He was mad at me for not choosing Jason over Charles. I know Jason loves me. I do know that. I have tried to love him back that way, but I can't," she said in a sad rush of words.

Alex rubbed the stubble on his chin and scratched his bed-head hair. He seemed to want to say something, but he remained quiet.

"I know it's completely fucked-up," she said. "I would see those public service announcements about domestic violence and I would think that my situation was different, but I was just fooling myself. He had me so convinced I was never going to be loved by anyone else, and that if I even thought of leaving him, he would kill himself or me."

Alex squeezed her hand like he never wanted to let it go, then brought it up to his lips and kissed her knuckles, never taking his eyes off her.

The love that emanated from him made her feel safe for the first time in a long time.

After a long pause, when the silence had once again settled in, Alex finally spoke up. "Thank you for sharing that with me. I know it couldn't have been easy. I want you to know that I think you're very brave."

"Can I ask you a question now?" she asked.

A wry smile danced across his face. "Anything."

She pointed an index finger at a puckered scar on his chest. "What's this from?"

Alex looked away. His clenched jaw twitched.

"You don't have to tell me. I—"

"No, I can tell you. I will warn you, though, that you might not like the answer. I know I don't," he said under his breath.

She nestled into her pillow, more relaxed than she'd felt all night, and thought that maybe telling his story would help unburden *him* as well.

"Let me be the judge of that."

***

He turned onto his back and looked up at the ceiling. He couldn't look at her when he told her the truth. He was far too ashamed.

"The scar is a constant reminder to me of my hitting rock bottom," he said, loathing the story he was about to tell.

Her eyebrows raised in wonder. "Oh?"

"You sure you want to know?"

She nodded. "It's only fair since you seem to know everything about me."

She had a point.

He smiled. "*Touché*. Don't say I didn't warn you, though."

He settled into the bed before continuing. "Okay, so I told you I'm a recovering sex addict, right? Well, when I was in my early twenties, I was serving overseas as a paramilitary officer with the CIA, in Iraq. I was working out of the US embassy's auxiliary office in Mosul. During my off-time, I would get restless and would go for walks through the market. There was a beautiful Kurdish woman named Chuwan."

He smiled at the memory of her. "Her name actually means 'beautiful' in Sorani. She sold fruits, vegetables and nuts at the market, and I was a sucker for the watermelons her family sold at their stall. We would flirt a little with each other, on the side, when her mother and sisters weren't looking. Well, one day she slipped me a note along with the change from selling me the melons. The note had a meeting place and time. We... well... anyways, long story, short—we got careless in our meetings and she got pregnant. She was coming to tell me the news the day her brother followed her and caught us... well, you know. He... um...."

He clutched the bed sheets in his free hand and cleared his throat. "He shot me and dragged Chuwan off. He just left me there for dead. If the call for afternoon prayer hadn't happened soon after, I would have bled out in the alley. I found out later that they beat Chuwan until she miscarried. She died a week later from an untreated infection from the miscarriage."

A stream of tears slid down his hot cheeks, and he left them alone. "My friend Doc and her husband Chris were stationed there at the same time. She worked in a women's clinic that helped women like Chuwan. She was the one who told me about what happened. It killed me." His voice quivered as he tried in vain to keep from full on sobbing in front of her.

"Chuwan had asked the nurses and doctors to find me and make sure I was okay, and to say she was sorry."

He took a deep, shuddering breath and continued. "At the time, when we were having our affair, I didn't care about what the consequences might be for her. All I could think about was the sex. After she died, I hated myself for what had happened. I... I... tried to kill myself, but Doc saved me." He purposefully left out the details of the night Doc had come upon him trying to hang himself in the empty mess hall.

He couldn't tell Katherine that part.

Katherine bit her trembling bottom lip. "I think I understand," she said. "When I was a Senior in high school, I got behind the wheel while drunk and hit my brother with the car, breaking both of his femur bones. He had to be in traction for the whole summer. I could have easily killed him... or someone else that night. Addiction is horrible thing that makes us do stupid things."

He turned his head back to face her for the first time since he had started his story.

"Alex, I understand. I do."

His heart swelled with affection for her. How could he not love her?

A sly teasing smile greeted him. "Tell me more about this Doc of yours."

"Well, her name is Ellie, but I've always called her Doc. She's a psychiatrist, but when I first met her she was an army medic. Because of my addiction I didn't have any friends back then. I guess Doc and Chris took pity on me. We didn't really get close, though, until after the incident with Chuwan. I should have been shipped back to the states after what happened, but Doc fought for me and got it taken off my record," he said, still grateful for his friend's help.

"Doc was the one who diagnosed my problem and tried to help me out. I did the whole twelve steps and going to meetings thing when I got back to the States, but it didn't work. Thankfully, Doc put me on some anti-anxiety meds, and suddenly I was able to function again. She's always been there for me. She and Chris mean the world to me. They're my family."

"And you're just friends?"

"Yes." He laughed. "She has super clear boundaries in that department. Once, early on in our friendship, I got a little drunk and confused and tried to kiss her." He felt the heat rush to his face.

"Oh?"

He rubbed his jaw at the memory of that embarrassing night. "Yea, she clocked me good... made it very clear that it was not appropriate or appreciated. I'm like her idiot little brother."

Katherine laughed a little as she stifled a yawn. "I'd love to meet them some day."

He pulled the blankets up and tucked them around her, then brushed a strand of hair from her face and whispered, "Get some rest. I'm right here. I'm not going anywhere."

She seemed to relax under his watchful guard. Her eyes slid closed and sleep quickly took her away.

He lay on his back, listening as her breathing slowed and became regular.

The news of Sara's violent death, coupled with talking about Chuwan, had been too much for his frayed mind to handle. He had been surprised that his boss at the CIA had called Doc. A part of him wondered how much the CIA knew about the nature of their friendship.

I'm getting sloppy.

Pushing all those thoughts away, he rolled onto his side and watched the love of his life as she slept. After a while, his eyelids grew heavy and the strong tide of sleep pulled him under. His last thoughts were of Sara, of how he hadn't gotten closure... and never would.

Chapter 13

Brian Williams' Estate
Hinsdale, Illinois
June 8, 2008
6:00 AM

Jason woke with a start. His forehead and the side of his face had been resting painfully on the keys of his laptop. He kneaded the sore indentations on his cheek with his fingertips.

He hadn't written like that in a long time. The writing exercise had been therapeutic, even if it had been mostly garbage. He had exorcised some demons last night when his fingers danced along the keys in a fast-tempo tango, which took him through the first four chapters of what looked to be the beginning of a novel inspired by the recent events—a tragic love story.

He tapped the keyboard to wake up his computer, and scrolled through to the beginning so he could read some of what he had written.

This isn't half bad.

Somewhere in between the dark prose and the crisp dialogue, he had written Katherine out of his hopes and dreams for the future. He loved her enough to know he couldn't make her happy, and the letting go actually brought relief. Now if he could hold on to that and not slip back into his hound-dog ways, he could perhaps find happiness himself. He was done begging for the scraps of her love and affection.

She was in good hands. He had seen the look in Alex's eyes when they pulled up last night. It was the look of a man lost in a woman—one he knew well. A part of him almost felt sorry for Alex.

If he left early, he could get back to Virginia in time to set in motion some of the plans that had begun to form in his mind. Things were going to change in a big way for him; it was both exciting and terrifying all at once.

After cleaning up and packing his things, he made his way down to the kitchen and poked around until he found everything he would need to make coffee. Just as he pressed the brew button, a man's voice startled him out of his reverie.

"You're leaving?"

He nodded, not really wanting to go into it with Alex, who looked at him with pity. *Fuck him and his pity.* "Yeah, I think you and Brian have things covered here just fine without me."

"Jason—"

He held up his hand to stop him. "Don't. It's okay. Just promise me that you will keep her safe."

There was no sense in letting the other man know about his broken heart. She would be in good hands with him. *He's no Charles, that's for sure.*

Alex cleared his throat and crossed his arms across his bare chest. "I will. I'll do my damnedest to keep her safe."

Jason leaned back against the counter, wanting to believe the man was up for the job. "Good. I know this goes without saying, but please treat her right, man. She's been through so much already. I just want her to be safe and happy."

Alex bit his upper lip and nodded. "We want the same thing, man."

He reached up into the cupboard and pulled out another coffee mug. "Coffee?"

Alex nodded. "Yes, please."

The two men sat down at the table together in an agreed upon silence, having already said everything that needed to be said. Jason did a mental run-through of the long list of things he needed to do when he got back to D.C.

He was so preoccupied that he didn't hear Katherine come into the room.

"I don't suppose you boys left me any coffee." She walked over to the coffeemaker and started to poke around.

Jason was the first to break the silence. "Top cupboard to your left."

"Thanks." She opened the cupboard and reached up on her tiptoes to get a mug down.

Her shirt lifted, revealing bruises in the shape of fingerprints, and he forced himself to look away. When she sat down at the table between them, the tension in the room became palpable.

Brian's wife, Betty, came breezing into the room moments later with Brian in tow. "Good morning, everyone. I'm sorry I wasn't able to greet you when you arrived last night. I have a new showing at the gallery next week and it has just plum worn me out. Is anyone hungry?"

A cacophony of grunts and nods affirmed that, yes, everyone was indeed hungry.

Brian chuckled and announced, "I'll start another pot of coffee."

***

Alex changed into a gray t-shirt and a tight pair of Levi's. He desperately needed a smoke and, remembering that Betty had been a chain smoker years ago, thought she might have a pack he could bum. He paused in the doorframe beside the stove, where Betty was cracking eggs.

"Betty, love, I don't suppose you're still a smoker?"

She chuckled. "No, I quit a few years ago." She leaned towards him and added in a hushed whisper, "But I may or may not have a hidden stash in the upstairs bathroom."

Brian turned and caught his wife's eye, scolding her.

Alex smiled. "Thank you." Before he left, he turned and kissed the older woman on the cheek, making her blush.

He made his way up the stairs to the guest bathroom. Just as Betty had hinted, a whole carton of cigarettes lay nestled in the closet.

Score!

He ripped into a pack and pulled out a cigarette. *Lighter? Shit, it's downstairs. Wait a minute....* He pushed aside some monogrammed towels and found a pearled lighter.

"Thank you, Betty."

The window stuck, but after a few good shoves he had it opened. He lit the cigarette and took a nice long drag before blowing the smoke outside. *Fuck, that's good.* As he smoked the last of the cigarette, someone knocked on the door.

"Come in." He was surprised to see Betty push open the door and close it behind her. He chuckled. "Want one?" he offered with a wink.

She shook her head. "No, but I think I will just sit and enjoy the secondhand smoke. That way I can keep my promise to Brian."

"You sneaky old woman, you," he teased.

She swatted a hand at him.

Laughing, Alex lit his second cigarette and blew the smoke towards her instead of out the window.

She closed her eyes and deeply inhaled. "Oh yes," she moaned.

He chuckled again. Their kids didn't know how good they had it. His parents hadn't given two shits about him.

Betty inhaled deeply the cloud of smoke he had created above them. "So, what's the deal with you and Katherine?"

A short laugh escaped his parted lips. "You aren't pulling any punches, are you?"

She inhaled again and smiled. "I'm too old to pussyfoot around."

The cigarette dangled precariously between his pinched lips. "*Touché*, Betty." He took a short puff and looked away from her intense gaze.

"Well, out with it already." She impatiently waved her hand in front of him.

"Okay, all right. I don't know what there is to tell. I like her. I like her a lot, and I think she may like me too."

She shot him an irritated glare. "Tell me something I don't already know, Don Juan."

He laughed a little and shrugged. Her myopic preoccupation with his love life was amusing and irritating in equal measure. "I don't know. This isn't exactly the best time to be starting something with someone. Don't you think?"

She shrugged back before handing Alex another cigarette.

"Are you trying to kill me, old woman?"

Her smile deepened as he lit up his third cigarette in as many minutes.

It didn't matter that his stomach was starting to roll and his head was buzzing.

"If you wait for everything to be just right, you'll never do anything. Trust me."

He held the cigarette loosely between his fingers, and tapped the top with the pad of his thumb as he thought about what she had just said.

With his gaze still on his hands and the lit cigarette, he cleared his throat and told her the truth of the situation. "She was hurt pretty bad. I worry that she's been too damaged by all of this to ever be ready for a relationship. It doesn't help that I've never had a girlfriend before."

Her wizened eyes looked up at him, and she placed her wrinkled hand on his knee. "The not knowing and acting anyway is part of living your life. You can't be afraid of everything that may be lurking around each corner."

"Maybe so, Betty." He sat back and looked outside at the boughs of the oak tree that swayed in the breeze outside the window.

***

"Excuse me, you two. I need to go check in on my wife. I think she has inhaled enough secondhand smoke by now," Brian said as he got up to go upstairs.

Jason finished his eggs and wiped the corners of his mouth with the cloth napkin.

Katherine cleared her throat. "You're leaving?"

Jason nodded. "Mmm hmm, I need to get back to Washington. There are some things I need to do."

Her heart sank at his news, but she needed to let him go. It wasn't fair to keep stringing him along and giving him warrantless hope.

"I think you're in capable hands." He looked away from her towards the door, like he couldn't wait to bolt.

"What about you? Will you be safe?"

He chortled.

It pained her to realize that her concern for *him* was too little too late.

He caught her gaze and let out a loud exhale through his nose. "I'll be fine, Kat. I'm going to hand over the paper to Lisa for a little while, and go spend some time with my grandfather and do some real writing."

She couldn't have been happier to hear his news. He was long overdue in achieving his own dreams. "That sounds wonderful! I know how much you hate working for the paper."

He placed the napkin on the table and put his dirty dish on top of the growing stack beside the sink. "Well, I'd better get going. I've got a long day of driving ahead of me."

She stood and went to hug him goodbye, but stopped herself. Something had shifted between them. New boundary lines had been drawn.

"Goodbye, Jason."

"Bye." He picked up his bag and laptop, then headed out of the kitchen and out the front door.

She cupped her face with her hands and sobbed. What if she never saw him again? He needed to be free of her so that he could live his own life, but his absence created an unfillable hole in *her* life. It was her fault. She brought him nothing but misery and despair.

The sound of the chair across from her scraping against the wood floor brought her back to the moment. She parted her fingers and gazed at an exhausted Brian, who stared back at her.

"Katherine, there are some things we need to talk about."

Alex entered the room and sat down at the table with them. He smelled like cigarettes.

Her eyes widened and her grip on the table tightened. Couldn't she get a moment's break from reality? Was that too much to ask?

"Katherine, honey...." Brain patted her hand.

She couldn't help but flinch, a reflex born out of the trauma. When she glanced over at Alex, he gave her a half smile in return, which told her she wasn't going to like the news.

"Katherine, hon," Brian continued. "In the course of the investigation we discovered something surprising, something that we don't quite understand."

"Just tell me, already." Her irritation over it all was rising with each passing second.

Alex reached his hand across the table, towards her. "Katherine, your father is alive."

She gasped. *That can't be! They must be mistaken.* She just stared in disbelief.

Alex left his hand just millimeters away from hers and caught her eye. "I got a tip from one of my sources in the CIA that someone fitting the description of your father was working in Detroit as a general contractor. I traveled there to see it for myself, and I positively ID'ed the man. He's alive."

It felt as though the air in the room had been sucked out. She pushed back from the table, struggling to breathe. "Oh God!" She rushed out the backdoor in just a few strides, grateful when they didn't follow after her.

Chapter 14

Brian Williams' Estate
Hinsdale, Illinois
June 8, 2008
8:00 AM

Alex walked out back to the pergola to talk to Katherine, who seemed lost in thought, staring at the garden.

He cleared his throat. "Do you want to talk about it?"

She shook her head.

He shoved his nervous hands into his pants pockets. "Okay, but we'll have to talk soon about the plan Brian, Richards, and I have set in place to keep you safe. I'd like your input."

She drew her knees up under her chin and hugged her legs to her chest. "I know."

He sighed and sank into the chair next to her. "You should know that the investigation wouldn't be where it is now if you hadn't given Jason those jump drives. Because of you, we might actually be able to get enough evidence to prosecute and bring these people to justice."

She tilted her head towards him with her chin resting in the crook between her knees. Her eyes squinted at him. "They were able to decode it?"

"Yeah, the CIA has been pooling its resources to make this happen, but the Attorney General still needs you and at least one other witness to testify."

"That's where my father comes in? You need him to come out of hiding, or whatever it is he is doing, and testify about what he knows about The Syndicate?" She brought her hand up and cupped it across her forehead to shield her eyes from the unrelenting sun.

"Yeah, but that's not going to be easy at all." He fished out the pack of cigarettes he had pilfered from the upstairs bathroom, took one out and lit it.

To his surprise, she reached over and took it from him. As she took a short puff, his phone rang.

Frustrated, he pulled it out, answering it on the third ring. "Bailey."

"Bailey, I need you back ASAP," his supervisor at the CIA barked at him. "We've got a tactical team who can transfer her to the safe house. We'll just need the location."

"Sir, I don't think that's a good idea."

"I didn't ask you if you thought it was a good idea or not. The girl will be perfectly safe. You can even review the group yourself."

Out of the corner of his eye, he caught Katherine watching him with interest.

"With all due respect, sir, that isn't good enough. I'm going to stay with her at the safe house. Did you receive the paperwork from Dr. Forester and Special Agent Richards?"

"I don't know what kind of stunt you're pulling, but you're never going to be allowed in the field again. Are you sure this is how you want this to play out?"

"Yes, I'm sure. She's too important to lose."

His supervisor continued to go on and on, but Alex had stopped listening. He caught Katherine's gaze and held it—a myriad of emotions swam through her lipid blue orbs.

"Thank you for your concern, sir. I'll keep in touch." He ended the call and tossed the phone on one of the lawn chairs.

Katherine took a long, deep drag of the cigarette.

He didn't like her smoking. It didn't suit her. He snatched the cigarette back, took a long drag, and blew rings of smoke up over his head. Making rings always calmed him.

"Fuck!" he exclaimed to the sky.

When he looked back down, their eyes met.

Oh, what you do to me....

The air between them crackled. For a moment, he thought about kissing her, and when he pushed the urge back down, he could swear a look of disappointment crossed over her.

Danville Press
Danville, Virginia
June 8, 2008
4:00 PM

Jason drove straight through to the paper in Virginia. His assistant Editor-in-Chief had been calling for days, but he'd ignored all the calls, letting them go to voicemail. He believed in his staff's ability to function without him. When he arrived at the paper that afternoon, he was pleased to see they had done well in his absence.

The news that awaited him, though, took his breath away. The front page of the paper that day read:

> *Local editor from the Danville Press was pushed in front a Metro train.*

His chest tightened and his breathing became labored to the point that he had to sit down. He thought back to the last time he had seen Sara. What had been her role in all of this, and did this happen because she had warned him? So distraught by all that happened, he hadn't noticed someone standing in the door frame of his office until he heard a sharp knock on the already open door.

"Can I come in?" a hesitant, but familiar, voice asked.

Jason looked up from the police report and the articles to see a familiar face. "Charles?"

He stood and rushed the man, pinning him hard against the door. He could kill him for what happened to Katherine.

Charles did nothing to stop him. As Jason's forearm dug into the asshole's throat, constricting his breathing, he turned red and then purple.

Right before Charles passed out, Jason let him go. *He* was no murderer. "You aren't even worth the effort to kill you."

Charles' hand went up to his neck as he struggled to force air back into his lungs. "You...." He struggled to take in air. "You have every right to want to kill me." He sat down in the chair on the other side of the desk. "I fucked up. I know that."

Jason folded his arms across his chest in an effort to keep himself from attacking the scumbag again. He was afraid that next time he might not be able to show any mercy.

The man's eyes filled with self-loathing. "I wish you would kill me. I'm too chicken shit to kill myself."

Jason attempted to keep his breathing tempered and his mind clear. "What do you want?"

Charles' face sunk. "Is she safe?"

In all the years Jason had known him, he'd never seen Charles this upset before.

"She's with her partner. They—"

Charles held up his hand to interrupt him. "I know, I heard." His face twisted in agony. "Is she going to be okay?"

Jason slumped down into his office chair—too tired for this. "That's kind of a loaded question. Is she alive? Yes. Are the physical wounds healing? Yes. Will she ever heal mentally? Emotionally? I don't know."

Charles' body rocked back and forth. "I never, ever wanted anything like that to happen to her, you have to believe me."

Jason shook his head. "Bullshit! You almost killed her, I don't know how many times. How does what you did not come out the same in the wash as what that animal you left her with did to her?"

"How dare you!" Charles' voice grew louder. "I *love* her."

Jason shook his head. "You have a pretty shitty way of showing it."

Charles clenched and unclenched his fists.

"I didn't come here to fight with you."

Jason pushed back his chair and started to pace. "Why *are* you here?"

The once-mighty man looked up at him with a look of desperation. "I want to turn myself in, but I need your help."

Jason stood dumbfounded for a moment. "Um... okay, what do you want from me? Why don't you just go to the police or the FBI?"

"I need your help in getting in touch with the right people. I don't know if you know, but there are people in the FBI that are dirty when it comes to this investigation. I need to get to Katherine's boss, the man you've been working with—Richards."

Jason's eyes shot up to meet Charles'. He hadn't seen this coming, not in a million years.

Chapter 15

Brian Williams Estate
Hinsdale, Illinois
June 8, 2008
4:00 PM

Katherine stooped over a row of cherry tomatoes, eating more than she was picking. Each one exploded in her mouth with a rich, tangy flavor she couldn't get enough of. It was the perfect distraction from the constant pain and panic attacks she had been experiencing all day. Recovery was a long and painful process, she knew, but knowing this didn't ease her discomfort in any way. Finding joy in the simple things seemed to be the best way to go.

Betty elbowed her in the side. "Save some for the salad."

She smiled at the older woman, embarrassed. "Sorry."

The lines around the woman's eyes softened and she smiled back. "Your hair really is quite lovely red. I'm glad we dyed it back."

Katherine touched the soft ends of her newly washed and dyed hair. "Me too." She tucked a lock of it behind her ear before stooping back down to pick away at the weeds.

The other woman had been tickled pink when Katherine started making suggestions about the gardening, pulling on her knowledge from her days at the nursery. They had spent half the day toiling under the hot sun, talking about natural insecticides and plant food.

Betty popped a tomato into her mouth and stretched her back. "It is such a beautiful day to be out in the garden."

Katherine squinted and took in the sight before her. There was something to be said about getting ones hands dirty and putting sweat equity into a project.

Alex, who had been watching the Tigers and Indians game, stepped outside for a smoke. He quickly lit his cigarette and wandered over to the garden where the women were working.

She could feel the heat of his gaze, and wondered if he liked the red hair? She looked up from the vegetable rows and was taken aback by the look in his eyes.

I guess he does like it.

He smiled and raised his hand in greeting as she tucked away a shy smile and waved back.

Betty looked up and caught the wordless exchange between the two young people. "Alex, blow that smoke over here, will you, dear?"

Alex chucked. "Oh no, I made a promise not to let you anywhere near this."

He put out his half-smoked cigarette, making Betty groan in protest. Before he went back inside, he paused for a second at the patio door, catching Katherine's eye one more time.

As the door closed, Katherine let out a breath and smiled to herself.

"He's a good man. Not bad on the eyes, either," Betty said.

Katherine chose not to take the bait. "Oh, you think so?"

The coy old woman straightened her back and looked down at Katherine. "Yes! I would assume you would too!"

Katherine looked up at her and broke into a fit of laughter. She was rewarded by a sharp swat to her side.

"Oh, you!" After a moment of silence, Betty continued. "You know he likes you? A lot."

Katherine bit her lip and paused. She had never been open to talking about her personal life. "I know. I like him a lot, too."

The other woman clasped her hands together at her heart. "Oh, good."

"How long have you known him?"

Betty stood up to stretch her back again and wipe away the sweat from her brow. "We've known Alex for quite some time now. We met through a friend of mine. We were still living in D.C. and he had just gone on furlough after a long time in the Middle East.

"An art therapist friend of mine showed me one of her client's work, which she thought I might be interested in exhibiting in one of my shows. It was Alex's. He's a really talented artist. He had some beautiful sketches of the city and the people in his neighborhood, but the ones that most impressed me were drawings of a Middle Eastern woman. They were so dark and moving that I just fell in love with them. I just had to meet the artist." A faint nostalgic smile tugged at the corners of her mouth.

"When I met Alex, I fell in love with him too. He's such a sweet, sensitive man. Brian and I sort of adopted him. We tend to do that sort of thing. He had no family to speak of and was kind of a mess back then, and needed to be tended to, much like this overgrown garden."

"I had no idea." Katherine tugged some weeds up by the roots as she thought over all this new information.

***

Alex and Brian stretched out on two separate but matching La-Z-Boy chairs, watching the Tigers cream the Indians. Only one beer remained of the six-pack Brian had stored in the mini fridge between the chairs. For the first time in a long time, Alex began to relax. It had always been this way when he visited with the older couple. They were the closest thing he had to parents, even though they were only fifteen years his senior.

A commercial break came on at the bottom of the sixth inning, during which Alex took a long sip of his beer and turned to Brian. "Your wife is working hard on her cupid campaign. She already has Katherine and me getting married and making babies."

The older man grinned, his pale blue eyes bracketed with fine lines. "She is a force to be reckoned with. I didn't stand a chance, and neither do you."

Alex took a long drink from his beer. "Am I crazy if I think I might want all that, too?"

The other man just smiled and shook his head in a knowing way. "Yeah, you don't stand a chance."

From inside his pocket his phone rang with Doc's ring tone. "Sorry, I have to take this."

He quickly put the footrest down and answered the call. "Hey, Doc, I'm sorry. I know I was supposed to call you today."

He grabbed his beer and went out to the front porch to talk. It was comforting to hear Doc rant into his ear about how she was worried—Chris, too.

"Doc, I'm doing okay. I'm taking my medication. I'm staying away from the computer and the TV. Well, except for the baseball game I was just watching." He laughed a little. "Baseball isn't going to mess with my sobriety, though."

Doc sighed in his ear. "I just don't want you to get hurt in all this."

He nodded, even though she couldn't see him, which made him smile. "I appreciate your concern. How are *you* feeling? How's Chris? How long is he on leave for again?"

They soon fell into normal conversation about everyday things. He wasn't ready to tell Doc he was in love with Katherine and wanted to have a real relationship with her, a real life. Her blessing was important to him, and he worried she wouldn't approve... yet.

CJ's Biker Bar
Off I-70
June 8, 2008
8:00 PM

Jason sat with Charles at a corner table, drinking scotch. The bar was far enough out of the way that they wouldn't run into anyone they knew, and it seemed like as safe a place as any to have a clandestine meeting.

Charles unabashedly told Jason everything about how he was recruited, what roles he played in the organization, and the laws he broke in the process. He was very clear about laying out how everything was tied to certain people within the FBI, who were obstructing justice in exchange for large sums of money or were being blackmailed into compliance.

Apparently, Charles had been collecting information for months as a means to protect himself, but now he was going to use this knowledge to protect Katherine and bring The Syndicate down. He had papers and recordings that implicated Senator Mitchel in some of the illegal dealings. The most damning of all was proof that Senator Mitchel had hired the hit man who shot Katherine in March.

Jason took careful notes, recording every detail. He asked all the right questions so that, in the end, they had compiled a report that would piss off a lot of people. For the first time since they had known each other, they were working together for a singular purpose—make the men involved pay for what they had done.

Charles paused to take a long drink of his scotch, and continued. "There's more."

Jason looked up from his notes, not so sure he wanted to know anymore. "What?"

Charles took a deep breath. "The Syndicate had Sara under their thumb. She was being blackmailed into being a sort of double spy. They used her to get information they suspected was in your possession. I don't know if you know this or not, but she worked for the CIA with Alex. I think they might have been lovers."

Charles gulped down the last of his scotch. "I was ordered by them to kill her. I'm the one who pushed her off the train platform."

Before Charles could say more, Jason took a long gulp of his scotch, letting the burning liquid sting his throat and chest. His head spun and his stomach turned. Everything in his body told him to run, but he stayed still.

Charles wet his lips with a quick sweep of his tongue. His voice had begun to tremble. "Scott thought she was going to talk, and turn in the two of us in exchange for immunity. There were some extremely incriminating photographs that linked the dear

Senator and I to known individuals in the conspiracy—not a smoking gun, but enough that the prosecution could have gone forward with it, gotten warrants and what not. It gave her a big upper hand, which made her a giant fucking target. Dumb bitch never should have let those pictures see the light of day. The Syndicate intercepted a call between her and a CIA handler. She had to come out of the shadows to turn herself in, and that's when I was to remove the threat... or be thrown to the wolves myself."

Jason's fist clenched together, snapping his pencil in two. "You son of a bitch! You murdered her?" He spoke in a hushed whisper, looking around to make sure no one was listening to their conversation. He had always known Charles was an ass, but he had never thought him capable of murder.

Charles held up his trembling hands in defense. "I'm not proud of what I did. I can't sleep or eat, and my fucking hands won't stop shaking. I'm here trying to make things right. After what happened to K-Katherine...." His breath hitched. "I knew I couldn't keep doing this."

Jason pinched the bridge of his nose. *Why do I keep letting myself get pulled into this mess?*

"You should also know that I killed the man who hurt her, too. His body is dumped in some burnt-out house in Detroit." The tremble in his hands caused his tumbler to shake and rattle on the table.

Jason reached across and stilled the other man's hand. "What the fuck, Charles?" He drank the remaining two fingers of his three-finger scotch. He didn't relish his appointed role as confessor, and had no council for the man.

"I know this is fucking messed-up, man. That's why I came to you. You've always been an honest, stand-up guy. You're the only person I can trust."

Jason's nerves were flayed open, leaving him raw and exposed. "I wish you hadn't come to me. I was trying to get away from all of this. I left her, for fuck's sake, just to be done with this." He motioned for the barkeep to bring another round of drinks.

"But she's safe, right?" Charles asked.

Jason nodded, not wanting to give away too much. He didn't trust Charles. "I don't know where she is, and I wouldn't tell you even if I did know. She's safe—as safe as she can be."

Charles let out a shaky breath. "Good. I don't want to know anything else. It's better that way."

The barkeep brought their drinks, and Jason drank his in one gulp, making him gasp. Once he had caught his breath, he pulled out his phone and called ASAC Richards.

"Hi, this is Jason."

"Is everything okay with Katherine?"

"Yes it's fine," Jason said. "I have someone with me that I think you will want to talk to. We need you to keep quiet about it. It's a matter of life or death, and it may well be what breaks your case."

An hour later, ASAC Richards pulled up outside the bar. When he walked inside and saw who Jason was sitting with, he reached for his gun holster.

"What the fuck!" Richards' face burned red.

Jason stood up and placed himself between the two men. "Just hear what he has to say."

Richards took his hand off his gun and sat down at the table. "This had better be good. Start talking."

Charles took a deep breath and started his sordid tale.

"Charles, I'm going to have to put you under arrest. You understand that, right?" Richards asked.

Charles nodded. "Take me now or I'm a dead man."

Brian Williams' Estate
Hinsdale, Illinois
June 9, 2008
11:45 PM

Alex lay in bed watching Katherine sleep when his phone started to buzz on the bedside table.

Grumbling, he grabbed it and walked out of the bedroom. "Bailey."

"Alex, I have some good news and some bad news," Richards burst out.

Alex ran his fingers through his bed-head hair. "Do I need a cigarette for this?"

"Charles turned himself in to the FBI. His lawyer is talking with the Attorney General's Office now to work out a deal of some sort to avoid capital murder charges. We have him in temporary custody now, but will be transferring him to the State tomorrow morning." The man sounded positively giddy.

Alex exhaled. "You're kidding me!"

Richards chuckled. "It's a long fucking story, and it's not the hour to hash out that shit, but yeah. Katherine's friend, Jason Knettle, set up the whole thing. I met up with them earlier tonight at some dive bar outside of town."

He had never in his wildest dreams thought that Charles, of all people, would turn state's evidence. "What prompted his change of heart?"

"Katherine's attack fucked him up. He takes full responsibility for what happened, as he should. He confessed to killing the man who attacked her, which is where one of the capital murder charges comes in. I'm just playing a hunch, but I have a feeling that there is more to all of that. He also confessed to murdering that woman that was pushed in front of the Metro. Apparently, she was a part of all of this as well. Apparently, she was going to turn him over to the CIA."

Alex's gut twisted and churned at the news.

"You there, Bailey?" Richards asked.

Alex forced air into his lungs. "Yeah, I'm still here. What was he able to give up in return?"

"Well, we have enough to nail Senator Mitchel to the wall for illegal campaign contributions, conspiracy to commit murder, obstruction of justice, bribery, extortion, racketeering, money laundering, and the list goes on."

Alex swore he could *hear* the other man smiling. "I have no words."

Richards harrumphed. "You're telling me! He was able to confirm that Fullmore and some low level people are accepting bribes to look the other way, or are being blackmailed, but he didn't know a lot of the details, so we'll still need you to back up these claims with all the paperwork I'm going to be sending you. Once we get all our ducks in a row over here, I will also be sending you all the documentation that Charles has, as well. I think between the two, we should be able to find enough to indict Fullmore and his cronies. It will just take some digging. I know you'll be able to figure it out, though, in no time."

Alex bit his lower lip. "Sir, what's the bad news?"

"The AG's office won't send down indictments until our case is a little more airtight. We need a bulletproof paper trail, and for Katherine's old man to testify. The problem with that is that we don't know where he is anymore. My sources think he's been spooked and gone deep into hiding."

Alex padded into the kitchen, pulled a beer out of the fridge, and sat down at the table, using the end of table to pop off the top. "Fuck," he muttered under his breath. "What's the grand plan then, sir?"

His former boss stifled a yawn. "We need you to find him. Use your sources, whatever you have, and find him. Maybe if Katherine talks to him, he'll come forward. In the meantime, we need to get her installed in a safe house. Charles is going to wait out the trial in prison. I need you in the field for this, Alex."

He swallowed hard. The pressure to do it all had been building up inside of him all day. "You know I can't. I need to be here with her."

"I don't suppose you would go if I ordered you out into the field either, huh?"

He paused and drank half the beer in one long gulp. "No."

"Fine."

Alex smashed his face with his hand. He was caught between his duty to follow this through and his desire to protect Katherine. "I'll call in all my sources and assets and see what I can dig up." That would just have to be enough.

"Do you have everything set with the safe house?" Richards asked.

Alex looked at the clock. "Yeah, we're heading out there tomorrow. Thank you for keeping me in the loop. I'll see what I can do on this end. Don't worry, sir, we'll nail them to the wall."

After a long pause, Richards asked, "How is she?"

He pursed his lips, pausing to consider the loaded question before him. "Not well. She needs me here."

"Damned if this isn't the biggest mess," Richards said. "Just help in any way you can, okay, Bailey?"

"Yes, sir, I will. I'll... uh... talk to you later."

"Yeah, bye."

Alex ended the call and tossed the phone down on the table.

He hadn't heard Brian walked into the kitchen, and was startled when his friend said, "Who was that on the phone?"

"My ASAC. It seems Charles is turning state's evidence."

Brian's mouth dropped open in shock. He took a seat across from Alex and shook his head. "Wow. So, what's the plan?"

Alex traced a knot in the wooden table. "I'm going to take Katherine to the safe house tomorrow, and the FBI and CIA are going to turn over every couch cushion in the hopes of finding her dad, who's disappeared again."

Chapter 16

Brian Williams' Estate
Hinsdale, Illinois
June 10, 2008
8:00 AM

Alex awoke to the sound of birds chirping outside his window. A sleep-heavy arm and leg had him pinned to the bed. During the day, he could barely get away with a small touch, but in her sleep, she wound herself around him like twine. He was afraid to move, lest he wake her up and end the wonderful feeling of her body pressed against his. He closed his eyes with a sigh and snuggled against her. From outside came the sound of the neighborhood coming to life—people driving off to work or taking their kids to school.

It was Monday. He and Katherine would be leaving for the safe house today.

Alex was pulled out of his train of thought when her leg, which had been draped between his, tightened its hold on his midsection, and the hand that had been resting on his chest slid down to his hipbone that jutted out over the waistband of his boxers. It would be the easiest thing in the world to cross the mere inches that separated his lips from hers.

This sexual hiatus he was embarking on was so much harder than he thought it would be. Each small touch of her body against his enflamed him. He let out a small hissing sound as he tried to bring himself back under control, rousing Katherine. Her eyelids fluttered and opened to meet his intense gaze. For a moment they both lay there embracing each other, but it didn't last long. The shadow of fear and anxiety darkened her eyes, and he tried to temper his frustrations when she recoiled away from him.

"I'm sorry." A hint of irritation laced his apology—spoiling it.

They were on shaky ground. He had told her he was falling in love with her, but she had yet to say anything about how she felt about him. When he had left her in Florida, they had not made any promises, it had all been way too soon for that. Now, with all that had happened, he wished that they could just start over.

She scowled at him. "Don't. Don't you dare be sorry."

Before he could even process what was happening, she had already jumped out of the bed and stalked off in the direction of the bathroom—toiletries in hand.

He needed a cigarette before dealing with that kind of complicated girl shit. His knees creaked as he swung his stiff legs over the side of the bed. The cigarettes and lighter were still in the pants from yesterday, which he had strewn on the floor with the rest of his clothes.

The flame of the lighter popped up and lit the end of his cigarette. He drew in the sweet tobacco smoke and his anxiety began to abate. The bed springs creaked as he sank down onto the old mattress and smoked the cigarette down to the nub. He lit another—it was a two cigarette kind of morning.

At some point yesterday, Betty had left one of her old ashtrays in the bedroom for him. It was the small things, he thought.

***

Katherine stood in front of the bathroom mirror holding the sides of the sink as she tried to catch her breath. Anger rolled and bubbled inside of her, unbidden. She was ashamed by her unwarranted outburst. Alex hadn't deserved that; he had been so patient with her the last couple of days. She cupped her hands together, splashed cold water on her face and patted it dry with the guest towel. As she straightened back up she was forced to look at her reflection.

She didn't recognize the battered woman reflected back at her. Her full-rounded features now looked more like those of a POW returning home from years of imprisonment and torture—with harsh blue marks across her neck, a split upper lip, and yellow and green shading around her eyes. She dared to touch the fingerprints bruised into her skin—branded.

Alex had told her, what seemed like a lifetime ago, that he would wait for her, but that was before this.

She choked back a sob, determined to shake off the despair that clung to her like barnacles on a bed-calm ship. After brushing her teeth and downing the half dozen pills the hospital had prescribed, she stalked back to the bedroom with the intent to make things right.

He looked up from his phone and caught her penitent gaze as she stood paused in the doorframe of their room. He released his thumbnail from between his teeth, letting his hands fall.

The room smelled like smoke.

"Hey," he said.

She leaned into the frame for support and cleared her throat. "Hey." She wished that single word hadn't sounded so awkward. She didn't know how to get back to where they were before, but she knew she wanted to get back there.

Before, she thought. Now everything would be marked as *before* and *after*. She wet her lips with a quick sweep of her tongue and cleared her throat. "Um, about earlier—"

"It's okay, I get it. You don't have to explain yourself." Despite his words, angry lines still marked his forehead.

He gave her a small, tender smile, which relaxed away some of the tension from her slight frame. She noted the thick cords of tension in his broad shoulders—knowing she had played a part in putting them there. She longed to go to him, touch him there and make it better. She bit her lip, embarrassed by this sudden impulse.

He caught her intense gaze and raised his eyebrows. "I should get dressed. We have a lot to discuss this morning." He cleared his throat and looked away. "I got a call from Richards last night."

His cold, all-business tone made her heart sink. She watched as he grabbed some clothes from his travel bag—jeans and a t-shirt, his "non-work" attire.

"I'll go see about breakfast and you can fill me in then," she said as he walked out of the bedroom past her. She couldn't help but notice that he was careful to give her a wide berth so there would be no accidental touches.

As he walked off to the upstairs bathroom to shower, she dressed in a t-shirt and jeans herself. She then headed out to the kitchen to see about getting them something to eat—anything to avoid the agony inside.

Unknown Location
June 10, 2008
8:00 AM

Charles followed the guard down the empty cellblock. His hands, which held his neatly folded and pressed clothes and sheets, trembled.

His very expensive lawyer had been working all night with the Attorney General's Office to make a deal that would allow him to avoid the death penalty for the two murders he had committed. His lawyer told him he would be serving time in prison, at least six months, until the deal was finalized. After that, they hoped the A.G.'s Office would allow him to serve out the remainder of his sentence at home, under house arrest, or at least in a minimum security, so-called "country club." Though grateful to avoid capital murder charges, he wasn't at all looking forward to the long six months alone behind bars. Still... better than being caught on the wrong side of an Ocean City goon's gun.

All he had to do in return was testify against everyone around him for all the despicable things they had done. Not terribly difficult; he hated them all. His lawyer and the prosecution had assured him he would be safe in prison. In fact, they had cleared out a whole cellblock for him. His testimony was *that* valuable to the case, an investigation that had spanned more than three decades, he learned.

He entered his cell and unfurled his mattress, and the guard clanged the cell door shut behind him, making him jump. He slumped down onto the thin mattress and watched as his only connection with the outside world walked away down the block. He was more alone than he had ever been. Six months alone with little to no contact with the outside world... it might just break him.

He wallowed in self-pity until the picture of Katherine—they had allowed him to bring that in with him—fell to the floor at his feet. Whatever he had to endure, it was nothing compared to the hell she was in. No, he deserved this and so much more.

He bent to pick up the picture with trembling hands, held it with reverence, and traced his shaking finger along her profile. *Katherine.*

I-90
Danville, Virginia
June 10, 2008
9:00 AM

Scott sat in the back of his town car waiting to be taken to his district office in Richmond, Virginia. He had tried several times to get ahold of The Syndicate's top men to find out if there was any news on Charles' whereabouts. His little house of cards had started to wobble.

His sister and that partner of hers had gone into hiding. Even the dirty Ocean City slime balls couldn't find them. Either no one was talking or they had strayed from the traditional channels. As far as the police and FBI were concerned, they had fallen off the face of the earth. He was beginning to see that this wasn't going to bode well for him. For a moment he thought about hopping on his private jet, and leaving The Syndicate's echelon to take the fall.

Fuck them and their money! But he had a wife and a high profile job and couldn't just disappear.

If The Syndicate had just listened to him about Charles in the first place, he wouldn't be in this mess. Now he was out of the loop, dead weight that needed to be excised from the group. If only he had been in charge; none of this would have happened, and Katherine would have never gotten away with what she did. Her betrayal was going to cost him his freedom. If given the chance again, he wouldn't fail in stopping her this time.

He slammed his fist into the seat.

Fuck family loyalties! She needs to pay.

Brian Williams' Estate
Hinsdale, Illinois
June 10, 2008
9:00 AM

Alex sat in silence across the table from Katherine, eating his breakfast. The quiet of the house amplified each small noise so that each bite Katherine took of her toast seemed to echo through the room, grating on Alex's overworked nerves.

He wished Betty and Brian hadn't already left for work. They were excellent distractions.

He thumbed through the paper and took sips of his coffee, tired and frustrated, and thought it better that he kept quiet. He didn't want to risk hurting Katherine's feelings with the sharp words that hung on his barbed tongue.

Her loud chewing and constant fidgeting made it nearly impossible for him to concentrate on the paper. Taking away one of his stress-relieving outlets, during one of the most stressful times of his life, was beginning to seem like the stupidest decision he had ever made.

He carefully folded the sports section over and laid it down on the table in front of him to look at the baseball box scores, since he had missed watching the last half of yesterday's game. The black and white rules of baseball had always been a comfort to him. It was a simple constant—a straightforward action and reaction. He found deep comfort in its simplicity.

Out of the corner of his eye he caught her watching him over the lip of her cup.

The irritation he'd been suppressing the last few days bubbled up and out of his mouth before he could stop himself. "What?"

She blushed and looked away. "Nothing."

That's it!

He slammed his coffee cup down, causing it to spill. "I'm going outside to smoke."

Once outside, he lit up a cigarette and pulled out his phone to text Doc.

> *I'm losing it! Why do you women have to be so damn complicated?*

His phone buzzed back a reply:

> *Why do you men have to be such callous pricks? It's only been a couple of days!*

The bluntness of her comment struck a chord with him and he burst out laughing, choking on his cigarette smoke. He held his cigarette between his bowed lips. *Touché*, he typed back, then thought for a second and added:

> *This whole sexual fast thing may get ugly.*

Doc's reply came several seconds later:

> *If you care about her as much as you claim to, then it will all be worth it.*

Her words hit him hard. He did love her, he was sure of that. Doc was right, he resolved. Not that this surprised him. He *was* being stupid and selfish.

***

Inside, Katherine sat at the kitchen table. Her stomach rolled and twisted again, making her feel as though the small amount of food she'd managed to ingest was going to make a return visit. Her fingers covered her mouth as she concentrated hard on not vomiting. The sound of the back screen door opening and closing with a thud did nothing to calm her nerves. Today was going to be a bad one.

Alex paused in the doorway of the kitchen. "Are you ill?"

She shook her head no.

His long legs carried him across the room in two easy strides. He dropped down on his haunches, trying to catch her eye. "Katherine?"

When his hand touched her knee, her eyes began to pool. She turned her head to meet his concerned gaze, and fell into his warm embrace as hot tears streamed down her cheeks. She felt as though her heart might split into two from the force of her tenacious distress, which threatened to rip them both asunder.

She tightened her hold on him when his tears mixed with her own.

His legs began to tremble under their combined weight. Using the table as leverage, he stood with her still in his arms.

She sat on his lap as he settled into the chair, and they sat still like this for some time, and might have for longer if not for the intrusive sound of the doorbell ringing two times—the mailman's usual signal that he'd left a package on the front porch.

Alex reached up, brushed the tear-matted hair off her cheek, and tucked it behind her ear.

A stormy gaze greeted her when their eyes met, and her breath hitched at the intense feelings it brought out in her. She wanted to kiss him so badly that, before she knew it, she was already lowering her lips to his. Her parted lips caressed his, and as she continued kissing him, his breathing became ragged. His heart hammered against the side of her chest.

She let out a trembling exhale as she broke the kiss.

A slow smile crept up the sides of his mouth as she focused on him, testing the waters. His hands held her on his lap as hers looped around his neck. He kissed her again, causing her small smile to crack wide open, and soon she was grinning back at him.

What just happened?

She brushed her lips with her fingertips, already missing his kiss.

He chuckled, and his eyes crinkled as a wide smile snaked across his face.

She rewarded him with a hard jab to his gut, which made him laugh harder. For a moment, they returned to the sweet spot of new lovers, but the moment passed, replaced by the creeping darkness.

The need to not be touched overwhelmed her. She jumped up from her spot on his lap as if she were on fire, and made a beeline for the sink and the dirty dishes. She cleared her throat and began fussing with the breakfast plates, but the memory of the kiss brought a fresh, shy smile back to her face.

I'm a fucking mess.

Her emotions were torn between the light after-kiss feeling and the anxious, fearful one that hung around her neck like a noose, tightening and choking her at the most random and inopportune times. A single tear slid down her cheek.

She suddenly remembered that Alex had said something earlier about Richards calling him last night with important news. It was the perfect topic to transition them out of the awkwardness that had settled in around them like a persistent fog.

She glanced over her shoulder at him. "What did Richards call about last night?"

He looked up from the spot of spilled coffee he'd been examining, a faint smile on his lips.

"Oh, yeah... God, I completely forgot about that."

His arm brushed against her as he snatched a rag from the sink. He wiped up the coffee spill and began to fill her in on what had happened with Charles, Jason, and Richards. He told her about the text message that Richards sent early that morning while she had been getting ready.

"Charles is working on a plea agreement, but for now he is in the custody of the Commonwealth of Virginia."

She gasped at the thought of Charles locked up in prison.

Alex huffed. "I've never heard of anything ever moving this fast before. Ever!" He washed his cup out and put in on the drying rack with the rest of the washed dishes. "We're expected at the safe house today."

The close proximity of his body to hers made her flush. "That's today?" Her voice wavered. She had begun to feel safe and secure with the Williams, and the thought of leaving the security of their homey four walls and roof frightened her to the core.

"Katherine, what can I do to make this easier for you?"

His question took her a little by surprise, even though she was learning that his modus operandi in all things was absolute directness.

She sighed and her shoulders drooped as she looked up at him. "I don't know. I really don't. I'm just having a hard time today."

He nodded. "Okay, but you'll tell me when you do know?"

She nodded slowly, unsure about what she felt for him, or what they were to each other. All she knew for certain was that it helped just being near him. She couldn't explain it to him, though, even if she tried, so she kept it to herself—for now.

Illinois, Just South of Chicago
June 10, 2008
Noon

They had been on the road for nearly an hour and not said a word to one another. Alex didn't know if she was angry, sad, tired, or who-knows-what, but the wall between them was both tall and wide. Instead of pushing things as he would have in the past, he backed off and let her have her space.

The safe house, a hip condo in Chicago's Wrigleyville neighborhood, belonged to an overseas agent he knew from Iraq. She'd gotten the place cheap through an FBI auction, and when she was posted overseas, she would sublet it to make extra cash.

When everything had gone down with Katherine, Alex had gotten wind that his friend was in between tenants. He'd used back channels to get ahold of her at the Embassy in Kabul for permission to use her home. Thankfully, she was one of the few agents he hadn't pissed off, and she agreed to rent it out for a few months until she got back in December.

With its many high-tech safety features, it made the perfect hideout. Only Brian and Richards knew the location, unlike the situation before; no one to pay off this time.

As they drove up Lakeshore Drive, Alex pointed to Lake Michigan, which sparkled under the bright summer sun. "Isn't that beautiful?"

She grunted in agreement.

He squeezed the steering wheel and kept on driving. Finally, they pulled up to their temporary home. "This is it." He shut off the engine and pocketed the keys.

Katherine nodded and got out of the car. She stood in the V created by the open door and stretched her long, too lean body.

It momentarily mesmerized him. *Fuck. I need to stop staring at her like some lunatic. Move, you idiot!*

He snatched their bags from the back seat and led the way up the winding walk to their new home for the next few months. The entry required a special code and a key card, which he'd obtained a few days ago. A green light lit up, and he pushed open the door and held it open for her with his leg. He followed after with the things Betty had picked up for their "vacation," as she had called it.

"What do you think?"

She looked around the open floor plan condo with a look of disinterest. "It's nice."

"It has a state-of-the-art security system. The owner dabbles in it as a hobby," he said.

Her lopsided smile made him sad. The light in her eyes had gone out, and he longed for it to return.

Maybe the surprise will help turn things around.

"Do you want to see what I have for you up on the roof?"

She shrugged. "Okay, but you know I hate surprises."

"You're going to love this one, trust me."

He led her out the secured back entrance and up the private fire escape to the roof.

Katherine gasped. "Oh, Alex! It's beautiful!"

A hydroponic garden covered the entire roof, with everything in full bloom.

"The owner is a master gardener. It's all yours to enjoy." He felt a bit like Oprah on those *My Favorite Things* episodes.

Katherine flew into his arms and kissed him full on the lips, taking him off guard. "Thank you! Thank you!" she said as tears slid down her cheeks.

He smiled. "Anything for you."

Her rosy cheeks and shy smile, mixed with the dusting of freckles on her nose, made him want to kiss her again. Instead, he pointed towards the direction from which they'd come. "Why don't we get settled and then get some lunch?"

"Yeah, sure."

Once back inside, he picked up their bags and walked through the condo to show her the back bedroom. "This bedroom is yours. It has an attached private bathroom."

Her perfect bowed lips parted as if to say something, and then shut again.

He tilted his head in concern. "What is it?"

She shook her head and held out her hand to keep him at a distance. "It's nothing. Thank you."

Alex bit his bottom lip and narrowed his eyes. "Katherine—"

"Alex, I'm fine."

Suddenly, he realized why she might be upset. "Katherine...." He tilted her chin up. "Do you want me to sleep in the same room as you, like before?"

She lowered her gaze and wrung her hands. "Yes," she whispered.

He sighed and brought her into an embrace, and kissed the top of her head. "Okay, but I call the left side of the bed," he said, trying to lighten the mood. He was rewarded by a muffled chuckle vibrating against his chest.

He smiled as he let her go. "Want to order pizza and have a picnic on the roof?"

"Yes, that sounds perfect." She dabbed at the corners of her eyes.

Chapter 17

CIA Safe House
Wrigleyville Neighborhood
Chicago, Illinois
June 10, 2008
8:00 PM

Alex had just finished washing up their dinner dishes when the doorbell rang, startling Katherine. It pained him to see the small ways in which the attack continued to hurt her. He brushed the small of her back with his fingertips to let her know that he was there and that she was safe.

"I'll get that," he said. "It's probably someone from the Chicago Office with the evidence boxes Richards wants me to go through."

He tapped on the security camera's view screen and saw several FBI agents standing at the front door with a dozen or so banker's boxes.

"Fuck me," he said under his breath.

Katherine scrunched her forehead in concern. "What's wrong?"

Richards, you bastard!

"A loophole, it seems." He clicked open the front door and waved his arm towards the spare bedroom. "Good evening, gentlemen, just put it all in the room on the left."

Fucking Richards is going to dump all the grunt work on me. Great, just great.

The true intent of the addendum to his leave paperwork had now been made crystal clear. His gaze shifted from the boxes of work back to Katherine. She was worth it, he reminded himself.

"Who did you piss off, exactly?" Her beautiful blue eyes twinkled up at him.

She thinks this is funny!

"I—I think it's safe to say that Richards is a little pissed at me for taking this leave of absence." He rubbed his temples with his fingers, feeling a headache coming on.

He walked the men to the door, shaking each of their hands in thanks. When the last of them had left, he fell back against the closed door. "Well, I guess I know what I'm going to be doing for the next ten years."

"At least you'll have something to do." As a witness, she could no longer participate in the investigation.

He tried to be understanding, even if he was a little jealous. "You must be getting bored if you're bemoaning missing out on grunt work."

The clock on the wall told him it wasn't too late to catch the last half of the game.

"Come on," he said, leading her by the small of her back. "Let's watch the end of the Tigers game. Hopefully it won't depress me further."

Mack's Auto Center
Ocean City, Maryland
June 10, 2008
9:00 PM

Mack had been working late when he heard the shuffle of feet coming from the back of the shop. It was never a good sound to hear. They always came in through the back as if they were in some fucking Saturday afternoon spy movie.

"Mack, where's Billy?" the man in the crisp suit asked.

"Billy ain't here. His boy had a baseball game tonight." He hoped the man would leave.

"We've got a problem. The cops are sniffing around and some FBI agents have gone missing."

Mack stretched his back before carefully placing his tools back in the lock box. "I don't know anything about that. I just fix cars. You'll have to talk to Billy 'bout that."

"Talk to me 'bout what?" Billy sauntered into the shop like he owned it.

Mack could smell the booze on him and noticed his knuckles were raw. The prick was always banging Mack's baby sister and nephew around. It wasn't right, but no one said anything. His sister had told Mack on numerous occasions to mind his own damn business and leave Billy alone, so he did.

Whatever business Billy had going with the suit, he wanted nothing to do with it. He walked off to his office and shut the door behind him. The security cam showed his brother-in-law handing the man in the suit a fistful of cash—hush money, no doubt.

Even though Sally wanted him out of her hair, Mack needed to make sure his little sister was okay. He picked up the phone and dialed her number, and when she answered on the first ring, he hung up.

She's alive. He crossed himself and sat down to work on the books.

CIA Safe House
Wrigleyville Neighborhood
Chicago, Illinois
June 16, 2008
8:00 AM

Katherine and Alex, at the CIA safe house for a week, had settled into a routine and began joking with each other about the realities of sharing a small space. She had lots of small habits and idiosyncrasies that he hadn't known about despite his extensive profiling. They seemed endearing to him now, but he suspected they would most likely grate on him over time.

For now he was happy. He never thought he would be suited for such a domestic arrangement. Even though it had been just a week, he grew fonder of her by the day. This realization motivated him to keep on track with the busy work, putting in long hours all week in his new makeshift office. The reality of good police work was not as glamorous as it was portrayed on TV, not as simple as just push-pinning a bunch of papers to a cork board and suddenly making grand connections.

Though... that would be pretty fucking awesome.

That morning, he awoke at the crack of dawn to start on the mountain of files. By 8:00 AM he had smoked his way through half a pack of cigarettes, and the room was starting to look like the Scottish Moors.

It had taken him several days to organize the evidence in a way that made sense to him. He had then made several detailed lists, along with a page or two of some theories that he and the team had developed. Today marked the first time he was able to check things off.

Finally, some forward momentum.

Top on the list was to request information from the phone company and some financial institutions, but the thought of creating more paperwork piles made him nauseous.

Might as well get it over with.

Two hours later, he sat back with his head against the oak headboard, and actually dozed off, only to be jolted awake by Katherine knocking on the door. He slid off the bed, careful not to disturb his piles, and opened the door.

The sight of her took his breath away. *I'm doing this for her,* he reminded himself.

"Hey, how long have you been at it? I didn't even hear you get up this morning." Her fresh-faced smile renewed his spirit.

"Before dawn." He stifled a yawn.

She looked incredible with her sleep-tousled hair, a bright green tank top and very short blue jean cutoffs. He couldn't think of anything else except kissing her. Her shy smile told him that she might be thinking the same thing.

"What're your plans for today?"

"Gardening, and I have a Skype therapy appointment after lunch." She frowned up at him in a way that made him want to spend the rest of the day cheering her up.

"I know you must be bored. I wish you could help me with this mess, though if you did, I don't know how much work I would get done." He offered a suggestive rise of his brow.

Her cheeks stained red and she said, "Hurry up and save the day, G-man. This G-woman is getting restless."

"Well, you had best be moving on then and quit distracting me."

"All right." She turned on her heels and walked off down the hall to the fire escape.

He hung his head into the hallway, following her with his eyes. When she looked over her shoulder at him, he winked, making her smile. He heaved a deep sigh and closed the door to his paper-mache cave. Play time would come later.

Virginia Peninsula Region Correctional Facility
Williamsburg, Virginia
June 15, 2008
6:00 PM

Charles shifted in the metal chair as he waited for his lawyer in the prison's legal counsel room. He had been in prison for a little over a week and was already losing his mind. It helped that his lawyer, one of the top-rated criminal defense attorneys in the state, was also a total knockout.

Penelope Eakins, Esq. walked into the room with a huff and tossed her briefcase on top of the metal table in the middle of the room. "Mr. MacAvoy, I have your plea agreement here for you to sign. They agreed to all of your terms. You're lucky, and will only have to serve three months prison time and twenty years house arrest." Charles sighed with relief.

"I also have the other paperwork you wanted worked up. Are you sure you want to go through with it?"

He nodded. "I couldn't be more certain."

CIA Safe House
Wrigleyville Neighborhood
Chicago, Illinois
June 16, 2008
11:45 PM

Alex was buried knee-deep in the phone and bank records that had been delivered earlier that day by a courier from the Chicago Field Office. So far he had been unable to find a clear enough chain of evidence that would connect A.D. Fullmore to Senator Mitchel or The Syndicate. Although they had Charles' testimony, they needed irrefutable proof. The team needed him to find something that would make it easy for the prosecution to connect all the dots for the jury.

He was somewhat glad that he couldn't share with Katherine everything he was discovering, especially the part about her twin brother being the one to order the hit on her in March.

His cell phone rang beside him. *Doc.* He smiled and put down the papers and picked up his phone. "It's awful late to be making calls. Is everything okay?"

"I haven't heard from you in over a week. I got to thinking dead-in-a-ditch thoughts, and couldn't sleep until I was sure that you still roamed the Earth as a living, breathing being," she said in an anxious rush that made him laugh out loud.

"Oh, friend, I'm very much alive. I'm sorry I haven't called. I've been buried under mountains of paperwork. I don't know if Richards told you, but he would only sign my leave paperwork if I allowed him to put in some addendum about helping out with the case or something or other. Next time I need to have my lawyer look that kind of shit over. He sent me fifteen banker's boxes of evidence to comb through."

Doc laughed. "That's what you get for up and leaving us."

He settled into the bed and rested his head against the fluffy decorative pillows. "I miss you, too."

"How are things going?"

A smile crept across his face. "It's going better than I expected. I could get used to this playing house business."

"How's Katherine?"

His smile widened and his cheeks grew hot. Just hearing her name did things to him. "She has her good days and her bad days, but she is so resilient. Pretty sure I wouldn't be doing so well if I was her."

"You really like her, don't you?" She sounded genuinely surprised by this.

Why is this so hard for her to understand?

"Yeah, I've been trying to tell you this for a while now, Doc." His voice rose alongside his growing irritation. "Just because I'm a sex addict doesn't mean that I can't love someone."

"I know you can love someone, Alex." She sighed. "I just don't want you to get hurt."

He was getting a little tired of her go-to line regarding Katherine. The only person that was hurting him now was Doc.

After a long, uncomfortable pause, she continued. "I didn't call you to fight."

He unclenched his jaw. "I don't want to fight with you, either."

"Can I tell you the real reason I called?"

He exhaled, relaxing his tensed muscles. "Sure, why?"

"I selfishly wanted to be the first person to wish you happy birthday," she said.

"Thanks, Doc. I totally forgot about my birthday." He laughed and looked at his watch and saw that, sure enough, he was officially another year older.

The tension between them fell away and they slipped into their usual conversational tones, chatting about her pregnancy, and about Chris shipping off with Special Forces for six months. When they hung up, it was after 1:00 AM and he was bleary-eyed and hungry for sleep.

The muscles in his back and shoulders protested as he stretched and made his way through the darkened hallway to their bedroom. He quickly shed his pants and shirt and crawled into bed beside Katherine. As was becoming habit between them, she curled up against him in her sleep, and he used his index fingers to tuck away the loose strands of fiery red hair behind her ear.

So beautiful.

He tipped up her chin and softly kissed her sleep-slackened lips.

Still half asleep, she smiled rested her head on his bare chest.

He circled his arms around her and fell asleep with a small, contented smile on his face.

***

Despite the late hour he took to bed, he was wide awake at the break of dawn. His stomach growled and he thought of pancakes. He had been working hard and deserved a treat, and a big birthday breakfast would be a change of pace from his usual diet of coffee and nicotine.

He slipped out of bed, careful not to wake Katherine.

In the kitchen, he turned the radio on to the adult alternative station and got to work. It didn't take long for him to pile up a big stack of pancakes beside him. Just as the song on the radio changed to "Leather and Lace" by Stevie Nicks, he heard a stifled giggle behind him. He turned to see Katherine poised in the entrance, dressed in one of his t-shirts, her hand covering her smiling face. He turned off the burner, pivoted to place the finished pancake on top of the already large mound, and took two long strides across the room.

He pulled her up against him and dipped his face down to hers. "Good morning, Beautiful." He smiled as he waltzed her around the kitchen, singing in her ear along with Don Henley's part of the song. The words hit home for him.

I need to know.

When she tipped her face up to his, he asked, "Could you? Could you love me, Katherine?"

Her eyes widened and she blinked back tears as she nodded an emphatic yes.

"Really?" His breathing hitched.

She nodded again. "Yes," she said, her voice just above a whisper.

As if to prove her point, she rose on her tiptoes and kissed his smiling lips. Intimacy between them was still new and rife with agonizing fits and starts.

He knew her regimented course of intensive therapy and medication were helping, but that it was a slow process. That made moments like this hard for him, as their circumstances forced him to ride the brakes through these passionate exchanges, when all he wanted to do was coast through the experience with her.

When her body stiffened, he pulled away from her kiss. Her anxiety was riding shotgun this morning.

His heart hammered in his chest and he was left a little breathless from their short kiss. "Wow." He smiled. "Best birthday present ever!"

She tilted her head to the side and a wounded expression flashed across her face. "Today's your birthday? Why didn't you tell me?"

He shrugged, embarrassed. "I've been so busy that I didn't realize it until this morning."

Much to his delight she bounced on the balls of her feet. "We have to get a cake!"

He smiled down at her upturned face. *God, what she does to me.* When she again rose on her tiptoes, he was ready for it—a lazy Sunday morning kiss. He pulled her up against him, and could see the frustrations play out in her eyes, making it harder to keep himself under control.

As usual, it didn't take long for things to get heated. She deepened their kiss, moaning with pleasure as she pulled him in tighter.

He slipped his hands underneath the t-shirt and rested them against the small of her back, holding her close. When his phone buzzed on the counter with an incoming text message, she groaned, echoing his own frustrations at the interruption.

"Hold that thought." He crossed to the room and picked up his phone. "Shit," he mumbled under his breath.

She turned her head. "What?"

"I have to take this, excuse me," he said in a rush as he breezed past her and out the back door.

This was a call he would have to make in private. He caught her disappointed look out of the corner of his eye, but this couldn't wait.

As he jogged up the fire escape, he deleted the message.

I have a hog that you might be interested in. I have five minutes to talk if you want more details.

He had her listed in his phone as a bike repair shop. When she answered on the first ring, he let out a sigh of relief. "Are you safe? Do you need to be pulled out?" he asked in a rush of concern.

"Keep your panties on, I'm fine. Billy just stepped out for smokes and I've been trying to find a time to call you. I heard you might be looking for information on that Syndicate group in Virginia," she said, perhaps dangling the carrot to see if he would jump.

He bit his lip hard. *Damn her!* He had put out some feelers for information from some of his assets and sources, but had kept Sally out of the loop. The cost for her information was too high for him right now.

"What makes you think I want anything on them?" He hoped to get more information before he showed all his cards.

She huffed. "You don't fool me, Spook. I don't have time for this cat and mouse shit, anyways. Billy will be home any minute and he doesn't really like me talking to you." Her comment served as a jab, reminding him of the time Billy had caught them together outside some dive bar in Maryland.

He let out a tired sigh. This woman exhausted him. "What do you want, Sal?"

"I want the same deal as before."

He ran his fingers through his messy hair. *Fuck!* He couldn't say no. She always brought him solid information. "Deal. Text me when you have something, and I will do everything I can to get to you. I'll need at least a five-hour window, though."

"Not in the D.C. metro anymore, are you?" She was far too clever for her own good, but that had always been part of her appeal.

"Just call me when you have something." The terms of their arrangement could be hashed out later.

"Billy is back. I have to go. I'll text you when I have what you need," she said in a rush, and then the line went dead.

Alex sank down on the step of the fire escape. Sally was one of his most reliable assets for getting good, on-the-ground information for criminal activity in the D.C. Metro. She might come through for them, but her terms had always been information in exchange for sex. Before, that kind of an exchange had never been a problem—quite to the contrary.

Katherine had changed that.

Ever the good soldier, he followed protocol and called his boss, who answered on the third ring.

"I thought you were on leave, Bailey," he said with no small amount of sarcasm.

Alex sighed. "Sally just called."

His boss grumbled on the other line. Everyone at the agency was aware of what a handful Sally Ride could be.

"She's your asset. Leave or no leave, you're gonna to have to manage her."

Alex's head dropped. "Yes sir."

He ended the call and slammed his fist against the decorative pergola.

Happy... fucking... birthday to me.

Rayburn Building
Washington, D.C.
June 16, 2008
11:45 PM

Scott Mitchel sat cross-legged on the floor of the tunnel that connected the Rayburn Building to the U.S. Capital. It was a quiet place to sit and think over what his next move would be. He had received a message from his contact at the FBI saying that it looked as though Charles had been arrested and charged with the murder of the two men in Texas and the CIA cunt. The man said one of his subordinates, Emmanuel Richards, arranged for the arrest without his prior knowledge or consent. He also said that someone on the outside had arranged the meeting between the FBI and Charles MacAvoy, but it was unclear who that man was at the moment.

He'll pay, whoever he is. Scott clenched and unclenched his fist.

As he thumbed through his burner phone, he found the number he was looking for and called it.

His right-hand man, Jean, answered on the second ring. "What's up, boss?"

"I need you to put some tails out on everyone associated with Katherine. Has anything shown up on travel manifests?"

"No. Your sister and that CIA agent appear to have holed-up somewhere."

Scott pinched the bridge of his nose. "Call me if anything out of the ordinary happens."

"Yes sir!"

He ended the call and rested his throbbing head against the cool wall. Charles was going to ruin everything for him. There had to be a way to get to him and end that threat once and for all, even if he had to do it with his own bare hands.

Chapter 18

CIA Safe House
Wrigleyville Neighborhood
Chicago, Illinois
August 21, 2008
9:00 AM

Alex grumbled as he packed his suitcase for the trip back to the East Coast. He had been issued a new CIA identity so he wouldn't show up on anyone's radar, because they'd managed to catch some chatter from various groups—there was a price on his head. No one knew yet the extent of The Syndicate's connections, so they had to play it safe. The last thing he needed was to get shot.

In a few minutes, he would be leaving for an indeterminate amount of time. Betty and Brian had agreed to come and stay with Katherine while he was gone, but he still felt anxious at the thought of leaving her side. He couldn't shake the memory of what had happened to her the last time he'd left. That night they had lain awake all night, talking and fooling around. In the two months they'd been living at the safe house, the physical aspect of their relationship had begun to evolve.

A couple of times, things had gotten pretty hot and heavy between them, but their mutual anxieties always prevented things from escalating too far. Despite this, he'd never been so happy in his entire life. Even though things were still new between them, he had pledged faithfulness to her. She never said anything, but he could tell that she worried about of his addiction. With her help, he was working the steps of the program, and for the first time in a long time he was proud of himself—no small feat.

The day before, Alex had gotten a call from Sally with information she would only share in person. After talking it over with Richards and Magellan, they decided it was vital for him to come back to the East Coast to present his findings to the joint investigative team, and to get the information from his source. He had a full report that outlined a strong enough paper trail to help the case along. There hadn't been a smoking gun, but the information he'd gathered, coupled with whatever Sally had found, might be enough to prosecute. None of his other contacts had come up with anything regarding Katherine's father, but there was talk about still going through with the case.

The impending trip and the thought of seeing Sally again made him nervous. If Katherine had noticed his apprehension, she never said anything, and for that he was grateful. He was still too ashamed to own up to some aspects of his past. His relationship with Sally had always been complicated, and he didn't think he could explain it to Katherine.

He looked up from his suitcase just as Katherine sulked into the room. He pulled her into his arms and kissed the top of her head. "I wish you could go with me."

She wrapped her arms around his mid-section and snuggled her head against his chest. "Me too."

He tipped her chin up and brought his mouth down to hers in a soft kiss. "Hmmm." A shot of electricity shot through him as he deepened the kiss. In her embrace, all his anxiety and fears disappeared. When it was just the two of them, he could forget all about his shameful past behavior and be a better man.

Still, he paced himself. By now he had grown so attuned to her every response that he was able to take them right up to the line she had drawn in the sand between them.

"When are Brian and Betty supposed to get here?" He gave her a suggestive wink.

She smiled slyly up at him. "We have about five minutes." She bit her bottom lip as he backed her up against the bed, causing them to both topple over onto it.

"Let's make the best of our last five minutes alone," he said as he gazed into her loving eyes. Her long legs wrapped around him, making him hiss into her open mouth.

Two can play at that game. He nipped at the curve of her pale neck.

Her breath quickened and she raked her fingers through his hair. She rolled and pinned him down, then dipped down to kiss him passionately on the lips.

Her actions made him tremble and gasp, and he fought to control himself. *Baseball, think of baseball.*

They both jumped at the sound of the doorbell.

He grumbled under his breath at the intrusion, and would need a minute before he was presentable to company.

Katherine bit her lip, apparently trying to refrain from giggling at his obvious discomfort. She straightened her clothes and bounded off, leaving him alone.

He fell back onto the bed trying to calm his roaring heart. *Loving her is going to be the death of me.*

Dulles International Airport
Dulles, Virginia
August 21, 2008
11:30 AM

"Hey, is it lame that I miss you already?" Alex asked.

On the other end of the line, Katherine chuckled and whispered into the speaker, "No, but only because I miss you, too. Betty brought puzzles for us to work on."

He laughed. "I'm sorry. I promise I'll hurry up and get back to you as soon as I possibly can."

"You'd better."

"I love you," he said in a husky voice. He was overjoyed when she responded in turn. He hung up the phone and put it in his carry-on bag.

As he shouldered his way through the crowds of people at Dulles International, he spotted a very pregnant Doc waiting for him at baggage claim. He broke into an easy run, knocking against people to get to her. When he finally made it to her side, he lifted her off the ground and spun her around.

"Look at you! You've never looked more beautiful."

She had a glow and a fullness about her that made her look like an entirely different person. This was the longest she had ever carried one of her babies, and he was hopeful right along with her that perhaps this was the season for their dreams to be actualized.

Doc held him at arm's distance, inspecting him like a mother might. "You look pretty good yourself. You've gotten some color." The cold tips of her fingers brushed against his cheek.

He flushed in embarrassment at her attention. "I've been helping Katherine in the garden."

She smiled, letting her hand fall from his reddened cheek. "Come on, we'd better hurry up and get your bags. I'm double parked."

He chuckled and followed after her in search of his luggage.

***

That night, after dinner, he sneaked out onto the deck to call Katherine. When he ended the call and went back inside, Doc sat at the table waiting for him.

"It's been almost three months since you've lectured me in person, so I guess I'm due, huh?" he said, gearing up to receive his routine wrist slapping.

She nodded to the chair in front of her, indicating she wanted him to sit down.

"What's up, Doc?" He turned on the charm like he always did to diffuse the tension in the room.

She shifted in her seat. "How are you really doing?"

He shrugged. "I'm doing okay, I guess."

"You guess," she said under her breath. "So the medication is working?"

"Yes, it's a lot better. I've even cut down on smoking."

"No nightmares?"

He used his finger to traverse the circular knot in the wood of the table. "No, I still have nightmares," he said under his breath.

"Want to talk about it?"

Alex laughed. "Do I ever?"

He could have left it at that, but Doc was tenacious when it came to his well-being. For better or worse, she had made him her responsibility, and for the most part he didn't mind that.

"Doc, it's the same old thing. She left a hole inside me that is never going to go away. This stuff with Sara and Katherine just brought it all back up again. I'll be fine." No sooner had he said the words than the realization hit him: he really *was* fine.

The look in her eye told him that she didn't believe him. "Are you staying sober?"

He smiled with pride. "Yeah, I'm working the program."

Her left eyebrow shot up in surprise. "Oh, I thought that was all bullshit?"

"Yeah, well, I guess it isn't."

She nodded. "You know what that means? No masturbation and no sex outside a committed relationship."

"I'm almost three months sober." He confidently met her worried gaze.

She let out a loud exhalation. "That's wonderful, Alex!"

He nodded. "The last time was with Sara, the day she turned over Katherine's location."

"Oh, Alex," she said, putting her hand on his and squeezing. "None of that is your fault." She wet her lips before continuing. "How are things between you and Katherine... physically?"

He was surprised to see the faint blushing of her cheeks after that question. She had never been embarrassed to ask him anything before, and her uncharacteristic embarrassment in turn caused him to grow self-conscious. His own cheeks grew hot, and he had to look away from her. For the first time in their friendship, he didn't feel like sharing something with her.

"That's personal, Doc," he said, stonewalling her.

She seemed pleasantly surprised by his tight-lipped response.

He had always been very open and sometimes too descriptive about his sexual exploits. This was the first time he ever played the *don't kiss and tell* card with her.

She said nothing.

Now it was his turn to be surprised. As the silence extended, he felt comfortable enough to open up a little about his current fear. He took a deep breath and spoke the ugly truth, which he hadn't even quite admitted to himself.

"I think maybe I'm not ready to sleep with her. Her not being ready just gets me off the hook from thinking about why I don't want to."

Doc stood up and hugged his head to her swollen abdomen. "Give it time. You've both been through a lot. I want you to know how proud I am of you."

His shoulders slumped as he sunk into her embrace. He had missed her, even if she did make him talk about things he didn't want to.

I-90
Danville, Virginia
August 21, 2008
8:00 PM

The throbbing in his head had reached epic proportions. He had just received a text message that Special Agent Alex Bailey had been spotted at Dulles, but that his CIA detail would make it impossible to get to him. Things were happening and Scott Mitchel was impotent to do anything about it. If something didn't happen soon, he would be forced to take drastic measures.

A second text message made him snap back to attention.

> *Jason Knettle is involved with Charles MacAvoy and the plea deal he made. We have a tail on him and have bugged his home and office. He won't shit without us knowing about it.*

Scott sighed and leaned back against the leather interior of his town car.

Et tu Knettle, et tu!

Church Hill Neighborhood
Richmond, Virginia
August 28, 2008
8:00 PM

Alex sat outside on Doc's deck with a beer in hand and his feet propped up on the railing as he dialed Katherine.

She answered on the first ring. "How did it go?"

He chuckled at her directness. "It couldn't have gone better. All the hard work is going to pay off big time. They have some loose ends they need to tie up, and I have an asset I'm meeting with later, but it looks like indictments are going to come down this fall."

"Oh, that is wonderful!" she nearly shouted. "I'm so proud of you! We'll have to celebrate when you get back."

His voice dropped an octave. "Oh?"

"Oh, yes." Her sultry tone made his toes curl inside his shoes.

His face flushed and his heart skipped a beat in anticipation. "I like the sound of that. It kind of makes me want to play hooky and go home now." He couldn't wipe the silly grin off his face if he tried.

She chuckled. "Oh no, you have to finish up all your work before you can play."

He grumbled good-naturedly, making her laugh even more. *God I love her laugh.*

"I should be done and flying home to you on Monday." His anxiety returned with a flourish. "How was your day?"

She went into a long discussion about all the changes she and Betty had been making to the garden to get it ready for fall.

He settled into his chair and listened attentively, asking all the right questions.

Hardtails Biker Bar
Elkdon, Maryland
August 31, 2008
5:00 PM

Alex sat smoking in the back of the darkened bar, waiting for Sally. His anxiety over the meeting had him slipping into bad habits. In order to set a professional tone, he had dressed in a full suit, and some of the looks he was getting from other patrons made him a little uneasy.

The buzzing of his phone told him that the show was about to begin.

Meet me out back.

They had a bad history of things happening in alleyways behind bars. As much as he didn't want to meet her out there, he knew she'd already set her mind. He got up from the seat and slipped out the back door, by the men's bathroom.

Sally jumped him the moment he stepped outside. She kissed him full on the lips, then dropped to her knees to undo his dress pants and bring her very skilled mouth down on him.

His eyes rolled back in his head as a swell of anxiety coursed through him. His brain was sending out "cease and desist" messages that his body was ignoring. He told himself he needed to break this cycle before he did something he couldn't take back.

I can't do this to Katherine. Hell, I can't do this to myself! I need to stop this before it's too late...

And it was almost too late.

He grabbed her by the shoulders and brought her back up to her feet. "Whoa, Sally." He swayed a little, overwhelmed by the rush of blood away from where he needed it most.

As he fixed his pants, he caught Sally narrowing her eyes at him. For good measure, he put some space between them, since he didn't think he had it in him to stop her if she tried it again.

She crossed her arms over her chest and gave Alex an angry glare of warning. "What's the deal, Alex?"

Gooseflesh broke out all over his arms and legs. *Shit!* She had used his name and not *Spook*. He needed to think fast, because she was dangerous enough when you were on her good side.

He cleared his throat. "I want to talk to you about the terms of that agreement. We can't do *this* anymore."

Her icy blue eyes narrowed down to two angry slits. "What, my blow jobs are suddenly not good enough for you, Spook?"

Alex shook his head and tried to backtrack his way out of the verbal hole he was sinking into. "God no, you're very good. Best blow jobs I've ever had." He shoved his nervous hands into the pockets on his dress pants. "It's just that...."

He tried to think but was finding it very difficult, as he was equal parts terrified and turned on. When a sly smile crept across her lips, his heart jumped.

"You fucker! You got yourself an old lady, didn't you?" Her full lips curled at the ends in an amused smile.

"Yeah, I guess I did." He let out a relieved sigh. "So I don't think it would be a good idea to continue with what we've been doing."

Sally burst out laughing. "Alexander Bailey got himself a girl. Damn, I thought those rumors of you and that bitch from the FBI were BS. I thought, no-fucking-way is that prick not still chasing every tail he can get." She laughed so hard that tiny tears slid down the sides of her cheeks.

He didn't appreciate her laughing at him and his apparent failings, but it was better than the alternative.

"We're cool, Spook. Though I will say, I wish I had known that the last time really was our l*ast* time. I would have savored it a little more." She licked her lips, teasing him.

A shiver rippled through him and his mouth went dry. "Yes, well... do you have any information for me?" They needed to focus on the real reason for the meeting.

"Oh, yeah! Don't I always?" She paused, as if for dramatic effect. "I found out some fucked-up shit that you are going to really love."

He slowly let out the breath he had been holding.

She told him about her brother-in-law's cousins, Marcus and Skins, and how they were found dead at the hands of The Syndicate. Apparently, they had taken Marcus out after he "raped some chick of theirs."

Alex clenched his hands into a tight fist, but otherwise just nodded and kept his cool.

She then went on to say that some dude they had paid off to go into hiding went even deeper into hiding, and that he was holed up somewhere in Illinois just outside Chicago.

Then she pulled a padded envelope out of the storage bag on her bike and handed it to him. "This is the security footage from my brother Mack's shop. He lets some of his asshole buddies of his use the place to make deals."

He nodded. "Okay, I'll bite. What's on this one?"

Her familiar sly smile danced across her face. She got off on this stuff. "One of those FBI stooges that they pay off to keep quiet." She looked pleased as punch with herself.

Now it was his turn to smile. "Damn, Sal, you did good!"

She beamed as he bent to peck her cheek.

"Thank you. I aim to please," she purred.

As he started to pull away from her, she took him by surprise and grabbed him firmly between the legs, making him gasp. "Are you sure you don't want to fool around a little bit, Spook? Because it seems to me that a part of you still wants to."

She made him squirm and shudder, but he calmly took her hand and extracted it from his person before he embarrassed himself. "Yes, well, he and I aren't always on the same page. He's gotten me into too much trouble, so I've put him in timeout."

Her saucer-sized blue eyes twinkled with amusement in a way that had always led to them doing things that got them in trouble.

It had been good....

"Wow, it's been awhile, hasn't it? You sure ya don't want me to help you relieve some of that pressure?"

He gulped hard. "I'm sure." The slight quiver in his voice gave away just how uncomfortable he was with the whole situation.

"I'm just messing with you, Spook. Be good to your old lady. Don't step out on her." She took his hand and shook it with an exaggerated serious look on her face. "It was good doing business with you, Spook."

He straightened his tie and jacket. "Thank you, Sal. I'm glad I could entertain you." He bowed slightly, which made her smile.

As he walked back to his car, he let out a deep shuddering breath, pulled out his phone, and texted Katherine. He didn't quite trust the integrity of his voice yet.

I just finished my last bit of business. I'm anxious to get home and celebrate. Love you!

She responded quickly:

Everything okay?

He took a deep breath and thumbed a reply:

Yes, it's just been a long week and I miss you.

He imagined her wearing that giant floppy hat and working in the garden. The thought made his heart ache.

Her reply made him even more anxious to get back to her:

Hurry home.

CIA Safe House
Wrigleyville Neighborhood
Chicago, Illinois
September 1, 2008
10:00 PM

Alex's flight had been delayed twice and then canceled, but he had managed to get the last flight out on standby. Upon finally arriving at the condo, he dragged himself and his bags through the darkened house in utter exhaustion. The sound of snoring coming from the guest bedroom made him smile.

As quietly as he could, he set down his bags in his and Katherine's room, and began to strip out of his sweaty suit.

She sat up in bed and squinted at him. "You're home!"

"I'm sorry I woke you. Go back to sleep." He tossed his dirty suit in the laundry pile.

She excitedly threw off the covers and scrambled out of bed. "Not on your life."

Her warm arms hung around his neck, and as tired as he was, he kissed her the way she wanted to be kissed. She was wearing one of his t-shirts again to bed, which awoke his senses and propelled him to gather her up into his arms and lie her down on the bed. Her hungry gaze met his, and his control started to slip. Her kiss and her hands were insistent despite the anxiety he sensed. They weren't ready for this, but that didn't stop her.

She slipped the t-shirt off her slim frame.

Another woman with her mind set.

He began to tremble from the sheer force of holding back. While his body was green-lighting this project, his brain flooded him with burning anxiety, which rippled through him like a wild fire. He was grateful when his phone rang not once but three times in rapid succession.

When he started to move away, she pulled him back to her. "Alex."

He shook his head and climbed off her to get his phone, which had fallen out of his pants and onto the carpet. He had three missed calls from Chris.

No one ever calls with good news at this hour.

His heart sank and his throat went dry as he clicked his phone to call Chris back.

His friend answered on the first ring.

"Hey, Chris, is everything okay?" As he listened to his friend relay the devastating news, his heart beat like a reckoning. He couldn't lose Doc. "Oh God! Is she okay?"

Katherine pulled her shirt back on and sat beside him on the bed.

"Do you want me to come back?" He paused. "Yeah, call me later when she gets out of surgery. Okay. Please give her my love."

He ended the call and hot tears streamed down his face. "Doc... she um... lost the baby. She's lost a lot of blood. The doctors don't know if she's going to make it," he choked out.

He let her pull him back into the bed with her, where they laid until he stopped crying and fell asleep.

Chapter 19

Wrigleyville Neighborhood
Chicago, Illinois
September 5, 2008
Noon

Katherine and Alex walked hand in hand to the local hole-in-the-wall diner down the street from their condo. The Chicago street bustled with families and young people walking along the sidewalk to the L stop. Katherine stopped at her favorite flower cart to buy deep purple mums, which he carried for her as they walked the rest of the way to the diner.

He took time eating his breakfast and drinking the bottomless cups of coffee. With the bulk of his investigative work done, he was able to enjoy a brief reprieve, and all during brunch he couldn't take his eyes off her.

Her long auburn hair hung in loose curls that cascaded past her shoulders and down her back. The summer in Chicago had done her good. She had never looked more healthy and vibrant.

It had been good for him, too. He no longer drank or smoked to excess, and his sexual hiatus was entering into its fourth month, something he was very proud of—it was the longest he'd gone since losing his virginity at fourteen.

Alex had spent some of his first week off researching the various bed and breakfasts in a small town that boasted about its apple orchard. They could pick apples, eat donuts and drink hot apple cider—normal couple stuff. He hoped this might quell the deep-seated fear within him that she would come to her senses one day and leave him.

He no longer had his trusted confidante to talk to. Doc's stillbirth had caused severe hemorrhaging that required an emergency hysterectomy; there would be no more babies for her. Since she'd gotten out of the hospital, she wouldn't talk to him; his calls all went to voicemail. She had managed to shut everyone out, including Chris.

Katherine looked at him with concern as she reached across the table for his hand. "Hey."

He shook his head to clear it of all his dark thoughts. "I'm sorry." He returned his attention back to her. "I have a little surprise for you this weekend."

"Oh?" Her left brow raised into a high arch.

He smiled. "Yeah, if we're all done here we can get started. I already have a rental car packed and waiting for us."

Her hand flew to her throat. "*What?*"

He raised his hands to reassure her. "I know you hate surprises, but you'll like it—trust me." He rose from the booth and offered her his hand.

Her shoulders relaxed and the three lines of worry, doubt, and mistrust retreated from her forehead. "Well then, let's get going." She took his hand.

Nancy's B&B
Speer, Illinois
September 5, 2008
3:00 PM

After almost three hours of driving, the bed and breakfast where they would be staying came into view. Katherine fiddled with her seatbelt and stared out the passenger window. Alex had been so patient with her, but could she really trust him to wait? Was this his way of trying to take their intimacy up a notch? Over the course of the summer, they had tried several times, unsuccessfully, to make love.

Alex put the car in park and looked over at her with a look of concern.

She tried to hide her panic and insecurities behind a half-hearted smile, but he knew her well enough to see through her charade.

"Katherine...." His voice registered just above a whisper.

She looked away and tried to compose herself.

"Katherine...." His voice rose, but he didn't try to touch her.

For that she was grateful.

"Katherine, honey, please look at me."

She turned to face him, her hands shaking in her lap.

"You're in control, just as always. I'm not asking or expecting anything. This is just where we're going to stay tonight. We're going to spend all day tomorrow at an orchard. Honey, I'm sorry. I should have just told you beforehand."

She wiped at the tears that had begun to fall. Things needed to change; she couldn't keep feeling like this all the time. *When am I ever going to feel normal again?* "I'm sorry."

"Don't ever be sorry for that." He shook his head and rubbed at the stubble on his chin.

It always surprised her how much he loved her, especially considering how little he got in return. Overwhelmed by what she saw in his eyes, she leaned forward and laid a delicate kiss on his lips. But it wasn't enough.

For the first time in months, she *wanted*.

She tugged him closer and deepened the kiss, but as she was throwing caution to the wind, he held back, creating a maddening tug of war.

Alex won by breaking off the kiss and sitting back. "I love you, Katherine, and I really, really want this too, but I'm also afraid."

His words were a hard slap to the face. Just as she was breaking down her walls, he seemed to be putting his up.

Frustrated, she stormed out of the car and marched up to the steps of the B&B.

***

Alex tried to calm his thundering heart before getting out of the car. He popped the trunk and took out the travel bags he had packed for them the night before.

After he checked them in, he carried their things up the steep steps to their room.

Katherine followed behind him, radiating an angry silence.

That all changed when he opened the door to their room. He had gone all out and dug into his savings to get them the biggest and best room, but it was worth every penny when he saw the look of awe on her face.

"Alex!" She turned to him, beaming. "What did you do?"

He shrugged as if it had been no big deal.

She wrapped her arms around his neck, burying her face into his collarbone. Her anger from moments ago seemed to melt away into tears that wet his neck and the collar of his shirt. He held her tight, until she stopped crying and pulled away.

He kissed her and whispered, "I'm here. I'm not going anywhere."

She breathed in heavily and her body relaxed.

He nodded his head in the direction of the grove of trees. "Want to take a walk? The grounds are supposed to be amazing. They have a three-mile hike through the grove, which should be really beautiful this time of year, and I don't know about you, but three hours in the car has me kind of stiff. I could use a little exercise."

"Yes, I would like that." She linked her hand with his.

He smiled down at her. "Great, let's go!"

I-90
Danville, Virginia
September 5, 2008
4:00 PM

The Senator sat in his town car looking through the latest intelligence reports, his heart hammering against his chest. Something was wrong. He had gotten a call that morning from one of the operatives in the FBI, who was equally concerned by the lockdown The Syndicate had initiated. If the FBI had anything, then the Attorney General would be acting soon.

The partition between him and his driver slid down half way, and a pair of dark brown eyes regarded him through the rearview mirror. "We're here, Senator."

"Thank you, Alejandro."

Apparently, you really do need to do things yourself if you want them done right!

The Senator was never one to get his own hands dirty. There were filthy animals that could easily do it for him, and for the most part they did. This time he would have to roll up his shirtsleeves and join in the fray. His future may very well depend on it.

His sister was no longer enemy number one. No, someone else had easily placed himself in his sights in front of her: Charles. If something were to happen to him and he couldn't testify, the FBI wouldn't have much of a case against Scott. Dollars to donuts there was one man who might have an idea of how to get to him—a weak, ineffectual man who would bend easily to Scott's will or snap like a twig.

Nancy's B&B
Speer, Illinois
September 5, 2008
4:00 PM

Alex held Katherine's hand as they walked between the orange, red, and yellow-leafed trees, grateful for this quiet time with her. It surprised him how easily he had left his past all behind to be with her. When he spotted a red bald cypress tree, he remembered that first night in the bar. With the tips of his fingers, he led her by the small of her back towards the tree.

He reached up, plucked off one of the needles, and held it up to her hair. "Almost a perfect match."

Katherine blushed almost as red as the needle in his hand.

He leaned down and kissed her softly, and as he pulled away, she stopped him and kissed him harder. She tugged on his shirt and backed up so that he pinned her up against the tree, with his body flush against hers. When her hands slid into the back pocket of his jeans, he groaned and gasped for air, feeling consumed by her passions. She wasn't holding anything back, and even though she no longer seemed afraid, he struggled for control of his own desires.

He was fighting a losing battle, as it was clear his body was done waiting. *If you wait until everything is perfect, you will never act. Isn't that what Betty said?*

Katherine pulled away from the kiss, her eyes pleading with him. "Make love to me, Alex."

His mind became muddled with a high-octane mixture of love and lust. His breathing grew ragged, making it even harder for him to think.

Don't think! Act! "Here?" he asked.

She laughed, a little out of breath herself. "Do you think we can make it back to our room?"

He nodded and yanked her by the arm down the path that led back to the B&B.

Her girlish laughter echoed through the canopy of the fall leaves.

This is love.

Danville Press
Danville, Virginia
September 5, 2008
4:00 PM

Jason sat at his desk with the proof for the day's paper spread out before him. A half empty glass tumbler sat beside him with what was left of his alcohol stash.

Lisa Eddie, his Editor-in-Chief, tossed a crumpled piece of paper that hit him square between the eyes. "Take it easy over there, Hemmingway. Write drunk, edit sober, remember?"

He grumbled and downed the last of the scotch.

Lisa rested her feet on top of his desk, tipping back on the back legs of the chair, a red pen balanced behind her ear and a pair of reading glasses perched on the edge of her nose. "We need to get moving on this or we're going to miss our deadline, boss."

He frowned at her feet. "Just make yourself at home, Eddie."

A smile crept across her face, and she blatantly placed her hands behind her head in a relaxed posture. "Don't mind if I do."

"You have a hot date tonight or something? That why you're in such a hurry to get rid of me?"

"Actually, yes I do. I'm getting picked up in an hour."

He pushed off the desk and stood up. Today was one of those days when he would jump at anything to avoid having to do any actual work. "I'm going to get some coffee. You want any?"

"Yes, but only if you're going out to get some. If you even try to bring me the sludge from the kitchen in this shithole, I will hurt you."

He rolled his eyes. "Sure thing, princess. Remind me why I hired you again? It seems fucked up that I pay you to harass me and to fetch you overpriced lattes."

His friend and colleague for over fifteen years chuckled. "Hardy har har. You know you would be lost without me."

"Yeah, I guess there's that." He snatched his jacket off the back of the chair and put it on. "Okay, I'll be right back."

Eddie waved at him, not taking her eyes off one of the articles she was editing. "Sure thing, boss."

He walked through the familiar aisles of the darkened bullpen, which during the day was bustling with energetic, over-caffeinated writers. He had been a little heavy-handed with the drinking all afternoon, leaving him unsteady on his feet, which made an echoing sound on the hard linoleum.

He hadn't seen the man sitting in the shadows, perched on the edge of one of the desks. "Coffee's going to have to wait."

Jason froze in mid-step and his mouth went dry. Adrenaline coursed through him, sobering him up a little. A single beam of light streamed into the room and reflected off the cold metal glint of a gun barrel aimed directly at his head.

"Sit down, Jason."

Jason trembled as he reached behind him to sit down at one of the desks.

Out of the shadows stepped Scott Mitchel with a small gun in his hand.

"Jesus Christ, Scott. What are you doing?"

"Taking matters into my own hands, something I should have done from the very beginning. I did nothing wrong, and yet a bunch of ignorant grease monkeys are going to drag me into the mud with them."

Scott wound a tight rope around Jason, tying him to the chair. The rough cord bit into his skin at even the slightest movement.

"Didn't your old man get shot in here?" Scott looked around the old newsroom that had been around since the 1950s.

"Shut the fuck up, Scott," Jason said through clenched teeth.

The door to Jason's office opened with a flourish as his loudmouth editor filled the doorframe with her tall lanky body. "Jay, come on, man. Quit fucking around. We've got work to do."

A loud crack echoed and a whoosh of wind whirled past him. He watched in agony as Lisa fell hard to the ground.

His head snapped back to Scott. "I'm going to kill you, you son of a bitch."

Scott shook his head and chuckled. "You go right ahead and try. I'd actually like to see you stand up and be a real man for once."

Jason fought against the rope holding him in place. It ripped and tore at his flesh, and blood ran down his arms and pooled into his open palm. His brow furrowed and his lip curled as he looked over at Lisa bleeding out a few yards away from him. "There's no getting away with this. If she dies, you're going to spend the rest of your life rotting away in prison."

Scott sat backwards on the chair in front of him. "I think we both know that my days are numbered. I don't plan to go down without a fight, though."

"What do you want?" Jason asked between clenched teeth.

"I want Charles MacAvoy... dead." He used the same tone he might employ when asking for a glass of water.

Jason huffed in exasperation. "You're insane. You know this, right?"

He didn't see it coming, but he felt the impact of the hard metal against the side of his face. Scott pushed off the chair and loomed over Jason as blood pooled inside his mouth. It made him gag and choke as it ran down his throat. He sputtered, causing blood to splatter onto Scott's crisp white shirt. One of Jason's bottom teeth now lay sideways in his mouth.

The fucker knocked my tooth out! He spit his tooth and more blood from his mouth.

Scott looked down at his soiled shirt with a look of disgust.

A hard blow to Jason's other cheek sent him reeling.

Scott reached into Jason's pants pocket for his wallet, and took out three crisp twenty dollar bills. Jason watched with incredulity as Scott pocketed the money with a shrug. "This should cover the dry cleaning."

Jason's head lulled to the side. He had lost the ability to sit up, and was now held up only by the binding that held him against the hard back of the chair. He had to fight to stay conscious. Blood pooled in his mouth and continued to run down the back of his throat, making him feel queasy. The Mitchel family was literally going to be the death of him.

Scott smirked. "I just don't get it, Knettle. Why would you help Charles out? When they told me what you did, I couldn't believe it. He treated the love of your life like a punching bag. This was your chance to make him pay. Instead, you helped him plea out of a capital murder charge."

The swelling in Jason's eye left him with only one eye to look up at his psychopathic ex-friend. Scott's words washed over him, and he realized he didn't have a rational answer for him—at least not one he would want to hear. Jason had always been opposed to the death penalty, and it wasn't like Charles was getting off scot free.

He licked his sore lips as his head lulled to the right. "Are you worried they may make you bunk mates?"

Scott rolled up the sleeves of his shirt.

Jason watched him carefully, wanting to be prepared for the next blow. When Scott sat back down instead, Jason let out a short breath of relief; he wasn't sure he could take another hit.

"When is Charles being transferred to house arrest?"

Scott's intense glare made him sweat. Jason wet his lips again and grimaced as he swallowed hard. He had been in contact with Charles. Despite his wishes to be done with the man, it seemed Charles was not ready to wash his hands of *him*.

Why can't they just leave me the fuck alone?

Scott eyed him as though he could read his mind. "I know you have kept in touch with him. My contact at the prison said he's been talking to you, but no one seems to know when his release date is. Something tells me that *you* know."

A sudden rush of clammy heat overcame Jason, and he vomited blood and scotch down the front of his shirt.

Scott pushed the chair back to avoid the mess. "Good God, man, get a hold of yourself."

Jason groaned as his stomach continued to spasm, and the pain was more than he could take. At that moment, through the corner of his one good eye, he saw movement. Scott was too busy inspecting his clothes to see, but someone was crouched low behind one of the desks just a few yards from where they sat.

A light went on in Jason's muddled mind. *Marianna!* Eddie's cop girlfriend was early for their date.

He rolled his head back to Scott. He would need to keep him occupied. "Okay, I'll tell you as long as you promise that I never have to see any of you again."

Scott looked up from his shirt stains. "Yeah, sure thing. What do you know?"

Jason shifted in the chair. "The last I heard, he's getting released to serve out the rest of his sentence in his new house outside of Danville. It's that old mansion off Marion Lane. He wanted me to coordinate with a security team to get it ready."

Scott sighed and smiled—a look of victory unfolding across his arrogant face.

Jason smiled despite the swelling and, unable to stop himself, started to laugh.

Scott frowned. "What's so funny?"

He laughed even harder when Marianna pressed the barrel of her service weapon against the back of Scott's head. "Drop your weapon."

Scott's face fell, but his finger, still on the trigger, pressed down.

Jason was already so riddled with pain that at first he didn't even register that Scott had shot him... until he saw the dark red sticky blood running down his shirt and pants. The last thing he saw before the darkness came was Marianna knocking Scott out with the butt of her weapon.

When he came to, the newsroom was bustling with cops and medics. Several EMT's were working on him. He tried to move his arm but he couldn't, and searing pain shot through him.

"Sir," an EMT said. "Please don't move. You've been shot, but you're going to be okay."

An oxygen mask covered his swollen face, the straps digging into the tender spot on his jaw where his tooth had been. He blinked hard, causing tiny tears to slide down his cheeks, but the familiar figure leaning over him brought him an immediate sense of relief. *Marianna.*

"Hey there, nice to see you're still a member of the living."

"Lisa...." he said, surprised by the hoarse sound of his voice.

She held up her hand to shush him. "She's going to be okay. It was bad, but it looks like you both will live to write another day."

He let out a deep sigh of relief. *Thank God!*

She sank down onto her haunches. "Senator Mitchel was taken into custody by the local PD. It's going to take a lot of paperwork since I'm out of my jurisdiction here. They're going to want to talk to you as soon as you're up for it. Make sure your lawyer is there. Okay?"

He blinked a short nod with his one good eye to let her know he understood.

She pushed the hair back off his forehead.

The soft touch comforted him, and he sighed quietly as his tired eyes slid closed.

"Get some rest. You can fill me in on all of this later. Just close your eyes and rest."

Richmond Memorial Hospital
Richmond, Virginia
September 5, 2008
10:00 PM

Emmanuel Richards and a fresh-faced officer from the Danville PD stood outside the open door to Jason Knettle's private room. Richards paused outside the room and looked over his shoulder at the officer behind him. "I'm running this show. Take the notes you need for your records, but don't you dare fuck this up for me. You hear?"

The officer nodded emphatically.

Richards was glad that he still had it in him to put the fear of God into a young man when he needed to. "Good."

He walked into the darkened room, pleased to see Jason sitting up in bed and talking on his cellphone as if he hadn't been shot just six hours prior.

Jason grimaced as he chuckled. "I can't thank you enough, Mari. I don't even want to think what would have happened if you hadn't shown up when you did."

Richards stepped farther into the room with his hands in his pants pockets, pushing back his opened suit jacket behind him.

The Danville police detective followed behind him at his heels, where he belonged.

Jason looked up and met his eye. "Hey, Mari, I gotta let you go. The cavalry just showed up for my statement. No, I don't need a lawyer, thanks. Yeah, I'll take it easy. Just take good care of Eddie. You know it will take us both to keep her out of that office." He chuckled again. "Later."

After ending the call, Jason tossed the phone onto the bed and looked up at Richards and the plainclothes officer with a grim look on his face.

"Hi, Jason, it's good to see you again. This here is Detective Hoover from the Danville PD. He and his men made the arrest tonight. We need to get your statement for our records."

"I don't really have anything to tell you," Jason said.

Richards hunkered down into the seat beside the bed. "I talked with your editor. She didn't fare as well as you did, but it looks like you both got pretty fucking lucky."

"Lucky," Jason said with a huff, twisting the bed sheets with his one good hand. He cleared his throat and grimaced as his hand moved up to favor his swollen jaw.

Richards had heard about the lost tooth. It had to hurt like a motherfucker. Once he had lost two teeth boxing in the Navy, and the memory of that pain was still fresh in his mind twenty years later.

"How are you holding up?" he asked, and nodded his head to Jason's mangled face.

"Like I went through a meat grinder." Jason let out a short laugh that made him grimace again.

"Your statement is really important to this case. Do you think you can tell us exactly what happened tonight?" He slung his foot over his knee and sat back in the chair.

Jason sighed and looked away, his eyes pooling. "Yeah, let's get this over with."

Richards pulled out a tape recorder and put it on the hospital bed table. "I'm old, so if you don't mind, I'm going to record this."

Jason nodded. "That's fine."

"Why were you at the office today?"

Jason raised the bed so that he was sitting up, but his eyes never left the bed sheets. "We were working to get the Sunday morning paper out. This is the first time in the history of the paper that we won't be providing our subscribers with a Sunday paper. My father is probably rolling in his grave. The paper was his life. He died for the fucking thing."

Richards couldn't help but feel sorry for the guy. He hadn't asked to be involved in this mess, and yet here he was recovering from being shot. Yet as sorry as he was for the poor bastard, he needed Jason's account of what happened. This had to be done by the books if they were going to keep Senator Mitchel behind bars. They couldn't afford for him to be out on bail.

"So you were working on the paper... and then what?"

"I stepped out of my office to get Eddie and me some coffee."

Richards leaned forward so that his good ear faced him. "Eddie. Lisa Eddie, your Editor-in-Chief?"

"Yeah," Jason said as single tear slid down his cheek. "I was walking through the bullpen in the dark when I heard a gun being cocked and Scott telling me to stop. He tied me up to one of the chairs."

"Just for the record.... Scott is?"

Jason's face reddened and his voice rose. "Scott Mitchel, the illustrious Senator for the great Commonwealth of Virginia. My once-friend, who held me at gunpoint, knocked out my tooth, and mercilessly shot me and one of my closest friends."

A pretty nurse with chestnut-brown hair poked her head into the room. "Is everything okay, Mr. Knettle?"

Jason held up his hand to dismiss her. "I'm fine. I'll calm down."

The nurse looked to Richards and Hoover. "You gentlemen are on warning. Mr. Knettle needs to keep his blood pressure down."

Richards nodded and flashed her one of his southern gentleman smiles. "Sorry, ma'am, won't happen again."

The nurse narrowed her eyes at them, but nodded and walked back out.

"I'm sorry that this happened to you, Jason." Richards patted his hand.

"Yeah, me too." Jason wet his split lip with a quick sweep of his tongue.

Richards got up and brought him his cup of water.

Jason took the cup with his good hand and took a sip. "Thanks," he said as he handed his cup back to Richards.

"I'm sorry, but I really do need a clear account of what happened. So he tied you to the chair, and then what happened?"

Jason leaned back against his pillow. "Lisa came out to yell at me to hurry up, and Scott shot her like it was no big deal. He just let her lie their bleeding on the floor outside my office."

Richards sat down on the end of the hospital bed. "Then what happened?"

Jason took a deep ragged breath. "He hit me a few times with the gun, knocked out my tooth. Some blood got on his shirt so he took money out of my wallet, saying it was for the dry cleaning bill."

What a lunatic. "Did he say what he wanted?"

Jason nodded. "He wanted to know Charles MacAvoy's release date. He wants him dead so that he can't testify against him."

Richards crossed his arms over his chest, his upper arm buttressed by his middle-aged belly. "What did you tell him?"

Jason looked him straight in the eye. "When he demanded the information, I noticed Officer Marianna Espinoza. She and Lisa had a date tonight. She's a cop with the first precinct in Richmond. She had her gun drawn and was creeping up behind Scott, so I tried to distract him with what little information I knew. Marianna told him to drop the gun, which he did only after shooting me in the shoulder. The doctors say it was clean and I should heal fine."

Richards took a deep breath and looked over at Detective Hoover. "Do you need anything else?"

Hoover shook his head. "No, that's good. I'll go and interview Ms. Eddie now. Thank you for your time, Mr. Knettle."

The young officer turned back to Jason at the door. "I'm going to make sure that sick bastard stays behind bars for a long time." With that he was out the door and down the hall.

"Does Katherine know?" Jason turned his head back to look at Richards.

The edge of the bed squeaked as Richards sat down. "I left a message. They're out of pocket this weekend."

Jason nodded. "Have you seen how the news is spinning it, saying Scott is being questioned in connection with a shooting? No one is telling the truth."

Richards sighed. "Son, I don't understand the news media. No offense, but it seems to me that they never get it quite right."

"Maybe I need to do something to change that."

The determination in his voice had even a cold-hearted skeptic like Richards believing.

He looked down at his buzzing phone, saw a new message from Alex, and handed the phone over to Jason to read.

Jason read it out load. "Just saw your text. We are so glad to hear that Jason is okay. Katherine's worried about him even though I told her he was going to be okay. I think she is also quite distraught because it was her brother. She feels responsible, even though that's ridiculous. I don't think she will sleep well until she hears from Jason, so please allow him to call her on the secured line."

Richards watched as the young man's eyes pooled. "Do you want me to call the number for you?"

Jason nodded, and his Adam's apple bobbed up and down as he swallowed hard.

Richards dialed the secured line and Katherine answered on the first ring. "Hey, Kat, I'm here at the hospital with Jason. I heard you want to talk to him."

"Yes!" Her voice filled the small room.

Richards handed the phone to Jason, whose voice trembled. "Hey, Red. Yeah, I'm okay. Please don't cry. Really, I'm okay, and Lisa is too."

Richards slid off the bed and stepped out to give them some privacy. At least that's what he told himself. He really just needed a smoke.

Chapter 20

CIA Safe House
Wrigleyville Neighborhood
Chicago, Illinois
October 15, 2008
10:00 AM

Alex woke up from his post-coital nap to the sound of his phone vibrating on the bed stand beside him. He blindly reached for it—still half asleep. "Bailey."

Beside him, Katherine stirred. "Who is it?"

Alex held up his finger to silence her so he could listen to the caller.

"Hey, Bailey, it's Brian. I got a call that the police and the FBI caught the old man and are holding him for questioning at the fourth precinct in Chicago. I don't know if you want her to know or not—we'll leave that up to you—but he said he won't talk to anyone but her."

Katherine shifted beside him, and watched him with her head in the palm of her hand.

Ever since their weekend stay at the B&B, they had spent most of their time between the sheets, making up for lost time. Their fun time was going to come to an abrupt end now.

He sat up in bed and swung his legs over the side. "Thanks for letting me know. Yes, I'll let her know and coordinate with the Chicago Field Office to make the arrangements for the meeting, and I'll call you if anything changes. "

"Sounds good. Talk to you later."

He wordlessly ended the call and placed his cell back on the nightstand.

He rubbed his face and raked his fingers through his hair. Sally's information on the whereabouts of former US Marshal Mitchel had been solid. He knew he should be happy that Katherine's old man had been found, but he worried too much about what this would do to her.

She bristled beside him. "Alex?"

He turned his head back towards her but avoided looking her in the eye. "They found your dad and brought him in last night. He says he won't talk to anyone but you."

She sat up with a start.

He took a deep breath and twisted his body towards her. "We're supposed to meet with him as soon as possible at the Chicago Field Office."

She paled and opened her mouth to speak, but abruptly closed it again. Instead, she jumped out of bed and ran into the bathroom.

Damn it.

After a couple minutes, he stood and padded into the bathroom, where Katherine was already in the shower. He pulled back the curtain and climbed in.

Despite the running water he could hear her soft sobs. He touched her shoulder and folded her into his embrace. "I'll be with you the whole time."

"Thank you." She wrapped her arms around him and kissed him.

Chicago Field Office
Chicago, Illinois
October 15, 2008
1:00 PM

Alex's heart skipped a beat as he rounded the corner.

Katherine was dressed in a black Donna Karan suit, minus the jacket. Her black pencil skirt hugged her like a glove, and her

Louboutin heels... well, they made her look sexy as hell. She was suited up for warfare, but in that moment all he could think about was later, when he could take it all off her, except for maybe the shoes—they could stay on.

He bit his bottom lip, shook his head, and took a deep breath as he set down a hot cup of tea in front of her.

Her hand trembled as she pushed it away. "I can't." Her hand moved to her stomach, and she looked as if she might throw up.

"You ready?"

"I don't know if I'll ever be ready, but I want to get this over with as quickly as possible."

The chair raked across the linoleum as she pushed it back to get up, and she followed him to the room they had set up for the interview. As they neared the door, she turned to stop him. "Can you stay out here? I think I want to do this alone."

He nodded.

She tugged his arm and looked up at him with her sparkling blue eyes. "I need to do this on my own." He reached up and cupped her cheeks in his hands, and she leaned into his touch, her eyes slipping closed for a moment. "I know you're right here waiting if I need you. I need to do this for me."

"Okay, but I'll be watching and ready, just in case." He hooked his thumb over to where the monitors picked up the security feed.

A smile rippled across her trembling lips. "Thank you." She kissed the palm of his hand.

His stomach bottomed out as she stepped away from him and his hand fell back to his side. The security feed showed the small room with a long table and two chairs. He sat down in front of the monitor and watched as the door closed behind her with a *thunk,* making her pause for a moment in her step.

"Come on, baby," he said to himself as his knee bounced up and down.

When she stepped forward again, he let out a breath of relief. The sound of her pulling the metal chair away from the table reverberated throughout the room. She sat down, scooted the chair closer to the table, and folded her hands in her lap. He worried his bottom lip between his teeth as he watched her stare down her father. The two sat there in complete silence while the clock in the room ticked past the seconds, and then minutes.

"Jesus," he said under his breath.

After five minutes had passed, Katherine cleared her throat and spoke in a strong authoritative voice—her FBI voice, he thought with a smile.

"You wanted to see me?" She offered an inquisitive arch of her eyebrow.

Alex shivered at the coldness that emanated from her.

Her father seemed unperturbed by it as he sat there, studying her.

Once a cop, always a cop.

Slowly, the corners of Mr. Mitchel's mouth cracked into a smile. "You've grown so much, Kit-Kat."

Katherine sat still, unmoved by his familiarity.

"You look so much like your mother." The old man's expression softened, but her flat affect seemed to disappoint him. "You were such a little firecracker. Now look at you." He puffed his chest pushing out in pride. "They tell me that you work for the FBI as a criminal profiler, and that you were the one to set this all in motion."

"You said that you would cooperate with the investigation if you saw me. You've seen me," she said, her tone as frigid as before.

Her father's face fell as the wall between them grew tall and wide.

Alex knew all too well how painful it was to be on the other side of that wall.

"Katherine," the old man said. "You have every right to hate me for deceiving you and the rest of the family. I need you to know that I did what I thought was best for you all. I was stuck. I had already taken some bribe money to look the other way, and when I had a change of heart they came down hard on me, threatening to discredit me, and to hurt you kids and your mom. I made a deal with them that, at the time, seemed like the only option. I really thought you would be better off this way. It seems you're doing well here at the FBI."

She huffed angrily at her father's words. "And on what are you basing this astute assumption?"

Her father's mouth fell agape. "I guess... I guess I don't know. I'm sorry if I presumed wrongly."

Despite the old man's otherwise calm exterior, Alex could tell he was starting to crack.

Katherine wet her lips with a quick sweep of her tongue, and her eyes narrowed. "That's an understatement. Scott's a part of The Syndicate now, did you know that? Did you know that they killed Adeline to keep me quiet? Did you know Mom has been in and out of institutions since you *died*? Did you know that I was kidnapped, beaten, raped, and left for dead by The Syndicate?" She verbally vomited her rage at him through the rapid-fire succession of barbed questions.

Mr. Mitchel paled at her harsh words. "No, I didn't know that." The old man's hands trembled and his eyes pooled.

"No, I think it's pretty clear that you don't know anything," she replied under her breath as she examined her own clasped hands.

With tears in his eyes, her father tried to meet her gaze. "Kat, I am so sorry. I don't know what else to say. I...." He choked on his words.

She pursed her lips and looked up in an obvious effort to hold back the tears that threatened to fall. Even after clearing her throat, her voice still wavered. "Your cooperation with this investigation would be appreciated," she said in her professional tone again. "We'll need you to give an affidavit stating everything you know, and produce any evidence you have to corroborate those claims."

Her dad nodded and reached across the table towards Katherine, but she pulled her hands back.

"Maybe, in time, we can get to know each other better," he said.

She looked down at the table, gave a small, almost imperceptible nod, and stood up to leave. "Someone will be in shortly to explain the process and what we need to move forward. Goodbye, Mr. Mitchel." She turned and walked briskly out of the room.

Her father slumped in his chair when she left.

As the door closed, Alex saw her bravado give out, and he was there at her side immediately. He took her into his arms as she sobbed into the scratchy material of his suit jacket.

He pulled away far enough to wipe away her tears. "Come on, let's go home."

CIA Safe House
Wrigleyville Neighborhood
Chicago, Illinois
October 21, 2008
6:00 AM

Following the meeting with Katherine's father, the field office requested assistance from Alex, who agreed to help. He'd told her how he'd anticipated them just needing an extra set of hands to handle the large volume of paperwork that came with taking Mr. Mitchel into custody. He was surprised when they assigned him to be the ASAC for the Chicago side of the investigation.

She was surprised too, but after living and breathing the investigation, he was probably best suited to fill that position.

They put him in charge of managing the evidence collection; the evidentiary chain of custody; the staff assigned to the task force; and made him the point person for the representative from the AG's Office. The office was charged with assisting the D.C. headquarters with preparing for the upcoming indictments. Arrests were scheduled to occur the day before Halloween, and Alex was assigned to be one of the arresting officers in the bust.

He worked long, hard hours, and she missed him, but she kept herself busy planning for their move back to Virginia in November.

The date of her deposition came faster than she'd expected. For security reasons, she gave her testimony to the AG's staff at the Chicago Field Office. On her last day, one of the staffers had asked if Katherine had a tampon on her, and she realized with a start that it had been a long time since her last period. The app on her phone said it had been two months since her last cycle.

During one of her scheduled breaks, she sneaked out of the office, with one of her bodyguards in tow, to go to a drugstore and pick up a pregnancy test.

The next day, she awoke early and crept out of bed and into the bathroom to take the test. She didn't want to worry Alex. It was silly even contemplating it, since the doctors had told her after the attack that it would be almost impossible for her to get pregnant. Still, as she waited for the results to show, she paced back and forth inside the tiny bathroom.

She wasn't opposed to having children, and if by some miracle she was pregnant, who was she to question that? An anxious prickling of fear crept up on her. What would Alex think? They had only been lovers for such a short time, for God's sake! That weekend at the bed and breakfast....

As much as she wanted to avoid looking at the stick, she forced herself to do it. Sure enough, two lines stared back at her. *Pregnant.* She slid her hand down her belly—they had made a baby.

Alex sat up in bed just as she walked out of the bathroom. His face scrunched in instant concern. "Hey, are you okay?"

She watched as his eyes traveled down to her hand holding the positive test. His hand covered his face, hiding a smile. "Katherine...."

She held up the stick for him to see. "It looks like we're pregnant."

He scrambled out of bed—getting tangled in the sheets in the process-- and ran to her. He lifted her up into the air and spun her around, all the while peppering her with kisses and whispering words of love against her ear.

She let herself sink into his embrace and feel the joy of the moment, which she would surely remember fondly for the rest of her life.

Chicago Field Office
Chicago, Illinois
October 24, 2008
3:00 PM

Alex was still floating on cloud nine when he got a call from Chris that yanked him back to earth—Doc had attempted to commit suicide. The painful reality of never being able to have a child proved to be just too much for her to bear. Chris, a stoic military man, sobbed on the other end of the phone, and for a heartbreaking moment, Alex had misunderstood him and thought Doc was lost to him forever.

Chris had called in all the favors that he could, and begged him to help protect her from the career consequences of attempting to take her own life.

Alex called Richards, who had just been promoted to Section Chief, and had him help find a way to ensure that Doc had a job to come back to. They filed paperwork indicating she had gone on a sabbatical. No one had to know the truth.

They were able to pull some strings and get her placed in a private facility, where she voluntarily committed herself.

The joy of his impending fatherhood was lost in the shadows of his grief for Doc. He couldn't help but wonder if he would lose her now that he and Katherine were expecting. He hadn't told Chris, and didn't know how he could.

He was supposed to fly into D.C. in a few days, and figured he would try to see her then. He needed to know that she really was going to be okay.

Washington, D.C.
October 30, 2008
9:00 AM

It rained that morning, a cold, hard rain that left their flak jackets soaked through. Despite the abysmal weather, it was a very satisfying day for two men in particular. In a synchronized tactical mission, those two men led one of the ten arrest teams about to bring down one of the largest criminal organizations in the history of the United States.

As Richards, Alex, and the rest of their arrest team stormed through the fourth floor and read A.D. Fullmore his rights, Richards wore a grin so big that his cheeks might be sore for a whole day afterwards. Nothing in his entire career had been, or would ever be, more satisfying than seeing Fullmore and his cronies being arrested by his men. They would pay for the pain and suffering inflicted upon their fellow agent.

That night, the two men sat a dive bar around the corner from the Hoover Building. They spent the solemn celebration getting as drunk as possible while still staying upright. Their victory that day had come at a cost, and they mourned in silence for everyone who had paid dearly during the course of the investigation.

Virginia Peninsula Region Correctional Facility
Williamsburg, Virginia
October 31, 2008
8:00 AM

Alex sat in the cold, hard chair waiting for the guards to bring out the prisoner, his arms crossed over his chest to keep himself in check. The latent rage over the course of events that led to his sitting there had begun to undo him. After a day of arrests and then drinks with his boss, he was more than just a little exhausted and hungover. He needed to do this, all the same.

Seeing Scott Mitchel in chains and an orange jump suit was what he needed, and what he hoped would help him move on. As an added bonus, the Senator seemed none too pleased to see him, which just made it all the more enjoyable.

Alex picked up the phone and indicated through the Plexiglas that Scott should do the same.

Scott picked it up and spoke into the receiver through his gritted teeth. "What do you want, Alex? To gloat?" A fiery rage burned in Scott's eyes.

Alex smiled a victor's smile. "How are you enjoying your stay, Senator?"

Scott glared at him, and for a moment Alex thought the man would hang up and walk away, but he didn't.

"I just wanted to see your face and tell you that you lost." The last of his calm vanished, and his shaky voice gave away his extreme hatred of the man in front of him. "I also wanted to tell you that, despite your best efforts, Katherine is not only alive, but well. You're going to be an uncle, not that you'll ever see the kid, but I thought you might want to know."

Scott's face seemed to soften for just a moment. "She's pregnant? Fucking whore sure didn't take long."

Alex's smile slid off his face. "I'm going to make it my life's work to make sure you never see the light of day, Mitchel."

Scott chuckled. "Yeah, good luck with that. One day I'll be out, and there will be hell to pay. Just who do you think I'll go after first?"

Alex shook his head. "Goodbye, Senator." He hung up the phone and stood.

He needed to get to work and finish up his paperwork. The sooner he could get back to Katherine, the better.

FBI Headquarters: Hoover Building
Washington, D.C.
October 31, 2008
6:00 PM

Section Chief Richards worked his way through the crowded bullpen to where a disheveled Alex sat at a desk, buried under stacks of paperwork. "Hey, Bailey, you hungry?"

Alex looked up through bloodshot and sunken in eyes, lost in a haze. "Hmm... what?"

Richards shook his head. "You look like shit, man. Have you eaten anything? Slept?"

Alex shook his head. He looked as if he might have come back to the office after the bar last night. "There's too much to do. The faster I can get this done, the faster I can get back to Katherine."

Richards nodded and handed him a cup of coffee. "Take a break and come with me to get something to eat. You have to eat."

Alex warily pushed away from his desk. "All right, but something quick."

Richards slapped him on the back. "Come on, man, my treat."

Alex smiled at his boss. "Well, why didn't you say so in the first place?"

***

Richards pulled his FBI-issued sedan into the parking lot of a small, out-of-the-way cafe called "Lucy's Fried." Alex had grumbled the whole way about how he needed to get back and didn't have time for such a road trip, but Richards ignored him and reassured him that it would be worth it.

Alex pushed open the car door with more force than necessary.

"Jesus, calm down man! Smoke a cigarette or something," Richards said, growing more and more irritated by him.

"I'm trying to quit." He toed the gravel.

Richards cocked an eyebrow in surprise. "Oh?"

"Katherine's pregnant," he said under his breath.

Richards stopped in his tracks. "What? That's wonderful, man."

Alex smiled. "Yeah, I kind of want to be around for the kid, so I'm trying to be good."

"Congrats, man. I'm happy for you." He patted Alex on the back.

Alex nodded. "Well, let's get inside and eat so I can get my work done and get back to her."

Richards' smile faded. "Okay, don't get mad at me, but I have an ulterior motive for bringing you out here. Just promise me that you'll have an open mind?" He opened the door to let Alex walk in first.

Alex stopped in the doorframe when he saw who was sitting inside, surrounded by Federal Marshals. "Fuck, Richards, really? How is he even here?"

Richards nudged him into the cafe. "He's being transferred to house arrest. Since he's been so cooperative—a model prisoner, I'm told—my warden buddy is doing him this small favor."

Alex glowered at him and asked in a hushed whisper, "What favor might that be?"

"Charles has something for you and Katherine that you definitely want." Richards gave him a shove forward.

Alex gave Richards a look that said he doubted it, but he went in anyways and sat down. "Talk fast, Charles. I don't have the time or the patience for your bullshit."

Charles sighed and pushed a manila envelope across the table to Alex. "Divorce papers. All she has to do is sign them. I'm giving her everything."

Alex didn't respond.

Charles reached into his pocket, pulled out a key, and handed it to Alex. "This is to Moran's storage in Maryland. All her stuff is inside. Everything that the government doesn't seize is going to her."

Alex nodded. "You could have sent this by courier. Why the meeting?"

"I wanted to give it to you in person. I needed to look you in the eye and say I'm sorry. I need you to let Katherine know how sorry I am. I fucked up, I see that now. I want her to be happy. I know you may find this hard to believe, considering all that has happened, but I love her. I always have, and I probably always will. She deserves someone so much better than me, though. I'm told you make her happy. Treat her right."

Alex clenched his fists. "Are we done here?"

Charles nodded. "Yeah, I said what I needed to say."

Alex pushed off from the table, snatched the papers and key, and stormed outside.

Richards ran out after him with a takeout bag. "Come on, man, wait up!"

Alex was fuming, but Richards couldn't for the life of him figure out why, given that he held in his hands the means to make an honest woman of Katherine. It was *good* news.

Alex fished out a cigarette and a lighter, and lit up as he stalked across the gravel parking lot to Richards' car. "I have an errand I need to run. Can you take me?" He visibly relaxed a little.

Richards nodded. "Of course, man. Where to?"

CIA Safe House
Chicago, Illinois
November 1, 2008
6:00 PM

Katherine paced back and forth impatiently in their condo, waiting for Alex to get home. His plane had landed an hour ago! After two days of arrests, mounds of paperwork, and a battery of tests and interviews, he was given the go-ahead to return to Chicago... back to Katherine.

He was officially out of the CIA and set to start his teaching position at the FBI's Quantico Academy after the New Year.

Brian and Betty had spent the better part of the two days with her, but the remaining six hours she just had the posted guards outside. She was anxious for Alex to be back, having been a nervous wreck the entire time he was gone.

Just as she was about to pick up her phone and try his cell, the door lock clicked and opened. Katherine rushed him at the door, nearly knocking him down.

Alex hungrily gathered her up in his arms, kissed her, and carried her straight to their bedroom. There would be time for talking later.

***

The next morning, Alex awoke sometime past 10:00 AM. Though content curled up against Katherine's naked backside, he rolled out of bed, pulled a small box and a manila envelope out of his knapsack, and hid the small box behind him.

He woke up Katherine and handed her the envelope. "Open this," he said with a grin.

Still half asleep, her eyebrow cocked in curiosity. "What is it?"

Alex nodded towards the envelope, biting his lower lip in expectation.

She sat up in bed and pulled Alex's shirt on. Once settled, she tore open the envelope, pulled out the papers inside, and gasped in surprise.

Alex nodded. "Charles had divorce papers written up. He's giving you everything, uncontested. All you have to do is sign and initial on a few dotted lines, and you're a free woman." He grinned again.

A small paper fluttered from the stack onto the bed in front of her. It was a handwritten note.

> *Dear Katherine,*
>
> *As long as I live I will always love you, but I know that I ruined what we had. You deserve someone so much better than me. I am sorry for everything and wish I could make it better, but I know I can't. The only thing I can do is let you go.*
>
> *Love Always,*
> *Charles*

Katherine reached for the pen on her bed stand, signed and initialed on all the highlighted parts, then closed the papers and sighed with relief.

Alex slid the small box he'd been hiding across the bed and in front of her.

Katherine looked from him to the box and back again in stunned disbelief. With trembling hands, she opened the box to reveal a beautiful Claddagh, a traditional Irish wedding ring.

She pulled it out of the velvet slip and held it up to the light. "It's beautiful!"

Alex beamed as he took the Claddagh and slid it down the ring finger of her left hand—a perfect fit. Tears of joy slid down her cheek, and he swept them away with the pads of his thumbs.

Katherine laughed through the tears. "Damn pregnancy hormones."

"I love you, Katherine. Will you be my wife?"

She nodded. "Yes." A fresh set of tears slid down her cheek.

Their lips met in a soft, gentle kiss.

Alex, so filled with joy, couldn't stop smiling. He looked down and touched her belly, and spoke to their unborn child. "Did you hear that, little buddy? She said yes!"

Chapter 21

Pittsylvania County Courthouse
Chatham, Virginia
November 26, 2008
5:00 PM

Though they had enjoyed their time in the cozy Chicago condo, they were both glad to be home in Virginia. Katherine would have to testify in a few short weeks, and they wanted enough time to get moved back into Alex's apartment, which he had sublet to a colleague while they were gone. They had debated about whether to hold off getting married until the baby came or after the trial, but had decided life was too short.

It had snowed the night before, but it didn't stop their plans. They were eager to make their family official, so with marriage certificate in hand they trudged through the snow to the Pittsylvania County Courthouse in Chatham, Virginia.

The simple civil ceremony was attended by Betty, Brian, Jason, Christopher, Section Chief Richards, and enough security to keep the President of United States safe. The added security was part of Charles' wedding present to the young couple. He footed the bill for a high-end security detail that was on them 24/7.

Alex bristled at it, but he couldn't say no to an offer that kept his family safe.

Through the whole ceremony, he couldn't help brushing his hand against the barely perceptible bump on Katherine's abdomen, like a touchstone. He needed to be reassured that it was all really happening, and not some fantastical dream.

Afterwards, they made their way to a small cottage inn to eat dinner and stay for the night. For security purposes, Charles had booked the entire inn.

Even though Alex had cut down, he still smoked the occasional cigarette; some habits were just too hard to let go. He was standing outside on the patio, shivering and smoking his first cigarette of the day, when Christopher stepped outside with two stout beers in hand.

He handed one over to Alex and motioned for them to sit down on the patio chairs. "Congratulations, man."

They clinked their glasses together and sat in a companionable silence while watching the sun set over the small grove of trees behind the inn.

After a few minutes, Christopher cleared his throat. "I know she'll be sad that she missed this."

Alex swallowed back the ball of emotions rolling up his throat. "I wish she had been here, too. She would have made a great best man."

His poor friend gave a half-hearted chuckle in response as he unscrewed the top of a flask, took a long swig, and chased it down with his beer. "She'll come around." Christopher bobbed his knee up and down.

"Katherine's pregnant, isn't she?" Christopher's voice cracked.

Alex wiped away a single tear that had fallen down his cheek. "Yeah."

Christopher shook his head. "I have to say, Bailey, I never thought I would see the day that you became a family man."

Alex smiled, put out his cigarette, and nursed his beer. "Did you know Ellie has a picture of us in her office, of that night we sang *Ebony and Ivory* at the Embassy karaoke night?"

Christopher laughed. "Jesus, we were so drunk that night."

Alex smiled at the nostalgic memory as they clinked their glasses together again. "I know you were pretty fucked-up back then, but damn we had good times, didn't we?"

"Yes, we did, even when we were getting kicked out of every poker night the Embassy staff hosted."

"They just couldn't handle losing to our brilliance." Sadness crept over them as they took another drink from their mugs.

Alex smiled. "Ellie had her hands full with the two of us idiots."

"I have to go back to Germany next week to finish out my tour. It's only for another two weeks but... I don't know how I'm going to go."

Alex shook his head. "I'm so sorry, man. I know you worry about her being alone. I wish she would let me see her."

Christopher finished off his beer in one gulp. "Yeah, me too... me too." He stood up and placed his hand on Alex's shoulder. "I'd better get going if I want to make it to the hospital before visiting hours are over. I'll bring her some cake. She loves wedding cake—always used to say it tasted like hope."

Alex covered his friend's hand with his own. "I'm really sorry, man. Call me when you get back stateside. Maybe we can get a poker game going."

Christopher smiled a sad half-smile and walked back inside, leaving Alex alone with his memories.

Holy Cross Hospital, Psychiatric Ward
Just outside Richmond, Virginia
November 26, 2008
7:30 PM

Christopher held out his phone to show her the pictures he had taken of the wedding.

She thumbed through them and handed it back to him. He smelled like cigarettes and alcohol.

"You smell like him," she said. "Maybe I should take up smoking."

He reached inside the paper bag at his side. "How about some wedding cake instead?"

She took the cake and the plastic spoon. *No knives or forks allowed.* She poked at the cake and only took a few bites.

"I wish you would let him visit you. I think it would do you both some good."

Ellie shook her head and pushed the cake away. "I can't have him seeing me like this."

"What, you don't want him to know that the great and powerful Doc is really human, with failings of her own?" His tone dripped with bitterness and anguish.

I suppose that's my fault. Fuck him and his heartbroken puppy dog face. He doesn't understand me or my relationship with Alex. He never did. I just want to be alone. I can't lose face with Alex. Not now.

"You can leave now."

Christopher pushed off the table and stormed out.

She watched him walk away, knowing she should feel something, feel bad about how she treated him, but....

Fuck him.

Chapter 22

Moultrie Courthouse
Washington, D.C.
December 19, 2008
9:00 AM

Time passed by in a flash, as it always did when Alex was happy. Before he knew it, the time had come for Katherine to testify.

The sound of reporters and onlookers was deafening. Reporters shoved microphones into their faces and asked rude, leading questions. Some were related to the case, but others were personal and made his face flush with anger.

Their driver had let them out at the front of the courthouse, because the roads were a mess, and they had no choice. It made him extra vigilant, even with the added security Charles' team provided.

As they walked up the steep steps to the courthouse, he held her by the elbow and whispered in her ear, "I love you. You're doing the right thing. I'm so proud of you."

He hoped his words would drown out the hateful things being shouted at her, words he tried to block out himself. When she paused on the steps, he squeezed her arm again. "You're doing great."

Her wide-eyed gaze caught his and he smiled for encouragement. "I know you're scared, but you've got this."

They started back up the steps, and a familiar face appeared at the top. The woman's expression sent a chill down his spine.

As if in slow motion, she pulled her hand out of her trench coat, and the early morning light caught a piece of metal in her hand.

Gun!

The woman locked eyes on Katherine, her sister-in-law.

Alex shoved Katherine out of the way. The only sound he heard was the crack and whine of the gun going off.

The impact took him by surprise. He hadn't anticipated getting shot himself, but as he fell back on the steps, he knew he would do it again in a heartbeat.

Knettle Creek Cabin
Millburo, Virginia
December 19, 2008
Noon

Jason decided to take some time off for the holiday to do some writing at his grandfather's cabin. He was pulling up the gravel drive when his phone started to blow up with incoming messages.

He threw his truck into park, picked it up and thumbed open a text message from his Editor-in-Chief, Lisa Eddie.

Check your email!

Jason pulled up the new mail message she had sent.

To: Jknettle@DanvilleNews.com
From: Leddie@DanvilleNews.com
Subject: Special Agent Alex Bailey shot outside courthouse!
Date: December 19, 2008

Dear Jason,

This just came across the wire. I am going to lead with it in tonight's paper. Leave it to the AP to refer to us as reporters. WTF!

FBI AGENT GUNNED DOWN OUTSIDE D.C. COURT HOUSE

Washington, D.C. (AP) FBI Special Agent Alexander Bailey was shot on the steps of the Moultrie Courthouse. D.C. police are reporting that the intended target was Special Agent Katherine Mitchel, his wife, who is pregnant with their first child. Police arrested Kimberly Anne Mitchel, wife of Senator Scott Mitchel, who is serving time for the shooting of two reporters. Special Agent Bailey is being treated at Providence Memorial Hospital and is said to be in critical condition. The Agents were at the courthouse to testify against Senator Mitchel, Katherine Mitchel's twin brother and one of the key defendants in The Syndicate trial.

Call me!
Lisa Eddie
Editor-in-Chief
Danville News and Views

Jason threw his truck into reverse and headed back to the paper in Danville. It was going to be a long night to get the special issue out.

He tried to focus on the logistics of work, but all he could think about was Katherine. Besides the wedding, he hadn't had time to see her, and he couldn't bring himself to call her—not even now. Instead, he would chain himself to his desk with the rest of his staff, and polish off a bottle of scotch and a box of pizza. Somehow that would have to be enough.

He pulled into the parking lot of the paper and got another notification, this time from Charles.

I just heard about the shooting on the news. Have you heard anything? Is Katherine okay? Please let me know as soon as you hear anything.

Jason shot back a quick text.

Katherine's okay. Alex was shot by Scott's wife.

Charles responded almost immediately.

I'm hiring more men to watch over her and to set up a security system at her apartment.

Jason wanted to tell him that he couldn't protect her from everything, but he knew it would fall on deaf ears.

Providence Memorial Hospital
Washington, D.C.
December 19, 2008
8:00 PM

Katherine sat at Alex's bedside, holding his hand and watching the machines beep and click as they breathed for him. The doctors said they didn't expect him to regain consciousness until at least tomorrow. He had spent six hours in surgery, a thoracotomy, to repair the damage.

One of the bullets had nicked his aortic valve. His beautiful heart had been damaged in order to save her life and that of their unborn child.

Tears streamed down her cheeks in an endless succession. Nurses had been sneaking her food and drinks from the maternity ward fridge, and the OB on call in the ER had checked on her and did an ultrasound to check on the baby. After having a bag of IV fluids, the mild contractions she was experiencing went away, and they left her to be with Alex.

As hard as she tried, she couldn't help but replay the events of the morning over and over in her mind. They had been pushing past all of the reporters and onlookers trying to get inside the courthouse, where she would testify later that morning. He had been whispering loving and encouraging words in her ear to combat the throng of negative words and slander being slung at her.

He had pushed her out of the way, knocking her down two steps in the process. The familiar crack and whine of a discharged weapon shattered the air around her, and her tailbone had hit the hard cement with a thud.

Alex fell to the ground beside her, and blood had pooled between them—red, so much red.

Her security detail had said she passed out. She didn't remember much after that point.

She was beyond exhausted now, but her body wouldn't let her rest.

At some point her body must have finally given in, because she felt herself being shaken awake. She grumbled as she sat up.

Brian stood over her with a forlorn look. "Kat, honey, you need to get some real rest—not in a chair. Come on, the nurses have a bed you can use."

She looked back to Alex, reluctant to move. *If I leave his side, will he die?* It was a stupid irrational fear that had plagued her all day.

"I'll sit with him tonight." Brian rubbed her shoulder.

"You'll get me if anything changes?"

"I promise," he said.

She struggled to stand up from the chair, still clutching Alex's hand. She loathed letting him go, but she needed to get some rest. Alex would want her to take care of herself and the baby. She let herself be led away.

When she looked back, she let out a small sob at the sight of Brian holding her husband's hand. The man had become something of a stand-in-father for him, and Katherine was grateful for him and Betty.

Providence Memorial Hospital
Washington, D.C.
December 20, 2008
7:00 AM

Katherine had been tossing and turning all night before finally falling asleep sometime around 4:00 AM. She was lost in a dream when someone shook her arm.

"Katherine, wake up!"

Brian. Oh no, Alex. Something is wrong with Alex!

She bolted up on the cot. "What is it? Is he okay?" Her heart raced, making the baby dance inside of her.

Brian smiled and nodded. "He's awake and he's asking for you."

She pushed past him and dashed off in the direction of the ICU.

Alex lay in his bed awake and extubated. "Hi."

Katherine choked back a sob. "Hi." She sat down on the chair beside the bed and brought his hand to her lips.

He nodded towards her belly with deep concerned etched across his face. "Is the baby okay?"

"Yes, he's fine." She smiled down at the love of her life.

His eyebrow shot up in surprise. "He.... We're having a boy?"

She nodded, wiping away the tears that fell freely down her cheeks. "Yes, they did an ultrasound. Last night when they told me we were having a boy, I thought that Bailey might be a good name for him."

Alex blinked back the tears that had begun to well up. "Really?"

They made quite the pair, a couple of cry babies, she thought as she laid her head down on the pillow beside him. She let loose a shaky sigh. "I was so afraid you would never wake up."

"I know. I'm sorry I scared you. When I saw the woman...." His voice faltered with emotion.

"Scott's wife," Katherine said, and a chill ran through her. She hadn't quite processed the idea that her sister-in-law had tried to kill her. The police had captured her on the scene before she could take her own life.

"Yes, she had a gun pointed at you... and I...." The machines monitoring him beeped more incessantly, indicating his heart rate and blood pressure had elevated.

Katherine shushed him. "It's okay. We're okay. You saved us. Now we just have to work to make you all better. You still owe me a honeymoon." She winked, trying to distract him.

"Hmm, I like that idea." He smiled and started to slip back into sleep.

"Just rest. I'll be right here." She touched his face and hair.

Alex smiled lovingly up at his wife as he drifted off to sleep. His heart rate and blood pressure returned to normal.

Katherine looked up to see a nurse standing by.

Later that evening, he awoke again, this time more alert than the last. He even took a few bites of the bland dinner the hospital offered.

Katherine couldn't stop touching him, as if trying to reassure herself that he was still alive. After he took his last bite of lime Jell-O, he put down his spoon and reached for the bump under her shirt. His calloused thumb and fingertips stroked the stretched skin of her stomach, and his whole face lit up with an awestruck smile.

She couldn't help but return the smile, and a little of the tension in her started to dissipate. When she bent over him to kiss him, his monitors blipped for a second.

"What you do to me," he said with a mock swoon, making her cheeks hot and red with embarrassment.

Alex turned the ring on her thumb over and over, his ring that the doctors said he couldn't wear. "Didn't we just meet?"

She chuckled. "I guess we kind of just did. We just fit a lot of life into a short amount of time."

He beckoned her back to him for another kiss, but Katherine shook her head. "No way. I'm afraid I might kill you."

He laughed heartily but winced from the pain of it.

Katherine's chest seized at his obvious distress.

"Speaking of first meetings," he said. "What did you think of me then? Be honest. I can take it."

She laughed. "I thought you were incredibly sexy."

"Sexy, huh?"

She rolled her eyes. "I also thought you were a lot of trouble."

"And am I? Trouble?"

She smiled and patted his hand. "Oh yes, but only the best kind."

His smile slipped away and he grew serious. "I fell in love with you that night at the bar. I didn't want to admit it, even to myself, but I was gone from the moment I first laid eyes on you. You don't know this, but I fought for this assignment. I wanted to be close to you from the very beginning."

Katherine blushed under the weight of his gaze, and his words made a chill ripple through her. She took his hand and brought it up to her pursed lips.

"I love you, Katherine. You're the best thing that's ever happened to me, and no matter what happens next, I'm glad we had this time together." His eyes brimmed with a reflecting pool of unshed tears.

Katherine's eyes pooled. "Please, don't talk that way." *He's trying to prepare me for losing him.* After everything she had already lost, she refused to lose him, too.

She ignored the looks the doctors gave each other when they talked about his prognosis. She chose instead only to hear their optimistic words.

That night he awoke with a fever and was delirious. The doctors assured her this was common and not to worry, but she noticed too that the nurses seemed more vigilant and somber in their efforts to care for him. She tried her best to comfort him during his moments of consciousness, but she saw the fear that lurked behind his eyes—a fear she shared with him.

The next day, the fever broke and he seemed to be out of the woods.

Still, she carried her worries around like a handbag. She couldn't let go of the fear.

***

Despite the doctors being able to get his post-operative infection under control, Alex struggled to get better. When the doctor walked in with the test results they had been waiting on, Katherine's stomach bottomed out.

"I'm sorry, but I have some bad news, Alex." The doctor shifted his gaze between the two of them, finally settling on Alex. "The test results have come back, and it appears as though the infection you had following your surgery did some damage to your heart valve. It has progressed to pericarditis, which is an inflammation of the pericardium. Your heart's mitral and aortic valves have been damaged."

His words became jumbled in her mind as she grew hot with panic. All she heard was the roar of her breaths coming in and out in rapid succession.

Even though his hands fidgeted with the bed sheet, Alex otherwise seemed calm, as if he were discussing car repairs with a mechanic. "How serious is this?"

The doctor cleared his throat. "Alex, your heart is only functioning at twenty-five percent capacity. You're going to need a new heart. The hospital's transplant committee is meeting tonight to discuss putting you on the transplant list. The problem is that you're a smoker. You have to be tobacco free for six months before they will give you a new heart. In the meantime, we're going to do what we can to get you to that time marker. When you're stronger, there are a few procedures to help you meet that goal."

All other sounds in the room were drowned out by the sharp deafening ring in her ears as her blood pressure skyrocketed. She clutched hold of the arm rest on her chair as her field of vision stated to tunnel.

Alex looked at her, grabbed hold of her hand, and squeezed it in reassurance.

She smiled weakly back at him.

***

A week after he had been shot, Alex's heart was still not functioning better than twenty-five percent despite the treatment and course of action the doctors had taken.

The stress of the incident and his poor prognosis had put a strain on Katherine and the pregnancy. After several hours of contractions, she got in to see her OB.

Alex stared up at the ceiling, willing his child to be okay.

"Knock, knock." Chris stood in the doorframe. "Hey, man."

Sheesh, he's looking at me like I'm at death's door. "Come on in, man. I'm not going to bite."

His best friend walked inside and shed his heavy jacket.

"I just got back. I called your cell and your girl told me what happened." Chris sat down and leaned against his knees.

Alex reached for the TV remote. "Want to watch a game with me?"

Chris leaned back in his chair and sighed. "Yeah, man, sure."

The two men sat in near silence, only occasionally commenting on the players or a bad call by the ref. A sense of deep relief washed over Alex for the first time in a while. Aside from the whole hospital business, it was all very familiar and comfortable.

During a commercial break, he flipped to the news.

> *"The grand jury convened this morning on The Syndicate trial. A spokesman for Senator Mitchel reports that he is not guilty of the crimes he is being accused of. Today the jury heard testimony from Section Chief Richards of the FBI. We received word from a representative for the Attorney General's Office that Special Agent Katherine Mitchel's testimony has been rescheduled for January, though no date has been announced."*

Alex grumbled under his breath as he flipped it back to the game. After a few minutes had passed, he finally broke the silence that had settled in between them. "You haven't talked about her."

Chris sighed. "Yeah, well, I'm a little pissed off with her right now. Fuck her. What about you? This heart thing serious?"

Alex shrugged. "Serious as a heart attack."

His friend was not amused. Apparently dying wasn't a joking matter.

Alex shrugged. "I don't know, man. I try not to think about it too much."

"I hear that." After a long pause, Chris cleared his throat. "You should know, I told her about you getting shot, and about your heart. I told her because I wanted to upset her. How fucked up is that?"

After some thought, Alex said, "I'm glad she knows."

His friend gave him a twisted, self-conscious grin. "So I'm not an asshole?"

"Oh, no, you're still an asshole." Alex smiled.

Chris punched him hard in the arm. "Thanks a lot, man."

He twisted his bed sheet. "I wrote her a letter and put it in the mail yesterday, so she would have known anyways. I guess I got mad, too. I don't know."

Chris sighed and pulled a deck of cards out of his pocket. "Up for a game?"

"Absolutely, though if you want to help with the medical bills, you can save yourself the effort and write me a check right now."

Wills Family OB/GYN
Washington, D.C.
December 30, 2008
12:00 PM

The paper covering the exam table stuck to her legs as she shifted her weight. Her taught abdomen contracted again, for the fourth time that hour, and the knock on the exam room door startled her. She was tired, having not slept properly since the shooting.

When her doctor walked in the room, her palms dampened. *Please be good. I can't take any more bad news.*

"Mrs. Estrella," the doctor said as she washed her hands in the basin. "The fetal fibronectin test was positive, which means you are at risk for preterm labor. I'm putting you on medical bedrest."

Katherine let out a nervous huff of air as the panic at this news began to sink in. "Is the baby okay?"

Doctor Wills nodded. "He's fine for right now. Your cervix isn't shortening, but I'm concerned about these contractions you keep experiencing. I'd like for you to be in the hospital for at least a week to get things a little more under control. Sometimes a little rest and fluids can turn things around."

Katherine's heart pounded in her chest, and a faint fluttering erupted inside her belly, like a dozen butterflies flapping their wings against her rib cage. She rubbed her bump to reassure the child within.

Dr. Wills put her hand over Katherine's. "We're going to do everything we can to make sure this little guy stays in as long as possible. Okay?"

Katherine nodded as tears broke loose from the corner of her eyes and landed on the sheet covering her naked legs. "My husband...."

Dr. Wills squeezed her hand. "I called Providence. They've got an excellent Neonatal unit and are expecting you."

Katherine sighed as she wiped away at her tears.

Dr. Wills let go of her hand and reached for the fetal heart rate monitor. "Why don't we take a listen?"

Katherine lay back on the exam table and let the doctor run the monitor over her lower abdomen. The whirring sounds of her insides filled the room, followed by the distinctive thump of her son's heartbeat.

"Strong heartbeat. Good fetal movement."

Katherine sighed a little, letting the sound comfort her.

Chapter 23

Providence Memorial Hospital
Washington, D.C.
January 5, 2009
9:00 AM

Katherine felt the passage of time in a way she never had before. Each moment seemed to expand and contract upon itself.

As her doctors and nurses fought to keep her child inside her womb, two floors below her, the man she loved fought to stay alive. In the span of a week he had started to go downhill, even suffering a minor stroke. The side effects of the stroke were minimal, but the doctors made it clear that he might not be so lucky next time. More tests and more procedures followed—each one more ineffectual than the last.

She prepared herself to lose him.

Her nurses gave her looks of concern, as her medical records showed her history of depression and that she had suicidal ideations. Their pity cut her.

Despite the best efforts of those around her, she slipped back into the darkness. Despair clung to her. Aside from the hour a day her doctor allowed her to visit with Alex, she spent her days and nights on her left side, lying on a rock-hard bed in the labor and delivery ward. The cacophony of laborious women, mixed with newborn wails, dug at her resolve to be strong for Alex and their unborn son. This wasn't the way it was supposed to be.

That morning, as the orderly wheeled her down to his floor, she felt the reassuring fluttering of her son reacting to the pounding of her heart.

Alex turned his head to see her being rolled in, and put on a crooked smile that didn't reach his eyes. They performed a perfunctory dance for each other, as if everything was fine and dandy. She wasn't sure who they were performing for, exactly.

"There's my favorite girl." His words slurred and he reached for her with his left hand—the right one was weak and useless.

"Hey," she said, trying to not cry at the sight of his sagging eye and mouth. She grasped his hand in hers, brought it first to her lips and then to her belly.

His thumb rubbed her bump. "Hey there, little Bailey."

"He's very active this morning. I swear he knows when it's time to see you."

He looked away from her.

Alex's doctor knocked on the open door and came inside. "How are you feeling this morning, Mr. Estrella?"

Alex cleared his throat and swallowed hard, his Adam's apple bobbing up and down. "I'm okay."

His false bravado made her angry.

"The nurse tells me that your fever is gone. If we can keep it that way, we're going to go through with the surgery tomorrow morning."

Alex nodded and squeezed Katherine's hand. "Sounds good, Doctor."

"And how is little Junior doing?" the doctor asked Katherine.

"He's doing great. I should be released to go home tomorrow."

I hope!

Alex smiled weakly as he rubbed small circles on her knuckles with his thumb.

"Well," the doctor said. "I'll leave you folks to your visit. Alex, I hope to see you on my OR board tomorrow."

"I'll do my best," Alex said.

The doctor walked out of the room, leaving them alone again.

He turned his head to face her. "Katherine, if I don't pull through—"

She covered his mouth with her hand. "Don't."

He clasped her hand in his and kissed it. His eyes slid closed and he took a deep shaky breath. "Please, I need to talk about this."

He squeezed her trembling hand. "I love you, Katherine. I don't want to leave you, and I'm going to do everything I can to stay with you as long as humanly possible, but if I can't, I need you to know how much you mean to me. Also... I want you find happiness without me."

Katherine choked and sputtered as tears rushed down her cheeks. "Alex..."

He took two shaky breaths, and his heart monitor beeped as his blood pressure and heart rate began to climb. "I wrote him a letter."

She looked away from him as the tears slid down her cheek. *This is too much.* "He won't need one. You're not going anywhere."

Alex nodded and pulled her in to an embrace that simultaneously comforted her and broke her heart.

Will this be the last time?

Everything between them was punctuated with that thought—the last kiss and 'I love you.' She knew from the look in Alex's eyes that the same thought plagued him.

***

Later that night, Katherine awoke with a start and sat up in bed, her heart racing and sweat dripping down her face.

A nurse rushed into the room. "Mrs. Estrella, are you okay?"

"Bad dream," she said, gasping for breath. "I need to see him. I know it would break the rules, but I need to see him."

The nurse's face fell. "Ma'am, I don't think that's a good idea."

"I need to see him!"

The women sighed. "All right, but it will have to be quick, really quick."

As the nurse wheeled her down the half-darkened halls, the quiet of the place struck a chord in her. The muffled wails of newborns were replaced by the wrenching sobs of mourning families. The cardiac unit was the quietest. The whir and blips of the machines in the partially darkened rooms seemed so ominous and sad to her.

Alex was asleep. The rise and fall of his chest brought her more comfort than she would care to admit.

The nurse kneeled down to look her in the eye, and whispered, "It was just a dream. He's very much alive."

Katherine put her hands on the chair wheels and scooted into the room. She watched his hand twitch involuntarily, his forehead smoothed out by sleep. He looked so peaceful. If not for the rise and fall of his chest, she imagined that this is what he would look like dead. She reached out to touch his hand, startling him awake.

"Huh!" When he rolled over and saw her, he smiled in confusion. "Katherine?"

"I had a bad dream," she said.

He reached a hand out for her.

She went to him and fell into his comforting embrace. "Tell me again."

He kissed the top of her head. "I love you, Katherine."

She nestled against him. "I love you too, Alex."

"I know," he said, his voice cracking.

"I don't want to lose you." She lifted her head off his chest and kissed his tear-stained lips.

He cupped the back of her head in his hand as he deepened the kiss. When he pulled back, he slid his hand down to her bump and said, "I love you both so much."

The nurse, who had been waiting patiently, cleared her throat.

Katherine and Alex exchanged smiles, and he winked. "Uh-oh, we're in trouble."

"See? I told you that you were trouble," she said.

"Only the best kind," he said, reminding her.

She bent over and kissed him one last time, making his heart monitor blip. "Go back to sleep. I'll see you in the morning."

He lay back down with a ghost of a smile on his lips.

***

"Here are the clothes you asked for." Betty handed Katherine a duffle bag.

"Thanks, Betty." She took the bag and went into the bathroom to get dressed.

The pants were snug but she was able to hide the opened top button with her long FBI academy sweatshirt. Through the bathroom door she heard Betty humming to herself.

"When is the surgery?" Betty asked.

Katherine opened the door and stepped out. "In an hour."

The nurse came in with the discharge paperwork and a wheelchair to take her to the cardiac wing.

Once she had finished up the paperwork, she and Betty went straight to Alex's room.

He was sitting up in bed fidgeting as usual. The news was on.

> *"Later this month, Katherine Mitchel and her ex-husband, Charles MacAvoy, will take the stand. It is currently unknown what kind of deal he struck with the prosecution. A representative with the Attorney General's Office stated earlier today that he is being held under house arrest in an undisclosed safe house. We also received word that the prosecution has a surprise witness scheduled for the end of January. Back to you, Tom."*

When Alex saw Katherine and Betty, he shut off the TV and smiled at her. "Did I have a really awesome dream last night or did you really sneak down here?"

Katherine sat down on the edge of the bed and kissed him.

He slipped his hand underneath her shirt and cupped her belly, and when she pulled away, his green eyes twinkled.

A nurse cleared her throat as she entered the room. "We're gonna take you a little early, Mr. Estrella. The OR time got bumped in your favor. The sooner we get you in, the sooner you can get back to kissing that wife of yours." She winked and gave him a shot through his IV port. "This will make you feel all kinds of good."

Alex laughed and squeezed Katherine's hand. "Nothing can make me feel as good as my wife does."

"Ooh... listen to you. Hang on to this one, honey." The nurse tapped Katherine's shoulder.

"I'm trying to."

"All right, shug, I'll be back in fifteen minutes."

Alex smiled up at Katherine and kissed her hand. He didn't seem to have heard a word the nurse said. "Just lie here with me until they come back, okay?"

Betty walked over and kissed Alex on the cheek. "I'm going to go raid the snack machines. I'll be in the waiting room, Kat, honey."

"Alone at last," she whispered.

Alex's hands slipped underneath her shirt and his mouth sought hers out. "God, you feel good."

She broke their kiss and met his eyes, which were looking sleepy. "Close your eyes."

He nestled back down onto the bed and closed his eyes, and she ran her fingers through his thick wavy hair, making him sigh. "I love you," he said.

When the nurse and orderly walked in a few minutes later to get him, he had already fallen asleep. She kissed him one last time and got up from the bed.

***

The small waiting room made her feel claustrophobic. Much to her credit, Betty tried everything to distract her, but Katherine only half listened as her new friend planned out a baby shower.

Minutes turned into hours, and the conversation lulled.

Katherine dozed off in the reclining chairs. She awoke at one point to Betty knitting booties for the baby.

Four hours into the surgery, she awoke again when Betty asked the nurses' station for an update. No new information.

Two hours later, the double doors opened and Alex's doctor stepped out into the waiting room.

Katherine stood up with her hand on her belly. When she saw the look on his face, her breath caught in her throat.

"Mrs. Estrella, I'm sorry. We did everything we could. His heart just wasn't strong enough."

Her knees gave out, but Betty was there to catch her and hold her up. Katherine felt numb. She had no tears left to cry. All she could think about was that last kiss and 'I love you.'

Holy Cross Hospital, Psychiatric Ward
Just outside Richmond, Virginia
January 6, 2009
Noon

Doc sat at the window in the recreation room, looking out at the grounds through the mesh metal grating that covered the window. It was one of those rare, quiet afternoons in the hospital psych ward. One of the orderlies was going around delivering mail, and she was surprised when he handed her an envelope covered in a familiar small print scrawl.

Alex wrote me a letter?

She wanted to toss it aside, like she had all the other ploys by family and friends to be let in, but this was Alex. Somehow that made it all different.

She took the letter, sat in the chair by the window, and carefully opened the envelope.

> *Dear Doc,*
>
> *I was thinking about that ugly box you had in Iraq, the one with the peeling yellow flowers, the one you kept all your letters from home in. You were always a sucker for*

handwritten notes, so I thought I might reach you through this letter. I need your help.

I need to tell you about my best friend, Elliana. She tried to take her own life, and when she failed in her attempt, she wrote me and everyone else who loved her out of her life. I'm so angry with her, Doc.

I'm not angry at her for that, though, because I know what it feels like when that seems like the only way out. I'm angry for what she did afterwards. She didn't trust me to be the kind of friend she had always been to me.

Did you hear that I was shot? Yes, again! This time it nicked my heart. I've had several procedures but my heart doesn't seem to be up for the fight. I want to live, Doc. I want to make things right with Elliana before it's too late.

What do I do, Doc? How do I reach her? How do I let her know how much I love her and miss her? How do I tell her that I want her to know my wife, and to be a part of this new life with me? I know that maybe this is selfish, but I don't want her to miss another moment.

And I don't want to miss another moment of her life. I want to show her that I can be the rock she has always been to me.

But I worry that I may not have all the time I need for that.

Call me, if you can. Let me know what you think. Or you can call to yell at me. Just call me, please.

Love always,

Alex

Doc wiped away the tears that had begun to fall down her cheeks. With great care, she folded the letter back up, opened her closet, pulled out the battered flower box, and put the letter inside.

She took a deep breath and walked back into the commons area to the payphone. *Only a place like this would have a payphone.*

The quarters slid inside the slot with a clink, and a dial tone rang in her ear while she dialed a number that she would know by heart for the rest of her life. Her heart raced as she listened to each ring, and it sank as the call went to voicemail. She left him a message, a long one that would fill up his mailbox memory space.

His letter had made her think that maybe it was time she checked herself out. She made a plan to talk to her therapist about it on Monday, and to tell Christopher when he came on Tuesday.

Alex's letter had changed something inside of her. Suddenly a switch had been flipped and she began to see the shards of hope shining through the cracks—the few spots where she wasn't quite broken. She remembered what he said when he had tried to take his life, so long ago, and she took comfort in those words now.

***

After talking it over with her therapist, she realized that she needed to leave Christopher if she wanted to get better. Being around him was too hard for her. As part of her discharge, she agreed to a strict outpatient treatment plan that included medication, extensive individual therapy, and support groups.

That Tuesday afternoon, she waited for Christopher's visit with anticipation, excited to tell him that she was ready to leave the hospital. But the moment he walked into the common room, she knew... and the excitement fell away.

His puffy red eyes, and the distant way he looked at her, sent a chill down her spine. His crisp gray suit was the one she'd bought him for his great aunt's funeral. His mouth moved, but it was as if someone had turned the sound off.

The only thing she heard was a deafening ringing in her ears.

He's gone.

He wouldn't be returning her phone call this time. Her best friend in the whole world was gone and she hadn't even gotten to say goodbye. Her pride and anger with him had ended up robbing her of sharing his last moments on Earth with him.

As the realization sank in, she collapsed, blacking out.

Charles MacAvoy's Estate
Danville Virginia
February 9, 2009
4:00 PM

Charles entered his home, and would-be prison for the next twenty years, with no small amount of apprehension. Though he had only been in jail a short time, he had already started to hear some buzz that The Syndicate was trying to get things up and running again. They were looking for new management.

From behind him came the sound of heels clicking on the steel gray tile of his entryway. His very hot and very capable lawyer, Penelope Eakins, Esq., stepped into his line of vision, and his heart started to race.

"I have all the paperwork on the short sale. The house is officially yours. Congratulations." She handed him the paperwork. "I also have the paperwork back from the security detail you had put on your ex-wife." She handed him another envelope.

"How is she?"

"Not well." Her plump red lips formed a thin line.

"Is there anything more I can do?"

Penelope shook her head. "No, she needs time, something you can't really give her. The FBI will push for her to get some counseling, but really it will just take time."

"Any news on Scott?"

Penelope crossed her arms over her ample chest. "Yes, there was a fight at the prison this morning that resulted in one of the kingpins being stabbed with a shiv. No one can prove it, of course, but word is that Scott Mitchel was behind it."

Charles' stomach flip-flopped as he turned on the four o'clock news.

"Channel 12 News, The News Channel You Can Trust!

"Good evening everyone. Our top story of the night sounds a bit like a daytime soap opera. Today the prosecution

revealed the identity of their secret witness in The Syndicate trial. The witness is none other than Officer Tom Mitchel, father of Senator Mitchel and Special Agent Katherine Mitchel, who was thought to have died in a car bomb explosion several years ago. The prosecution would not comment about Officer Mitchel's testimony or his supposed return from the dead.

"Katherine Mitchel, whose husband, Special Agent Alexander Bailey, died as a result of a gunshot wound on the courtroom steps, was exempt from giving her testimony due to an undisclosed medical problem. Her deposition, which was given over the summer, was used in court this morning. Her testimony corroborated that of Charles MacAvoy."

Charles turned off the TV and turned to his lawyer. "Are you staying tonight?"

She carefully toed off her expensive shoes. "Yes."

He nonchalantly tossed the paperwork on the bare floor, and kissed her.

Alex and Katherine's Apartment
Alexandria, Virginia
March 28, 2009
7:00 AM

Katherine sat at her kitchen table with her cup of English breakfast tea and the day's paper. The early morning sun shone through the shear curtains in the kitchen, and the weight of her grief didn't seem as heavy that day. She had gotten dressed and combed her hair—an improvement over recent times.

Betty and Jason would be pleased. They had been tag-teaming her all winter to make sure she was okay.

She had Skyped a few times with the psychiatrist she'd spoken with over the summer, but mostly the passage of time alone had slowly begun to eat away the tethers of her grief. She knew Alex would want her to be strong and move on—for the sake of the baby.

She opened up the paper and read the front page headlines, all about The Syndicate. The detailed articles almost glorified the defendants, who had all received guilty verdicts. The author of one article speculated that her brother and some of the other high-level members of the group could each face up to ten years of prison time. Her brother's sentence would be added to the two years he got for shooting Jason and Lisa. Her sister-in-law was still awaiting trial for shooting Alex—*that* would now be a murder rap.

Katherine still received death threats but was well-guarded at all times. Charles, whose business had been doing well, hired a state-of-the-art security team to install a high-tech security system. She chafed at his continued involvement in her life. Of everyone involved, he seemed to be the only one who came out on top, and she hated him for it.

She stretched out on the couch—too tired to do anything else—and fell into a deep sleep with her hand cradling her seven-month bump.

She awoke with a start when a contraction gripped her like a vise. She clutched her belly and sucked in a breath. "Oh, Jesus, no."

The guards posted outside her door rushed in at the sound of her cry. One of the men picked her up and carried her down to the car while another called Betty.

When they arrived at the hospital, her contractions were gripping every five minutes. They gave her medicine to help the baby's lungs.

Once she had been admitted, they hooked her up to the contraction and fetal heart rate monitors—they were piggy-backing one on top of the other.

When Betty arrived, Katherine had entered into transition labor. "I'm here, love." Betty rubbed Katherine's back.

Tears streamed down Katherine's cheeks. "It's too early, Betty."

The older woman continued to rub her back and remind her to breathe.

Thirty minutes later, Katherine felt the hard pull to push. Her room was a flurry of activity, which acted as background noise to the clamber of worries and concern racing through her mind.

One hour later, Bailey came into the world at 2 pounds, 15 ounces. Katherine cried for the both of them.

Danville Press
Danville, Virginia
June 7, 2009
1:00 PM

Jason unbuttoned his suit coat as he stalked into his office with a huff. The door bounced against the frame as he slammed it shut.

Scotch!

He yanked open his desk drawer, pulled out a bottle, threw the lid across the floor, and drank straight from the bottle.

No one should ever have to bury a child. No one!

Through the whole service, all the way up until they lowered the baby into the ground beside his father, Katherine had been a pillar of strength. Then the gears had ticked off each inch of ground as the casket was lowered, and she began to cry.

She didn't wail or wretch at her clothes or throw herself onto the tiny casket. No, she stood there with silent tears sliding down her reddened cheeks. It was almost worse that way.

He took long gulps of the burning scotch and felt his own tears start to fall.

The door to his office swung open with a flourish, and Lisa and Marianna walked in arm-in-arm with another bottle of scotch and three solo cups. "We thought we'd join you."

Jason sighed as the two women made themselves at home. They had been doing that a lot lately. While he was touched by their concern, he really did want to be alone.

Lisa gave him a knowing smile. "You're not getting rid of us Knettle, so ya might as well get comfortable."

"Being my mother hen isn't in your job description."

"Sure it is. It's part of that *Other Duties* line item."

Jason chuffed out a laugh. "Oh, is that what that means. I thought it meant I could make you scrub toilets and shit like that."

Lisa tossed a cup at Jason, hitting him square in the head. "Let's get drunk, Boss."

He couldn't argue with that.

FBI Headquarters: Hoover Building
Washington, D.C.
June 7, 2009
10:00 AM

Ellie had been besotted with grief the night she tried to take her life. It was her last-ditch effort to escape her perceived failure to bring a child into the world. She could find no hope in a world where her children could not live beside her.

Christopher had wanted them to work it out together, but she wanted nothing to do with him. Every time she saw him, she saw her boys—boys who'd never taken a breath outside her body, who would never nurse from her breast, crawl on the wood floors of their home, learn to ride a bike, go to school, marry, or have children of their own. The vast void of their unrealized possibilities suffocated her.

She left the hospital, Chris moved out, she returned to work and began to live a life that somewhat resembled the one she had lived before. At the most random times, memories of Alex would haunt her. In the valley of her grief, she hadn't seen that dawn was beginning to break, and that Katherine's friendship could be the catalyst she needed to turn her life around.

She had heard the rumors around the Bureau when Katherine's son was born too early. She had even pitched in when a collection envelope was passed around.

A few weeks later, when Katherine's file fell on her desk and she read the mandatory counseling form her superior had filled out, her heart shattered. Though she knew it was wrong, she made room in her schedule to take her on as a client.

Chapter 24

US DEPARTMENT OF JUSTICE
Federal Bureau of Investigation
Dr. Elliana Forester
FBI Employee Assistance Program
Therapy Notes

June 27, 2009
First session notes: Katherine E.

Katherine E. presents as a 35-year-old Caucasian female, recently widowed, who has worked for the FBI for 12 years and was an integral part of a large 30-year+ investigation of a crime ring. Katherine E.'s chief complaint is stated as anxiety and depression after the recent loss of her infant son. The infant died as a result of Respiratory Distress Syndrome. She doesn't give a name for the infant, but instead refers to him as "my son." She has been having trouble sleeping, and when she does sleep has violent nightmares regarding her involvement in the recently concluded investigation.

She says: "I see red. Blood. Red blood. It's everywhere, and I can't find the baby."

She states that she had been asked by her superiors, out of concern for her well-being, to take advantage of the FBI's EAP. Her progress in our sessions will dictate whether or not she is allowed to work in the field.

She is resistant, stating that, "I don't see how being here is going to make anything better. Not that I don't think you're good at your job."

Katherine E. stated that she has suffered from insomnia and depression on and off. She is a recovering alcoholic and proudly stated that she has been sober for 12 years. Her father had been murdered on the job in a car bombing, but was recently found to be very much alive. She currently doesn't have any relationship with her mother, who has been in and out of institutions for most of her adult life. Her sister was murdered and her twin brother is currently in prison.

Katherine E. stated that she has always been able to do her job regardless of what stress she had in her personal and professional life. She does not mention anything about her recently deceased husband.

Katherine E. is not oriented to person, appearing instead to be oriented to place and time. Her thinking is clear but not always linear. Her memory does not appear adequate. Affect is guarded, and sometimes it appeared she was fighting back tears when talking about her infant son.

Supported client in positive coping skills. Will be using a mixture of dialectic behavioral therapy (DBT) and cognitive behavioral therapy (CBT).

Possibly suicidal. Will see client two times a week to increase coping skills and create a positive support system.

Ellie finished typing the last of the report for Katherine's file and heaved a great sigh. She should assign Katherine to a different therapist, as there were so many things wrong about having Katherine as a client, she couldn't even begin to count them. Yet no matter how wrong it was, she just couldn't turn her away.

For one hour, she was Doc again... and that meant everything to her.

Church Hill Neighborhood
Richmond, Virginia
May 3, 2011
11:00 PM

"Let me help you with that." Katherine took the empty beer bottles and placed them in the recycle bin.

Ellie turned off the TV and followed her into the kitchen. "Where do you think Jason went off to? Think he's seeing someone?"

Katherine put their dishes in the sink. "I don't know. Has he said anything to you?"

Ellie shook her head and bit her bottom lip. They were both avoiding discussing the things truly on their minds, avoidance was a coping mechanism they shared.

"What about you?" Ellie picked stray popcorn bits up off her shirt. "Have you and Ben gone out again?"

Katherine washed the last bowl and put it in the drying rack, and paused.

Ellie saw her cheeks turn pink; Ben was the first guy Katherine had seen more than once. "Yeah, we're going out tomorrow night."

Ellie smiled. "Good. I like him. He seems like a nice guy."

"He is. When does the moving truck come tomorrow?"

"Noon." Ellie looked down at the kitchen floor. It was dirty.

"What's wrong?" Katherine asked.

"All the memories I've had in this kitchen. I need to get out of here and start fresh—for my own sanity—but leaving is a lot harder than I thought it would be."

"Well, Jason and I will keep it in tiptop shape, so if you ever want to move back, the place will be yours. Maybe with roommates, but yours all the same."

Ellie laughed. It was a comfort to her that Katherine and Jason would be living in the house while she was in Texas. For the last six months, they had all lived together, a motley crew, but it had been far and away one of the happiest times of her life.

Katherine wiped her hands with the dishtowel. "You're not packing the new TV-VCR thing you just got?"

Ellie bit her lip and answered. "No, I don't need it anymore."

Katherine's nose scrunched up in the way that it always did when something didn't make sense to her.

Ellie sighed and sank into one of the kitchen chairs.

"What?" Katherine pulled out a chair and sat across from her.

Just like Alex used to.

"It's silly, really. I was going through all my old stuff and deciding what to toss, what to sell, and what I wanted to keep. One of the boxes in the back of the attic had old videos, like of my med school graduation. One of them was from when Chris and I were in Iraq, when I was pregnant the first time—the year I met Alex. Chris had been over the moon about the baby and filmed us constantly."

Katherine looked down at her hands clasped on top of the wooden table. "Oh...."

Ellie exhaled a trembling breath. "I had forgotten what his voice sounded like. I guess I just needed to hear him call me Doc... one more time."

Katherine buried her face in her hands.

Ellie sniffed as she got up from her chair and walked around to sit beside Katherine. She wrapped her arms around her friend. "I'm sorry."

Katherine looked up at her with red-rimmed eyes. "Don't be sorry, Ellie. I'm just jealous of all the time you got to spend with him. I sometimes feel foolish because we weren't even together a year. I wonder if he had lived if we could have made it work, or if how I felt about him would have lessened over time. Is that weird?"

Ellie looped her arm with Katherine's and buttressed her head up against her friend. "No, honey, that's not weird at all."

Katherine leaned into her and sighed. "I am happy, Ellie, even though I didn't think I ever would be. But... I get the feeling that *you* aren't."

Ellie swiped the tears from her cheeks and chuckled. "Whatever gives you that idea?"

Katherine laughed a little and snuggled in closer. "I love you, Ellie, and I want you to be happy. I'm not thrilled that you're moving a thousand miles away, but I do understand the need to get away."

Ellie's heart leaped in her chest. "I love you, Katherine, and I'm going to miss you, too. I don't know what I would do without you."

Katherine smiled her sweet Pollyanna-esque smile that always warmed Ellie's heart. "You would get on just fine without me. You're a lot stronger than you give yourself credit for."

Ellie almost believed her.

Mary Martha Chapel
Richmond, Virginia
June 20, 2015
3:00 PM

Katherine stood in front of a full-length mirror to check her makeup and make adjustments to her small veil. The cream-colored wraparound dress showed off her athletic form. Even at forty, she had still managed to look fit—something she was proud of. A floating pearl necklace adorned her pale neck, and she had to force herself to keep from touching it.

As she was applying her lipstick, her best friend, a vision in pale yellow, filled the background of the mirror. The lipstick shook in her trembling hand, giving away her true feelings.

"You look beautiful, but if you keep shaking like that you're going to look like the Joker," Ellie said with a twinkle in her eye.

Katherine caught Ellie's gaze in the reflection of the mirror, and her own eyes started to pool. She turned to face her friend and they embraced. "Tell me I'm doing the right thing, Ellie."

"Oh, Katherine, love, I wish that I could, but only you can know that." Ellie squeezed her tight.

As they pulled out of the embrace, Ellie reached in Katherine's bag for a tissue, but found instead a handkerchief with the initials A.B. After a short pause, she handed it to her friend.

Katherine looked down at the scrap of cloth, which had seen better days. "My something old and borrowed." She took the fabric and blotted away the tears that threatened to put her carefully put together face to ruin. "Betty hand-stitched them for him, you know?"

She smiled at the memories they invoked. "He gave me this one the night we met. We were standing outside a bar after a run-in with Charles, and I burst into tears. I was so embarrassed!" Her thumb traced the careful stitching. "He told me to just hold onto it, and I never gave it back to him. I used to carry it with me everywhere. I even had it...." She swallowed hard before continuing. "I had it with me the day he died."

"Katherine, do you love Ben? Love him enough?"

She nodded. "Yes, I think so. I have to stop comparing everything to what I had with Alex. I know that. Ben is a good man."

Ellie shrugged. "Then I guess you have your answer."

Katherine sniffed as she clutched the kerchief to her chest. "Yeah, I guess I do."

"We should probably fix up your makeup then. Shall we?" Ellie's lips curled into a sad half-moon smile that never made it to her eyes.

Katherine gave her friend a quick hug. "Thank you."

"All right, enough with the waterworks. Let's get down to business."

Katherine took out her makeup. She had a wedding to go to—her third. *Maybe this time it will stick. After all, the third time's a charm.*

Chapter 25

Unknown Building
Unknown Location
October 11, 2024
6:00 PM

A lull had fallen on those born under The Syndicate, and for the men and women who had brought them to justice. They had all moved on—buried their loved ones, moved away, married, and did all the things people do as they live out their ordinary existence.

While the others had been pacified by the ordinary world, one man had been waiting and plotting for the next chapter. It was all about to begin, and no one knew it was coming.

He had worked all through the night, planning and setting everything in motion. Being in charge wouldn't be easy, but at least this time things would be done right. As he signed the final release form and messaged it to the Litchfield Psychiatric Facility, a sharp thrill ran down his spine—the intoxication of power.

In just a few hours, he would have at his disposal a most terrifying creature—a creature whose black soulless eyes would leave even Charles Manson quaking in fear.

"Billy," he said, calling out his lowliest but most loyal man.

"Yes, Boss?"

"I've sent in the release paperwork. He'll be eager to get back to work, and I have lots of work to keep him happy." He handed the other man the paperwork.

Billy held them between his shaking hands. "Y-yes, Boss."

"Good. Just be sure and keep him on the list. Oh, and Billy... don't fuck this up."

***

Later that night as Bill lay sleeping under the influence of a powerful sedative, Sally went to work. She couldn't believe her luck. Her stupid husband had been given the high distinction of being the new boss man's pet.

Every night, while he slept off the drugs she'd slipped into his dinner, she copied the papers he was supposed to be delivering to the high-level operatives. They had resorted to an old-fashioned paper trail because digital fingerprints were so much harder to clean up.

She had to give it to the new boss: they shared that mistrust of technology.

She stored copies of all the documents in a secure facility outside of town. She just had to sit and bide her time. It was about to start all over again, except maybe this time they would be stopped once and for all.

Hollywood Cemetery
Richmond, Virginia
October 19, 2024
3:00 PM

Katherine tucked her graying hair behind her ear as she walked down the winding path to the gravesites of her previous husband and infant son, whom she'd lost so long ago. She sat between the two graves and pulled out a joint. She lit it, took a hit, and settled in. After twenty-six years of sobriety, cancer had finally knocked her off the wagon; the marijuana helped temper the pervasive nausea that was part and parcel of her cancer.

She gathered her wool sweater around her rail-thin body, one of Doc's that she had stolen years ago. Her sunken eyes and the fine lines that etched her mouth gave away not only her age, but the hard life she had lived—battle scars, she called them.

"Alex...." Just saying his name brought tears to her eyes.

God, I'm stoned.

"I'm sorry I haven't been here to visit with you and Bailey." She took another short puff. "I just couldn't bring myself to come here. It was too hard. When I lost you and Bailey, all I wanted to do was die, just so I could get back to you both."

She took out one of his old handkerchiefs and wiped away the tears. "I got remarried, and he's a good man, but he isn't you. Everyone kept pushing me to date, to find someone." The memory of that time seemed so long ago now. "So I did. I was lonely. I needed someone to pass the time with. It was hard at first, like I was being unfaithful to you. Ellie...."

She paused to correct herself. "Doc kept telling me that you wouldn't want me to pine away for you until the day I died. She and I have grown very close over the years. I don't think I could have made it those first few years without her. You always said she and Chris were your only friends, and I can see why. This may surprise you, but she and Chris divorced awhile back. She's remarried and living in Texas, but she comes to D.C. once a year and stays with me. She just flew home yesterday. I didn't tell her about the cancer, though she mentioned how thin I was getting. It was exhausting trying to hide it from her, but I just couldn't tell her."

Katherine tightened the sweater around her as the cool breeze sent a chill down her back. "She would worry and fuss. You know how she can get. I need to process it first. I know she's going to be pissed at me, though."

She took another long drag. "The cancer's spread faster than they had thought it would, and there's nothing more they can do. I have another three to six months, if I'm lucky. They said to put my affairs in order. So I need you and Bailey to get ready for me, because I'm finally going to come home to you."

She stood and reached for a bright red branch from the bald cypress, broke it off, and placed it on Alex's grave. "See you soon."

Her heart felt lighter. She wasn't sure if it was because she had gotten all of it off her chest, or because she was stoned. Either way, she felt freer than she had in years.

Soon it will be my new beginning, my new chapter.

Church Hill
Richmond, Virginia
June 12, 2025
8:00 PM

Jason sat in the dark with a bottle of scotch beside him as he flipped through the digital newspaper he was proud to call his own. It had been a trying week for him, and he needed to forget, so he drank until he couldn't feel anymore. She was dying—his best friend, the woman he loved.

Two weeks ago they had fought over whether or not he should be there at the end. She had wanted to say her goodbyes before things got bad.

The liquor burned his raw throat as he pulled up an online forum discussing the true crime novel he was working on. That was the other thing they had fought about.

She'd said no good would come of digging up the past, insisting that he'd be poking a bear that for all intents and purposes was asleep. In the end, she agreed to allow him to write the story, but cautioned him once more to find another project.

It was risky, sure, but he felt compelled to get the truth out. So many false reports had dominated the media for years. John Q. Public had no idea the extent of the crimes that The Syndicate had unleashed upon the communities and people around them. They didn't know the personal cost that everyone involved had paid.

The fallout from that year was still being felt seventeen years later.

He wanted to honor those who had gone up against the beast with all they had. Most of the news stories practically glorified The Syndicate, and he was tired of it.

As he drank the last of the scotch and felt the hard pull of darkness that came with his blackouts, his smart watch's message notification set him off like a tuning fork.

It was over. She was gone.

He felt the ending and the new beginning unfolding at once. The story wasn't over; it had just begun.

Epilogue

Church Hill
Richmond, Virginia
June 15, 2025
5:00 PM

I reach into my handbag and pull out the folded paper that Katherine's husband had handed me earlier at the funeral—her last letter. It shakes in my trembling hands.

Once I read it, it will really be over, and that thought alone paralyzes me. I hand the letter to Chris. "Will you read it? I just can't."

He nods in understanding, unfolds the letter, and begins to read it in his calm, baritone voice.

> *Dear Ellie,*
>
> *This is the hardest thing I have ever written, because I know that you won't be reading it until I have passed on. It's a lot of pressure to come up with the right last words for your best friend.*
>
> *Are you mad at me for not telling you about the cancer sooner? I'm sorry if I hurt you. That's the last thing I wanted to do. Maybe I should've told you when you were here last, but I selfishly wanted to enjoy our final visit together. If I had told you, you would have had me laid up in bed the whole two weeks and started researching alternative treatments or planning a fundraiser to pay my medical bills. These are all things that I love deeply about you, by the way.*

I cherish the time we've had together. Those six months we spent as roommates were some of the most carefree, fun experiences of my life. Leaving you is the hardest part of all this. I know it may sound off, but I'm ready to go. I want to see my son again. I want to see Alex. I want to tell your babies about how wonderful their mother is and how much I miss her, even in heaven. And I will miss you.

I ask that you might keep an eye on my dad and Betty. Ever since Brian died, I've worried about Betty. Her health has not been good, but she will most certainly tell you differently. So don't believe her for a second.

I've given permission to Jason to write about all this, so if you want yourself to come off well, you might want to talk to him. I'd say to keep an eye on him too, but he doesn't care to be minded these days. The consummate bachelor seems quite happy to stay that way. He is hell-bent on being the quintessential Hemingway in the woods, like his grandfather. He forgets that his grandfather had love once – a wife, a family. I blame myself a little for this.

I want you to find love again, too. Live your life! Life is short. Happiness is fleeting. Enjoy each lovely moment as it happens. Find the joy that is out there and share it. But above all, find love.

Love always,
Katherine

Chris folds it back up, looks at my tear-filled eyes, and hands it back to me.

I put it back in my purse.

He shifts in his position on the step and nods. "I remember." He pauses as if weighing his next words. "I think I know what she meant to you, and how she helped you... helped you when I couldn't."

My breath catches as I bring his hand up to my muted lips. A single unbidden tear slides down my cheek and onto our clasped hands, which are now baptized in our joint tears. He pulls me in closer still. Our heads nestle together in a familiar way that makes me think of home. A small imperceptible turn and the space between us ignites, and we join in a tender and familiar kiss.

When he breaks from the kiss, his thoughtful and loving gaze penetrates through me in the way it always did. In his eyes are the remnants of all the hurt.

The burden of that regret has been sitting in my back pocket all through the years. I have often wondered if I would ever get a chance to tell him I'm sorry, to tell him it was a mistake to leave.

Now here he is, sitting beside me, and I've said nothing. So of course, I blurt it out in an awkward jumble. "I'm sorry."

His gaze lowers to our clasped hands, and finds the scar on my left wrist with his thumb—evidence of our old wounds. He pulls my wrist up to his chest and presses it against his beating heart. "Please don't be sorry."

His forgiving words lift an age-old burden from me. A deep sigh escapes my lips and I begin to relax.

His fingers work over mine, paying close attention to the bare ring finger.

I wait for the inevitable questions, the thought bubbles that float around us begging to be spoken.

He clears his throat. "I heard... I heard that you got married and ah... were living out west. That you had a couple of boys." The last few words come out strained and laced with hurt from a shared wound.

"I'm in the middle of a divorce, and the kids are his from his first marriage. It turns out I make a horrible stay-at-home army wife. His kids hate me and—"

He cuts off my anxious words with his eager mouth, and the kiss deepens, leaving me breathless. He reaches up and cups the side of my face in his soft, warm hand, pulling me in, leaving me wanting more.

It was always this way. From the moment I first met him at basic training, there were serious sparks. It didn't take us long to become an item, engaged and married. Even near the end of our marriage, when everything was falling apart, we were drawn to each other. It was part of the reason I left for Texas in the first place. The passion never died out, even in the face of hurt and blame.

The passing years have tempered the hurt, but the love and passion remain in full force. I feel like Alice. It would be so easy to plunge down into this familiar yet unknown rabbit hole.

My muddled mind gives up trying to figure it all out as he deepens the kiss and pulls my compliant body closer to his.

The sound of the doors opening behind us startle us out of our embrace, and our cheeks color in embarrassment as we stand up like two teenagers caught making out in the basement. He holds my hand in a firm grip, as if afraid he'll lose me in the crowd of mourners filing out of the building and past us.

They're so lost in their own grief that they don't even seem to notice us. We step aside to allow several groups to pass us. Katherine's pallbearers carry her casket out the heavy wooden doors and down the steps to the hearse parked out front.

"Goodbye...."

As the hearse pulls away, Christopher pulls my body against his and brushes an errant hair behind my ear, something he always did that is both familiar and foreign to me now.

Shyness creeps across his usually confident features. "Want to go and grab a bite to eat or something?"

This chance—a gift, an answered prayer—leaves me feeling much like the young girl I used to be, full of hope and promise. "Yes, I think that would be lovely."

These past seventeen years we both grieved over the lives we didn't live. We can let it go now. We can start again. Maybe this time we can make it right.

THE END

ACKNOWLEDGEMENTS

I am full of gratitude to everyone who supported me in this effort: family, friends and readers. I would like to give a special shout out to my beta readers Jessica Dominguez and Jennifer Arsaga, who have gone above and beyond in their support. I have an amazing team of fact checkers but I would like to give special thanks to Rayne Soza, who puts up with my often times bizarre medical questions. I'd also like to thank Melinda McIntosh, my diehard cheerleader, who keeps me going when the going gets tough. Last but not least I am grateful for the friendship and support of two amazing writers, Cassidy Cayman and Melissa Storm, who have helped me turn a love of writing into a blossoming career.

ABOUT THE AUTHOR

USA Today Bestselling Author, K.M. Hodge grew up in Detroit, where she spent most of her free time weaving wild tales to spook her friends and family. These days, she lives in Texas with her husband and two energetic boys, and once again enjoys writing tales of suspense and intrigue that keep her readers up all night. Her stories, which focus on women's issues, friendship, addiction, regrets and second chances, will stay with you long after you finish them.

When she isn't writing or being an agent of social change, she reads Independent graphic novels, watches old X-files episodes, streams Detroit Tigers games and binges on Netflix with her husband.

Sign-up for her mailing list to receive a free gift:
www.KMHodge.com/Subscribe

She enjoys hearing from her readers, so don't be shy about dropping her a line, or just following her, at any of these links:

Website: www.KMHodge.com
Goodreads: K.M. Hodge
Amazon: www.amazon.com/K.M.-Hodge/e/B00V1P18HW/
BookBub: www.bookbub.com/authors/k-m-hodge
Facebook: @KMHodgeAuthor
Pinterest: https://www.pinterest.com/kmhodge0635/
Twitter: @KMHodgeAuthor
LinkedIn: www.linkedin.com/in/kelly-manfredini-4094b

MORE FROM K.M. HODGE

Don't miss the entire "The Syndicate-Born Trilogy," which is actually four books with the prequel added in:

1) *Red on the Run*
2) *Black and White Truth*
3) *True Blue Son*
4) *The Sally Ride Chronicle* (A Prequel)

The series has garned critical acclaim, been an award winner, and thrilled thousands of readers. We know that, having now finished the first book in the series, you'll want to jump right into the rest of the series.

You can find the individual book listings at our website, and on each book's pages, links to purchase the books, by starting out at the webpage below:

www.EvolvedPub.com/SyndicateBornTrilogy

MORE FROM EVOLVED PUBLISHING

We offer great books across multiple genres, featuring high-quality editing (which we believe is second-to-none) and fantastic covers.

As a hybrid small press, your support as loyal readers is so important to us, and we have strived, with tireless dedication and sheer determination, to deliver on the promise of our motto:
QUALITY IS PRIORITY #1!

Please check out all of our great books,
which you can find at this link:
www.EvolvedPub.com/Catalog/

Thank you!

Lightning Source UK Ltd.
Milton Keynes UK
UKHW010451090223
416681UK00005B/1230